TRANSPORT 2

The Flood

PHILLIP P. PETERSON

Translated by
JENNY PIENING

Edited by
LAURA RADOSH

Chapter 1

Twenty years ago:

"PRIVATE PENWILL, give me the lowdown. How much longer will our supplies last?"

The lanky soldier in charge of the warehouse glanced up from the papers on her desk and gave a brief salute. With her protruding cheekbones and skinny arms she looked like she suffered from an eating disorder, but Captain Marlene Wolfe knew that her subordinate was blessed with a healthy appetite. In fact, Marlene suspected that Ann Penwill sometimes siphoned off an extra ration from the supplies she managed.

Marlene followed her to the back of the tent, where boxes of food were piled up in big crates. Private Penwill pointed at one of the stacks. "That's all we have left. We've used up about half our supplies. If we don't cut back rations, I'd say we have three months, tops. We need to have found a solution by then."

"And how long—maximum—could we survive if we do cut back?" asked Marlene.

Ann Penwill tilted her head to one side as she considered. "The current rations provide about three-thousand calories a day. Soldiers who are moving around a lot or doing manual labor need more. If we reduce the amount of work they have to do, and risk the consequences of further weight loss, we could manage for a while on a thousand calories a day. In my opinion, any less would be verging on starvation. But you'd be better off asking Doctor Lindwall."

"I'm going to see him shortly. So, you'd say three months if we eat normally and nine months if we cut down to the minimum?"

Penwill nodded. "Yes. Although there's another, bigger, problem than the food supplies."

"What's that?"

"Our store of drinking water will be depleted first. Four weeks at most."

Wolfe smiled. "We've managed to solve that problem, at least. Dr. Dressel and Lee have created a condenser, which is able to draw enough water from the air. It's lucky this planet has such high humidity. The first attempts were successful, and in two days at the latest we'll have fresh water, once the engineers have connected the thing to the reactor."

"Well in that case all our problems are solved," Penwill retorted sarcastically.

"Stay positive," said Marlene. She turned on her heel and headed toward the door.

"Sir?"

Wolfe turned around again.

"Will we make it back home?"

Marlene smiled encouragingly. "Of course we'll make

it back home. We'll find a way."

But from Penwill's rigid expression she knew that her subordinate wasn't convinced.

"Listen, Ann. It's too early to give up hope. We don't know exactly why the transporter won't accept Earth as a destination anymore. But I can assure you that the best scientists are working on the problem back at home. And we also have our fair share of top physicists and engineers, some of whom I would even go so far as to describe as geniuses. Have a little patience and confidence in their abilities. We'll find a solution."

Ann was silent for a moment and then nodded. Wolfe smiled at her subordinate again before leaving the tent. As soon as she was outside, she let out a deep sigh.

The supply tent was on a hill a little way off from the main camp. The crew tents, which housed all thirty-five members of the expedition—soldiers and scientists—were around six hundred feet to the left of the supply tent. On another little hill behind the camp were the laboratory module and more tents, where the scientists and technicians worked. The hill was surmounted by a three-hundred-foot-high antenna and several narrow towers with meteorological and physical instruments.

Marlene took in the scenery. Although she had been here for three months already, the environment still seemed unreal. As far as the eye could see, there were only gentle, rolling hills covered in grass-like stuff, which clung on to the rocky substrate with its sucker-like roots. Above this landscape arched a deep-blue sky, interrupted here and there by fluffy, slow-moving clouds. The sun was at its zenith, so that Marlene's body barely cast a shadow. At first glance, it looked like a landscape on Earth. Ireland perhaps, or northern France. But if you looked more closely, you noticed that the colors were strange. Too bright, the hues too saturated, as if you were looking at an image that had been visually enhanced to make it look like an alien world.

And that's exactly what it was: an alien world. And to her right, in a hollow, stood the infernal thing that had brought them here and doggedly refused to take them back home. The alien transporter was like a foreign body in this bright, warm environment. The highly sophisticated piece of technology—forty feet in diameter, spherical, and so black it was like a dark spot floating in Marlene's eye—had been stranded on this planet for millions of years.

Suddenly, an opening appeared in the curve of the black sphere and Dr. John Dressel, their head physicist, stepped out into the open. Their eyes met. The small, stocky scientist shook his head and Marlene Wolfe understood him immediately.

Nothing—again!

Twice a day, Dressel went into the sphere and tried to set the destination code for Earth. But the field for starting a transport never appeared on the black console.

It had been three months now. Initially they had been due to stay here for three weeks.

What on earth had gone wrong?

Marlene no longer knew how often she had been asked this question over the last two months.

The memory of that day was still fresh in her mind: the day she and her Special Engineers unit had received the command to report to Nevada for a mission. There she had met with General Morrow—a gruff, old-school commander—in a high-security facility. She could hardly believe what he was telling her, but then she saw the mysterious black thing in an underground cave. A door to the stars! Found on the ocean floor off the coast of California, salvaged and brought to the high-security facility in Nevada.

Marlene had never been interested in space travel, and even less so in science fiction. And yet she and her unit were commanded to step into this teleportation device, constructed by an alien civilization, and to set up a base on a distant planet. The experiment was supposed to last three weeks. Their job was to babysit a team of scientists—when their time was up, they would be relieved by another company. But the replacement had never arrived. Then they had tried to get back home on their own, only to discover that Earth could no longer be selected as a destination—as if the corresponding station on their home planet no longer existed.

Since then, Marlene had tried to keep up morale among her soldiers and the scientists. But as more and more days passed with no change, her confidence began to crumble. She did not reveal her feelings to the others, but slowly she began to fear that they would never get away from here. It was their good fortune that they had come with far more supplies than they thought they would need, as they had been given the job of setting up a depot for planned follow-up missions; otherwise, they probably would have all starved to death by now.

As green as the planet was, there was no food here. And all attempts to cultivate the seeds they had brought with them had failed, because there was no fertile topsoil.

Meanwhile, Dr. Dressel had reached the top of the hill. He was out of breath and the expression on his face was resigned. "Nothing."

Marlene nodded. "I could tell. Your face says it all."

The scientist breathed heavily. Back on Earth, Marlene had already complained that some of the scientists were far too unfit for the military. And this guy was probably only in his mid-thirties, for Christ's sake!

Dressel adjusted his glasses and shook his head. "I just don't get it! It never works! There are no problems with the other destinations; at least we can dial them. The code for Earth is the only one that the transporter won't accept."

"I know. We've had the same problem for over two months now."

"We can't wait around here forever. We have to start considering alternatives."

"And what do you have in mind, Doctor? Do you have a concrete suggestion?"

Sheepishly, the physicist looked down at his feet. "No. I don't. We don't know enough about how the transporter works. That was the job of the team back on Earth."

"What do you think could have happened?"

Slowly they walked back down the hill to the crew tents. Dr. Dressel ran a hand through his thick, black hair, which—no matter how often or how much he combed it— was almost impossible to tame. And although he shaved every morning, by lunchtime his chin and cheeks were covered in stubble, adding to his general look of dishevelment. A short, military haircut would have suited him better.

Dr. Dressel hesitated. "There are plenty of possible explanations. Maybe they carried out an experiment with the transporter back on Earth and it went wrong. It could have been accidentally destroyed or damaged. Or maybe the devices only have a limited power supply, which has now run out. Or something entirely unexpected happened. Ultimately, we can only speculate—until we get back to Earth and find out the truth."

Marlene Wolfe thought uneasily about the nuclear warhead underneath the Nevada transporter. General

Morrow had told her about it. Perhaps there had been a real threat and her superiors had decided to destroy the transporter. In that case, they were stranded here forever and could look forward to starving slowly to death. Whatever the problem was back on Earth, the scientists obviously weren't getting to the bottom of it. Their chances of returning were diminishing by the day.

They had reached the camp. Wolfe turned to the physicist and folded her arms across her chest. "We won't give up hope. We have plenty of supplies, enough to live off for a few more months. Until then, I'd like you to think about what other options we have to get back to Earth. If you want to carry out any experiments with the transporter, now's the time to get started."

Dressel laughed. "Experiments with the transporter? We don't have the right people for that, or the necessary equipment."

Wolfe shook her head. Her voice went up a notch. "For God's sake, half of the men and women on this expedition are scientists. Many of them have doctorates and are among the best in their field. Think of something!"

The physicist nodded slowly. His shoulders hung down limply. "Alright. I'll talk to my colleagues about possible options."

"By tomorrow evening, I would like you to have produced a list of at least ten suggestions for us to discuss together."

"Ten suggestions? I seriously doubt—"

"Ten!" Marlene narrowed her eyes to slits.

The scientist hesitated a few seconds, then lowered his head. "Okay." He left without giving Marlene a second glance.

"Sir?"

Captain Wolfe turned around. She had to tilt her head

back to look Private Lawrence in the eyes. "What is it, Ernie?"

"Lieutenant Hawke has been looking everywhere for you. He wants to talk to you." The deep bass of his voice seemed to emanate from a subwoofer somewhere deep inside his body. With cropped blond hair and a belligerent expression, Lawrence liked to play the tough guy. Now he came right up to Captain Wolfe, practically butting into her with his impudently folded arms. But Marlene had known him long enough to know that beneath all his swagger, he still respected her. In this company of inexperienced pioneers, she was in fact glad to have one fighter she could rely on. And she knew that she could trust Ernie, even if she suspected that he saw himself as Lieutenant Hawke's subordinate rather than hers.

"Where is Hawke?"

"He's waiting for you at the command post."

He's waiting for me*? Has he forgotten that I'm the Commander in Chief here?*

"Go and tell him that I'll be there as soon as I've completed my inspection."

Which was actually his *job.*

"He said it was urgent, Sir."

Marlene could hardly suppress a smile. Lawrence saluted quickly and stomped off without a word.

Wolfe shook her head and walked quickly to the medical tent. The entrance was closed. She pushed the tarpaulin aside and stepped inside. The interior was dominated by a white operating table. To its right were camp beds, to the left were various shelves and cupboards. Dr. Lindwall was sitting at a desk at the far end of the room. Slim and of average height, the doctor was leaning over a bowl, out of which smoke was rising. He hadn't noticed her, probably because of the loud rock music that was blaring from the little stereo system in the corner. A smell reminiscent of incense hung in the air, like in a church during Easter Mass.

"What are you doing?" asked Marlene with a frown, and stepped closer.

Dr. Lindwall gave a start and looked up. Marlene saw that the bowl was filled with smoldering bushels of the grass-like plants that covered the planet.

"I . . . um . . . just a little experiment," stammered the doctor. Although he was barely in his mid-forties, his thick hair was almost completely grey. He fumbled for the volume button on the stereo system and turned down the music.

"I doubt you'll be able to find out anything our biologists don't already know. Jenny, in particular, has done hardly anything all week except analyze this stuff."

Lindwall picked up the bowl and placed it on a table behind him. "Yes, you're probably right." He cleared his throat. "What can I do for you?"

"Your daily report will do for starters."

The doctor rummaged around for a clipboard that was buried under a pile of paper. "Nothing much. Travis Richards scalded his hand on a piece of lab equipment. But it's not bad and a salve should do the job. Sammy Yang came in complaining about his back again. I suggested he swap his camp bed or try out a different sleeping position. Another member of the expedition had a genital infection. Despite the lack of privacy, there's been an increase in sexual activity lately. There have also been more people asking for contraceptives."

Marlene shrugged. "That's hardly surprising, with an equal number of men and women living in close quarters for such a long time."

Lindwall fiddled with his ballpoint pen. He kept

clicking the nib in and out. Wolfe was irritated by the noise. The doctor seemed to be very jittery today. He was sweating, although it wasn't really warm. Surely Lindwall wasn't ill? A flu epidemic in the camp was all they needed now. "Is everything okay, Doctor?"

"Everything's great. I'm fine. Listen, although the soldiers and scientists are in excellent health, I'm slowly starting to worry about the psychological effects of the situation we're in."

"You're not a psychologist, Doctor," said Marlene curtly.

"It doesn't take a psychologist to notice that the mood here is going rapidly downhill. At first, people were just a little worried, but over the last few days they've started to really freak out. Many of them think we're never going to get back to Earth."

"What exactly are they saying?"

"They often talk to me during their weekly routine checkups, because they know I'm bound by a duty of confidentiality. Many of them believe the connection to Earth has been cut off completely, because somebody made a mistake. And some of them, particularly the soldiers, are complaining that nothing is being done anymore at our end and that all we're doing is waiting."

This gave Marlene food for thought. If the soldiers and scientists started to lose trust in their leaders, there was danger of a mutiny—particularly if they didn't believe they would be making it home anymore. She regretted she hadn't made more time to listen to people's concerns. She resolved to talk to them at the earliest opportunity, but first she needed to be clear about what should happen next. She could no longer afford to simply wait. But what was the alternative? It was vital that she showed strong leadership.

"Doctor, I have a job for you. I want you to talk to Private Penwill and come up with a plan for rationing our food. We still have plenty of supplies, but they won't last forever. Work out how long we can make the supplies last in the worst-case scenario, and report back to me tomorrow."

The furrowed his brow. "Are we really already at the stage that we need to start rationing? Have you also given up hope?"

Wolfe shook her head vigorously. "I haven't given up anything. But it won't harm to be prepared for all eventualities."

Dr. Lindwall reached for a coffee cup. Only now did Marlene notice that his hands were shaking. Some of the black brew slopped over the edge of the cup and left dark stains on the papers.

"For God's sake, Doctor. What's wrong with you? You look exhausted. Something's up with you and I want to know what it is. I can't afford to have a sick team."

The doctor put down his cup and stared at the floor. Whatever it was, he obviously found it embarrassing.

"Speak up, Doctor. Can I help you in some way?"

Lindwall looked her in the eyes and shook his head. "I've run out of cigarettes," he said sheepishly.

Now Marlene understood. Usually there was always a cigarette glowing somewhere within his reach. He couldn't even stop himself from smoking in the hospital. She smiled. "Well, then you'll have to learn to get by without nicotine. The withdrawal symptoms will pass. See it as an opportunity to give up smoking. You're actually the only one here who was still smoking." She stopped short and looked at the still smoldering bowl on the table behind him. "Is that why you were burning the grass? Did you

11

hope there was something in it that would give you a kick?"

The doctor turned red.

Busted!

Marlene grinned. "I'm afraid I have to disappoint you. I've read Dr. Baldwin's report. There are no active substances in the stuff."

"Too bad," murmured Lindwall.

"I expect your report about rationing supplies by tomorrow evening, Doctor."

Without waiting for an answer, Captain Wolfe turned on her heels and left the tent.

She walked along slowly between the crew tents. There were two expedition members per tent. Only she, Lieutenant Hawke, Dr. Dressel, and Dr. Lindwall, as leaders of the expedition, had their own tents. Most of the soldiers and scientists were still very young; hardly any of them were over thirty. The team of scientists included several students who were financing their studies with a military scholarship. One of the conditions of the scholarship was that they could be called to take part in a military mission. Marlene wasn't surprised that the teams were anxious; but the fact that they were already discussing their concerns with the doctor suggested that the situation was coming to a head—usually they vented their frustrations on each other first. She knew it hadn't reached a critical stage yet, but if they had to wait much longer for contact with Earth, there was a real danger it might. Then the men and women would follow someone else; someone who offered them an apparently simpler solution.

She pushed aside the opening of the command tent and saw Lieutenant Hawke sitting at one of the two desks. Marlene's second-in-command was tall and strongly built, and had a pointy nose. He was leaning back in his chair with his spotlessly clean boots on the table, carefully squirting gun oil on the slide of his pistol. He acknowledged her arrival with a nod, placed the little bottle of oil on the desk and picked up a white cloth, which he wiped almost tenderly over his weapon. Although there were no enemies here far and wide, Ben always had his pistol on him. Marlene thought it was ridiculous; she hadn't taken her pistol out of the cupboard for weeks now.

"You took too long, Marlene," said Ben in a high-pitched, crotchety voice, which jarred with his brawny physique. She knew that beside his burning ambition to lead his own company, he had a problem with her because she was a woman. She could have requested that he be transferred, he'd given her enough reasons to do so, but it just wasn't her style to solve problems that way. "You wanted to speak to me, Ben. What's up?"

Ben smiled coldly. "We've been here for three months now. We were supposed to be relieved two months ago. We should start talking about possible alternatives."

Marlene sat down at her desk and took a weighty document out of a drawer. Then she stood up again, walked briskly over to the big whiteboard, and affixed the document to the pale metal surface with a magnet. She turned around, looked Ben in the eyes and tapped purposefully on the document.

"This is our order with the parameters of the mission. To set up a base, support the scientists in their work, and hold the fort until we are relieved after approximately three weeks. *Approximately*!

Back on Earth, they seemed to have known there might be setbacks. That's why we were sent here with so many supplies. It also says here that we should not conduct any experiments with the transporter technology, and that under no circumstances should we select a destination other than Earth. We have supplies to last us at least six months, perhaps even a year, if we ration. I think it's premature to start disobeying orders. It also wouldn't make much sense. But it might reassure you to hear that I've asked Dr. Dressel to come up with some options for Plan B."

Hawke's jerked his head forward. He laid his weapon and the cloth on the table and stood up. He came menacingly close to Marlene and pointed at the list. "This no longer applies."

Wolfe didn't budge an inch. "And now *you* make the decisions?"

He shook his head. "There's nothing to decide. It's obvious. We've lost contact with Earth, so we are no longer bound by their orders."

Marlene guessed that he had come up with an idea. Despite his blatant disrespect, she was curious. "Okay, so what's your suggestion?"

"Let's start by summing up what we know: We can't get back home. We've had zero contact with Earth, and we can't select it as a destination. We also can't assume that the situation will change."

"Go on."

"Second: Although we have a lot of supplies, we won't be able to survive on Russell's Planet in the long term. All there is here is that inedible grass, and our attempts at sowing seeds have all failed, because there is no topsoil."

"I know all that, we've been through it a million times."

"Ergo, the only solution is to find another planet on which we can survive and that offers us a perspective for the future."

Marlene nodded. "That's true, but unfortunately we don't have any information about the other destinations. You were at the meeting. We can't just try out any old code

—that's how several people ended up dead when they experimented with the transporter last time. It took them to destinations with higher gravity or lethal atmospheres. There's no way of knowing in advance where you'll end up."

Hawke stalked over to his desk and picked up a piece of paper. "That's why we need people, guinea pigs, who we can send in the transporter. We'll do that until we've found a suitable planet.

Marlene laughed. "As far as I know, Russell's Planet is the only one they found that at least had a breathable atmosphere. Many people would die in the process of finding another one—that is, if we even find another one. It would be a death mission. How would you go about it? Look for volunteers? Draw lots?"

Hawke folded his arms. "This is a military operation. Sure, we have civilians with us, but they're superfluous to our mission. We will explain the emergency on the base, intern the civilians and send off the most expendable ones first. I've already made a list, which ranks the scientists in order of usefulness. Starting with assistants like Radinkovic, Grant, and Young."

Marlene's face flushed with anger. She couldn't believe the words coming out of her deputy's mouth.

Ben continued before she had a chance to respond. "It's the only way. Extraordinary problems require extraordinary measures."

Marlene's voice trembled. "You've clearly lost your mind. I will never approve such an inhuman idea." She stepped forward and ripped the list from his hand. "Well that says it all: the people you can't stand are right at the top of the list." She crumpled up the piece of paper and threw it in a high arc into the wastepaper basket.

Ben's expression was steely. "What do you suggest

instead, Captain?" He spat out the last word with undisguised contempt.

"First of all, we won't jump the gun if it isn't absolutely
necessary. Then we will talk to the scientists, in particular,
to discuss our options and reach a decision together. And I
will not listen to any more of this. I can assure you that
what you suggest is not going to happen."

Hawke opened his mouth and closed it again, his fists
clenched.

Marlene continued. "Your attitude really gives me
cause for concern. We'll have to talk about this again soon.
Do you have any idea what would happen in the camp if
word of something like that got out? You must be out of
your mind." She was whispering, because she didn't know
who might be passing by the tent at that moment.

Had he already talked to other soldiers about his idea?
Maybe with Ernie Lawrence, who was known for shooting
his mouth off? It couldn't go on like this. Hawke's suggestion was so beyond the pale that she had to deal with it.
She could discharge Ben as her deputy, but that would only
set the rumor mill buzzing. No, the best thing would be talk
to the team right away and find out what ideas they had
come up with. Above all, she had to make it clear that
drastic measures like Hawke's plan were out of the question. It would be wisest to also involve Ben and give him a
task—one he couldn't wreak any havoc with.

"Ben, by tomorrow evening I want you . . ." She
pricked up her ears. Outside she could hear hurried footsteps and Rhonda's shrill voice, although she didn't catch
what she was saying. Shadows glided across the wall of
the tent.

"What's going on?" muttered Ben. He stood up just as
the tent door was ripped open and Corporal Grant
stormed into the command post. He was wide-eyed and

completely out of breath. He didn't even make an effort to salute. "Sir, they've come. They're here. . . ." He stumbled over his own words.

Marlene raised her arms. "Calm down, Dillon. What's going on?"

Corporal Grant took a deep breath. "The transporter. Two men have come out." He was grinning from ear to ear. "We can go back home."

Marlene looked at Hawke, who also couldn't hide his amazement. "Let's wait and see."

She hurried after the corporal. Others had noticed the commotion and were looking out of their tents to see what was going on. Obviously there was a better view from the lab container, because the scientists were already running out of the lab toward the transporter. That could only mean one thing! She hoped that they weren't mistaken. *Please, please!* Finally the alien object came into view.

The transporter was open. Two strange men were standing stock still in front of it and looking around. They were wearing combat uniforms, like everyone else in General Morrow's unit. Their saviors had come at last. Almost immediately, the two men were surrounded by a clapping, cheering throng of people. Camille Ott, the young soldier who had only been assigned to her unit recently, jumped up and down and screamed like an excited child. Two scientists in lab coats hugged each other in relief.

"Finally."

"Home! We're going home!"

"What took you so long?"

Marlene reached the transporter, and pushed herself between Dr. Potter and Sergeant Grazier. One of the new arrivals noticed her rank and sprang to attention. He was a little taller than Marlene, and had short brown hair and grey eyes. A thin, jagged scar ran down his face from his temple to his smoothly shaven jawbone.

The other man was a little smaller, but still taller than Marlene. He was hopping agitatedly from one leg to the other. They didn't react to the cheering going on around them. One of the men stepped forward and came to a halt two steps away from her. His face was devoid of emotion, and instinctively Marlene knew that the two guests had not come to bring them back to Earth. Something about the situation was wrong. She saluted and introduced herself. "Captain Marlene Wolfe. Welcome to Russell's Planet."

They shook hands; the man's face remained rigid. "I'm Russell Harris, and this is Christian Holbrook."

"We've been waiting a long time," said Marlene.

"I know, I'm sorry," answered Harris.

"What happened?"

The man's voice was loud enough for everyone to hear him. His words came out smoothly, as if he'd been rehearsing what to say for some time.

"I'm one of a group of former prisoners who were selected for experiments with the alien transporter. Some of us died in the process."

"Prisoners?" asked Marlene. Morrow only mentioned volunteers.

"Yes. I myself am a former officer of a special forces unit. Christian is a former astronaut and trained our group. I remember when you left for this planet; in fact, we met at the time."

"I can't remember. Continue!"

"We found out that the transporter had an artificial intelligence and we made contact with it through telepathy. As a result, we found the remains of the aliens who built the transporters and who distributed them throughout the galaxy."

"The remains?"

"Yes. The aliens wiped out their own planet with their technology. Earth would probably have succumbed to the same fate if we had continued to experiment with the transporter. That's why I and several others destroyed the transporter on Earth with a nuclear bomb after escaping to another planet. We know you can't survive here, which is why we decided to find you and invite you to our planet, which offers good living conditions for a colony."

She didn't follow the last few sentences. In her head she could only hear the same words, over and over, which were the essence of what he had said:

The transporter on Earth has been destroyed. I will never go back home!

Harris continued talking, but his words didn't register. From the crowds of soldiers standing around them she could hear screams. She looked into Sarah Dening's horrified eyes. Beside her, Travis Richards had slumped together, and behind her, Ben Hawke was giving free rein to his fury. He wasn't the only one.

"Bastards!"

". . . Never go back home?"

"Please, no!"

Harris had finished his speech. He looked at Marlene with an expressionless face. He knew exactly what was coming next. Private Lawrence grabbed Holbrook by the collar and swung him round.

"I'm sorry," said Harris quietly.

Marlene shook her head slowly. "I just can't believe . . ." Her voice faltered as the magnitude of the situation dawned on her.

I will never go back home!

A surge of violent anger welled up inside her. Without being fully aware of what was happening, her hands balled into fists—she could feel the adrenalin coursing through her body. Suddenly, one of her fists was flying into the broad face of the traitor. Pain seared through her hand. She must have broken at least one finger. Blood sprayed in her face and into the air. There was a crunching noise, and then Russell's head flew backward, pulling his body with it, before hitting the black outer wall of the transporter with a thud. He slumped like a bundle of wet clothes to the ground, unconscious.

Chapter 2

"Damn it," Russell swore. He had completely disengaged the clutch, but it still made a grinding noise as he changed from third to second gear.

"The transmission again?" asked Marlene Wolfe, who was sitting beside him in the jeep's passenger seat.

"Yup."

"I thought Albert repaired the thing last week."

"He did, but it looks as if the gear train is coming apart again."

"Our little fleet spends more time in repair than on the road these days."

Russell gave her a sideways glance and grinned. Her laconic remarks during their joint excursions had become something of a tradition. He liked Marlene, and knew that the feeling was mutual. Their relationship had been frosty in the early days, after she'd broken Russell's jaw at their first meeting. He had guessed that the repair to the jeep wouldn't last long. The quality of the steel that Albert and his helpers produced in their forge was improving all the time, but they would never be able to produce parts to the same standard as the industrially manufactured ones they were used to from Earth. The seven jeeps they had brought with them from Russell's Planet were in bad shape, so that never more than four or five vehicles were roadworthy at the same time.

"The word 'road' doesn't quite hit the mark."

The rudimentary lanes that they had created in the area surrounding their settlement were not exactly easy-going on the vehicles. The roads running through the foothills of the nearby mountains were impossibly bumpy, while the one in the marshy lowlands, which they had built to get to the oil spring and refinery, was more of a muddy track.

"Hopefully the jeep will hold out until we get back to the camp," said Marlene.

"I reckon it will. But then this bucket of bolts really needs to go to the garage. That clattering noise at the back can't bode well for the axle bearing."

"We should have walked."

"Then we would have been gone the whole day," responded Russell.

"Exercise is healthy."

Russell nodded. He had never shied away from physical exertion. But today he was glad they had the jeep at their disposal. He felt tired and sluggish. He blamed it on his age. Last week he had celebrated his sixty-second birthday. Or rather, Ellen and Albert had forced the celebration upon him. He hadn't been in the mood for it. Birthdays and holidays were things that he had left behind on Earth. But others desperately held on to old traditions and meticulously maintained the terrestrial calendar alongside the New California one, which—due to the different duration of days and years—was far from simple. "I'm glad that we could spare ourselves the hike today."

"Headache again?"

Russell nodded. He put his exhaustion down to his advanced age and his increasing physical inactivity. The headaches were probably the result of unsettled sleep the night before.

"You don't look too great, either," said Marlene. "Too pale. You should go to Dr. Lindwall for a checkup."

He waved her suggestion aside. "I'm fine."

They took the last few curves of the narrow mountain road, which was surrounded on either side by steep cliffs, and then the landscape changed abruptly. The narrow canyon opened out onto a verdant plain where, a few miles in the distance, the broad river delta of the New Mississippi began. Further to the east, the delta flowed through a dense jungle that covered a vast area stretching to the distant ocean, around a hundred miles away. "The view always blows me away," said Marlene.

"Same here," replied Russell.

The canyon formed a natural connection between the highlands, where the colony was situated, and the fertile lowlands. The upper end of the pass leading out of the narrow valley was just a few miles from Eridu, their settlement. At the lower end, they had erected a permanently manned observation post. A lookout and a hut had been erected in front of a nine-foot-high fence, because many different animal species populated the lowlands, some of which could only be described as extremely dangerous monsters. In the early days, lone animals or whole herds had come up to the highlands and attacked their colony. They had built the watchtower just a few months after their arrival and the first reconnaissance missions. Since then, there had thankfully not been a single attack on Eridu. There seemed to be no more aggressive animal species left in the highlands anymore.

Russell drove the Jeep up to the little wooden hut that served as sleeping quarters for the two-man lookout team. Chris Neaman came toward them from the door of the hut. He looked bleary-eyed, but cheerful. Russell saw his comrade Ernie Lawrence standing on the watchtower with a sniper rifle. He, too, gave a brief wave and then continued to scan the sweeping grasslands through his binoculars.

"Hey Russell, hi Marlene," said Chris.

Russell turned off the engine and jumped out of the jeep. He immediately felt dizzy and stumbled forward a few steps. Chris caught him before he fell to the ground.

"Everything okay?" he asked.

Russell gave an impatient wave of the hand. "Yeah, yeah, I'm just out of sorts. Nothing serious. Old age."

"You're not that old," retorted Marlene.

"Someone who was always as fit as you shouldn't collapse just getting out of a car at the age of sixty. You really need to go to the doc for a checkup."

"I know, I know. When I get a chance." Russell quickly changed the subject. "How's it going?"

Chris shrugged. "Nothing much to report. Killed five wotans and two hyenas."

Wotans is what they called the monsters that had made life difficult on the first reconnaissance mission to the planet. Hefty and headless, without any visible sensory organs, one of them had stormed at the astronaut Walter Redmont, knocked him over and pinned him to the ground. Russell had had to avert his eyes as the creature secreted acid onto Redmont's skin and dissolved him alive. The animals often travelled in packs and were immensely dangerous.

The hyenas seemed to be their little brothers. They ran incredibly fast on thin, springy legs, and, in contrast to wotans, had small, knob-like heads from which they could spray acid up to a distance of thirty feet.

"Sounds like a lot," said Russell. "Since the start of your shift?"

Neaman shook his head. "Since last night."

Russell raised his eyebrows. "In just one night? We've never seen that many."

Chris shrugged again. "The last shift also mentioned they'd seen more. It's not a problem—gives us something to do! Five days can really drag."

"You only have to do three shifts a year," said Marlene. "And it gets you out of working the fields."

"I prefer that to hanging around here."

"I guess everyone has a different opinion on that one," Russell retorted. "I always prefer . . ."

"There's another one!" Ernie called down from the watchtower in his throaty voice.

Russell couldn't see anything beyond the gate with the barbed wire. He ran to the tower and clambered up the ladder, Marlene and Chris hot on his heels.

Russell looked in the direction that Ernie was focused on with his binoculars. Now he could see a blurry, brown dot at the edge of the forest, slowly coming their way. "I can't see it clearly."

Ernie handed him the sniper rifle. "Take it."

"Hey, thanks a lot."

Russell took the semi-automatic M-110 and lay down on his chest on the wooden floor of the watchtower. He flipped up the lens cap, took a deep breath and put his eye to the scope.

"A sniper," murmured Russell in alarm. Snipers were another species from the lowlands that could have escaped directly from hell.

The animal was vaguely reminiscent of a dachshund,

but suppler and larger. The pointed head moved back and forth, scanning the area. The flexible, thin legs enabled the creature to shoot forward in jolting movements.

"Are you sure?" Marlene whispered, although the animal was still far away.

"Yup, without a doubt," Ernie confirmed, still looking through his binoculars.

"We've never seen one like that here," said Chris.

"I know. And that worries me." Russell checked the weapon. There was already a cartridge in the chamber.

"What's it doing?" asked Marlene.

"No idea," Ernie replied.

"It's coming slowly toward us. It seems confused. You can tell this isn't its territory," said Russell.

"I'm not surprised. We've only ever seen snipers close to the sea."

"Yeah, and Travis Richards almost died from his wounds."

Russell remembered it well. It had been on an expedition to the lowlands, during which they'd come across some unfamiliar and frightening animal species. Unawares, Travis had gotten too close to one of the lurking snipers. Suddenly, he had collapsed, and thin fountains of his blood spurted several feet into the air. Russell had shot the sniper dead. When they did an autopsy on the creature, they discovered that it had a stomach-like organ from which it could emit crystals under high pressure at supersonic speed. Snipers were even more dangerous than wotans.

"Holy shit! There come another two!"

Ernie was right. Two more of the sinister creatures flitted out of the forest and followed the trail of the first one.

Russell noticed some shuffling going on beside him, and became aware that Marlene and Chris were also reaching for weapons and getting into position. He didn't let himself be distracted and continued to keep his eye on the scope. Beads of sweat trickled down his forehead. He knew that the animals were damn quick and veered one way and then the other as they ran. It would be difficult to hit one if they decided to run toward them. But at least the snipers were still a good way off. He judged the distance to be around half a mile. That was the furthest distance at which you could aim reliably with an M-110. If the target was standing still.

"What should we do?" asked Neaman. "Should we fire?"

The leader of the beasts kept turning its head to the side as if it were looking for something. Russell reckoned that the creatures might start running at any moment. But they weren't moving directly toward them. "We'll wait until they're a bit closer."

"Maybe they'll move away again," murmured Ernie.

"I don't think so," Russell replied. "They're carnivores. Hunters. They don't come out of cover unless they're planning something. I think they've caught our scent but don't know exactly where we are. When they're only a third of a mile away, we'll shoot. I'll take the one in the middle. Marlene, you take the one on the left and the other one is yours, Chris."

"Okay."

Fascinated, Russell watched his target through the lens. The slim, long body with the springy little legs looked utterly alien. There was no fur covering its thick, gray-brown skin. The wide mouth on the tiny head resembled a thin, jagged line. The tiny eyes were no more than dots, and the creature had no discernible nose or ears—but Russell was sure that it had highly developed sensory organs.

The two at the back had caught up and were trotting a few feet behind the leader.

"Another two thousand feet," whispered Ernie.

"Get ready," growled Russell hoarsely.

Slowly, the snipers moved in their direction.

"One thousand five hundred feet," hissed Ernie.

"On my command, in three, two, . . ." Russell didn't get any further. As if on command, the monsters ran off. "Shit! Fire! Kill them!" Russell struggled to keep his target in view. The monsters were fast. Damn fast. The ones on the edge ran off to the side before returning to their original course in a wide curve.

Russell fired.

As if the animal had known what was coming, it changed direction at lightning speed, taking a zigzag course before heading toward them in a straight line.

"Six hundred feet," bellowed Ernie.

Russell heard the shot. "Fuck," hissed Marlene.

Several hundred feet away, the monsters stopped for a moment, swerved to the side, stopped again and ran in the opposite direction. But their heads remained facing the watchtower. Just as Russell fired again, missing his target, he heard a buzzing noise.

"They're shooting at us!" shouted Chris. A piece of the wooden railing splintered into hundreds of pieces that flew off in every which direction.

A bang. Marlene had fired again. "One down," she hissed.

Russell tried to get his target back in view. He waited for that split second when the creature stopped before changing direction. There was that hollow buzzing sound again. Splinters of wood rained down on him from the roof. He concentrated on his target, which was dancing around the center of the viewfinder. The forelegs of the sniper came to a sudden stop, while the hind legs slipped out to the side. Now was the moment. Time seemed to stand still as Russell shifted slightly to take aim at the tiny head. He had stopped breathing many seconds ago. He crooked his finger pull the trigger. The head of the animal exploded in a fountain of red and yellow.

Got it!

What was the last one up to?

Another buzzing noise. Marlene suppressed a scream.

Don't let it distract you. Eliminate the danger first!

Just as his new target came into view, it slumped down. Chris lowered his gun.

"We've taken care of those pieces of shit," bellowed Ernie. Russell turned around. Marlene was clutching her lower leg and pushing up the green cotton pant leg.

"Are you badly hurt?" He saw red marks on her pants.

"Just a graze. I was lucky." She was pale, but Russell knew the feeling and the shock of being injured in battle and not knowing in the first instance if it was bad or not.

Russell propped himself up on the floor and stood up. The snipers were lying lifeless in pools of blood some distance from the barbed wire fence. They hadn't even got close to the landmines in front of the gate. Russell looked around. The shelter was riddled with holes. He shook his head. It was sheer luck that none of them had been seriously hurt or even killed. In the past, they had been able to keep the beasts at bay with ultrasound, but that had only worked for a short time.

"That was fucking close," Chris wiped his brow.

Ernie grinned. He was addicted to adrenalin kicks like this. Russell had never understood why Lawrence had joined the Special Engineers unit. He would have been better off in an infantry unit.

"I just don't get it," said Russell.

"What do you mean?" asked Marlene, who had taken a first-aid kit from the wall and was wrapping gauze around her wound.

"In twenty years, we've never experienced an attack like that. And we've never seen any snipers here. I don't like it."

"Maybe they just happened to be in the area and picked up our scent," suggested Chris.

"In wotan territory? I doubt it. And the fact that more and more creatures are appearing in the area around the watchtower seems to suggest something else," said Russell.

"And what would that be?" asked Marlene.

"I have no idea. Perhaps a natural migration. I really don't know. We should talk about it with Jenny. Maybe our biologist has an idea. In the meantime I suggest doubling the number of people on watch."

"Oh no!" groaned Chris. "That would mean being on duty six times a year."

"Tough shit!" said Marlene. "Russell's right. Imagine if a group of those creatures broke through and got into the colony. If they surprise us at night, we're dead meat."

Russell, Chris, and Marlene climbed back down the ladder and returned to the jeep. Ernie continued to survey the area beyond the gate through his binoculars.

Marlene opened a box on the truck bed and handed Chris a clunky-looking field telephone.

"This is the actual reason we came here," said Russell. "Be more careful next time, we've got hardly any spare parts left."

"Okay, Okay. Pretty stupid we can't use the radios."

Russell nodded. The narrow canyons made radio contact with Eridu impossible. So they had pulled a copper cable through the valley, using up half of their cable supply in the process.

"When we're back at camp, I'll send back-up right away. We need four people here. We're not taking any risks," said Marlene.

"Sounds good." Chris turned around and took the field telephone with him to the wooden barrack.

Russell climbed into the driver's seat. After Marlene had swung herself into the passenger seat, he started the motor and reversed with a judder.

"I don't like it," he murmured.

"I agree. Something's going on."

"I'm worried about the next supply run to the refinery. It's nearly time to go again."

Marlene grunted. "In any case, we should increase the number of lookouts."

Russell pursed his lips. The nearest oil reserves lay about six miles away, in the jungle. Years before, Albert, Dr. Cashmore, and Lee Shanker had erected an improvised refinery right next to the oil spring. It was fully automatic, and provided the expanding colony with valuable raw materials for producing petrol, benzine, and lubricating oil. They had even been able to produce rudimentary plastic from the hydrocarbon compounds, although only in small quantities. In any case, the tanks of the refinery had to be emptied every few months and brought back to Eridu. More than once they had been attacked by wotans on one of their regular trips.

"Yeah, we'll definitely need more lookouts."

Wistfully, Russell thought about the plan to build a pipeline from the oil springs to the edge of the colony. Then they could erect the refinery directly next to their colony, and spare themselves the dangerous trips into the jungle. But they didn't have enough resources. Like so many other plans, the pipeline idea had slipped right to the bottom of the pile. It would be a project for a future generation.

Russell took the curves fast. He liked it when the rear axle skidded through the gravel on sharp curves. Suddenly he slammed on the breaks and swore. Something was lying in the middle of the road.

"Jesus Christ!" He jumped out of the vehicle and ran toward Drew Potter. She was kneeling on the ground holding a flat stone in her hand. She had frozen to the spot when the jeep skidded to a halt just a few feet away from her.

"I nearly ran you over."

The geologist rose to her feet. "Jesus! You scared me to death racing round the bend like that."

"And why on earth are you kneeling in the middle of the road?" asked Marlene, who had come up beside Russell, arms folded.

Drew stood up and laughed. "Road? What road? I don't see a road here, just the natural floor of the canyon. And anyway, there isn't exactly much traffic here, so I wasn't reckoning with a crazy boy racer!"

"Sorry. What are you doing here, anyway?" asked Russell.

Drew took his hand and placed something in it.

"Pebbles?" he asked.

"That's evaporite. With deposits of sodium chloride," said the geologist, as if that explained everything.

Russell exchanged a quick glance with Marlene and stared at Drew in silence.

"Alright, I'll explain. This stone is formed through contact with water. The salt crust is not very pronounced, which means that the contact can't have been very long ago. On Earth, you only find these stones near the coast."

"But the coast is hundreds of miles away from here," Russell pointed out.

"Right. And that's not the only unusual thing. You would only expect to find these stones below this point, in the lowlands, at most half-way up the pass. In Eridu and the highlands above it, erosion is caused primarily by wind and precipitation, as you would expect."

"You mean storms and rain?" Russell asked.

"Right. Both of them wear away the stones and both erosion processes can be recognized by the patterns on the surface of the stones."

"Is this of any practical importance to us?" asked Marlene.

Drew rolled her eyes. "We should find out as much as we can about our new home. Up to now, I've spent all my time searching for natural resources and raw materials for you. Now the time has come to find out more about the geology of this planet."

"I don't dispute that. But will what you just told us affect us in any direct way?"

The geologist looked up at the precipitous, bleak walls of the canyon. "I don't know. Probably not. But it's very unusual. Do you see these horizontal grooves in the stone?"

"Yes, on Earth I remember seeing that kind of thing by the sea. On rocks that waves broke against all the time," said Russell.

Drew nodded. "That's right. Those are traces of abrasion—erosion caused by waves and tides. There are abrasion marks on all the rocks from here down into the valley —and they are very pronounced. I would bet my bottom dollar that not long ago, all this was under water, which then drained off again very quickly."

"Not long ago? You mean on a geological scale?" asked Russell.

"No, I mean literally. Not long ago. A few decades."

Russell tipped back his head to look up at the rock formations of the canyon. Suddenly the lines transformed into waves and the rockface was colored jet black. He gasped for breath, but the suffocating feeling remained.

"Russell? Is everything okay?"

Marlene's voice came from far away. His legs gave way. He stumbled forward to support himself on the car, but he couldn't keep his balance. He smacked onto the hard ground and fell unconscious.

Chapter 3

Twenty years ago:

"THE MEETING IS HEREBY OPENED. Quiet at the back, please!" said Marlene. The chattering in the corner of the room didn't die down. She raised her voice. "Kenneth, Stanislav! Please!"

Stanislav Radinkovic, one of the ecologists, looked up guiltily and stopped talking.

The mess hall, assembled out of prefabricated parts and the biggest building on the base, was full to the rafters. They had taken out the tables and set up rows of folding chairs, but there were not enough for everyone to have a seat. There were people leaning against the walls and others sitting on the ground. Everybody from the base had come, just as she had ordered. Twenty-nine men and women, of whom nine were soldiers from the Special Engineers unit, herself included, and the rest scientists and assistants. Marlene Wolfe was sitting at a long table at the front of the room, flanked by Lieutenant Hawke, who was fidgeting with his ballpoint pen, and Dr. Lindwall, who was leafing through some papers he had lain out on the table. His hands were trembling and he was chewing loudly on a piece of gum. Marlene guessed that he was still suffering from nicotine withdrawal. Sitting beside him was John Dressell, head of the scientific expedition. At the end of the table, in handcuffs, and guarded by Ernie Lawrence and Chris Neaman, crouched the two men who had abruptly destroyed all their hopes one week earlier: Russell Harris and Christian Holbrook.

They had interrogated the traitors until they had discovered every detail of what had happened. Marlene had not known that General Morrow had sent prisoners in the transporter and that he was responsible for a number of deaths. In principle, it was no different from Ben Hawke's suggestion. And it had obviously been approved by the president. Marlene had been shocked when she found out. She would never have countenanced something like that. Since then, she had been wrestling with her conscience; not only about what to do with the traitors, but also about their situation in general. Over the past few days, it had become clear to her that she couldn't make this decision on her own. Although this was a military opera-tion and she was the captain, the decision affected them all. A return to Earth was impossible and her mission was thereby ended. They found themselves in a new situation. Their base had turned into an independent colony and the expedition members had become involuntary colonists. Marlene did not want to establish a military dictatorship. The only problem was, they could not survive on Russell's Planet. The upcoming decision needed to be made democ-ratically.

That was her opinion, but unfortunately not that of her deputy. Hawke leaned over to her. "Think about it again. We don't have to go through this bullshit," he whispered in her ear. He had been in favor of proclaiming martial law, and restricting the freedom of the scientists. Their first act should be to set an example: Harris and Holbrook should be court-martialed as traitors, and shot.

She shook her head. If they did that, they would possibly rob themselves of the only chance of finding a planet on which they could survive, because neither Harris nor Holbrook had revealed the code to the planet to which they had fled before destroying the transporter on Earth. Hawke had suggested torturing the men to find out the code, but Marlene refused.

Marlene stood up. Immediately the ripple of voices died down. Marlene took her time, and looked as many people in the eye as she could. She wanted to give them the feeling that she was addressing each and every one of them in person. "Our situation has fundamentally changed. You know that we are stranded here and that we cannot return to Earth."

Angry muttering rippled through the room. The men and women knew exactly who was to blame for that.

"The first point we need to decide today is what should happen with these two men."

"String 'em up!" cried Eliot Sargent from the back row. There was a murmur of approval. On the very day the two men had arrived, there had already been an attack. Holbrook had got away with a deep wound to his neck after the soldier Andrea Phillips had attempted to slit his throat with a knife. Marlene had put Andrea under arrest and protected the men against further attacks by personally locking them into the lab and keeping hold of the only key. Although of course it had been she who had first laid a hand on Mr. Harris and broken his nose. It had been a kneejerk reaction and she

37

had immediately regretted it. However, she had not apologized.

"The death penalty is one possibility. We will decide that together today," said Marlene.

"You're the commander!" pointed out Igor Isalovic from the second row.

Marlene shook her head. "Our mission has become obsolete, since we no longer have any hope of returning to Earth. I can't be in command of our colony for the rest of our lives."

"Colony?" asked Dr. Cashmore in the first row.

"Yes. Our camp has become an involuntary colony. This is no longer a military mission. And we need to decide our fate together. I will give up my command as soon as we have democratically elected a council, which will oversee the future of our colony for a fixed amount of time. Since we have little choice but to establish a new colony, it should at least be based on the same democratic principles as our homeland. America was also founded as a colony, and we must not forget that many of the early settlers came unwillingly, but turned America into their home. I would like to follow their inspiring example and hope it gives us the strength and fortitude to come to terms with our difficult situation. And I would like the decisions that we make to be consistent with the beliefs and principles of our forefathers."

"Hear, hear!" Sammy Yang called out. A few people nodded. Marlene had the feeling she'd struck the right tone with her impassioned words. She walked around the table and stood next to Harris and Holbrook. "And I am not sure our new colony should start off with two death sentences." She paused histrionically.

"But that is for the community to decide. One thing is for sure: We cannot stay here, or else we will die. Let's not forget: these prisoners also offer us a perspective. I would like everybody to listen to what they have to say. Mr. Harris?"

Russell Harris stood up slowly. He knew his life was at stake here, but nonetheless he radiated a strange tranquility, as if this was nothing new for him. Harris had told her that he had once been a soldier in an elite unit. She assumed he had probably survived some dangerous missions. As much as she hated him for getting her and her men and women into this mess, she was curious to hear his story. She hoped the assembled group wouldn't condemn him to death before she got the chance. Harris cleared his throat.

"First of all, I would like to thank Captain Wolfe for giving me this opportunity to speak to you. I am aware that I and my colleagues are responsible for the fact that you can no longer return home. I apologize for this with all my heart. We, too, would have wished for a different outcome. After we found out the transporter technology posed a threat to very existence Earth, we decided to pay the price and—"

"Traitor! You should burn in hell!" Chris Neaman called out.

"Quiet! Let him speak," Marlene spoke calmly but firmly.

Harris did not respond to the remark. "We are only a small group of survivors. Myself and Christian Holbrook, and—on the planet to which we fled from Earth—Ellen Slayton, Albert Bridgeman and Jim Rogers. Five people. We can survive, but there are too few of us to establish a colony. We would like to invite you to come with us to our planet to start a new life together and establish a permanent colony. We have everything on our planet that we need in order to survive. The weather is pleasant, there are edible plants, and the soil is suitable for growing your seeds. There is no way back. Not for you and not for us. Let's build our future together."

Eliot Sargent stood up. His face was flushed. "Who gave you the right to destroy the transporter? What gives you the right to decide which technology is available to mankind and which isn't? The transporter was a gift that could have helped us make unimaginable progress. We could have colonized the galaxy with it. Perhaps the secrets of the technology would have helped us solve all of mankind's problems. You're the worst kind of scum that planet Earth ever produced." He spat out the last words so loudly that Julia Stetson, sitting beside him, had to cover her ears.

Sarah Demig, who was sitting one row in front of them, waved his remarks aside. She turned around to Eliot and spoke loudly enough for everyone to hear. "Oh, come on. The first thing humans have always done with any new technology they've got their hands on was to create new weapons. Perhaps the destruction of the transporter was the best thing that could have happened to Earth."

"Are you telling me that you agree with these traitors?" Eliot roared into her face. She simply shrugged.

"Hush now!" Wolfe raised her hands. "Dr. Dressel has prepared a report about the spheres, and whether they really posed such a threat."

The chief scientist stood up. "Over the last few days I have talked at length with Mr. Harris and Mr. Holbrook and found out as much as I possibly could. I have already been able to verify some of the facts. If you put yourself into a meditative trance-like state, you can talk to the artificial intelligence of the sphere by means of telepathy. Mr. Harris taught me how. I have already learnt a thing or two about the technology. The transporter works on the basis of an asymmetrical . . ." He hesitated and searched for words that the soldiers could understand. "Well, let's just say, the teleportation is made possible through the creation of a wormhole. The machine manipulates space-time and creates a strong gravitational field by means of some energy the source of which I haven't understood—similar to a black hole, but without an event horizon."

"Get to the point, Doctor," Captain Wolfe whispered.

The scientist paused, nodded and searched for the right words again. "In any case, the concept is inherently unstable."

"What does that mean?" asked Ben Hawke sharply. Every time Dressel slipped into science jargon, Hawke rolled his eyes.

"Well, it's like in a unstable nuclear reactor. In order to have a stable chain reaction, you have to constantly read-just the control rods. If you fail to do so, the chain reaction either breaks off or increases exponentially, like in Chernobyl. The transporter has to precisely regulate the creation of the wormhole."

"So what are you saying?" asked Marianna Waits. "That there might be chain reaction like in Chernobyl?"

Dressel shook his head. "No, worse. An event horizon would form and a stable black hole would be created, which would first destroy the transporter and finaly the whole planet."

"I thought that microscopically small black holes would immediately evaporate through Hawking radiation," said Dr. Cashmore. Although he was a chemist, Marlene knew that he devoted much of his spare time to reading about other areas of science.

Dressel nodded. "Generally, yes. But the event horizon generated by the transporter would be as big as the diameter of the inner sphere, the corresponding mass would be equivalent to about a thousandth of the mass of our sun."

"But that's impossible. How could that thing generate so much energy?"

"No idea. I assume the transporter pumps out vacuum energy. But that's speculation. In any case, during the formation of an event horizon, part of Earth's mass would immediately be sucked into the black hole that had been created. The rest would be ripped apart by cosmic forces, and hurled in every direction at almost the speed of light."

"How high is the probability that this all would have come to pass if these men hadn't destroyed the transporter," asked Wolfe.

"It's impossible to quantify, but I'm sure it would have happened at some point. Murphy's Law."

Ben Hawke snorted.

"Are you sure?" asked Dr. Potter from the first row. "Even if all safety precautions had been taken?"

"Absolutely. How can you establish safety measures if you don't understand the underlying principle? And they definitely would have continued to experiment with the technology. I would have done the same myself."

"Even if you knew that the technology is dangerous?" asked Wolfe.

"Yes, it would be almost impossible to resist the urge to discover the technology's secret. Imagine a horde of Neanderthals in the control room of an atomic power station, playing around incessantly with the switches. A reactor has emergency shut-off systems, but those can be deactivated too. At some point, someone would have found the right switch."

"But we're not Neanderthals," said Dr. Lindwall indignantly. The doctor took a piece of chewing gum out of his mouth and wrapped it in a tissue, which he slipped into his pocket.

The physicist laughed. "There's a far greater gap between us and these aliens than between us and the Neanderthals. They only died out thirty thousand years ago, while the builders of the sphere were millions of years ahead of us."

"We're getting off topic," Wolfe interrupted the discussion. "Dr. Dressel, you are also sure that the destruction of the sphere was justified?"

The scientist sighed. "Everyone has to decide that for themselves. All I will say is: I wouldn't have bothered putting aside any money for my retirement."

Wolfe nodded. "Thank you, Doctor. I would also like to point out that—"

"For Christ's sake!" Chris Neaman had stood up. He was puffing angrily. "Why do we have a chain of command? It would have been the task of the leaders on Earth to decide whether or not to investigate the technology. The Army also has plenty of outstanding scientists, who ought to be trusted to make the right decision. Every year, the USA spends billions of dollars on think tanks in Washington and elsewhere to analyze precisely these kinds of questions. But these idiots here . . . " he pointed with a quivering finger at Harris and Holbrook, ". . . made the decision all on their own. It's treason. High treason. For which there is only one possible punishment." He collapsed back into his seat.

Camille Ott stood up in the row behind. "I'm too young to have experienced it in person, but my parents often told me about their experiences during the Cuban Missile Crisis—when it seemed as if a nuclear war between the USA and the Soviet Union would begin at any minute. My parents feared for their lives. My mother told me later that back then, she woke up every morning thinking the day might be her last. At the time, I think most people would have given anything to reverse the discovery of nuclear fission."

"Bullshit," cried Travis Richards. He was leaning against the wall next to the entrance. His voice was quiet but firm. "You can't compare the two."

"Why not? Every time humans have invented a new technology, it's a sure bet that something will go wrong. We were always told nuclear power stations were safe. Then came Three Mile Island. People said it wasn't that bad, nobody was hurt. Then came Chernobyl. That time, there were victims. We were reassured by being told the reactor was a Soviet piece of junk. And then came Fukushima, and I'm sure that won't be the last reactor disaster."

"But you can't . . ." interrupted Neamen.

Camille ignored him. "It's the same with space travel. When the shuttle was developed, clever scientists calculated there would only be a disaster every few hundred years. Just five years later, the Challenger exploded during take-off. And despite every effort made to make it safer, a few years later came the Columbia crash. The Titanic was also supposed to be unsinkable. Whenever we think we've come up with a fail-safe system, something goes wrong. If you ask me, it's a miracle that humankind survived the last century. And there are greater dangers lurking on the horizon. Genetic engineering, nanotechnology, artificial intelligence. We throw ourselves enthusiastically into playing with these new toys, all of which have the potential to eradicate humankind. So we don't need hellish alien machines that can turn the Earth into a black hole on top of that."

Now she turned to Chris Neaman. "If we've spared the whole of humankind from this danger, then I think being stranded in space was a small price to pay. You want to execute these two men? I would give them a medal for bravery. That's my opinion."

"Does anyone else have something to add?" asked Marlene Wolf.

Marianna Waits raised her hand timidly. "Will we really never get back home?"

Wolfe shook her head. "Since the sphere on Earth has been destroyed, there is no chance. None of us will ever step foot on Earth again."

"I wouldn't say that so categorically," said Dr. Dressel.

Captain Wolfe turned her head and blinked. "What do you mean?"

"According to Mr. Holbrook there are other spheres in our solar system. For example on Mars. And they know that on Earth. I'm sure now that the transporter on Earth has been destroyed, the race will soon begin to find that sphere and take possession of it. It's only a question of time until the transporter on Mars has a manned station. If the government really wants it and is willing to provide unlimited resources, it could be done in five years' time. So we could get back to Earth via a circuitous route. Our exile is perhaps only temporary."

A wave of voices cascaded through the mess room. Marlene stared at Dr. Dressel. She hadn't reckoned with this. She had been under the firm belief that there was no way back. And now, suddenly, all was not lost after all. That changed the situation—fundamentally.

"Okay," she said. "That offers us a glimmer of hope that we can think about later. Nonetheless, we have to decide what our next step is. Clearly we have only two options: either we give free rein to our desire for revenge and execute Mr. Harris and Mr. Holbrook for treason. Or we accept their offer, join the other group and set up a colony on their planet, in order to hold out for as long as it takes to find a way back to Earth." *Or not.* "Does anybody have another suggestion?"

She looked around the room expectantly. There was some whispering going on. Neaman and Ott, in particular, were engaged in a quiet but heated discussion. She waited a few more seconds before continuing. "Alright. We'll take a break now. Take the time to talk things through with the others and then we'll put it to a vote."

Chapter 4

"Come on Russell, wake up!

The voice droned through Russell's subconscious. It weaved in and out of a dream about canyon walls closing in on each other and a vision of rising, blood-red water. He was trying to keep afloat, but the water was tossing him against the jagged cliff-face. He gasped for air as again and again he was pushed under the surface by the strong current. With now bloody hands he finally managed to cling onto a rocky outcrop and start to pull himself out. Behind him, he could hear a loud hissing noise and turned his head. Panic welled up as he saw a pack of greenish-gray monsters with open mouths and razor-sharp teeth coming toward him. He had to get away from here!

"Russell. You've got to wake up! Can you hear me?"

When the first of the monsters had almost reached him, the sun suddenly broke through a gap in the clouds. He was dazzled by the rays and blinked. One of the monsters had reached him, his gaping bloodthirsty mouth right in front of his face. Strangely, Russell didn't feel any fear. Why did everything look so fuzzy? He closed his eyes

47

and opened them again. He blinked helplessly, until the image came back into focus. The monster was changing into Dr. Lindwall. The tip of a toothpick was sticking out of the corner of his mouth.

"Finally! Look at me, Russell. Can you hear me?"

Russell nodded. He had a throbbing headache. The light came, of course, from the bright neon lights of the infirmary. He closed his eyes for a few moments until the headache was more bearable.

"Yes Doctor. I can hear you. What happened?"

A second face now swam into view. Russell was relieved to see his wife, Ellen. He had been dreaming, that much he knew. But how had he got here, and why? He simply could not remember. Ellen stroked him gently on the cheek and smiled. "You passed out. They brought you to the infirmary." Her voice was trembling slightly; it always trembled when she was worried.

"They?" Russell had no idea who she was talking about.

"Marlene and Drew. You were in the canyon. Half-way along the road back from the observation post. Can you remember?

The events of the day slowly came back to him. He had been at the observation post with Marlene. Then they had been attacked by snipers. Images from the battle danced before his eyes. Then the return journey through the canyon where they had come across Drew. The scientist had told them she'd found out something about the geology of the canyon. Then everything had gone black. He must have passed out.

"Must have been my blood pressure. Right, Doc?"

Lindwall looked at him critically. "Your wife told me you haven't been feeling too great these last days and weeks."

"Perhaps a little weaker and more tired than usual. Must be this cold I can't seem to shake off," said Russell. He didn't like to talk about it. Yes, he had been feeling under the weather recently, but not really ill. He didn't want to be an old wuss.

"You had a bad flu?" Lindwall scrutinized Russell skeptically. It wasn't impossible, since they had brought influenza viruses with them from Earth and there had been some serious flu epidemics, but one-off cases were almost unheard of, and due to the size of the colony—forty adults and as many children—Lindwall was generally well informed.

"Okay, not flu. A bad cold that's dragging on," replied Russell.

"What are your symptoms?"

"It started with a sore throat, which turned into a slight cough that won't go away."

"Combined with tiredness and feeling generally under the weather."

"Yes, I suppose so."

"Hmmm." Lindwall scratched his chin. "A protracted case of flu is possible, but unlikely. It would have had to turn into pneumonia to cause a circulatory collapse, and you'd have a fever and your phlegm would look different. Are you sweating at night?"

"Well, a little perhaps," said Russell, reluctantly. He wanted to get out of here. He didn't understand why the doctor was making such a fuss. He was getting old, that was all.

"Liar!" said Ellen gently but firmly. She stroked his back. "The last few weeks you were often soaked in sweat in the morning."

"But it's been pretty warm lately!"

"Well. . . . " said Dr. Lindwall.

"Now what?" asked Russell. "Are you going to do a blood test to find out what the problem is?"

"I already took some blood while you were unconscious. I'll check it out this evening. The automatic blood testing equipment has given up the ghost completely. Like so many things here." Lindwall spat the chewed-up toothpick, which he'd had in his mouth the whole time, in the direction of the trash can, but missed. He took another toothpick out of a little box and stuck it in his mouth absentmindedly. After twenty years on this new planet, the doctor still missed his beloved cigarettes.

"So I can go now?" asked Russell.

"I'd like to take an upper-body X-ray."

"I thought the X-ray machine had also given up the ghost," said Ellen.

"The machine was okay, I just didn't have any photographic plates anymore." He shrugged. "Dr. Dressel has found a way of improvising some replacement plates for me."

"How?" asked Russell, as he took off his shirt and walked over to the narrow X-ray cabin.

The gaunt doctor followed him, took a plate out of a container and slid it into the machine. "He coated glass plates with a silver-bromide emulsion."

"Silver bromide?"

Lindwall shrugged again. "Reacts with the X-rays. Our biologist had a canister of it in her lab. When it's run out, that'll be the end of X-raying for the time being. Over the coming years, we're going to have to say goodbye to a lot of the comforts and conveniences we're used to." The doctor furrowed his brow.

"I'm sorry if you'd rather be somewhere else," said Russell quietly. Even after all these years, he still had the feeling he had to justify himself.

Dr. Lindwall flicked a switch on the X-ray machine. "S'okay. The decision to destroy the transporter on Mars was reached democratically. I voted against it, but maybe it's a good thing humanity has no more access to this technology if it's as dangerous as Dr. Dressel says it is. I've come to terms with the fact that I'm never returning to Earth, but sometimes I wonder what kind of world our children are growing up in." He pointed out of the narrow window. "The nuclear reactor over there will be able to provide us with some of our energy even fifty years from now. But we'll have to plough our fields by hand when the jeeps are beyond repair in a few years' time. We don't even have horses or cows we can use, because there simply aren't any comparable animals here. We have a very peculiar mix of modern technology and medieval methods. And at the rate our equipment is falling apart, I would say we're sliding increasingly back toward the Middle Ages."

"Our engineers are already working on a tractor that could work with the combustion engine they created. We have oil, and if our children show initiative, they'll be living in a modern, digital society again within a few generations."

Lindwall laughed quietly. "You don't seriously believe that, do you? How many children do we have? The generation born here consists of forty children. The next generation, our grandchildren, might consist of around a hundred people: *far* too few for a modern, digital society. A modern chip factory needs—how many . . . a thousand?—in any case a great many workers that we simply don't have. The next few generations will have a universal education at their disposal. But we won't be able to go down the route of detailed specialization, which is necessary for modern technical achievement. Our level of development will be frozen at the level of the early twentieth-century for a long time, probably for hundreds of years. At the moment, our kids still have the luxury of accessing human knowledge using computers, but they won't last forever, either. At some point they will have to start developing everything themselves. And there isn't enough paper on this planet to even write down even the most basic knowledge. It will be a miracle if the society of our grandchildren doesn't revert to medieval barbarianism."

"Isn't that a very pessimistic view?" asked Russell.

"I also think we can trust our children and grandchildren to be more farsighted," added Ellen.

The doctor snorted. "War follows peace, creativity follows destruction, death follows life. We shouldn't believe that we are above this just because we left our home planet."

He took Ellen gently by the arm and pushed her out of the little room. He turned to Russell. "Take a deep breath and then hold it until I tell you."

Russell breathed in and stayed as calm as he could as the doctor locked the door.

There was a loud clicking noise and the X-ray was lying in the box.

Chapter 5

"Ben, is that you?" asked Drew, as she heard the squeaking of the front door.

This was followed by the familiar shuffling sound of Ben's footsteps, which answered her question and meant she didn't have to look up from her microscope. She had set up a little workspace in their hut, so she could work outside of the laboratory if she needed to. Right now, the geologist was busy with the stone samples that she had collected in the canyon.

Ben was usually busy with his own stuff, and they didn't do much together anymore, either inside or outside the house. The fact that her husband hadn't greeted her when he came in meant he was in a bad mood again.

"Where are the kids?" she heard Ben's voice from behind her. As usual, it was devoid of any emotion. After all these years, she still couldn't tell from the tone of this voice if he was happy, bored, concerned, or angry.

"Catherine is with Jimmy Harris and Dana is on duty on the fields today. How was your day?"

He husband didn't answer.

Drew turned around. Ben was standing there with folded arms. She turned off the light on the microscope and stood up.

Without warning, Ben's hand struck her in the face. "Clearly you've lost your mind," her husband said calmly.

She looked at him uncomprehendingly. What had she done wrong this time?

"What were you thinking?" Ben grabbed her roughly by the arm.

"I have absolutely no idea what you're talking about!" she shouted at him.

He hit her again. Drew tasted blood.

"You will never shout at me again. Never! Do you understand?" His tone of voice had not changed one iota since the beginning of the conversation. "I asked you if you understood me," Ben said menacingly.

Drew was whimpering with pain. "Yes! Yes!" she said hoarsely. "I understand!"

Ben let go of her arm. "What were you doing alone in the pass?"

"I was collecting stones." She simply did not understand why he was so angry. "The geology in the lower part of the canyon is completely different from——"

"I don't care about your stupid stones," said Ben. "But I don't like to have my wife found crawling around on the ground by Russell Harris and Marlene Wolfe."

So that was what this was about.

"The men were laughing about it. Do you know how it makes me look? Do you have any idea?"

She looked down at the ground as she couldn't bear the force of his gaze anymore. "How could I have known that Russell and Marlene would be coming around the bend? I didn't even hear their jeep," she whispered.

"I don't care!" said Ben. "I just don't want it ever to happen again, or there'll be a price to pay!"

Drew nodded slowly.

"Say it!"

Drew lifted her head, but was still unable to look him in the eyes.

"I will never do it again," she whispered.

Ben held her in a vice for a few more seconds and nodded. "Okay, we've got that sorted. I also don't want Cathy to continue meeting Jim Harris. Tell your daughter, or I'll have to do it."

Drew sobbed. "Yes, okay. I'll tell her."

Without another word, Ben turned around and disappeared out of the door before Drew sunk back into her seat. She sniffed, and tears ran down her cheeks.

Ben hated Russell. Still, after all these years. Drew tried to think back to the days when they had been happy together. They had gotten to know each other over twenty years ago during a mission in Afghanistan. It had been a peacekeeping mission. Ben and his team had built a bridge and Drew had been called in as a geologist to analyze the difficult substrates. Ben was the deputy company commander, sharp as a tack, and looking forward to leading his first mission. She fell in love with him at first sight. Despite his sometimes macho behavior, he could be very attentive and, compared to the other soldiers, he seemed genuinely interested in his work. They had just rented themselves an apartment together outside the base when they received the command for the fateful mission with the transporter.

Being stranded here had ruined Ben's career plan of becoming a company commander. When Marlene had disbanded the company and turned it into an informal militia that had more in common with the National Guard than with a specialized volunteer army, Ben didn't know what to do with himself anymore. He had never felt at home on New California, nor had he found a task to fulfill him. He was a military officer, after all, and not a technician, mechanic, or engineer, like many others from his company. The fact that Drew greatly enjoyed studying the geological peculiarities of their new home didn't make things easier for their relationship. As the years passed, he increasingly vented his frustration in violent outbursts. The first time he hit her, she had wanted to leave him then and there. But he had begged for forgiveness, and she had relented for the sake of the children.

From then on, his meltdowns became more frequent, and now she had come to the realization that she no longer had the strength to leave him. At least Ben didn't hit the girls. At least she hoped not.

Chapter 6

Russell was out of breath and coughing as he flung open the door to his hut. He was feeling dizzy, and the scratchy feeling in his throat wasn't getting better.

"Where were you?" asked Ellen, who was busy at the hearth. They used the open fireplace for heating and cooking. There were no fitted kitchens on this planet.

But a few years ago they had at least managed to produce glass, which meant the log cabins now let in more light. In the past, they had spanned pieces of leather across the windows. It was a simple life, but they had everything they needed. Russell didn't miss the trappings of modern civilization. He could survive perfectly well without a TV, telephone, computer, Internet, car and newspapers. In fact, he liked the fact that life here was focused on the essentials. Ellen felt the same way.

"I was at Chris's," said Russell.

"Chris Neaman?"

"Christian Holbrook," he replied. "I helped him to patch up his roof." He coughed again.

Ellen put down the wire brush, with which she had

been removing the soot from cracks between the stones. "Dr. Dressel said you need to take care of yourself. You look really unwell again and your coughing hasn't got any better."

Russell raised his arms helplessly. "I can't just sit around the whole day."

Ellen came up to him, gave him a kiss and stroked his cheek. "Nobody said you had to sit around. But you also don't have to climb around roofs with Chris. What would happen if you passed out up there?"

"I guess I'd fall down," replied Russell drily.

"Has the doc finally been in touch?"

"No, he said he'd come over once he's analyzed the blood sample and the X-ray. I don't reckon it'll be today."

"I hope it's nothing serious."

He could tell from his wife's tone of voice that his collapse in the canyon had alarmed her. He couldn't blame her; after all, over all the years he had never been ill. He wasn't too worried himself. He had never been one to take it easy, and he rushed around all over the colony whenever he was needed. Somehow there was always something to do, whether it was mending a roof or building a new hut. He had also never had a problem with doing fieldwork. He enjoyed the exercise. He was just getting older, that was the problem. He would have to slow down a bit, then everything would be okay.

"Nonsense!" replied Russell. "It's probably just a mild case of pneumonia. I'll get some antibiotics, and in a few days I'll be back to normal."

"Let's hope so."

Russell had hardly sat down on a chair, when the door crashed open and Greg came tumbling into the room. The boy had too much energy, thought Russell with a smile. But *I was no different at his age.*

The youngest of their three children was now eight years old. Greg ran straight to his father and stood in front of him, legs apart, hands on his hips. "Hey, Dad, Courtney said that on Earth there are houses as big as giant redwoods. And that more people fit inside than in the whole world." With "world" he of course meant New California, their colony. "Dimitri and I just laughed at them. They were lying weren't they, Dad?"

Russell stood up and couldn't resist giving him a hug. The boy let him, but didn't return the hug like he used to, probably because he found it embarrassing. This stung Russell. Even his youngest child was starting to spread his wings. "I'm afraid you're going to have to apologize to Courtney. The highest building on Earth was in Dubai, it was over half a mile high and as tall as our redwoods. I don't know how many people lived and worked in there, but I reckon it was over ten thousand."

Greg looked at his father with big, innocent eyes. "Ten thousand? You're kidding me, Dad!"

Russell sat down again, as he noticed that the dizziness was returning. "No, Greg. There really were buildings that high."

"And Courtney also said there were ships on Earth as big as redwood trees and that a thousand people could fit inside. But that's impossible!"

Russell felt a wave sadness wash over him. There were so many things his children would never get to see. For his son, who had never seen the ocean or even a big lake, the stories of Earth must sound like tales of a mythical land. In a few generations, when the last photos had also faded, Earth would become a legend and eventually a myth. It wouldn't surprise Russell if the name of their planet of origin was forgotten altogether one day.

"It's true, Greg. There really were ships that could transport that many people."

"Can't we build a ship like that here?"

Russell laughed quietly at the thought of steering a cruise ship over the oceans of New California. "I'm afraid we don't have enough people here for such a big ship."

"Maybe we could build a little one."

"The ocean is a long way away. It will probably take many more years until we have a settlement there and even longer until it would be worthwhile to build a ship."

"Well, I'd like to see the ocean. So much water . . ." His voice became hushed with awe.

Russell laughed. "You will, son. Don't worry. It might be a few more years until we're able to go on another expedition to the ocean, but then you'll be grown up and I'm sure you can come too."

Greg wriggled free from his father's grasp and ran to the door.

"Where are you going now?" asked Ellen, who was dragging the big table back in front of the hearth.

"I'm going to ask Dimitri if he feels like building a ship with me. Then we can take it with us in a few years when we go to the ocean. Can I, Mom?"

"Sure. Off you go."

Greg tore open the door and almost knocked over Dr. Lindwall, who was standing in front of it with a roll of paper.

"Come in, Doc. We're both here."

The slim and wiry doctor stepped inside. He didn't smile as he usually did in greeting.

"Sit down, Doctor," said Ellen. She pulled a chair up to the table. Russell stood up with difficulty and sat down opposite Dr. Lindwall. "Something to drink? A coffee, perhaps?" he asked.

Lindwall shook his head. He looked very serious. Like somebody facing a very unpleasant task. Russell could feel fear welling up inside him. Of course this must have to do with his diagnosis. How bad could it be? Was it his heart? His father had died at the age of sixty of a heart attack. Russell had been on yet another mission at the time, and only found out afterwards, long after the funeral had already taken place. Perhaps it was something hereditary.

Ellen sat down at the table, tight-lipped. In the space of a few moments, the atmosphere had changed completely. A minute ago it had been a warm and cozy little home; now it had been transformed into a bitterly cold court-room. And in a moment Russell would hear the verdict.

"I can see from your face that you haven't come with good news. Be straight with me. How bad is it?"

Wordlessly, the doctor rolled out his papers and unfolded the X-ray of Russell's thorax. Toward the top of the X-ray Russell could see the lungs. Dr. Lindwall pointed with his pen at a pale, almost circular spot to the side of the right lung. "That spot shouldn't be there. And there are high levels of CEA and NSE in your blood."

"NSE?"

"Neuron-Specific Enolase. A glycolytic enzyme. A high level of NSE is the main tumor marker of small-cell bronchial carcinoma."

Ellen's eyes became wide. Russell felt numb.

I have a tumor? Lung cancer? "Are you trying to tell me . . ." He couldn't continue.

Lindwall looked him straight in the eyes. "Yes. I'm terribly sorry."

"Are you sure? Are there any other tests we can do?" asked Ellen.

Lindwall shook his head slowly. "I also found some abnormal cells under the microscope in his sputum. On

Earth, we would double check with a CT scan and a bronchoscopy, but we don't have a tomography machine, and a bronchoscopy wouldn't help us here either."

The doctor's words reached Russell as if through a thick fog. All he could think was: *I have cancer!*

He had difficulty concentrating on what the doctor was saying. "How bad is it? Has it spread already?" He swallowed.

Lindwall spoke quietly. "I haven't found any metastases, but small-cell carcinoma spreads very quickly. If you can feel the first symptoms, it usually means the cancer is already at an advanced stage."

He took Russell's hand. This was an unusual gesture for the doctor, who normally shied away from physical contact. "Do you really want to know the details? Over the years I've discovered it doesn't necessarily help the patient, if they—"

Russell interrupted him brusquely. "It's my body. I want to know what condition it's in, even if I don't like what I hear."

Ellen was following the conversation open-mouthed.

The truth hadn't sunk in yet.

But for him it had: he would die, and not some time, but soon. He pulled his hand out of the doctor's, and folded his arms tightly in front of his chest.

"Two questions: what can we do, and how long do I still have?"

Lindwall raised his arms despondently. "On Earth I would have recommended a combination of chemotherapy with Cisplatin or Carboplatin, together with radiation therapy. But we have neither chemotherapeutic drugs nor radiology devices, so we can only treat the symptoms."

"Can't it be operated on?" asked Ellen. Her voice was suddenly high-pitched.

Lindwall shook his head. "Small-cell carcinoma is inoperable at this stage. It wouldn't change the outcome. It would be impossible to remove all of the metastases, and the remaining ones would spread very fast."

I want to know now, thought Russell. "How long have I got?"

Lindwall sighed, looked down at his feet for a moment and then raised his head. "Three months."

Oh God! Three months! In less than a hundred days I'll be dead!

Russell looked Ellen in the eyes. She stared back at him in disbelief.

"You should get your affairs in order and bid farewell to life." The doctor's words sounded funny. Perhaps doctors also found it hard to find the right words and therefore came out with clichés.

Three months! Jesus Christ! What can I do? There must be something we can do.

"And what happens next? I mean, what should I expect from now on?"

The doctor sighed. "For the next month you'll feel a lot like you do now. We can fight against the general feeling of sickness with vitamin shots and anti-inflammatories, although you might feel a bit weaker and more tired." He was obviously having trouble looking Russell in the eyes, because his own kept wandering around the room. "You might start to think and hope you're getting better, but the tumor cells will metastasize fast. You'll have more trouble breathing. You'll feel out of breath more quickly. Depending on how soon the tumor starts to press against other organs, you may start to feel pain, and fluid will build up in your lungs. Metastases in the brain can affect your behavior. You might become depressed, perhaps even aggressive—up to a complete change in personality, so that even your family doesn't recognize you anymore."

The doctor paused. "The last month will be bad. You'll hardly be able to breathe and we don't have much available here to change that. It's possible you'll be in great pain, for which we can give you morphine. Finally, you will slowly suffocate. At that point we will have to give you an anesthetic, so that you don't feel anything at the end."

My God! And that's all coming up soon!

"Thanks, Doc, for being so honest. I appreciate it," said Russell flatly.

Ellen started to sob.

The doctor pursed his lips, before continuing. "I'm sorry. Truly, I'm terribly sorry. I can't do anything to change the situation, but I'll try to make it as bearable as I possibly can, I promise."

Russell stood up. He wanted the doctor to leave so he could be alone with his wife.

Dr. Lindwall also stood up. "I'm here for you when you need me, please just let me know."

Russell nodded curtly and closed the door behind him. As if drugged, he swayed over to his wife and sat down beside her. She was still sobbing as he took her in his arms. She buried her head in his shoulder.

Three months! I've only got three months! He shook his head. *In fact, I don't even have three months. A month from now it'll go rapidly downhill. I will die a wretched death. And my wife, my children, will have to sit at the sidelines and watch me deteriorate*

Chapter 7

Eighteen years ago

"WHAT? WHAT IS IT?" asked Russell, as Katrina Cole stepped out of the infirmary and closed the door behind her.

"Calm down. She's still in labor."

Russell raised his arms helplessly. The contractions had started over twelve hours ago. This drama couldn't go on for much longer. "How is she?"

"She's doing fine. I'm more worried about you. Don't you want to go home for an hour and lie down for a while? Have you even eaten anything today?"

Was she joking? How could he possibly swallow a single bite in this situation?

"Ellen has eaten," said Katrina.

"Can I see her?"

Katrina shook her head. "It's better if you wait out here."

Russell just grunted. Katrina, who had been recruited

by Dr. Lindwall as a nurse and who had taken on the role of midwife today, turned on her heel and disappeared back into the infirmary, leaving the hapless father outside the barrack.

Russell sighed and continued his pacing in front of the door.

"Stop walking around in a never-ending circle," said Christian Holbrook, who was sitting on the stoop in front of the entrance to the infirmary. "If you carry on like that much longer, we'll have to refill the ruts that you've produced with your endless pacing."

"Put yourself in my situation! This waiting is driving me crazy."

The sun was starting to set. Last night, Ellen had already been tossing to and fro in bed. Early in the morning she had started groaning at regular intervals, as the first contractions started. Russell had brought her to Dr. Lindwall, in the firm belief that she would give birth within minutes. He had been very much mistaken. Now the sun was sinking in the west beyond the forest of redwoods, and only individual rays penetrated the mile-high treetops to cast their light on the walls of the barrack, which they had finished building recently to house the infirmary.

"It can't be normal to be taking this long," said Russell.

"Can you please sit down?" asked Christian.

"For the hundredth time: No!"

The former astronaut grinned, but quickly forced a serious expression back on his face. Russell was well aware that his friend found his helplessness highly amusing. If only this would be over!

Marlene and Albert came around the corner of the barrack. Marlene was laughing, and gave Albert, who was nearly twenty years her senior, a playful slap on the chest, as if he'd just been telling a naughty joke. In her other hand she was holding various pieces of paper. She smiled when she saw Russell and walked up to him and Christian.

"Still nothing?" asked Marlene.

"Nope. We've been waiting here for hours."

"Well, the baby obviously doesn't feel like leaving the comfort of his mother's womb yet."

"Ha! Little Jimmy just doesn't feel like catching sight of his Dad's ugly mug," said Albert with a grin. Russell stuck his tongue out at him.

"Why aren't you in there with Ellen?" asked Marlene.

Russell started to reply, but Christian butted in. "Lindwall threw him out, after he'd paced round his wife hysterically once too often."

Marlene laughed. "Well, you've obviously found a task that elite soldier Russell Harris isn't up to."

Albert grasped Russell's shoulders with both hands. "He can deal with guerillas, Islamists and aliens. But the arrival of a little baby has put him out of commission."

Russell extracted himself from Albert's grasp. "I hate not being able to *do* anything." He hopped nervously from one leg to the other. He knew he was making a fool of himself in front of his friends, but he had never felt this helpless in his entire life.

"Leave the work to others for once," said Marlene. "Doc Lindwall is an excellent physician and I'm sure Katrina is being an excellent midwife."

"What makes you so sure? She's never been present at a birth before."

From inside the barrack he heard a protracted groan that turned into a loud scream.

I can't bear this anymore!

Russell turned around and headed toward the infirmary door, but Marlene held him back. "Russell, Russell. Stay here. It's totally normal, calm down!"

Normal! The scream hadn't sounded normal at all!

But Marlene was right. Even if he went in now, there was nothing he could do. He forced himself to stay calm.

"Okay. You're right," he said. "So distract me. Tell me some news. What were you talking about? He pointed at the papers in Marlene's hand.

"The final plans for the workshop," said Albert. "We need a big stone oven with an air duct. It needs to be hot enough that we can smelt metals to produce tools and spare parts. The machines that we've got here won't last forever."

We're going to start building next week. Then we should be finished by harvest time," said Marlene.

"We should also talk about extending the infirmary," said Christian.

"Yes, the barrack we built is too small." She hesitated. "I'm not sure if I'm allowed to say this, but who cares. Your baby will have some playmates pretty soon," she said, looking at Russell.

"You mean . . .? Who?"

"Ben. He and Drew are expecting a girl. They're in the third month already."

Russell bit his lip: he knew Ben would rather bring up his daughter in solitary confinement than let her play with his son. Most of the colonists who had been brought here from Russell's Planet had come to terms with their situation, and reconciled themselves with Russell. Some, like Eliot and Donald, still threw insults at Russell when they crossed paths. But Ben *hated* him. Not that he insulted Russell or threatened him with violence—they had to work too closely together to plan the colony for that to be an option. But in his eyes he recognized only deep contempt.

When he was standing opposite him, the feeling of antipathy was like an electric current that made the hairs on the back of his neck stand on end. Russell hoped their relationship would improve at some point, but he had the feeling it would take a long time.

"Rhonda is also pregnant," said Christian.

Marlene blinked in astonishment. "Rhonda? I didn't know that. With Dr. Cashmore?"

Christian nodded. "They want to get married next month."

"Now I get it," said Marlene.

"What do you get?" asked Russell.

"A few days ago, Cashmore asked me if I could conduct a ceremony. But I didn't have any time and asked him to come back to me in a week. I didn't know it was about a wedding, or I wouldn't have brushed him off in such a hurry."

Ellen screamed again. Russell could hear Lindwall saying something to her, but didn't catch his words.

When is this ever going to end?

"I wouldn't be surprised if there are some more babies on the way soon—judging by the noise coming from Ernie and Andrea's tent nearly every night," said Albert, whose hut was next to Ernie Lawrence's. "Sometimes they wake me up at night."

"Then find someone with whom you can give Ernie and Andrea a run for their money!" said Russell.

Marlene blushed. He didn't know that she found these kinds of conversations embarrassing. He wanted to make a pointed remark, but Christian had already changed the subject.

"Should we be concerned, in the long run, about incest or genetic depletion?"

"No, not if we're careful our children don't get

together with close relatives," said Marlene. "I talked about it with Jenny. We are forty adults. It's cutting it close, but there should be sufficient genetic variation. She told me about Kiwis, these flightless birds in New Zealand. Apparently there were only five left in existence, but after their habitats were officially protected, they started to recover and now there are well over a thousand of them. We're passing through a genetic bottleneck, but we'll survive. The best thing we can do is to have as many children as possible."

"Well, Russell's making a good start," said Albert.

"Yeah, yeah, but it wasn't planned." They no longer had any contraceptives. The doctor's small supply had been used up after just a few weeks. To start, they hadn't wanted any children, but Ellen had got muddled up counting the days of her cycle—not a particularly reliable method in the first place. So when Lindwall had broken the news that Ellen was pregnant, they had been surprised but happy. And now Russell wanted to finally see his son!

As if on command, the door of the infirmary opened. Katrina had blood on her apron, but she was smiling mischievously. She held the door open and made an inviting gesture with her head.

Russell hesitated. "You mean . . . ?"

"Go on in!" Marlene spurred him on.

Slowly, Russell climbed the two steps up to the entrance, squeezing past Katrina, who patted him on the back. Dr. Lindwall came up to him as he took off his surgical gloves. He smiled and held out his hand. Russell grasped it.

"Congratulations, Harris. Go on through. Ellen is waiting. And so is someone else."

He hardly looked at the doctor and dropped his hand.

"I could really do with a cigarette right now," murmured Lindwall, as Russell pushed past him.

Russell stepped into the treatment room, where Ellen was lying in bed. She looked exhausted. A blood vessel had obviously burst in her right eye; he couldn't see any white. But she was smiling. In her arms she was holding a little white bundle. Just a little corner of pink-colored skin peeped out from the cover. Russell could see a tiny, closed eye.

Slowly, mouth agape, he walked around the bed. He knew he should have been paying attention to Ellen, but he couldn't help himself. He pulled back the white blanket and a tiny little arm stretched out toward him. He stroked the delicate skin gently with his index finger. He could feel a lump in his throat, and had to fight back the tears.

"Your son!" whispered Ellen.

My son!

Little fingers closed around his finger and held tight, as if they didn't want to let go again.

The damn burst and Russell started to cry.

"Jim!" he whispered.

Chapter 8

Marlene sifted through the papers in her tray; they were minutes from the last colony meeting. She squinted slightly as she tried to decipher Robert Cashmore's handwriting. After reading through the first page, she took a fountain pen made of hard redwood out of the coffee-cup-turned-pen-holder, dipped it into the ink that had been made from water and titanium oxide by the colony's chemist, and wrote her initials in the bottom right-hand corner of the page.

The paper was as yellow as antique parchment, but it was the best they could do with the wood chippings on this planet.

It irritated Marlene that they had created a completely new social order here, and yet simply couldn't manage without bureaucracy. After one of the first colony meetings, Dorothy Moore had challenged the legitimacy of the decision to clear part of the nearby forest, although the matter had been voted on. The argument had become so heated that Marlene had decided to keep minutes of future meetings and records of the resolutions that were adopted. Two months later she had run out of paper. But once again, Dr. Cashmore proved himself to be extremely innovative. Then, a few months later, most of the pens they still had from Earth ran out. Lee Shanker had come up with the wooden fountain pen solution.

Just as Marlene had signed off the last page, there was a knock at the door of the wooden barrack, which served as the colony's seat of government. Based on another far-distant seat of government, this one had been given the tongue-in-cheek name of "The Brown House". This is where they held their weekly council meetings and there were two desks where the members of the council could work.

"Come in!"

The door opened and Chris Neaman stepped inside. Like Ben Hawke, he had never found a new role for himself in the colony, and still saw himself as a soldier.

"Hi Marlene. Do you have a minute?"

"I've got more than a minute if you give me a second to file these papers."

Chris sat down on one of the two wooden chairs in front of Marlene's desk and fiddled with his coarsely woven sweatshirt. Although they were taken good care of, many of the uniforms they had come with had fallen apart long ago, and the spinning wheel that Albert had made, together with Sammy Yang's improvised loom, was increasingly put to use. Then it was up to every settler to sew their own clothes from the fabric. Five years ago, Donald Bell had managed to produce a multi-strand yarn from an indigenous plant, which they called "hemp" due to its resemblance to the plant on Earth. Since then, knitting had become an unavoidable pastime. Marlene had found it hard to suppress a grin when she had spotted even the rugged lone wolf Ernie swearing in front of his hut as he struggled with two knitting needles.

Marlene took the pieces of paper and reached into a little wooden box. She groaned when she noticed it was empty.

"Everything okay?" asked Chris.

Marlene leaned over the empty box. "We've run out of paper clips."

"I can run and get you some more from the warehouse."

"I think those were the last ones! Another thing we've run out of."

Chris shrugged. "I guess we'll survive a lack of paper-clips. And anyway, those things are just bent wire. Surely our engineers will be able to come up with something."

"They're busy with more important things," said Marlene. She punched the papers with a hole punch and filed them in a dog-eared folder that had also seen better days.

She returned the folder to the shelf and leaned back in the leather chair. "What can I do for you, Chris?"

The tall and lean soldier stroked his thick beard. "I'm worried about the observation post in the valley."

Marlene was surprised. "But just last week we increased the number of lookouts to four."

"The attacks on the barrier are becoming more frequent. Recently it was at least three per shift, so that I'm starting to worry about our supply of ammunition. Yesterday, Eliot Sargent also saw four creatures that we've never seen before roaming around the edge of the forest. And they didn't look friendly."

Marlene shook her head. "Thanks to the depot we

were supposed to set up on Russell's Planet, we've got enough ammunition to last a hundred years. I'm not worried about that. But the fact that so many creatures are starting to come up to the post is strange."

"If this goes on . . ."

Marlene waved a hand dismissively. "I don't want to speculate what it might mean. There's no point." She reached for the radio that was lying on a shelf next to her and pressed the speaker button.

"Infirmary, Wolfe here, please report."

There was a brief pause, then she heard the voice of Dr. Lindwall crackling through the loudspeaker.

"It's not a good time, can I get back to you?"

"No. I need to know if Jenny is with you."

"Yes, she's sitting here at the microscope analyzing plant fibers."

"Do you need her right now?"

"No, shall I send her over?

"Yes."

Without another word, the doctor broke off the connection. Marlene turned back to Neaman. "We should talk about this with our biologist."

Chris nodded, and there was a knock at the door.

"That was quick," murmured Marlene. "Come in!"

But it wasn't Jenny Baldwin, it was Drew Potter. She hesitated at the door. "Is this a bad time?" she asked shyly.

"We were expecting someone else. Is it urgent?" Marlene only noticed now that Drew had a black eye. Ben must have been hitting her again. She had tried to talk about it with Drew on several occasions, but Drew had always evaded her questions. Some time ago she had thought about stepping in, but what was the use if Drew denied everything?

Still she asked carefully: "Is everything okay?"

Drew nodded. "Great."

Marlene hadn't expected to hear anything different. Drew was an adult. She had to decide for herself what she could put up with.

"I carried out a few geological studies that I'd like to discuss with you," Drew continued.

"Does it have to do with the lines in the canyon?"

The geologist nodded again. "I analyzed stone samples from the area."

Marlene waited for Drew to continue, but she seemed to be waiting to be prompted. "And?"

"The entire southern half of the canyon seems to have been under water until relatively recently."

"Yes, you suspected as much when we met you in the canyon."

"Yes, but I've been able to establish that it was just thirty years ago, so around ten years before we got here. It also seems to be a cyclical problem."

"You mean, the pass is under water every few dozen years?"

"Something like that. I can't quite make sense of it." Marlene could hear the exasperation in her voice.

"Could it have to do with severe weather conditions? Big rainstorms that sometimes transform the pass into a torrential river? Could that be an explanation?"

Drew shrugged. "That would look different. I can't explain it. I've never seen anything quite like it on Earth."

"And what do you suggest now?"

"I would like to analyze the stones in the lowlands. A couple of miles away from the exit."

"But you already carried out research in the lowlands."

Drew sniffed. "That was just about finding oil and

other crude materials. I didn't have a chance to do any comprehensive field research."

"Well, I think we've got more pressing problems than scientific studies," Chris Neaman piped up.

Drew turned red. Probably she was embarrassed; Marlene had never seen the scientist angry.

"I have to agree with Chris. An expedition to the lowlands would be very dangerous. It would be difficult to defend ourselves in the jungle, not least because the number of animal sightings near the observation post has increased dramatically lately."

"Animal *sightings*?" Chris protested. "Last week they nearly had us for breakfast. You weren't there in person."

Marlene raised her hand to pacify him. "Yes, it was close. But I don't want to spread panic in the colony. And since then we've strengthened the observation post."

"Sure, but . . ."

The door swung open wide, and Jenny Baldwin burst into the hut. Neaman gave a start and swiveled round.

"Have you heard the news?"

"Heard what news?" asked Marlene sternly. She didn't like being ambushed in this way.

"About Russell!"

"What's up with Russell?" asked Marlene.

"Cancer . . . three months," said Jenny, practically tripping over her own words.

Marlene needed a few seconds to steady herself. She blinked at the biologist.

"What do you mean by three months. You're not trying to tell me . . ." Marlene fell silent as she took in Jenny's expression. "Oh my god!"

Marlene leaned back in her chair and closed her eyes.

Three months! Then I'll lose a good friend!

She could hardly remember how contemptuous she

had felt towards him when they first met. But when it had come to setting up the colony, there was hardly anyone who had worked as hard as Russell. First, he had earned her respect, friendship followed of its own accord. He was one of the first people Marlene turned to when everything got too much for her, and he had always been able to buoy her spirits. In turn, she had come to his defense in the early years, when animosity toward him still ran high. And now he was going to die of this pointless illness? Marlene didn't want to believe it.

They had all been relatively young when they had got here, apart from Albert, who was now seventy-three years old, but still in excellent health and with a ready grin on his face. Apart from Jim Rogers, nobody had died so far. There were hardly any illnesses here. They had been able to identify virus-like organisms in the animals, but they didn't affect human DNA. Most of their work was very physical, and so the colonists were generally in robust health, give or take the occasional minor accident. Over the last twenty years, Marlene had completely blocked out the fact that something as horrible as a fatal form of cancer even existed.

"Are you sure?" she asked.

Jenny nodded. "There's nothing here to treat it with. Dr. Lindwall says he isn't able to produce chemotherapeutic substances. He can administer morphine in the final stages, but that's it."

"Who else knows about it?" asked Marlene.

"Russell and his family, Dr. Lindwall, and now us. I wasn't actually supposed to tell anyone," the biologist admitted sheepishly.

Typical. Jenny's a gossip. The whole colony will know by this evening.

"I actually wanted to talk about a problem at the observation post, but I think we'll leave it for later. I'm not in the mood now."

"But . . ." protested Chris.

Marlene came around the table and laid a hand on Neaman's shoulder. "We'll talk about it tomorrow. Now I'm going to see Russell."

Chapter 9

"Wait up."

Ernie Lawrence turned around. His friend Grant Dillon, who had been stumbling along a few feet behind him, had stopped to sit down on a big rock at the side of the path. His backpack slid from his shoulders.

"What's the problem now?" asked Ernie. If they carried on like this, they would never reach their destination.

Grant loosened the laces on his left boot. "I've got a stone in my boot again."

Ernie remained standing on the dirt track, arms folded. "Your own fault. I don't know anyone who ties their laces as carelessly as you. You need to tie them much tighter. No wonder you're constantly whining."

Grant shook out the boot and put it back on. "But it's kinda dumb we have to walk so much here. Every time one of the tractors conks out, we have to walk four miles to the fields just to repair a jammed valve or some other minor thing," he complained.

"You're welcome to build yourself a hut next to the

fields, then you won't have to walk at all anymore. Be glad we're getting some exercise."

Ernie had never been able to sit still for long. He had felt at home in New California right from the start. There was always something to do, whether it was working on the fields or building a new hut. Life was harder, and there were no luxuries here, but Ernie had never minded, because in many ways life here was also less complicated than on Earth. After they were stranded, he had soon started getting along with Russell and the other "traitors" and taken their side. But he knew that Grant had seen things differently at first. The lanky mechanic, who was not the most talented at his profession, had left behind friends and plans for the future on Earth; in the beginning, he would have liked to murder Russell. It had taken him years to feel at home—which probably had something to do with getting married to Sarah Deming from the team of scientists. In the end, he had even voted in favor of blowing up the transporter on Mars, destroying all hope of ever getting home. Since then, together with Lee and Albert, he had been responsible for maintaining the colony's vehicles and machines, some of which were now practically beyond repair. It was to fix a broken tractor that they were now on their way to the fields. As on many previous occasions, Ernie was accompanying his friend to help carry the heavy tools. But if they had to stop every few feet, they would never get there.

"Are you done already, or do you want me to carry you too?"

"I'm ready. Chill out, will you?"

Grant snatched up his backpack and got back on his feet. "It's really dumb they didn't give us a jeep."

"They're all in use."

Slowly they walked through the forest of giant

redwoods toward the fields in the west. They had brought the jeeps with them from Russell's Planet. It hadn't been easy, they'd had to be completely dismantled in order to fit in the transporter. Then they had converted some into tractors, which were needed for working the fields. Two of them were used to transport people and materials to the observation post at the canyon exit, while the rest were nearly always undergoing repairs in the workshop. Recently, one of the cylinders had blown and since then, Grant and Lee had been busting their asses trying to build a replacement. Luckily, the Martin JLTVs were otherwise easy to maintain. The number of electronic components was limited and even after those broke, the jeeps were still fit to drive.

They had reached a junction in the middle of the forest that marked about half the distance between the colony and the fields, which were a good six miles away. A small path veered off from the dirt road to the right, and ended after several feet at a clearing, which was already in view. In the middle of the clearing, untouched for years, was the alien transporter.

Ernie shook his head at the sight of the weird machine with which they had reached this planet twenty years ago. "Whenever I see the transporter, I always expect some eight-legged monster to come jumping out of it."

Grant turned around and looked down the little path to the clearing. "Yeah, I still find that thing creepy."

The alien artifact sat there calmly on the mossy ground like a giant black pearl, surrounded by mile-high trees.

"I hope I never have to step back in that thing," said Ernie. The mere thought of it sends a chill down my spine."

"I wouldn't mind if it could take me back to Earth."

"You know that's not going to happen. Personally

there's nothing I really miss, except for a juicy steak of course."

Meat! I haven't eaten any meat for twenty years. How I would love to eat a steak or a burger again!

They had brought seeds with them, and some of the indigenous plants were edible, but the animals of New California were inedible due to their different metabolisms. Ernie had once tried a piece of grilled wotan, and then thrown up for hours. The soya-like substance that Igor had compressed into a burger tasted like lukewarm cardboard and didn't even begin to resemble the flavor of meat. Since then Ernie had been forced to become vegetarian—like everyone else in the colony.

"Did you actually vote in favor of destroying the sphere on Mars?" asked Grant.

Ernie nodded. "Dressel said the things posed a serious threat to Earth—that they might destroy it. So good riddance."

"But don't you sometimes miss your old life?"

Ernie laughed. "I didn't have a life outside of the company. My term of service was almost over and I had no idea what I wanted to do in civilian life. I guess for me, the only options would have been some kind of security job or becoming a mercenary for Blackriver. Here I've got my old company and my family around me. Life is simpler, clearer. And real men are needed here. I like it here, I don't want to leave." He gave Grant a slap on the shoulder. "And don't tell me you see things differently. What kind of life would have been waiting for you after your discharge? Working as a third-rate mechanic in some garage? Earning a pittance and living in a tiny apartment?"

Grant glared at Ernie. "Watch what you're saying. Third-rate mechanic? I would have gone to college and gotten an engineering degree. Then I would have gone to one of the big oil companies. Do you have any idea how much you can earn in two weeks on an oil rig off the coast of Alaska?"

Ernie laughed again. "Ah, come on. You're no cleverer than me. To get an engineering degree you've got to be good at math. It would have taken you ten years to get your degree and you would been up to your eyeballs in debt. And let's face it, you're not such a great engineer. How long did you need last week to change the valves on that jeep?"

"I do my work thoroughly, that's all."

"Five hours! And when you were finished, you still had screws and other parts left over. In the end Lee had to help you."

Ernie tried not to chuckle again. The whole thing had been pretty embarrassing for Grant, and the story immediately made the rounds in the colony. Due to his regular gaffes, many people were of the opinion that Grant would be better off working in the fields than in the workshop. But they simply had too few mechanics in the colony, and when the radio call had come through earlier that day, Grant had been the only one available.

Ernie marched on ahead, whistling merrily, while Grant trudged behind him, sulking. When they reached the edge of the forest half an hour later, they were still walking along in silence. They left the giant redwoods behind them and emerged onto a gently ascending plain. Verdant grassland reached all the way to the distant mountains in the west. More hills bordered the plains to the south and north, and between them, wispy white clouds slowly dissolved in the sun.

The scenery reminded Ernie of Montana, where he had often spent his vacations at his uncle's as a child. It was as if you were approaching the distant Rocky Mountains from the prairie of the Great Plains. He had once taken part in an expedition by foot, under Russell's command, to the mountains approximately thirty miles away. There they had discovered crystal-clear lakes, and breath-taking panoramas reminiscent of Montana's Glacier National Park. He had to admit New California had some incredible landscapes on offer.

They stopped at a junction, where a dirt road branched off to the north, and another to the west.

"Which way do we have to go?" asked Ernie.

"Igor said the thing conked out on the cornfields."

"So north."

They marched up a small hill, with wheat fields to their right and barley to their left.

"The wheat is almost ready for harvesting," said Grant.

"Which makes it all the more important that you get that old rust-bucket working again. I don't think the guys and gals will be too thrilled about harvesting by hand." Ernie remembered with dismay that he was scheduled for field work himself next week.

Grant just grunted.

From the top of a little hill they had a view across a small valley. The wheat field ended at the lowest point, where a little brook, emerging from the northern slope, flowed toward the forest. Beyond the brook, where the dirt track crossed over a little bridge, the cornfields began. Since they didn't have any animal products to eat, corn, along with legumes, was one of their most important sources of protein.

Ernie recognized the off-road vehicle that had been turned into a tractor and combine harvester by Albert, together with Grant and Lee. Grant was very proud of it and never tired of telling people how complicated it had been to build. Apparently they had had to design a special cutting unit that only threshed the corn ears and sliced up the rest of the plant, before spitting it out onto the field. The machine worked pretty well and had reduced the time it took to harvest a whole field to a day, even though parts frequently broke. Ernie wondered what Grant had in actual fact contributed to its construction.

The troop of harvesters was sitting around the tractor. Ernie spotted his wife, who was on field duty today. With her closely cropped hair and muscular body—the result of daily tough physical exercise—she resembled a man. But Ernie loved the way she looked, as well as her dominant character. She was standing next to Stanislav Radinkovic, who was leading the troop today and who kept pointing at the immobile tractor. Beside them, Jim Harris and Catherine Hawke were sitting in the tall grass. The two of them were clowning around, and it was easy to see what they felt for one another. They made an extremely unlikely couple. Everyone knew how much Ben hated Russell. The fact that his daughter might now be hooking up with the son of his arch enemy must be bugging him big time. A few other youngsters were lounging beside them, among them Peter Richards, Edward Grazier and Courtney Cashmore.

"Radi" Radinkovic had caught sight of Ernie and Grant and went up to them. Andrea followed two steps behind.

"Finally you've come. We been waiting hours here, and nothing to do because machine broken," complained Radi.

Ernie Grinned. Radi had emigrated to the United States with his family as a teenager, but still had a strong accent. The ecologist was an extremely able farmer with truly green fingers. Farming seemed to be in his genes.

Meanwhile Andrea had reached Ernie and came to a halt in front of him.

Ernie grinned at her. "Hey, honey, haven't you had enough of gardening yet?"

The next thing he felt was Andrea's hand giving him a gentle slap. He pulled her toward him and kissed her passionately. She embraced him with equal passion and pulled his head more firmly to hers. He became aware of the teenagers giggling in the grass, but he didn't care.

"Tractor don't drive no more. Harvested two rows, then broken!" said Radi. Ernie released himself from the embrace and looked at Radi, who had planted himself in front of Grant.

"Can you be a bit more precise? Is it the engine? Won't it start?" asked Grant.

"No, on. Engine good. Can't steer no more. Only straight ahead."

"It must be the suspension arm. It broke once before. Probably the weld joint. I'll have a look at it." Grant dropped his backpack on the gravel path and sat in the driver's seat of the jeep-cum-tractor. He turned on the ignition and the engine started without any trouble. He activated the combine harvester with a lever, put it into first gear, and then slowly took his foot off the clutch. With a judder, the vehicle started to move. Grant wrenched at the steering wheel, but he couldn't change the direction of the tractor. Cursing, he turned off the engine and jumped out of the vehicle.

"Well? What's the diagnosis, Professor?" asked Jim Harris with a smile. The sporty young man, who was the spitting image of his father, pushed his blond hair out of his face, but it was immediately ruffled up by the wind again. He had inherited his winning smile from his mother. No wonder Catherine had fallen for him. And she probably wasn't the only young woman in the colony to have done so.

"It must be the suspension arm. It's broken."

"And that means . . .?" asked Peter Richards.

"It means we have to first remove the wheels, and then I can see which of the two are affected, and then I'll dismantle it and take it back to the workshop to be welded."

"Welded?" asked Radi, aghast. "That will take at least a day. The crops must be harvested."

"Get another tractor."

"It's being used in field number eight for fertilizing."

Grant shrugged. "Nothing I can do about it." He walked over to his backpack and took out his tool kit. Ernie went and helped him with the jack. Together they jacked up the vehicle and removed the tires. Grant tapped the suspension arms on either side. "Seem to be okay."

"Perhaps it's something else," said Ernie drily.

Grant glared at him. "Then why don't you repair it, wise guy?"

"I was just saying."

"Get out of my face!" said Grant irritably to Ernie and the others who were standing around him. "Go sit over there and let me do my work!" He shooed them away.

Ernie shrugged, took his wife by the hand and pulled her along with him. They sat down together in the grass beside the track, and watched Ernie working on the tractor.

Grant needed two hours to remove both suspension arms. Finally the parts were lying in front of him in the grass. He wiped the sweat from his brow and swore. "Damn it, I just can't tell which one is broken." He looked up at Ernie. "I guess we should take both of them back to the colony and take them apart there. Then we'll see which of the two it is."

"And the tractor?" asked Radi.

"I guess it can stay here till tomorrow. Nobody's gonna steal it. Ernie, grab the tools! I'll take the parts and then we'll head back to the workshop."

Ernie shrugged, stood up and started to collect the tools that were scattered about.

"Is this normal?" Ernie heard Jim's voice. The boy had crept underneath the vehicle.

"What are you doing there? Is what normal?" asked Grant. He yanked himself under and crawled after the boy.

Ernie shoved some pliers into the tool bag and went over to vehicle to watch what was going on. He kneeled down and bent his head so he could look underneath the tractor.

Jim was pointing at a spot where the tie rod disappeared into a housing on the axle. "There's a corn cob in there!"

Grant cursed. Ernie could see it too. The green and yellow thing was stuck between the tie rod and the steering rack. It must be blocking the steering.

Jim grabbed it, and shook it until it loosened and came out. "I think I've repaired it," he said quietly, and handed him the offending item.

Grant crawled back out from under the vehicle and stood up. He looked at Ernie, completely baffled. Peter Richards snickered loudly.

Ernie joined in. "Well, Mr. Engineer, and what about the suspension arms?" he asked sardonically.

"I . . . I think they're still okay," stammered Grant.

Andrea was the first to burst out laughing, and Peter, Jim and Catherine quickly joined in. Ernie wanted to restrain himself, but the sight of Grant, with the maize cob in his hand, staring at the tractor open-mouthed, was too much for him. He clutched his stomach and cried with laughter. He fell to his knees, both hands on the ground, and gasped for air.

Eventually Grant recovered his composure, looked at the corn cob and threw it in a high arc over the combine harvester.

Ernie was still chuckling when there was a squawking sound from the radio on the tractor. "Field troop one, come in please." The distorted voice was that of Jenny Baldwin, who was on duty in the colony's radio hut today.

Andrea fetched the radio from the tractor and pressed on the speaker button, still chuckling. "Field troop one here. Jenny, what's up?"

"Is Jim Harris with you?"

Jim looked up. Tears of laughter were running down his cheeks.

"Yes, he's with us. Do you want to speak to him?"

"No, but he should return to the colony as quickly as possible."

Jim looked at Ernie in confusion.

"What's up?" asked Andrea.

"It's about his father."

Chapter 10

Fifteen years ago

"IT'S STARTING. WATCH OUT," said Dr. Cashmore. He flipped the switch, and the flasks on the table in front of him—which were attached via tubing to test tubes, heating elements and measuring devices—began to bubble.

Marlene swayed gently back and forth. Beside her, Russell Harris, Albert Bridgeman, Dr. John Dressel, and Dr. Jenny Baldwin were waiting for the result of the experiment. They were squashed together, since the laboratory container, which they had brought with them five years ago on the transport from Russell's Planet, wasn't very spacious. All of the equipment and utensils took up too much room. "How long will it take?" asked Marlene.

"Not long, a few minutes," replied the chemist quietly. He smiled as he ran his hand softly, almost tenderly, over the test tubes. Marlene thought he would have made a good minister or pastor, and in fact many of the colonists did seek out Cashmore to talk through their personal problems. More so even than Dr. Lindwall, who as a doctor should have been the one to help people with their psychological problems. The wiry scientist was wearing a white lab coat, which after five years was impossible to get completely clean despite regular washing. But he wouldn't be getting a new one. His hair reached down to his shoulders. Despite going grey, he looked younger with his long hair than he had in the past, when his hair had been cropped short.

Wolfe looked at Jenny Baldwin to her left. During an expedition a few months ago, the biologist had wanted to start classifying the indigenous flora and fauna in the lowlands. She and Russell had come across a swamp, at the far end of which bitumen bubbled up in a continuous stream from the ground. The natural asphalt pointed to the possibility of oil deposits nearby. In the course of a subsequent expedition two weeks ago, Drew Potter, the biologist, and Travis Richards, had undertaken a few test drillings, and after only about eighty feet they had struck oil. They had brought back several canisters of the black stuff to the camp and handed them over to Dr. Cashmore for analysis. The chemist had thrown himself into his new task with glee.

"In principle, the experiment is like a rectification column. The crude oil, cleaned and freed of suspended particulate matter, is in this container, which will now be heated up to four-hundred degrees Celsius. The escaping particles evaporate and move into the second test tube, in which there is a slightly lower temperature of three hundred and seventy degrees. Any heavy crude oil condenses at this temperature and drips into the vessel down here. Whatever remains flows into the next container and so on. By means of this column, we can separate the different component parts of the crude oil."

"And you think that the oil on this planet might be identical with that on Earth?" asked Russell skeptically.

Drew Potter answered on behalf of the chemist. "The living organisms here are made up of the same carbon compounds as the fauna and flora on Earth. So there is no reason to assume the components of the crude oil are any different." She hesitated. "Although I'm still very surprised at how similar the biology is on a cellular level."

"We've already been through that," remarked Albert Bridgeman.

But Jenny never tired of talking about it. "It's incredible really. The cells function in exactly the same way as on Earth. Of course, the DNA of the life forms here are different from the ones on our home planet . . ."

"This is our home planet," Wolfe interrupted testily.

"Whatever; they're similar. The cells contain mitochondrion, which on Earth has always been regarded as an evolutionary accident. The proteins also correspond with those on Earth, although I've already found several new proteins. But the differences are so minute, they're hardly noticeable. The other chemical components of the organisms are also almost identical. There are all the same vitamins here as on Earth, and almost the same trace elements."

"Which is lucky for us, otherwise we couldn't survive here," said Cashmore.

"So how's the experiment going, Doctor?" Albert interrupted the discussion. He had been so excited by the possibility of drilling for oil, he had already drawn up plans for a rudimentary refinery.

Dr. Cashmore turned around. "So, it's now reached the necessary temperature. Any moment now, the first condensates ought to drip into the container. There, you see!" He pointed at the first test tube in the row. From an opening in the container above it, a black, viscous substance dripped slowly but steadily into the glass vessel.

"Those are heavy oils, which can be turned into heating oil, for example. And there!" He pointed at another test tube in the column, which was filling up with a colorless liquid. "That's petroleum ether. Or ligroin, to be more precise. You can use it directly as fuel for simple gasoline engines." He tore a yellow testing strip out of a folder and dipped it in the chemical. The strip quickly turned green. The chemist compared the color to a scale. "The octane rating of 60 fairly low, but by adding tetraethyllead we can get it up to a usable level."

"I'm sure I could produce a simple combustion engine in our forge, given enough time," said Albert.

Marlene laughed. "We've got more than enough to do just cultivating crops so that we all have something to eat. For the time being, the jeeps we brought with us from Russell's Planet will have to suffice."

"But we also need to think ahead to the future," objected Russell. "At the latest when our children are a little older, we'll have to start thinking about whether we want to be a purely agrarian society or if we want to allow for a certain amount of industrialization. In that case, we need to start sharing our knowledge sooner rather than later."

"I agree," said Dr. Dressel. "The first children will soon be of an age when they would be starting school on Earth. It's essential that they receive schooling, and we should start organizing it as soon as possible."

Marlene nodded. "Yes, we'll discuss it at the next meeting."

In the five years since its foundation, the colony had made rapid progress. There was plenty of edible food in the form of plants and fruits, as Dr. Baldwin had been able to establish in her research. What's more, they had planted fields in the highlands beyond the forest using the seeds that had been originally intended for cultivation experiments. Meanwhile, they had wheat, corn, spelt, barley, and sugar cane. Perhaps one day they would be able to grow rice in the lowlands, where the ground was wet enough, but the danger posed by the wotans was still too high.

They had built log cabins out of wood from the giant redwoods, and after a few months they had settled into something of a routine. Many of the colonists, including Marlene, even started to enjoy their life in exile. Here, they could conquer a whole world and establish a new civilization, free from the constraints of distant Earth. It was hard work, especially for Marlene, who was president of the colony. At first, the unfamiliar challenge had almost driven her to despair. What did she know about establishing a new society? Then she had given up on trying to plan and understand everything down to the smallest detail, and had learnt to delegate responsibilities. From that point on, things became easier.

"We should hold the meeting soon. The list of issues that need discussing is growing by the day," said Russell.

"Yes, I wanted to wait for the results of our refinery experiment, but since that's obviously succeeded," Marlene pointed at the row of test tubes on the table that were filling with more and more differently colored liquids, "I'll hold the meeting this week. It's time to form a new council."

Dr. Dressel turned around. "Has another year really gone by? Time is passing quicker than I ever imagined."

"Time itself isn't, but the year actually is passing quicker," said Russell. Their new home planet circled the central star of the solar system in just three hundred and twelve days, although the days here were about half an hour longer than on Earth. They had gotten used to living according to their new calendar, but Marlene still found it difficult to accept that the year ended on November eighth.

"What's on the agenda for the meeting so far?" asked Albert.

"Besides setting up a school for the children, we also need to vote on building a refinery next to the oil fields—and what we want to and should produce with it. Could you prepare a report, Doctor?"

Cashmore nodded. "No problem."

"Good. In my opinion we should start by concentrating on fuel production. That will be hard enough. The refinery needs to be manned and guarded at all times, because there are wotans in the area. That will mean less people to work the fields."

"No, the refinery will be fully automatic," said the chemist.

"In any case, I am of the opinion that we should get started on developing the combustion engines." This had obviously turned into an obsession for Albert. "Then we can build engines for vehicles, as well as pumps and generators."

"Generators?" asked Russell.

"Yes, for producing energy. The reactor won't provide electricity indefinitely."

Marlene shook her head. "There's still enough uranium in the reactor to last another twenty years. There's no hurry." They had taken their small travelling-wave reactor with them from Russell's Planet, and it would ensure a supply of energy for some time to come. "And anyway, we can't build a generator since we don't have any copper for the coil windings. Maybe we can extract enough copper from the cables and machines we already have, but there won't be enough for the large-scale electrification of our colony," said Dr. Dressel.

"Drew has found copper deposits in the mountains east of the camp," said Jenny.

"In that case we could build a mine there and extract copper," said Albert.

Marlene laughed. "Hey, guys, we've only got around forty adults here and a handful of kids and toddlers. We've got enough on our plates growing food, and now we're adding a school and a refinery, we're at the limit of what we can manage. Perhaps once the children are older and the colony has reached a decent size. Until then, the forge will be limited to the production of tools."

Albert shrugged in resignation. "Whatever you say, Madam President."

Marlene rolled her eyes. Albert always did that when decisions didn't go his way. Well, she would have her revenge that evening!

Soon after arriving on the planet, they had voted for the first council of four members, who were responsible for deciding their fate, and since then new elections had been held every year. The other members of the council had changed, but Marlene had been repeatedly voted as president of the council by the overwhelming majority. Everyone presumed it would be the same again this year. They didn't have a parliamentary system—the colony was too small for that—instead, the council served a mainly administrative function. Compared to back home on Earth, they had a system of direct democracy and made important decisions based on the votes of all colonists.

"And what else is on the agenda?" asked Russell.

"Travis Richards has proposed the idea of introducing a monetary system."

"Money? Have we really got to that stage already?"

"I don't think so," said Marlene hesitantly. At the moment, every colonist had fixed tasks, aside from regular shifts in the fields, and the rations were divided up evenly among them all. In any case, there were no consumer goods that anybody could have bought with money. But some colonists were dissatisfied with their jobs, and although they tried to consider everyone's wishes when they divided up the work, there was no real individual freedom.

"At the moment we're living in a kind of communist system. If we want to have a free society at some stage, we won't be able to get around having money. Unfortunately we don't have any economists in our midst, but we'll discuss the issue."

Russell shrugged. "What else?"

"We want to wrap up some long-standing issues. Donald Bell has revised the draft for the constitution, and I'd like to bring it to the vote."

Albert groaned. "Again? It's never-ending."

Marlene nodded. "And I expect that some of the paragraphs will have to be revised again. For Dillon and some of the others, the paragraphs on individual freedom don't go far enough."

"Is it really that important to have a unanimous vote on the constitution?" asked Jenny Baldwin.

"Yes. I want all the colonists, without exception, to stand behind it." Marlene paused. "And then there's the question of another expedition."

Russell nodded. "Yes, that proposal came from me."

Dr. Dressel ran a hand through his tousled hair. "Is that really necessary? Shouldn't we concentrate on the area immediately around our colony? Expeditions are dangerous. On the last one in the lowlands, some of the team almost died."

Marlene nodded. She was filled with horror at the memory of their camp being attacked by wotans in the night. It had been sheer luck that Chris Neaman's leg hadn't needed to be amputated. "Yes, it was a close shave. But I agree with Russell, we need to get to know our new planet better. We only have one single drone with a range of thirty miles, but I'd like to know what's out there—including what dangers—in a sixty-mile radius. Better to take our chances on a carefully prepared expedition than to be taken by surprise in the colony by some unknown menace.

"And where to this time?" asked Jenny Baldwin. She smiled. As a biologist, she obviously wanted to be part of the expedition.

"South," said Russell. "We've explored the highlands up to the edge of the range of hills, but we don't know what lies beyond them."

"How many people do you want to take with you?" asked Marlene.

"Five. Including three fully equipped soldiers. And a biologist and a geologist."

"That'll be me," said Jenny with a smile.

"Anything else?" asked Russell.

Marlene shook her head. "Those were the most important points on the agenda. Or does one of you have anything else to add?"

John Dressel nodded. "I have something else. We need to talk about it finally."

Marlene was all ears. "What is it, John?"

"The other transporters in the solar system. We need to decide, or it will be too late."

Marlene bit her lip. She had pushed this issue to the back of her mind for a long time, but the physicist was right. After endless discussions, the general opinion in the camp was that the transporter technology posed a threat to humanity. At the most recent vote, two-thirds of the colonists had agreed that the destruction of the transporter on Earth had been a good decision.

"Five years have passed since we arrived here. With enough persistence and money, that's about the amount of time that would have been needed on Earth to get a rag-tag Mars mission off the ground. It's possible that people will reach the transporter on Mars soon. So I'm in favor of implementing the plan and destroying the remaining trans-porters in the solar system with the atomic bombs we have left. Either we do it now, or it will be too late," said the physicist.

Marlene was in agreement, but there were still a number of people in the colony who hoped to return to Earth via Mars, above all her former deputy Ben Hawke, who was anything but satisfied with his role in the colony. "Do we really have to do it, John? I mean, if people mess about with the transporter on Mars, it doesn't pose a risk to Earth. In the worst-case scenario they end up destroying Mars—which is a tolerable risk." Marlene immediately realized the enormity of classifying the destruction of a planet in the solar system as a tolerable risk, but she didn't have time to pursue this thought, since Dr. Dressel began to vehemently contradict her.

"I'm not bothered about the sphere on Mars. But they'll take everything they find out about the alien tech-nology back to Earth and start experimenting with it in research laboratories."

"But you're a scientist yourself. Don't you trust your colleagues to act responsibly?"

John Dressel laughed. "In the course of my career I've seen so much incompetence in laboratories and met so many scientists who were prepared to throw caution to the wind for the sake of spectacular research results." He shook his head. "No, I trust a few of them, but by no means all. And only all would be enough. Thanks to Russell I was able to communicate with the transporter intelligence myself. A technology that can manipulate the gravitational field unconditionally is so risky that a tiny mistake would be all it takes. Once you know how it works, you can produce stable black holes in small laboratories."

"But if it isn't that hard, humans will work it out anyway," Albert pointed out.

"No," replied Dressel. "Humans aren't even close to understanding the physical and mathematical foundations. By the normal route, it will still be thousands of years before humans take that decisive step."

"Well alright," agreed Marlene. "We'll discuss it at the meeting. Prepare a report, but be prepared for strong resistance."

"Will do. Anything else?"

"Yes, something else has occurred to me," said Marlene. "We need to finally agree on a name for our planet and the colony."

Russell nodded. "You're right. It's total chaos at the moment. Some people are calling it New California, others have gotten used to Avalon. I prefer the latter."

"Marianna Waits has cobbled together a group that wants to call it Honua," said Jenny.

"Honua? Where does that come from?" asked Dr. Cashmore.

"Marianna has Hawaiian ancestry. Apparently it's what they used to call Earth."

"Aha," said Russell. "And what should we call the colony? Do people have other suggestions for that, too?"

"Rhonda has often called it Kaupunki," said Drew.

"What?" asked Marlene.

"It's the Finnish word for city."

"Well, I dunno . . ."

What about Eridu?" suggested Dr. Dressel.

"Does the word have a deeper meaning?" asked Marlene.

"It was the name of the oldest city on Earth. A Sumerian city in Mesopotamia."

"We'll discuss it at the meeting," said Marlene, and brought the discussion to a close.

Chapter 11

"Holy crap!" Albert Bridgeman looked at Russell with undisguised horror. While Russell had been telling his friend about his illness, his eyes had been glued to the ground. Albert put down the jeep axle he had just welded beside the embers of the fire, so that it would cool down slowly. "Are you sure?"

Russell nodded. "Two months. Maybe three. Max."

His friend sat down beside him in silence. Since they had gotten to know each other on the suicide mission with the transporter twenty years ago, they had remained close friends. Albert was now seventy-three years old and had never been bothered about leaving Earth behind. He had thrown himself into setting up a forge, which meanwhile produced pretty decent steel alloys from the iron ore discovered in the mountains and the coal mined at the edge of the lowlands. He had also improvised the welding machine together with Lee.

"But Lindwall must be able to do something. Surely he can help you fight this," said Albert.

"He doesn't have the right medication and can't improvise anything out of plants, either. But even on Earth there wouldn't be a cure. I'm a dead man."

"Oh Jesus." Albert obviously didn't know what to say, and stared into the fire of the forge.

Russell lowered his tired eyes to the ground. "I shouldn't complain. I've had a full and exciting life. I could have died twenty years ago during the transports. Instead I've helped to colonize an alien planet and brought up three children."

He glanced up at his friend. Unlike most of the other colonists, Albert had remained single. But he didn't seem to miss not being in a relationship. He drew all his energy from his work and the forge. Right now, Russell envied him. He didn't have to worry about what would happen to his family after he was gone.

"Christ, Russell, you're only sixty-three!"

"Lately I've been feeling twice as old. If it's time for me to go, that's okay." He paused "But I'm frightened. Frightened of death and of dying."

Albert nodded slowly. "I think we all live with that fear, no matter what our age. Although I'm also approaching the end of my life, I don't let myself think about death. I hope it might never be necessary. I hope that at some point I just fall down dead and it's over. Getting ill and knowing that in the near future . . ." He didn't finish his sentence.

Russell picked up some tongs. The metal was pleasantly cool to the touch. "I don't want to lie in bed and slowly suffocate to death. And above all, I don't want my wife and kids to be sitting beside me watching me die a miserable death." Days ago he had lain awake all night and come to a decision. How was it possible to sleep when you knew that in a few weeks your eyes would close forever?

Albert glanced up. "You're planning something. The tone of your voice . . . You don't want to . . .?"

Russell interrupted him with a grim smile. "No, I won't kill myself. But I'm planning something else."

Chapter 12

Russell tossed and turned in bed. He had been sweating again, and the wet sheet stuck to his skin. It had been his last night with Ellen, and he should have enjoyed it, but his illness had taken away his libido, too. His wife was fast asleep, and he could hear her slow and regular breathing. When they first met, they had been prisoners. She had shot her psychically ill husband dead in self-defense. Russell himself, in a knee-jerk moment of insanity, had shot dead the drink-driver who had killed his family in a car crash. Joining the transporter project had saved them both from execution, but the mission had been so damn dangerous, they had hardly stood a chance of surviving. In between their individual transports—which were equivalent to a game of Russian roulette—they had fallen in love. Perhaps their relationship had begun, in part, out of a desperate desire for intimacy in the face of death, but even after they had settled into an unlikely yet stable life together on New California, their mutual affection had deepened, not least due to the children. After his first wife and son had been wrenched out of his life so violently twenty years ago, he couldn't have imagined ever having a family again. But with time the pain had subsided, and today he could watch his children grow up on New California without the sorrows of the past casting a permanent shadow over his new-found happiness. He would have loved to put his arms around Ellen and curl up close to her, but he didn't want to wake her.

It was early morning, long before dawn, when he finally got up. He slipped silently into the living room and closed the door of the bedroom. His kit was lying next to the hearth. He checked it again. The rifle, a hundred rounds of ammunition, a pistol with a spare magazine. Some tools, food for several days, a spare set of clothes, a first-aid kit. That would have to do—until the end of his life. He took a little bottle of oil, poured some onto a cloth and used it to clean the slide of his handgun.

A sound from behind him made him wheel round. Ellen stumbled into the room with bleary eyes. She sat down on the chair next to Russell and grasped his hand. He put aside the gun and the cloth, kneeled down in front of her and lay his head in her lap.

"I don't want you to go," she whispered.

"And I don't want to go," he replied quietly.

"Then don't!"

Russell was quiet for a long time. They had had this conversation so many times over the last few days.

"I have to go."

"Why?"

"You know why."

Although he didn't look at her, he knew from her trembling that she was crying.

"Yes, I know. But I don't understand."

Russell lifted his head and looked into her tear-filled eyes. "Because I don't want you to see what happens to me in the next few months. I don't want to die like that. Lying in bed, getting weaker, being sick, screaming, turning into a skeleton because I can't eat anymore." He paused briefly. "I want to have one final adventure."

"Wouldn't you rather die with your family and friends around you, than out there, alone?"

Russell was silent. He didn't know how to answer her question without sounding hurtful.

Ellen was encouraged by his silence and carried on talking. "I don't care what you look like at the end. And Lindwall can give you morphine for the pain. Then at least I can hold your hand when you leave us, and we can bury you here. If you're out there somewhere, we'll never know how you died."

Russell shook his head. "It won't take long. And it doesn't matter where my body is after I'm gone. It's one thing for *you* to watch me die. But then the kids have to watch too, and I don't want that. I want them to remember me the way I am now—and not see me gradually deteriorate."

"Do you prefer the idea of being eaten by wild animals?"

Russell looked at his weapon.

She noticed where he was looking. "That won't be much help against a whole pack of wotans."

Russell forced himself to smile. "Then I won't use it on *them. . . .*"

Ellen frowned. A solitary tear rolled down her cheek. "I can't change your mind." It was more of a statement than a question.

"No."

For some time they sat silently together, her hand warm in his.

"Then at least come back to bed for an hour." She stood up and led him back to the bedroom.

Chapter 13

Russell's gaze wandered over the plateau. The approaching dawn cast the barren landscape in a bluish, ghostly light. Despite the early hour, half of the colony had turned out to witness the departure of the doomed traveler. All the people whom he regarded as friends were here, as were the few involuntary colonists who had never forgiven Russell for the fact that they could never return to Earth. Heading up the latter group was Ben Hawke, who stood alone on a little knoll and watched the spectacle with folded arms.

"Which one do you want to take?" asked Albert. From the gloomy undertone of his voice, it was clear what he thought of his friend's undertaking.

Russell had found what he was looking for. "That one!" He pointed at one of the whales on the escarpment.

"Why that one precisely?" asked Albert.

"It looks so robust, but isn't too big. It won't fly as high and far as the others. How long do I still have?" Russell asked Christian Holbrook.

His friend looked at his watch. He had one of the few

watches that still worked; the mechanical wind-up mechanism didn't require batteries. However, due to the difference between the length of the days here and on Earth, the time needed to be constantly converted. But the astronaut didn't mind. "Half an hour until sunrise."

"More than enough. Come on!"

Russell went past the other whales. None of them would stir before sunrise. About a dozen of them had gathered on the plateau the night before to sleep. The spot was high enough and inaccessible enough to provide a safe resting place for the fascinating creatures. They had come across these whale-like creatures on their very first visit to the planet, serenely gliding across the sky like hot-air balloons. Heated up by sunlight, the creatures rose into the sky at sunrise and fed on microorganisms, which they absorbed through their skin. There was an abundance of these microorganisms in a layer of continuously humid air around a mile above the ground.

Russell came to a halt in front of "his" whale. In awe, he looked at the creature with which he would go on his final journey. Its skin was like brown leather. Very dark, to absorb the rays of the sun. It looked thicker than it actually was. Small, tentacle-like protuberances anchored the creature to the ground as it swayed gently back and forth in the breeze. It didn't appear to have any eyes, ears, or a mouth. Around twenty-five feet tall and wide, and twice as long, these flying whales were a breathtaking sight when they rose up into the air. Like balloons, they couldn't direct which way they drifted, but they could control how high they went thanks to several valve-like organs. The whales also had two protruding humps, one on either side. According to Jenny, these probably contained some kind of sensory organs—a kind of compass perhaps—but it was hard to know exactly without carrying out an autopsy. The biologist had always shrunk away from killing one of the creatures purely for research purpose. She still hoped to find a dead whale one day, but it seemed that the animals retreated to some distant place to die. How often had Russell dreamed of riding one of these creatures!

"Are you sure this is a good idea?" Christian whispered in his ear.

Russell smiled at him. "Actually, I'm absolutely sure it isn't a good idea."

The former astronaut looked at his friend in confusion but said nothing in return.

"If not now, when?" Russell added.

"You won't come back."

"That's the whole point."

Christian said nothing, but frowned.

Russell reached for the net he had slung over his shoulder, and threw it in a high arc over the whale. Attached to the net were loops he could grab onto. With a carabiner on his belt he was able to hook himself to the mesh of the net so that he wouldn't fall down even if there was turbulence. Albert and Christian helped him to fasten the net to the animal with ropes. When they were finished, Katrina Cole came up to Russell and tapped him on the shoulder. He turned around to the meteorologist and smiled.

"What's the forecast, Katrina?"

"The weather should be fair today. A light breeze from the south-west, on the ground as well as at a height of nine-thousand feet. In the afternoon, the wind will probably change to an easterly direction. Then you have to be careful that it doesn't take you out to sea."

"Don't worry, the whales don't land on water. If necessary, it would go down earlier and wait on the beach until the wind changes direction," Jenny Baldwin said, joining the group. The biologist had studied the animals and had already suggested their potential as a means of transportation some time ago. She was thrilled that someone was now daring to try it out, and hopped excitedly from one foot to the other. She was less thrilled about the fact that Russell wouldn't return to tell them about his adventures.

"At any rate, I think that you'll cover between fifty and sixty miles today. When you go down near the sea this evening, you'll be about twenty-five miles further north than we were able to get on the expedition to the sea that we started a few years back."

"So it's absolutely unchartered territory." He smiled at her.

"I can't really share your euphoria," said Jenny. "We don't know what kind of creatures live there. But we have already established that the lowlands are dangerous."

"I think I'll be safe on shore," said Russell.

Jenny nodded. "The whales wouldn't land there at night if they were in danger. But to find food, you'll have to leave the shore and go into the jungle. It could be that you don't survive tomorrow night." She stopped talking as Ellen and the children approached. "Good luck, Russell. You remember what I asked you to do, don't you?"

"Yes, I'll mark the spot where I land and leave notes. When you make an expedition to the north some day, you'll know how far I got." Russell hugged the diminutive biologist, who then stepped back.

Ellen hung back, and let a few other people go in front of her. She wanted to be the last person to say goodbye to Russell.

Dr. Lindwall came up and gave Russell a hand-sized, square black pouch with a zipper. "I've put together some medication. There's an anti-inflammatory, some painkillers and a few phials of morphine to self-inject. And some sleeping pills."

"I don't think I'll need the sleeping pills," said Russell.

The doctor shook his head. "If you take five of them at the same time with a dose of morphine . . ." He didn't continue.

Russell looked at the doctor and slowly nodded. "I understand. Thanks." He hugged the doctor, who usually avoided physical contact, but rigidly accepted Russell's embrace. "All the best!"

Russell hated good-byes. He would have preferred to disappear on the quiet, but that would have been unfair to his friends.

"It's time," said Marlene, who had suddenly appeared in front of him. Her expression was serious. Obviously she was sparing herself and him an attempt at a smile.

Russell nodded. "Yes, I know." He glanced at the heavy rucksack that was slung over her shoulder. "Do you want to come with me?"

Now she did smile after all. "No, Ben and I are driving down to the observation post in the valley."

"Problems?"

"Not as bad as the ones you're going to encounter today."

Russell raised his eyebrows inquisitively.

"And since you've always been honest with me, I'm going to be honest with you now: I think what you're doing is a fucking stupid idea."

"Christian told me the same thing."

"Well, if you didn't listen to him, I can spare you my lecture."

"Yup. Tell me something encouraging instead. You know what I asked you. You still haven't given me an answer."

Marlene glanced over at the couple's children, who

114

were patiently waiting a few feet away. "I'm quite sure they're capable of looking after themselves."

"That's not what I wanted to hear."

Marlene reached out a hand to Russell. "All the best, my friend."

Russell clasped her hand and looked silently into Marlene's eyes.

"I'll take care of your family," she said in a subdued voice.

Impulsively he gave Marlene a hug. "Thank you," he whispered in her ear. Slowly she disengaged from his embrace and stepped back.

Russell knew that the hardest goodbye was yet to come. He hugged his friends, shook hands, clapped shoulders. Then he was standing in front of Ellen, Jim, Grace, and Greg. Ellen's face was puffy. She had been crying again, but now she looked at him with a blank expression. Jim and Grace were old enough to understand what was going on and he had told them about his plan a few days ago.

Jim stepped forward. Eighteen years old, he was now taller than Russell. His brawny physique and warm—if currently somewhat forced—smile evoked in Russell painful memories of his own youth.

Good God I've become old. I looked like Jim when I joined the army. That was forty years ago, and I've spent half that length of time here. We were so busy building a new home, we never found time to think about ourselves. And now I've reached the end of the road.

"Dad . . ."

Russell wanted to say something, but he knew that his voice would break. Instead he stepped forward and took his first-born in his arms. He closed his eyes and tried to fight back the tears. After endless seconds he let his son go and turned to his daughter. At fifteen, Grace was in the process of turning into a pretty, well-adjusted, and intelligent young woman. How he would have loved to watch her further development. In a few years, she might have children of her own and he would have been a grandfather.

It's so unfair.

In farewell, he kissed her softly on the forehead before turning to his youngest child. It had been difficult with Greg. Russell had tried to gently explain to his eight-year-old son that he wouldn't be returning, but the boy simply refused to believe him, so Russell had decided not to tell him the truth. His youngest son believed that his father was simply going on a long journey and he refused to listen to any other explanation. He would grasp the truth himself after a certain amount of time had passed.

"Look after yourself while I'm gone," said Russell softly. "And listen to your mother!"

"Why can't I come with you?" grumbled Greg.

"The journey might be dangerous."

"But you've got a gun with you."

Russell laughed. "Yes, I've got a gun with me." He ruffled the boy's hair. "But you need to go to school and work in the fields. And Albert has promised that you can help him in the workshop with the cars."

"But I'd much rather see the ocean. Will you really land there?"

"Yes, if all goes well I'll be at the ocean this evening. Some day you will see it too. But that time hasn't come yet."

Russell leaned down and hugged his son, then turned to Ellen. He took her hand and looked into her eyes for a long time. They were brimming with tears and made her look glassy-eyed. He saw the fine lines that had been etched into her face over the past years. Just like on his face. They had been together for twenty years. A third of his life. They had been twenty good years. Everything they had achieved and built up was almost as unbelievable as the circumstances in which they had got to know each other, and which had brought them from the searing heat of Nevada to this alien planet.

She fell into his arms and hugged him tight. He had expected her to try and change his mind at the last minute, but she had obviously given up hope of that working.

"Look after yourself," she whispered in Russell's ear. She freed herself from his arms. Russell took both her hands and looked into her eyes again.

She smiled weakly. "I hope you have a good trip. Thanks for the good times we had together."

Russell leaned over and kissed her tenderly, then he let go of her hands and turned around. The first rays of sun were already bathing the nearby mountain peaks in light.

"I have to go," he said.

Slowly Ellen turned around and went with the others to the edge of the plateau.

Russell pulled himself up the net on the side of the whale until he had reached one of the humps three-quarters of the way up.

First Russell hooked his equipment to the net, then himself. He lay on the hump, about fifteen feet above the ground, and tried to relax. He looked back and saw the men and women of the colony at the edge of the plateau, from where a steep path led down to the settlement. Right at the front were Ellen, Jim and Grace. He couldn't see Greg, but there were simply too many people.

The humps vibrated slightly. The whale was waking up! The rising sun bathed the entire plateau in golden light. Russell could feel the warmth on his skin. Not long now.

One of the bigger whales swayed back and forth in the

wind, then its sucker-like tentacles released themselves from the ground. It rose very slowly, dream-like, into the sky. As if on command, the other whales surrounding Russell began to rise into the air.

He checked his carabiners again. Whatever happened, he didn't want to fall off—either here or at a height of nine-thousand feet, when the creatures reached their cruising altitude. When he looked up again, he realized that the whale had taken off. They were rising very slowly, he could hardly feel the movement. After several hundred feet he could feel the gentle but steady jet stream, and they drifted off to the north-east toward the sun.

Russell looked back. His friends and comrades were still standing at the edge of the plateau, following him with their eyes. A few of them were waving. Russell found it increasingly difficult to tell the people apart. In the background he could now see their settlement. The wooden huts, the army tents, and containers that they had brought with them looked like randomly scattered building blocks, sandwiched between the highlands and the nearby forest. Even from up here, the three-thousand-feet-high redwoods looked awe-inspiring. Somewhere in that forest was the black transporter that they had brought with them to this surreal place. Far in the west, he could make out the fertile lower mountain slopes with their rectangular fields. A dark dot at the edge must be one of the tractors.

Everything that he could now see had been his home for the past twenty years. He had helped build it up and make it into a place where he and his friends could not only survive, but even confidently look into the future. Of this he was proud, and his pride was mixed with melancholy. How he would have loved to watch his children as they took on responsibility for their lives and for this world.

Fucking cancer!

Russell craned his neck and looked to the east. The mountain range came right up to the escarpment of the plateau, and he could see the narrow canyon that led gradually upward. Below, he could see a thicket of fairly small trees, whose crowns were connected by an impenetrable tangle of climbing plants. It was impossible to see the ground.

After a few minutes, the whales reached their cruising altitude. Russell could feel it immediately. The air suddenly warmed up, so that he was no longer shivering. But although it was warm, it was also unpleasantly humid. Russell noticed that he was starting to sweat. He briefly considered taking off his jacket, but to do so, he would have had to free himself from the net and he didn't want to take any risks. The expanse below him was immense.

The strange atmospheric inversion was one of the biggest secrets of this planet. Katrina Cole had not been able to discover how this constant warm layer of air came about. One idea was that it had to do with the different spectrum of the sunlight, but Dr. Dressel was highly skeptical.

Russell had now left the colony far behind him. He presumed that he had already flown seven or eight miles. The little oil spring and their refinery must be a bit further to the south. It ought to be easy to spot, since it was in a clearing in the jungle, but he couldn't see it.

Russell turned onto his back to relax a little in the warm sun. Safely secured to the net with the carabiner, he closed his eyes. He didn't have any real plan of what he would do after he landed. He had food with him for two days, then he would have to go into the jungle to find more. With the aggressive animals on this planet, it was questionable how long he would survive. He reckoned on a few days at most, then they would get him, but he would rather lose his life fighting one of those monsters than be carried off by this damn cancer. Whatever the animals did to him, it wouldn't take as long as slowly suffocating to death. If there was no other way, he would turn his gun on himself or swallow the pills Dr. Lindwall had given him. But he didn't want to think about that yet. Until that time came, he was determined to fully enjoy this final adventure. He looked at the jungle far below him. He thought he could hear the screeching of wild animals, but he could be imagining it, because he must be flying too high for that. For a moment he closed his eyes and only then did he notice how exhausted he was. Last night had been too short, and he let himself relax for a moment. Without noticing it, he drifted off.

HE WAS AWOKEN by some kind of noise, and Russell got such a fright, that he instinctively shifted his weight. His upper body slipped from the hump of the whale on which he had rested safely up until now. Frantically, Russell grasped at the net, but he simply couldn't get a hold. He slipped down until his head was pointing toward the ground. Fortunately, the carabiner prevented him from slipping any further and hurtling down to earth. Groaning, Russell pulled himself up on the net until he was finally lying safely back on the hump of the whale.

The sun was now high in the sky, it must be around midday. Russell turned onto his right side. The highlands with the colony had disappeared in the haze. Angrily, he realized that falling asleep had made him lose his sense of direction.

But he could see a little chain of hills below, and sighed with relief when he recognized them. That was where they had set up a supply depot on the way to the ocean. A hut with supplies was still waiting there for the next expedition that might one day penetrate that far. Russell looked at his compass. A wind blowing inland had changed the course of the whales northward. The animal had fallen far behind the rest of the group. Perhaps he was the reason for this, after all, the whale had to carry not only its own weight but Russell's, too.

Then he looked ahead to the horizon and got a shock. What he had just taken to be the light blue of the sky, was in fact the ocean. Due to the haze, it was impossible to see exactly where sky and water met. But it was much too early! According to his calculations, the ocean must be at least another thirty-five miles away!

Russell leaned forward to look at the ground. The shoreline was ten miles away at most. Had he miscalculated due to his nap? No! The hills below him were definitely where the supply depot was. He had mapped it himself at the time. He could make out the highest peak, a little taller than the others, which Marlene had christened Mount Fairweather. When he looked back, he could still see the craggy cliffs that separated the jungle in the valley from the highlands and the mountains.

That could only mean one thing: the ocean had flooded the valley.

What on earth has happened? A tsunami?

Drew Potter's tests in the canyon! He had suppressed it; he had been too wrapped up in his illness. Not that many years ago, something had caused the water level to rise half way up the pass. Was a new flood on its way? Would the vast lowlands be entirely flooded? Russell shook his head in disbelief.

What would that mean for the colony? First, the oil spring and then the refinery would be destroyed by the encroaching water. That, at the very latest, would set off alarm bells in the colony, but by then it would be too late to rescue the oil reserves they had stored there. Then the observation post at the exit would be flooded.

Damn! And I can't warn them! If only I'd taken a radio with me!

Russell squinted in the direction of the shoreline. He couldn't tell whether the sea was still moving inland, or at what speed. It seemed to be advancing very slowly, in any case.

Then Russell heard a sneeze and got such a shock that he nearly lost his grip.

What the hell . . .?

He knew that sneezing. He'd heard it a hundred times before. And he hadn't expected to hear it again. It couldn't be!

He looked to his left, but could only see the leathery, brown hump of the whale's back. The noise came from the other side of the animal.

Russell grabbed the rope pulley, unraveled it and attached the carabiner to the net. He attached the other end to his belt. Then he clambered up the rope as fast as he could. Luckily the flight was calm and there was no turbulence. He was supported by the net, and a moment later he was sitting at the highest point of the whale's back and leaned over to the side. There he saw . . . his son!

"Greg! Jesus Christ!"

"Hi Dad!" His youngest looked up at him with a mischievous expression.

"Hold tight! Whatever you do, don't let go of the net!" said Russell, trying to keep his voice calm.

"Don't worry, Dad. I've hooked myself into the net, like you have."

Russell could see the carabiner on Greg's belt, but it

didn't reassure him. It didn't change the fact that his son was as good as dead!

"Why did you do that?"

"I wanted to come with you and see the ocean. Please don't be mad." Greg spoke the last sentence in a pleading tone of voice.

Russell's mind was racing. The boy had to get back to the colony. Somehow. He knew that they hardly stood a chance of getting back through the jungle unharmed. They couldn't call for help. And with every mile they moved further away from the colony, their chances diminished.

We have to land. Immediately!

The whale had turned northward and was taking a course parallel to the newly formed shoreline of the ocean. It would be at least another four hours before it landed at sunset. Russell had to force the animal to the ground. Somehow.

A yellow spot, a good arm's length in front of him on the flank of the whale, caught his eye.

Maybe it will work. Maybe not. But I need to try, at least.

He pulled himself forward along the net.

"What are you doing, Dad?"

When Russell reached the spot, he twisted half round so that Greg could understand him better. "We have to get down to the ground. I want to force the whale to land. Hold tight!"

"Why do we have to land? You said you wanted to fly until nightfall."

"Do what I say! Make sure that the hook is firmly attached to the net and hold tight!"

"Are you mad at me?" asked his son in a subdued voice.

Russell didn't answer and felt mad at himself. As a boy

123

he would have done the same thing; he should have guessed. Now his son was in mortal danger and it was his fault. If something happened to Greg, just because Russell had wanted to go on this last adventure, he would never forgive himself.

Russell reached down to his belt and pulled the sharp knife out of its sheath. He didn't want to harm the whale, but given the situation he had no other choice. With a sharp movement, he rammed the knife deep into the light spot on the animal, where he presumed the organic valves must be with which the whale controlled the height at which it flew. It felt as if he had stuck the knife through a piece of paper.

"Dad, what are you doing?" asked Greg in a shrill voice.

Russell pulled the knife back out. It was now coated in a yellow liquid. At first nothing happened, then he heard a thin whistling sound and warm air came out of the wound. The whole whale vibrated, then it started slowly to spin on its own axis.

It's working! We're going down!

It took a long time, but after a while, Russell noticed that they had left the humid atmospheric layer with the microorganisms.

"We're going down! Hold tight!"

"I'm already holding tight. Why did you do that?"

Russell tried to calculate the speed at which they were going down, which wasn't easy. But there was no denying that the ground was getting closer. The whale continued to turn, and in the south, Russell could make out the hill with the supply depot. In the hut there were also weapons and a radio! It was only one or two miles away. Maybe they would make it!

Now that they had left the hazy layer of air, the view

was also clearer. In the distance, Russell could clearly make out the edge of the plateau with the colony. He estimated that they were about twenty miles from the observation post. Before that were the oil springs. There they would be safe, but to get there they had to get through ten miles of impassable jungle.

"What's that blue over there?" asked Greg.

"That's the ocean." Russell turned to look eastward and still couldn't believe that the ocean had moved so far inland.

"That's the ocean? Wow. It's enormous!"

"I know, Greg."

"And what's that light thing over there?"

Puzzled, Russell looked in the direction that Greg was pointing. A pale shimmering sphere half protruded over the horizon of the ocean. Instinctively Russell wanted to answer: *That's just the moon!* But then he remembered where he was.

New California doesn't have a moon! What the hell . . . ?

He grabbed the little telescope on his belt and directed it at the pale source of light. Dark-gray areas and pale-gray areas, between them craters and hills. It was a moon, no doubt about it. It even looked like the Earth's moon. But in all the years they had been here, they had never seen it.

Why now? And why couldn't we see it from the colony?

He got an answer to his second question as they floated further down to the ground and the moon disappeared from view. The whole time it had been hidden behind the curve of the horizon. A few minutes later, as they neared the treetops, there was nothing left to be seen of the moon. At the last second, Russell looked back at the nearby range of hills in order to imprint the direction in his mind.

"We're nearly down, Greg. Hold really tight."

"You keep telling me to hold tight. I've been holding tight the whole time!"

Branches snapped noisily all around them as the whale caved into the treetops. Russell was briefly shaken, a thin branch scratched a bloody welt in his face and then, wheezing, the animal came to a standstill.

Several feet below, Russell could see the jungle floor. Luckily this wasn't a forest of giant redwoods!

Russell pulled himself along the net over to the hump on which his son was lying and staring at him with frightened eyes.

"Now listen to me, son. We're in danger. There are really nasty animals in the jungle. About one mile from here is a supply depot. With a bit of luck the radio will still work and we can call for help. We'll make our way there now, as quickly as we can. I don't want you to say a word and you mustn't leave my side. And above all, do exactly what I tell you. Understood?"

Fear flickered in Greg's eyes. He nodded.

Russell grabbed his backpack, pulled himself over to Greg and attached the carabiner on Greg's belt to his own. Then he tied the rope to the net and looped it through his second carabiner. He checked his pistol and stuck it back in the holster. His rifle he attached to his backpack in such a way that he could easily reach it once they were on the ground. Then he slowly lowered himself down the rope with his son.

A few moments later they were standing on the damp floor of the jungle. His son was about to say something, but Russell immediately put a finger to his lips. Then he looked around.

The jungle was not as impenetrable as some of the jungles he knew on Earth, but nonetheless he couldn't see more than forty feet ahead. Thin, brown tree trunks were capped by a thick canopy of leaves that blocked out a view of the sky. Bushes, about hip height, proliferated between the trees. Anything might be hiding in them. If some monster suddenly sprung out of the undergrowth, he wouldn't even have time to grab his weapon.

Russell wiped the sweat from his brow. It was oppressively humid under the canopy of leaves and the silence all around them was frightening—as if the jungle were just waiting to devour them. Strange and overpowering smells penetrated Russell's nose, like in a hothouse of a botanical garden.

Russell pulled the rope out of the hook, then he reached behind him for his automatic rifle, balanced it in his right hand, and with the other took his son by the hand. "Come on!" he whispered. "Slowly and quietly."

Russell made sure they were going in the right direction and set off purposefully. Greg was trembling. It was obvious that he had had something else in mind when he'd imagined this trip.

Russell kept stopping to hear if anything was approaching. They had gone no more than three-hundred feet when he was startled by a loud cracking noise. It came from above, somewhere from the dense canopy of leaves. He swung the muzzle of his gun in the direction of the noise and prepared to fire.

"What was that?" whispered Greg.

Perhaps just the wind.

Russell pulled Greg forward, his nerves as taut as his muscles.

"Ouch, you're hurting me!"

Russell loosened his grip. "Psst! Sorry."

Without a compass he would have lost all sense of direction by now. With a machete, Russell cut a path through the thicket of vine-like plants. *We're making too much noise and moving at a snail's pace.* But there was no other way. The vegetation was simply too dense. Russell looked at his compass again. They were going in the right direction, but he had no sense of how far they still had to go.

By the time the forest finally thinned out, they had been walking for at least an hour but covered barely more than a mile. Russell was dripping with sweat and had to gasp for air. Breathing in this high humidity was exhausting. The effects of medication he had taken that morning had almost worn off, and he was overcome by a wave of weariness, which enveloped him like a heavy blanket. He was dizzy and to top it all, he felt sick.

Another noise made him look up, but his visibility was blurred and the treetops seemed to be turning in circles. Russell fell to his knees and threw up on the ground.

"Dad! What's the matter? Dad!"

Greg's hand touched his shoulder. Russell wiped his sleeve across his mouth and looked ahead. He tried desperately to focus, but the effort made his head pound. The pain drove him almost to distraction.

"Dad! There's something over there!"

Russell squinted in the direction that Greg was pointing. He could barely think straight.

Please, please not a wotan!

"Help me! In my rucksack! The little black bag!"

His son opened the backpack and searched for the bag of medication. Russell watched as if were looking through a thick fog.

"Here Dad!"

Russell undid the zipper and rooted around among the medication that Dr. Lindwall had given him. After a few long seconds he found what he was looking for. He flipped open the lid on the little bottle with his thumb, tipped back his head and held the bottle to his lips until he noticed that at least three of the capsules had made it into his mouth. He swallowed the Dexedrine without water and hoped that it would soon take effect. Then he reached for the bag again and took out a syringe. He removed the cap from the ballpoint-pen-like mechanism, and rammed the needle into his thigh through the fabric of his pants. He pressed the plunger right down. His headache subsided almost immediately, as the high-dosage Tylenol got to work. Why the hell not, he no longer needed to worry about the fact that such a high dosage could cause liver damage.

Finally, he was able to focus again on what was going on around him. He could hear the rustling in the bush, only fifteen feet away. Swaying slightly, Russell got to his feet and swung his backpack onto his shoulder.

"Stay behind me! Walk backward!" he whispered to Greg.

With trembling legs, Russell walked backward toward a clearing, to get as much distance between him and the animal or whatever was lurking in the bush.

There! Like the sound of a rattlesnake. But they didn't exist on this planet. It must be something else. Something dangerous, perhaps.

He gave a start, when suddenly the head of an animal shot up out of the undergrowth. Its body remained hidden in the undergrowth. Its black, demonic eyes seemed to pierce his soul. Beneath the eyes were a barely defined nose, with two twitching nostrils, and a wide mouth with leathery lips. The face resembled that of a chameleon, although the texture of the brownish skin was totally alien.

"What is that?" whispered Greg.

"I have no idea. Stay behind me!" Russell retreated step by step, his gun at the ready.

They were about thirty feet away from the animal when it suddenly, and almost silently, burst out of the bushes. It looked like a fur-less dog. A greyhound; even the size was similar.

But the body didn't seem to belong to the face at all. It was considerably thinner than a wotan's, with clearly defined muscles rippling under its naked skin.

Looks like it's damn fast.

Once again, Russell could hear the grim rattling sound. He had hoped that the animal would lose interest once they were further away, but that didn't seem to be the case. The creature was without doubt a predator. And they were its prey!

As if in slow motion, the greyhound-lizard opened its wide mouth to reveal needle-like teeth. But worst of all were the black eyes.

Jesus, those eyes are demonic!

Russell felt a chill running down his spine. He had never seen this species on past expeditions into the lowlands.

"Dad, what is it?"

"Psst! Quiet!"

Russell continued to grope his way backward, his gun pointed at the creature. His hand was trembling, but he didn't dare to use his other hand to help. With his left hand he ensured that Greg stayed under cover behind his back. With every step back, the monster came one step toward them.

This was the wrong tactic! It can tell that we're afraid and backing off. It was biding its time to start with, now it's plucking up more courage.

"Stop!" Russell hissed to Greg. "Keep your head behind my back, damn it!"

The lizard-dog cocked its head slightly to one side. Something was pulsating on its thin neck, and at the point where the head joined the muscular torso, little balloons pumped up beneath the skin.

Jesus, what's it planning to do?

The monster made a sudden movement with its head, and Russell saw something flying toward him. Instinctively he flung himself to one side as a thick drop of slime hit the muzzle of his gun. There was a hissing sound and a burning pain shot through his left shoulder. Russell screamed. His gun flew through the air as he fell backward, pulling his son down with him. He stretched out his left hand to break the fall. From the corner of his eye he could see a brown bolt of lightning racing toward them. He grabbed his pistol, lifted it and shot. He emptied the entire magazine. The monster continued to hurtle toward them—and over them. It rolled head over heels several times before coming to a standstill.

Groaning, Russell rolled over, inserted a new magazine, and got ready to fire. He propped himself up on his left arm and pointed the weapon at the lifeless animal. He tried to keep his trembling under control. Slowly he stood up, without lowering the weapon. But it was no longer necessary, their attacker was dead.

Russell helped his son to his feet. "Are you okay?"

Greg nodded. His whole body was quivering, his eyes ripped open wide. "Dad, your shoulder!"

The adrenalin and the stimulants had blocked out the pain, but now he became aware of the terrible burning sensation again. Part of his shirt, the size of his palm, had disintegrated. It hissed and stank of rotting meat.

Acid! These damn creatures spit acid. If any more turn up, we're screwed.

They needed to get away and to the depot. It was the only safe place far and wide. God knows how many more monsters he'd alerted with his shooting! He would have to tend to the wound later. Russell bent the fingers of his left hand and shook his lower arm. At least the injury didn't seem to be too serious.

He was about to pick up his weapon when he noticed that the entire barrel above the magazine had melted away. The thing was useless. He cursed to himself. He had only taken along two magazines for the pistol, and he had already emptied one of them.

"Dad, I . . ."

Whatever Greg had wanted to say, he swallowed his words when another rattling sound came from the right. And behind them another sound.

Jesus Christ. How many of these beasts are there?

Russell grabbed his son by the arm and ran. They didn't have a second to lose. At least the jungle was less dense here—it reminded him of the forests in the remoter parts of Connecticut. Then he realized why: they were moving up and out of the swampy jungle and onto higher ground.

They reached the foot of the little range of hills. If they continued to run uphill they couldn't miss the depot, which was on the south side of Mount Fairweather. It couldn't be more than half a mile away. The trees were more dispersed here, and the rays of the late-afternoon sun penetrated the treetops. Russell kept hearing the ominous sound of the greyhound-lizards behind them. It didn't subside, so they must still be hot on their heels. Every time he turned round to look, there was nothing to be seen, but that could change at any moment. Russell was surprised that the creatures hadn't caught up with them, fast as they were. Perhaps they were pack animals and still getting into formation.

"Dad, I can't anymore," gasped Greg, stumbling forward with little steps.

"We're nearly there," panted Russell. His lungs were burning like fire despite the painkiller. When the effect of the medication wore off in a few hours, the pain would be intolerable.

They had reached the crest of the hill. Here, there were just a few lone trees, and for the first time, Russell could see Mount Fairweather to the west, towering miles up into the sky. The lush grassland ended abruptly at a sheer black rock face, which made it look like a small volcano. Small white clouds drifted over the peak.

For Christ's sake, where's the depot?

Russell and Greg ran toward the southern slope. They had already left the last trees behind them. Up here there was no cover. Russell looked back more frequently—and then he saw them.

Two, no three, of the greyhound-lizards were emerging from the cover of the forest and running in their direction.

Russell estimated that they were nine-hundred feet away at most.

And they're faster than us!

"Run! Run as fast as you can!" screamed Russell. He stumbled again. His chest was hurting and he coughed violently. He pressed the back of his hand against his mouth to muffle the sound. When he took his hand away, he saw a trace of blood and slime, which dripped onto the butt of his pistol.

They had reached the lower slope of Mount Fairweather and ran along the edge of the escarpment. The ground was still sloping upward slightly, and beneath their feet was soft, wet grass that squelched with every step they took.

Russell turned to look around again. The animals were now no more than seven-hundred feet away. The leader of the pack was running straight toward them, while the other two flanked it to the left and right, but a good forty feet behind, twitching their heads continuously to the side.

They really are pack animals. And intelligent, too. Jesus Christ!

Russell could see what they were up to. The next time they changed direction, one of the animals would break rank and cut them off. If they missed the depot, they were done for.

Dammit, where is the goddamn depot?

A copse of trees appeared in front of them. Russell couldn't see what lay beyond it. Had they lost their way?

They ran through the trees and after a few seconds had already reached the far side. Finally, Russell saw the depot behind the next knoll. Hope welled up inside him again. He hadn't got them lost. It was so close. They could make it. They had to make it.

He glanced around and saw the greyhound creatures running through the copse of trees, no more than a three-hundred feet behind them!

Russell simply couldn't understand why the beasts hadn't got them already; after all, he'd seen how fast they could run. Then he realized:

They enjoy chasing their prey. It's a game for them. But for us it's life or death!

Russell pushed his son forward. "Run!" he roared.

The final stretch seemed to drag on endlessly. Russell wasn't sure if the effect of the stimulant was wearing off, or if he had simply reached his physical limits, but his head was spinning again and he lost all feeling in his legs. He staggered.

No! This can't happen! Not this close to our goal!

With his last reserve of energy he reached the heavy wooden door of the hut. As he drew back the iron bolt, he saw from the corner of his eye that something brown was shooting toward him. With a thudding noise, the door was ripped out of his hand and crashed against the wall of the hut. The animal had wanted to jump at him, but had hurtled into the door as Russell opened it. The greyhound-lizard lurched backward as Russell pulled Greg into the depot. The animal was back on its legs and getting ready to pounce. But Russell was now also inside. He pulled the door shut behind them and slid the bolt across.

His knees gave way, and he slid down the wall of the hut to the ground. Greg sat down next to him, laid his little arm on his father's shoulder and began to sob bitterly. Russell hugged him while still gasping for air.

We're safe. At least for the time being.

Six feet away from where they sat, wrapped in plastic on a shelf, he saw the radio.

Chapter 14

"Those are wotans. A whole pack of them. What are they doing so close to the edge of the forest?" Marlene Wolfe lowered her binoculars and shook her head. Over all the years they had been here, she had never seen more than one or two wotans at a time.

"I told you so," said Ben Hawke. "Something's not right. Today wotans and a few days ago that sniper attack. And the hyenas."

Marlene nodded. "Something is driving them out of the forest. They can't get up the cliff, so they're moving toward the pass and the observation post."

"We need to increase the number of lookouts on duty."

Marlene raised the binoculars back up to her eyes. The monsters did not seem to be moving in their direction anymore, but rather to be waiting. Suddenly, there was a roaring sound from the forest, not unlike the sound of a stag, and the wotans stormed in a southerly direction along the edge of the forest. A few seconds later they were out of sight.

"Something frightened them," murmured Marlene.

"Or lured them."

"But what? I've never heard a sound like that," murmured Marlene.

Hawke did not respond. "I told you, we need more lookouts."

Marlene pursed her lips. She was not officially the military commander, but as the elected head of the colony, she was in charge of allocating jobs. "I'd really like to avoid that if possible. The harvest is coming up and we need all hands in the fields."

"If a whole herd of wotans is heading for the barriers, we're all screwed. Visibility just isn't good enough—especially at night. We should have strengthened the barriers a long time ago. Wooden fences with barbed wire aren't enough to withstand a concentrated attack. We should have built a solid, ten-foot-high stone wall to seal off the canyon. As I've been saying for years!"

Marlene had to admit he was right. It would have been a lot of work and sucked up countless precious working hours—they had voted against the idea again and again, especially as the animals had increasingly kept their distance from the observation post. Nobody could have predicted that the situation would change so suddenly. Or could they? She had been a good company commander for many years. Back then, safety and security had been her top priority, regardless of the amount of work involved. Hawke was right; they should have built the wall, but now it was too late. If she called an emergency meeting and the colony voted to build it, it would tie up so many of the colonists that they could say goodbye to half their harvest. And she didn't want to go through another winter like the third winter they had spent on the planet. The best compromise solution was to bring in reinforcements.

"Okay, we'll increase the number of lookouts to five."

"Starting when?"

"Starting next week."

"Fine," said Hawke.

"I would like to speak to your wife," said Marlene casually.

Ben swiveled his head in Marlene's direction and scrutinized her through narrowed eyes. His sharp nose, raised in the air, looked like an accusatory finger pointing in her direction. "Why?"

Marlene was surprised by the aggressiveness of his reaction. She knew that Ben saw himself as the boss of his wife. And she also knew that Ben liked to be asked permission to consult with her. Marlene had never understood why Drew continued to live with Ben, and his jealousy attacks were getting worse all the time. Quite apart from the blatant beatings! "I would like to ask Drew her opinion about the strange behavior of the animals out there."

Ben stared at her for another moment, before turning to gaze in the direction of the open grassland beyond the barrier. "Fine, I'll order her to find you tomorrow."

Order? Marlene looked at him askance. He didn't even seem to notice.

She decided not to say any more on the subject, but she couldn't let this go on indefinitely. She also decided to talk to Dr. Lindwall about Ben.

"I would have thought that you . . ."

Marlene didn't get any further, because Igor was shouting something. She turned around and saw him running toward her from the barrack.

"What is it?" She leaned over the wooden railing and saw that his eyes were ripped wide open.

"It's Russell! It's Russell!"

Marlene raised her eyebrows. What was the man

138

talking about? Her friend had gone away in order to die, and she certainly hadn't expected to hear from him again.

"Calm down! What do you mean it's Russell?"

"On the radio. I just finished repairing it, and it started making a noise. It's Russell! He needs help."

Marlene shook her head. Lee had sent Igor with her to the observation post so that he could check out the radio. No doubt somebody had just been waiting for it to be working again in order to play a very sick joke. It couldn't be one of Russell's friends.

"Nonsense. Russell didn't take a radio with him!"

Igor made a confused gesture. "He called from the old hut on Mount Fairweather. He needs help."

"Russell doesn't intend to come back. Whatever's happened to him, he doesn't need any help and he wouldn't ask for any."

Igor grabbed her arm. His slim hands were surprisingly strong. "He has Greg with him! His son got on the whale without anyone noticing!"

Holy shit!

Shortly before making her way to the observation post that morning, she had heard that Russell's son had gone missing and that people in the colony were looking for him. Christian Holbrook assumed that the boy had hidden himself somewhere because he was mad about his dad going away. It hadn't occurred to anybody that he could have fastened himself to the whale. Obviously Russell had forced the animal to land and made his way back to Mount Fairweather with Greg. But without backup, the two of them didn't stand a chance of reaching the next post.

Marlene hastened to the barrack, where the radio stood in the corner. The thing didn't work half the time because components were constantly conking out. Not that they needed it to contact Eridu; they had a cable phone for that. But they needed the radio for the upcoming trip to the refinery. Igor had worked on the device for hours, cursing all the while, and Marlene had been doubtful he would succeed in fixing it. She sat down on the wooden stool and picked up the mouthpiece.

"Russell. Is that really you?"

There was a lot static, but she could hear his voice. "Marlene? Yes, Russell here. I've got Greg with me, otherwise I wouldn't have got in touch. We're at the old depot on Mount Fairweather and are stuck in a trap."

"Copy that. Are you hurt?"

"Not badly, no. But we can't get away. The hut is surrounded by animals."

Marlene nodded. The area around Mount Fairweather was swarming with wotans. That was where they had nearly lost Lee on their last expedition. And there had been fifteen of them, armed to the hilt.

"Russell, we'll get you out of there. It might take a while, I need to get reinforcements first. Have you spoken to anyone in Eridu yet?"

"No, I couldn't get through to the colony. I don't know how long we can last. They're pacing around the depot like they're plotting something. Be very careful when you come. I've never seen these monsters before. They're fast and spit acid from a distance of forty feet."

"We'll come as quickly as we can, but it will take a few hours. Hang in there!" Marlene replaced the microphone on the hook and turned around.

Ben Hawke had slunk in quietly and was standing next to her. Igor and Donald Bell were leaning against the door. Outside, Jack Neaman and Eliot Sargent were at the fence. The regular lookout team of four men, plus Ben and herself. Was that enough people for a rescue expedition? Drive there, pick up Greg and Russell, and get out again.

"I think it's a mistake!" Ben interrupted her thoughts.

Marlene pinched the bridge of her nose. "You don't even know what I'm planning."

He shook his head. "Doesn't matter. I still don't think we should risk anyone's life to bring back Harris. He made his decision when he flew off this morning on that whale."

"He has his son with him, for Christ's sake!" Marlene flew into a rage.

"His problem," replied Ben gruffly.

Marlene shook her head, at a loss for words. Ben hated Russell, she'd known that for a long time. But the boy was another matter.

"I say we get him out of there," said Jack Neaman from the door. In his right hand, the eighteen-year-old was holding a rifle with a scope. Chris's son was one of the generation that had been born here and he was good friends with Greg's brother Jim.

"You should stay out of this, boy!" Ben snapped at him.

"So should you!" the young man retorted. "Eliot is in charge of the observation post today."

Ben's face flushed red and he opened his mouth to speak. He was about to blurt out a nasty retort, but Eliot got in before him.

"He's right. The team leader is in charge during lookout duty. And I say that we can't simply abandon our man and his son out there."

Ben scowled and stepped into the background. Eliot pointed at a map that was hanging on the wall. "We're here at the bottom end of the pass. Russell and Greg are here, about twenty miles away. The first five miles won't be a problem, if we take the route past the oil springs. The gravel track is in good condition, and as long as we take precautions, it shouldn't be too dangerous. For the last fifteen miles to the foot of Mount Fairweather we at least still have the old path that we hacked through the jungle five years ago on our last expedition.

"We don't know what condition it's in. The path won't exactly have improved over the past five years," said Marlene.

"Better than nothing!"

Hawke pushed his way back to the front and tapped on the map. "The route to the oil springs is dangerous. It was dangerous even before the attacks on the post. The twelve miles to the old supply depot are sheer suicide! And all that for a man who's going to die anyway!"

"He has his son with him!" shouted Eliot in frustration.

Hawke looked unimpressed. "Tough luck!"

"What would you do if it was one of your daughters out there? If Dana or Catherine had got onto Russell's whale? Would you be so indifferent then?" asked Marlene icily.

"I've brought up my children properly. They wouldn't dare do something that stupid!"

Donald Bell shook his head. The former scientist and astronaut had never liked Russell much. After the destruction of the sphere, he and Allison Hadcroft had been stranded for some time on Summers Planet—a bare lump of rock without an atmosphere. When Ellen finally turned up in her space suit weeks later, the air inside the research module was thick as soup and they had already decided to commit suicide the next day. No, he wouldn't bend a finger for Russell. "Kids are kids, and they do things that nobody reckons with. And the same goes for your kids! If there's one thing worth protecting on this damn planet, then it's our children, and in my view it makes no difference whether they're mine or someone else's."

"You want to risk your life for someone else's child?"

asked Hawke in a tone of voice that left no doubt as to what his own answer to the question would be.

The chubby-cheeked scientist glared at Ben. "I'm almost fifty years old and so are you! If we're not prepared to risk our lives for the next generation, then everything we've achieved here will have been for nothing." He looked at Marlene. "And if we carry on wasting our time debating, we might as well leave it altogether!"

"Quit bitching. Nobody is going anywhere until we've planned this properly." She turned round to look at the map again. "We need about forty minutes to get to the oil springs, and—depending on the condition of the tracks— two to four hours from there to Mount Fairweather."

"There's no way we'll make it back to the post by nightfall. It's another four hours until sunset; we won't even make it to Mount Fairweather in daylight," said Ben. He turned on his heel, as if there was nothing more to discuss.

"I have a suggestion," said Igor, who until then had remained silent. "We set off immediately with the two jeeps we've got here. All of us. We take all the weapons and ammunition with us that are here at the observation post. Then we'll reach the old depot at dusk, stay overnight in the hut, and drive back at sunrise."

"You want to leave the post unguarded?" Ben shook his head.

"Hang on, that's not such a bad idea," said Marlene. "I'll call for reinforcements right away. It'll take an hour for them to get here, but in that time it's highly unlikely that hordes of wotans will storm the post. And if the odd animal manages to slip through the barrier, the reinforcements will take care of it."

"But they won't have anywhere to take cover in the canyon."

"I think that's a risk worth taking. That's what we'll

143

do." She looked every one of them in the eye. "I'm not in charge here, and Eliot can't force you either."

Donald Bell nodded. "That isn't necessary. I'm in!"

"Me too," added Igor.

Jack Neaman nodded curtly and started to rummage around on the shelves for ammunition.

"What about you?" Marlene directed a steely gaze at Ben Hawke. He pursed his lips, opened his mouth to say something, and shut it again. It was obvious that he didn't give a damn about Russell and his son, but if he was the only one who didn't go, it would look as if he were afraid of the mission. After several seconds, he gave a curt nod.

"Alright, pack up all the weapons, ammunition, and equipment that we have and load it into the two jeeps. I'll talk to headquarters and make sure reinforcements are sent down, and I'll let Russell know that help is on the way. Hurry, we'll get going in ten minutes. And so that there are no misunderstandings: Eliot remains in charge."

Eliot laughed. "That's dumb! You have more experience and better leadership qualities. I'm not even a soldier. I'm a mechanic when I'm not holding a weapon in my hand. I hand over command to you, Ms. President!"

Marlene shrugged. "Okay. Let's go."

Chapter 15

"Give me the first-aid kit," said Russell, turning around to Greg as he placed the radio back on the shelf.

Greg looked around the small barrack in confusion. The walls were lined with wooden shelves that were filled to the last square inch with food, tools, equipment and weapons. At the time, Russell had thought it was a mistake to leave all this stuff here. Another expedition had been planned for the following month, but that was five years ago, and the second expedition had never taken place. They kept planning to abandon the depot and bring the supplies back to Eridu, but they simply hadn't got round to it. Now Russell was glad of the fact. "Over there, on the shelf under the skylight." Greg hurried over to the place where Russell was pointing, took the little red box and ran back to him.

He took the kit from his son's hand and tore open the protective foil. He took out the scissors and cut open his shirt from the collar downward.

Russell pulled his shirt over the wound and cried out in

pain as he tried to pull off the scraps of material stuck to his skin. Even worse was the smell. Like rotten eggs.

He heard Greg crying. "I didn't want this to happen. I'm sorry. I just wanted to be with you!"

"It's okay, it's not your fault." Russell had tears in his eyes. The pain was hellish. He took a piece of gauze and dabbed the white liquid that had once been his skin from the wound.

His son turned around. He took a quick look at the wound and immediately turned away again. "Was that the spit from the animal? Is it acid?"

Russell shook his head. "It's an acid burn, yes. But caused by an alkaline fluid. With acid, the skin would have scarred over right away. But here the tissue has liquefied and the hole is deeper. I have to clean it off very carefully."

"Will . . . will you get better?"

Russell almost laughed. He would never get better again, with or without a wound. Instead he forced himself to smile at his son. "It's not so bad, luckily most of the spit missed me. Don't worry."

"Are they coming to get us?"

Russell nodded. He had dabbed off the wound. The skin was scarring in parts, but oozing in some spots. He groaned as he tied the bandage around his shoulder. "Yes, they're coming. But it will take a few hours. Until then we'll hide out here."

"Can't the monsters get in here?"

"I don't think so. But we have to be quiet so that they don't hear us."

"Are they still out there?"

Russell secured the bandage with a pin and took a deep breath. The pain was bearable if he didn't move. But he had no choice. "I don't know. I'll go and have a look." Russell crept over to the ammunitions cupboard. There were several pistols, two high-caliber rifles with scopes and two assault rifles. Russell took one of the two M-16s, inserted a magazine and cocked and racked the slide. He slipped an already loaded VP70 into one of his pant pockets along with some M67 hand grenades. Then he propped himself up and peeked out of the little window.

The window faced south, and the gentle incline outside provided an open view across the grassland down to the edge of the forest about half a mile away. The sun was far in the west, over where the oil fields must be. From the north, grey rain clouds were drawing in.

Greg had crawled over to him and was about to stand up.

"Stay down!"

The boy kept his head below the window frame. "Can you see anything?"

"No. All quiet. They seem to have gone away," whispered Russell. But he didn't believe they really had. The persistence with which the monsters had followed them made him doubt that they would give up on their prey that easily, especially since they had him and Greg in a trap. Russell guessed that they were somewhere nearby, lying in wait for their opportunity. He only hoped that the beasts would leave them in peace until Marlene had arrived with her crew.

Feeling very weak, Russell slumped down beside his son and leaned against the cool outer wall of the hut. The effect of the medication was wearing off, and it felt as if a jackhammer were pounding in his head. Within seconds he felt nauseous, and vomited all over the wooden floor. He wiped a sleeve over his mouth.

"Dad? Are you okay? Is it the wound?"

Russell shook his head. "No, that's not because of the wound. I need to apologize to you, I should have told you from the start." Russell paused and waited for a reaction, but Greg just stared at him.

"I'm ill. Very ill. The reason I just barfed is because of the medication that Dr. Lindwall gave me."

Greg continued to stare at him unblinkingly. "Will you die?"

"Yes," Russell turned away. "I will die. And soon."

He felt a warm hand in his.

"And that's why you wanted to go." It was more of a statement than a question.

Russell nodded and turned around to his son. His big green eyes reminded him so much of Ellen's. His vision blurred.

"Yes, son. You're right. I went away in order to die."

"Why, Dad? Why didn't you say anything?" Greg didn't look reproachful. But his eyes were moist.

"I couldn't, Greg. I simply couldn't. Please don't be angry with me."

Greg shuffled closer and hugged Russell tightly. "I'm not angry with you, if you're not angry with me."

Russell sniffed. He didn't want to start weeping in front of his son, but he couldn't hold back the tears. "I'm not angry. I never have been and never will be!"

For a long time they hugged each other in silence— father and son in a lonely hut, surrounded by monsters on an alien planet at the wrong end of the galaxy.

Chapter 16

"There's another one over there! It's trying to cut us off!" cried Marlene.

Ben sat upright in the passenger seat and fired a single shot in front of him. The hulking creature rolled across the track and came to a standstill in front of a tree trunk. Its hind legs twitched briefly and then it stopped moving completely.

The jeep swayed as Marlene drove over a big stone. The old track was in worse condition than they had expected. Since passing the oil spring, they had made painfully slow progress on their way east. Again and again, they were attacked by wotans. Igor Isalovic, Jack Neaman, and Donald Bell, in the rear jeep, had to deal with the worst of it. Shots were fired whenever one of the animals broke out of the undergrowth and headed for the vehicles.

Of course they had also been attacked back on their first expedition, but not like this. Why were there so many more animals? Had their numbers increased for some specific reason?

Marlene saw a movement from the corner of her eye. "Left!" she shouted. Ben turned around and fired. The wotan, already dead, thudded against the front left wheel of the jeep and was flung backward. The jeep veered sharply to the right and Marlene was worried it might tip over, but by turning the wheel hard, she was able to get it back under control.

Ben sat down again. "I don't need to tell you that I still find this whole thing a dumb-ass idea. We'll all die, just to save one person's life."

"Two people!"

"I wasn't counting Russell anymore."

Marlene didn't respond. "Six miles. We can do it!"

"I'm starting to worry about our ammo supply. And if one of the jeeps is hit and we're forced to stop, they'll eat us alive!"

Marlene bit her lip. Unfortunately Ben was right. Their only chance was to keep moving. If they stopped, they wouldn't be able to stave off the attackers. She was beginning to ask herself if they shouldn't have waited for reinforcement after all.

Be that as it may, it's too late to turn around now. We won't make it back to the oil spring by sunset. Our only chance is the supply depot on Mount Fairweather.

"Shit, something's happened to the other jeep! They've stopped!" Eliot shouted into Marlene's ear from the back seat.

She looked in the rear-view mirror. She could see Igor clambering out of the immobile vehicle and slammed on the brakes. No sooner had the vehicle come to a stop than she jumped out. "Ben, Eliot, cover us at the front!"

Hawke and Sargent ran past Marlene. Ben crouched next to the front right wheel and Eliot next to the left one.

Marlene reached into a box on the truck bed and took out three incendiary grenades. She tore off the pin from the first one and threw it far beyond the stranded jeep. The grenade detonated with a bang and the track was flooded with glistening yellow flames. The heat was so intense, Marlene had to turn her head away. She threw the second grenade into the forest to her left, the other to her right. The flames joined up into a blazing wall that would protect them from the wotans on three sides. She ran to the stationary vehicle.

"What happened?" she asked Igor, who had already crawled under the jeep. It stank of petrol and she feared that the gas tank had ruptured. In that case they would have to abandon it here.

"The fuel pipe has burst. No gas is getting into the pump!"

"Can you repair it?"

"Yes, but I need a few minutes."

She wished she had Lee with them, who had a knack for repairing the jeeps. But she didn't show her concern.

"Good." She turned to Jack Neaman and Donald Bell. "Don't fire into the flames. Wotans hate fire. Keep an eye on the gaps between the flames!"

She turned back round to Igor, whose legs were sticking out from beneath the vehicle. "You've got five minutes! When the fires go out, the whole pack of them will come at us and we're done for."

"I'm working as fast as I can!"

Up in front, shots were being fired at increasingly short intervals.

"Quickly!"

"Get me the tape from the box in the back of the truck." As Marlene slipped past Jack, she heard the firing of a gun. She turned around and saw a wotan diving through the flames—directly at her. Instinctively she threw herself to the ground and rolled over, banging her knee on a sharp stone. She cried out, but the shot had hit its target. With an ungodly yowling, the animal fell back into the flames, twitched two more times, and died. The air was filled with the smell of charred meat. Jack reached out a hand and helped her to her feet.

"Good react!" she groaned, but the teenager had already turned around to face the flames again. Marlene went to the truck bed to find the box of tools.

"There's a whole horde of them approaching from the front!" bellowed Ben from the first jeep.

"I have to reload!" called Eliot. "Fuck, we need reinforcement!"

Marlene pressed the tape into Bell's hand and ran to the front jeep. She kneeled next to Ben, lifted her weapon and took aim at one of the wotans. The monster slumped to the ground.

"There are too many. They're . . ." shouted Ben. His last words were swallowed up by rifle fire.

He was right. We can't hold out against this attack!

She fired at a wotan. And another. And another.

"What's wrong with the damn jeep?" she yelled. From the corner of her eye she could see that the brightness of the flames was subsiding. The fires were fizzling out. If they didn't get away from here fast, they were screwed!

"Igor, dammit!" screamed Marlene. She fired at two more animals. One of them rolled right up to her feet and before dying with a rattling noise in its throat.

Ben had emptied his magazine. He pulled a replacement magazine from his jacket pocket, and yelled in Marlene's ear. "We're all going to die here and it's your fault!"

She took out another wotan that was storming toward them and was about to remind Ben that he had come along voluntarily, when she heard the engine spluttering to life behind them.

"We can move!" shouted Igor.

"Get in!" cried Marlene.

As the jeeps set off again, Marlene realized that Igor had finished his repairs not a second too soon. Dozens of wotans were now leaping through the black smoke toward them. Jack and Donald fired at them from the back seat of their jeep. Within moments, droves of them were lying dead on the track. Marlene hurtled through a deep pothole without braking. Ben was thrown upward out of his seat and swore like a recruit on latrine fatigue.

"Not so fast, or you'll ruin the axle. It's already been welded twice, for God's sake," yelled Eliot.

"I don't care, we have to get out of here!" screamed Marlene, without turning around. With all the noise we've been making, every animal in a ten-mile radius will be heading our way."

"With a broken axle they'll be having us for dinner!"

"We have no choice!"

Marlene continued at thirty miles an hour without reducing her speed. Where on earth did all these monsters come from? At least they were only wotans, and not snipers.

"The sun is starting to set," murmured Ben from the passenger seat. Marlene noticed how the light was fading. Up to a moment ago, the occasional ray of sun still broke through the canopy of leaves, bathing the jungle in a pale-green light. But now the forest became darker, the colors less distinct. Even the wotans were harder to spot against the backdrop of the forest.

"In half an hour it will be pitch dark," said Marlene, worry creeping into her voice.

"How much farther is it to Mount Fairweather?" asked Eliot.

"Too far."

Chapter 17

"Can we turn on a light?" asked Greg.

Russell shook his head. Better not. The sun had set behind the distant mountains. The black clouds had drifted past without bursting, and had left in their wake a pale-blue sky that was now turning gray. The first star of the evening twinkled down on them. The trees in the forest had turned into a blur of brown specks; it was impossible to tell one tree from another. Moisture rose up from the grass around the depot, turning into a fine layer of white mist that swirled over the ground. An almost intolerable silence overlaid everything, creating an illusion of peaceful-ness where in fact there was none. The beasts were most probably still in the vicinity. Russell would have liked to open the door and look on the other side of the hut where there was no window, but he was afraid that the monsters were only waiting for such an opportunity.

"Where are Marlene and the others?" whispered Greg.

Russell looked to the south, in the direction from where he was expecting the jeep to arrive. At first he wanted to say something reassuring to Greg; that that the team of rescuers would be here any moment; but he had decided not to tell his son any more lies. "I don't know. Marlene said that they would be here before dark."

"Can't you try and reach them on the radio?"

"No, if they're in difficulty, I don't want to disturb them. They know how to get hold us if they want to talk to us."

"What will we do if they don't come?"

"It's too early to give up hope."

"But what if they still don't come? Can we walk back home?"

It was as if a switch had flipped inside his son. *Back home* . . . Despite the twenty years that Russell had now spent on this planet, in the now-thriving colony they had worked so hard to establish, he had never really felt at home here. The environment they were pitted against was too alien. On Earth he could have lived anywhere. He had never found it hard to adapt to new surroundings. He'd even gotten used to Afghanistan after a few weeks. But although he had settled into life in New California and did not miss Earth, he still felt like a foreign body on this planet.

For Greg and his friends, however, who had been born here, New California was their home planet and the settlement of Eridu was their home. They were the first generation of humans to be born in a distant galaxy under a foreign sun. As close as Russell felt to his children and the other young citizens of their colony, this rift was unfathomably deep. While many of the older generation would immediately return to Earth if they were given the opportunity, most of the children would probably refuse to go with them—or never feel at home on Earth.

Why had this thought never occurred to him before? It was only here in this goddam depot, surrounded by monsters, that the fundamental difference between the two generations became clear to him. The children were the future. They would take charge of this planet, conquer it and make fun of their parents who always lived in the past and lamented the loss of a planet that they had been forced to leave decades ago.

"Marlene will come. And we'll go home!" said Russell with as much conviction as he could muster.

It was getting darker by the minute. The trees merged into a black mass. The strip of orange on the horizon was becoming darker. Russell cursed under his breath. He was searching for one of the night-vision devices when the radio crackled. He leaped over to the device, lost his balance and fell flat on his face. Greg helped him up as Marlene's voice sounded from the loudspeaker. There was hardly any background hissing, which must mean she was close.

"Russell, Marlene. Please report."

Hastily, Russell picked up the microphone and pressed the speaker button. "Russell here. Where are you?"

"About half a mile away. We'll be there in five minutes."

Russell looked out of the window. He thought he could see the gleam of car headlights through the trees. Perhaps it was an illusion.

"Happy to hear that."

"We need to know if the clearing is empty. Once we come out of the forest we won't have any more cover."

"I can't see anything out of the window, but my field of vision is restricted. I suspect that some of the acid-spraying beasts are still hanging around in the vicinity."

"We need to know exactly. Can you provide us with some light, as soon as we reach the clearing?"

"Yes, I can."

"Good. See you shortly."

Russell took a box of incendiaries from the shelf. They were filled with magnesium and would create plenty of light. He turned to his son and said: "I want you to lie down there by the wall. With your face to the floor."

"Why?" asked Greg quietly. "What's going to happen?"

"Nothing is going to happen. When Marlene and the others arrive, it could get a bit crazy, and I don't want you to get hurt if one of those monsters is lurking outside the door."

With the incendiary in his pocket and a rifle slung over his shoulder, Russell climbed up one of the shelves until he had reached the skylight. He suppressed a cry of pain as his injured shoulder bumped into a protruding box. Quietly he released the latch, lifted up the flap and stuck his head outside. Keeping his feet planted firmly on the uppermost shelf, he craned his neck first one way and then the other. At least none of the creatures were sitting on the roof.

However, he could hardly see anything in the dark. It seemed to be very quiet. When there were animals nearby, they usually made their presence known. Maybe they had given up. Russell turned to look southward. He had to squint, but then he saw a glimmer in the treetops of the forest. A few moments later, two pairs of headlights appeared on the hillside.

Russell pulled the pin on one of the grenades and threw it to the east. The ignited magnesium was so bright that he had to shut his eyes. He threw the next one in the opposite direction. With a loud hiss, a wall of flames was suddenly blazing on the clearing as the grenades exploded. The whole area was bathed in bright light. This would doubtlessly attract more animals, but once the rescue team was in the depot, they could wait till the creatures had moved on again. Russell looked toward the jeeps. Between the two jeeps, a lone wotan sprang out of the forest into the glare of the headlights. He was felled by a single shot. Russell looked around in every direction. No monster in sight!

He ducked back down into the hut, closed the skylight and climbed down from the shelf a little too fast, causing a sharp stab of pain in his left shoulder. Then he hurried over to the door and pulled back the heavy bolt. Rifle at the ready, he crept out into the open. The flames of the incendiaries bathed the open grassland around the hut in a flickering orange light. The crackling of the flames was loud—too loud to hear possible noises made by approaching monsters.

The jeeps drove through a gap in the sea of flames and reached the depot. The headlights faded and the puttering of the engine fell silent. A door opened and Marlene jumped out. She ran over to Russell, smiled weakly and they hugged briefly.

"Thank you," said Russell. "And I'm sorry."

"You should be. The drive here was anything but easy. If it had been up to me, I would have let you snuff it out here," said Ben Hawke calmly as he sauntered up to Marlene's side.

Marlene threw an angry glance at Ben and smiled at Russell. "Don't listen to him. He doesn't mean it like that. He came voluntarily—we all did." She turned around. "Looks as if the coast is clear."

"Right now, yes, but I wouldn't rely on it remaining that way. You better come in."

Marlene nodded. She turned to her crew: "Grab your weapons and equipment and get into the hut! Our journey is over for today."

"Hey Russell!" Igor slapped him on the shoulder. He didn't notice the bandage and Russell cried out in pain.

"Sorry," said Igor sheepishly. "Is it bad?"

"One of the beasts almost got me, but it'll be okay."

"I never thought I'd see you again."

"Same here. Didn't go quite as planned."

"That's for sure."

Russell was the last one to enter the depot. He closed and bolted the door.

"Aha, and there's our trouble-maker!" said Marlene, and planted herself in front of Greg, who had just stood up again.

"I'm really sorry. I just wanted to be with my dad." The boy was close to tears. It had obviously dawned on him that people had risked their lives for him and were still doing so. Russell still didn't want to lay any blame on his son. It was his fault, not Greg's.

Marlene hugged Greg and stroked his back. "It's okay, sweetie. We're not angry with you."

Greg started sobbing again.

Exhausted, Eliot leaned against the wall before sliding down to a sitting position on the floor. "That was some trip, guys."

Russell sat down beside him. "Did you have a lot of trouble? Wotans?"

"Man, you have no idea how many of those beasts were running around." Eliot shook his head as if he still couldn't believe how many creatures had made his life hell that day. "Must have been about ten times as many as we encountered on our last expedition. When we broke down, I thought we'd had it!"

Russell nodded. "Something's going on here. We made it to the hut at the last minute. There weren't that many, but they really frightened me."

Marlene kneeled in front of him. "You said something about greyhounds that spat acid?"

Russell nodded and indicated his shoulder. "Actually it's an alkaline, but it amounts to the same thing. Spat a nice big hole in my shoulder from a distance of thirty feet! And I only got a few drops. Most of it missed me, luckily."

"A new species?" Ben was skeptical.

Russell nodded again. "Yeah, I've never seen these monsters here before."

Marlene looked worried. "And then there are the snipers—more of them have been turning up around the observation post in the valley lately. It looks as if some kind of migration is in progress. That would also explain the high number of wotans east of the oil springs. The greyhounds may be pushing them out of their territory toward the post." She scratched her head. "Everything is heading toward the post. But why?"

Russell slapped himself on the head. "Jesus! Why didn't I think of it sooner?"

Marlene looked at him quizzically.

"The ocean!"

"What are you trying to say?" asked Ben.

Russell ignored him and looked at Marlene. "From the whale, I could see the ocean. But not where it ought to be." He paused briefly. "It's ten miles away from here at most. The coastline is shifting inland."

Eliot shook his head. "Are you sure? How can that be?"

"My God!" whispered Marlene. "Drew's research. The waterline in the canyon. It's happening again. Now. At this moment! The ocean is advancing westward. The vast lowlands will become the new ocean bed. The animals are fleeing from the water, that's the reason for their migration. If the water continues to rise, they'll head for the pass and the observation post will be trampled down by migrating animals. Millions of starving animals will force their way up the valley and invade the colony. We're screwed!"

Jack Neaman shook his head in confusion. "How can the ocean rise that high. Tides?"

"No. New California doesn't have a moon. So it also can't have any tides," said Ben.

Russell stood up and looked Ben in the eyes. "You're mistaken. This planet does have a moon. I saw it!"

"What?" Igor looked at him open-mouthed.

"I saw it from the whale. Beyond the curve of the horizon. It looks like the Earth's moon, but obviously takes much longer to orbit—probably dozens of years. Now the gravitational pull is causing the ocean to rise."

"A moon that orbits the planet in years? That's impossible. It would have to be so far away, it would be beyond the gravitational field of New California," objected Marlene.

"I only know that I saw it."

"We'll talk about it with Dr. Dressel. Maybe he can give us an explanation."

"Do you really think the colony is in danger?" asked Igor.

Marlene turned around to him. "Imagine a million beasts of prey all saving themselves from being drowned by fleeing the valley. Since they will have mown down anything that breathes by the time they reach the observation post, they'll be pretty hungry by the time they invade the colony."

"But they're only animals! We'll just strengthen the post at the pass."

Marlene laughed. "A fence won't be much help against that kind of deluge. Whatever obstacles we put in their way, they'll just knock 'em down. It's already started! The attacks on the observation post; the vast number of wotans we saw today. More and more waves will break down the fences. The first wave will consist of wotans that can't defend their territory any more. Then it'll probably be snipers and these acid-spitting dogs fighting over the former wotan territory."

The fire was dying down outside the window and bathed Marlene's face in a diabolical shade of red that gradually faded. She spoke her final words into darkness. "The last wave will consist of all the remaining beasts left on the plain. And that wave will overrun our colony."

Chapter 18

"Dawn is breaking," said Russell. He pressed a hastily prepared cup of tea into Marlene's hand.

"Anything to be seen?" asked Marlene.

"All quiet at the moment. We should get going soon."

"Yes, as soon as it's completely light. Wake the others!"

The night had been peaceful. They had taken turns keeping watch, with Russell the last one on duty. But nobody had really slept properly. Russell was shattered. He couldn't stop coughing and was nauseous. He had toyed with the idea of sending Greg back with Marlene and the others and staying here at the depot to confront the creatures alone. He was sure he wouldn't last long. But he had already caused enough trouble with his maverick behavior, and it was only fair that he now help the group that had come here voluntarily to get him and Greg back safely.

Russell sat in silence next to Igor, listlessly munching on the muesli that he had prepared with powdered milk. It was a luxury, really. Since they didn't have any milk-producing livestock, this was the last taste of milk they would experience in their lives.

But Russell wasn't able to enjoy it. He thought about the dangers facing the colony due to the advancing ocean and the hordes of animals. Marlene seemed to be convinced that the threat was imminent, but Russell wanted to hear the opinion of their biologist first. Still, he couldn't brush aside the thought that his wish not to die a pitiful death from cancer might be fulfilled. But not the way he had wanted. Instead, he would die along with all the people of New California—including his family.

Russell shuddered. It couldn't come to that! Perhaps their fears were unfounded and Jenny would laugh at them. But if not? Then they would have to find a solution. But first, they needed to make it back to Eridu in one piece!

"Okay, it's time for us to get going," said Marlene.

Igor and Ben stood beside the door. Ben pulled back the bolt.

"I couldn't see anything out of the window, so I think we might at least make it to the forest in one piece," said Marlene. She turned to Igor and Ben. "You two first, then Russell and Eliot. Greg, stay behind your father at all times and don't leave him for a second! Understood?"

The boy nodded. He was pale but seemed determined not to show his fear.

"Good. Jack and I will keep up the rear. No funny business. Get to the jeeps and go!"

"I hope we don't encounter as many animals as we did yesterday," said Eliot.

"Let's wait and see. Ready? One, two, three!"

Igor tore open the door and stormed out. Immediately, he stumbled backward into the hut, as if he'd run into a brick wall. At the same moment there was a hissing noise and the smell of burning meat rose in Russell's nose.

"What the . . ." cursed Ben, who was pushed backward.

Igor slumped against Marlene and slid to the ground. Instinctively, Russell wanted to reach out for his head to protect him from the impact, but he pulled back his hands at the last second. In front of his eyes, Igor's skull dissolved in a puddle of yellow, red, and white slime. The stench made Russell's stomach turn.

Greg turned away, retching, and vomited on the floor of the hut.

"Holy fuck!" screamed Ben, and after a brief sideways glance at the body stormed out of the hut. Rapid gunfire. Eliot followed Ben and also opened fire.

Russell and Marlene's eyes met over the steaming body of their comrade. "Jesus!" she whispered. With a single bound, she was also outside.

"Die! Die you motherfuckers!" Ben's shrill voice echoed across the clearing.

Through the open door, Russell could see only Ben's and Marlene's backs. He turned to Greg. "Stand by the wall and don't move until I say so!" Greg couldn't take his eyes off Igor, but he nodded.

Russell released the safety on his rifle and ran out behind Donald Bell, but the offensive was already over. The barrel of Ben's gun was still smoking. Eliot secured the left flank, Jack and Marlene the right. "Motherfucking monsters," screamed Ben.

Five of the greyhounds lay dead in front of the hut.

Russell shook his head. *They were waiting for us. The whole night. And they knew which side we would come out. Igor didn't stand a chance.*

Russell noticed a white spot on the wall of the hut next to the door. The wood was gradually dissolving. If Ben hadn't been spun around by Igor, he would have been hit too.

Jack kneeled next to Igor's body, wailing. "Shit! Fucking shit! My God, Igor! How could this happen?" He stretched out his arms and wanted to lift Igor up.

"Don't touch him!" thundered Russell.

Jack stared at him out of blood-shot eyes.

"He's covered all over in the stuff. If you don't want to lose your hands, don't touch him!"

"Pretty damn clever, these beasts," said Marlene, scanning the area. "They move in formation and hunt in packs. Like wolves."

"Perhaps a bit more dangerous," said Ben, sarcastically.

"How far can those beasts spit that stuff?" asked Eliot, turning to Russell.

"I got the wound to my shoulder from a distance of about thirty feet."

"Not quite the range of snipers, but they can certainly cause huge damage," said Marlene. "Let's get out of here quickly, before more of them turn up."

"What do we do with Igor?" asked Jack.

"We take him with us," said Russell. We'll wrap him in a poncho and load him on the back of the second jeep. Greg, can you get me a poncho and gloves from the shelf at the back?"

Ben and Eliot checked that the coast was clear, while Russell and Donald heaved Igor's body onto the jeep. The rising sun bathed the grassland around the depot in reddish light. Only a few little clouds scudded across the sky high above them. As the temperature rose, wisps of vapor rose from the ground, and were blown away by the wind in the direction of Mount Fairweather. The rocky peak loomed up in the north like a sentinel. But it couldn't provide them with any protection.

"Oh fuck!" Russell heard Ben's voice. He followed Ben's gaze and nearly froze with shock.

"Greyhounds!" he whispered to Marlene, who was standing next to him. "Dozens of them. We have to get out of here!"

The animals trotted slowly but steadily into the glade. They weren't on the attack, but once they caught the scent of humans, they could be here in two minutes. More and more of the scrawny creatures emerged from the forest.

"Mount! Immediately," said Marlene in a calm voice.

Together with Greg, Russell climbed into the back seat of the first jeep that Marlene was driving. Ben had already swung himself into the passenger seat. Eliot, Donald, and Jack drove in the second jeep with Igor's body on the back seat.

When Marlene and Eliot started the engines, the greyhounds perked up. Two of the animals started running straight toward them. The pack followed.

"Step on it! Quickly!" screamed Russell. He tried to judge the distance between them and the creatures. Perhaps a mile? Marlene drove off, wheels screeching, sped up to thirty miles an hour and headed for the edge of the forest. She swore loudly as she drove over a large stone that she hadn't noticed. Russell and Greg were flung back and forth on the back seat.

"Can't you drive faster?" asked Russell, who wouldn't take his eyes off the animals, who were now only about half a mile behind them.

Ben answered. "The axle has been welded too many times. If it breaks, we're screwed!"

"If those animals catch up with us we're also screwed."

By the time the two jeeps reached the edge of the

forest, the greyhounds were still over a thousand feet away. Marlene turned onto the old track, but the bumpy surface made it impossible to go above twenty-five miles an hour. Within moments they were surrounded by trees and bushes.

"I can't see if they're still behind us," Jack shouted from the jeep behind them.

"You can bet they're still behind us!" yelled Russell. "And they're faster than us. Get ready for battle!"

He took out a pistol and pressed it into Greg's hand. "You can remember how to shoot it, can't you?"

"Yes, you taught me yourself!"

Russell nodded. Back on Earth, he hadn't believed in letting children or teenagers handle weapons, but on this planet, you had to be prepared for all eventualities. All the children in the colony were taught to shoot as soon as they were old enough to help out in the fields. There was no knowing if a wotan or some other creature might suddenly appear.

"Only shoot when I say! Aim at the monsters that come at us from the side. Whatever happens behind us, leave it to the second jeep to deal with. Never aim at the other jeep!"

The jeep continued to judder along the track. Russell looked behind him. At any moment the first beasts would appear between the trees. The terrain would only slow them down slightly.

"I can see them, they're coming!" screamed Jack, panic rising in his voice.

Russell cocked his weapon and aimed past the second jeep. He could already make out one of the creatures that was tearing its way toward them between two trees.

Holy crap!

The jeep was lurching so erratically that Jack—who

was sitting in the passenger seat—kept moving in front of the target. He couldn't shoot without hitting him.

Shots were fired. One of the beasts appeared as if from nowhere next to the driver's seat of the jeep at the back. A big glob of venomous spit landed on the left fender.

Eliot ripped his pistol from its holster while holding onto the steering wheel with the other hand, and took aim. The greyhound tumbled over.

"Fuck!" Russell cried. Three more animals had almost caught up with the back jeep. Donald shot two of them and shook his gun, cursing, as it was obviously jammed. Countless more creatures came tearing out of the forest. "There are too many of them! They're gonna get us!" yelled Russell in despair.

"Wotans! From the front!"

When Russell turned around, Ben had already opened fire. About two dozen wotans were running toward them along the track. Ben had hit one, but the rest were not deterred.

We're dead! Russell looked down at the pistol in his holster and then at his son. The thought flashed briefly through his mind . . . he could shorten his son's suffering and spare him an agonizing death at the hands of these monsters.

Marlene screamed as the wave of approaching wotans reached the vehicle, but immediately fell silent. Bewildered, Russell realized that the animals were completely ignoring the humans and their jeeps.

They're simply running past us!

"What the hell . . .?" began Benn.

The horde of wotans came face to face with the grey-hounds approaching from the opposite direction. Spitting and snarling, the animals threw themselves at each other, until there was just a mass of entwined bodies rolling across the mossy forest floor.

Still unable to grasp what was happening, Russell lowered his weapon. "My God!" he whispered. The sound of the creatures' ghastly yowling sent a shiver down his spine. Beside him, Greg was crying quietly.

"That was obviously our rescue squad," said Marlene drily.

"What *was* that?" asked Ben. "I don't get what just happened."

"It looks like the wotans were defending their territory," replied Marlene. "Yesterday I was already wondering why they didn't follow us into the glade." The border between their territories must run along here. The wotans used to control the whole area around Mount Fairweather. The two species are rivals. The approaching ocean is forcing the greyhounds into wotan territory."

"But I don't understand why they didn't attack us at the same time as the greyhounds," said Russell.

"The greyhounds have probably always been the wotans' natural enemies. We haven't been on New California long enough and aren't an established part of the ecology. For both species we're just prey, and therefore pose the least danger. But when one of the groups has won, they can start to think about lunch—and that'll be us."

"We didn't plan it, but we couldn't have come up with a better tactic," said Russell.

"What do you mean?" asked Ben.

"By luring the greyhounds into the forest, we created a diversion for the wotans. Now they're busy and haven't got any time to think about us. With a bit of luck we'll make it unscathed back to the post. Otherwise they probably would have got us."

"It's still quite a ways to the post," interjected Marlene. "Around twenty miles."

"The herds of wotans seem to be well organized. Over the next hour they'll summon up all their forces to defend the boundary."

"Do you really think they're that intelligent?" asked Marlene.

Russell shrugged. "It certainly looks like it. Now we're going to pay for the fact that we didn't find out more about these animals earlier. All we can do now is speculate. But if they are able to act with intention, it means that our observation post will be in even greater danger once they can't hold on to their territory anymore."

"Danger is an understatement," said Marlene.

Russell nodded. "I'm afraid the very first wave of wotans might be strong enough to break through the barriers."

Chapter 19

"So that's the situation in a nutshell. Now we have to discuss what to do about it." Marlene laid the microphone aside and sat down between Russell and Dr. Dressel.

Russell stole a quick look at Ellen, who was sitting in the second row of the assembly room. A day had passed since their return to the colony. The rest of the journey had passed uneventfully, as he had predicted. There had been only a couple of lone attacks by wotans, and those had been easy to fend off.

When they arrived back in Eridu, there had been a big commotion. Ellen had flung her arms around Greg and then, sobbing, hugged Russell. Although he was happy to see her, he had accepted the hug reluctantly; he didn't know what to feel.

Some of the colonists snubbed Russell—in retrospect they regarded Russell's whale ride as a selfish ego trip, which had led to the death of one of their fellow colonists. Ben did not hold back on propounding his opinion that Igor's death was all Russell's fault. Through gritted teeth, Russell had to acknowledge that his adversary was right on that point. Of course there was nothing he could do about the fact that Greg had fastened himself to the whale, but that didn't change the fact that Igor would still be alive if he had not decided to make a final journey. When Sarah Deming slapped him and screamed at him after seeing her husband's dead body, it washed over him in a daze. Once again he was the bad guy of the colony.

But Marlene had come to his defense, and pointed out that it was thanks to Russell's journey that they had become aware of the new danger facing them. The previous day, they had sat down with John Dressel, Drew Potter, Jenny Baldwin, Dr. Cashmore, and Dr. Lindwall to assess the situation. They had quickly come to the conclusion that a danger such as this needed to be discussed with all citizens of the colony.

"Are you really sure that the situation will become as precarious as you say?" asked Travis Richards in his booming voice.

Jenny Baldwin stood up. "We don't know how many animals there are down in the lowlands. But from the data we have, I'd estimate that there are at least a million larger animals. Marlene is absolutely right in her prognosis. We know the topography of the lowlands well enough to know that the canyon provides the only access to the highlands." She looked over to Drew Potter, who nodded in agreement, then continued: "It seems to be a periodic occurrence. Every thirty years the lowlands are flooded and the animals migrate to the highlands. When the water recedes again, they go back."

"I don't get it," said Nathalie Grant. "Why don't the animals stay in the highlands, if they have to flee every few years anyway."

"Presumably because the lowlands are more fertile. Even if they are beasts of prey, we know that wotans sometimes feed on fruit that only grows in the lowlands. Now we also know why we came across wotans when we first arrived here: obviously, shortly before we came to New California, one of the flooding periods had just come to an end."

Eliot Sargent stood up. "And what the hell causes this regular flooding? I grew up by the sea and know all about tides. But a high tide that only occurs every few years doesn't make sense. And I also haven't understood this thing about a new moon. I thought New California didn't have a moon!"

"Apparently it does," said Dr. Dressel. "At the moment it's still hidden behind the horizon, but from the top of the nearest mountain you can already see the upper edge. In a day or two we'll be able to see it from Eridu."

"And where's it been the past twenty years?"

"It moves very slowly. My guess is that the moon only moves across the firmament once every twenty years. It is my assumption that we arrived here shortly after the tides were at their highest, and only then are the lowlands flooded."

"You mean the moon only orbits the planet every forty years? It would have to be millions of miles away!" said Dr. Cashmore.

"No, I didn't say that. It orbits in a little less than a day, which makes its angular velocity a little higher. That's why its position relative to the surface of the planet changes only very slowly."

"You've lost me," said Ben.

"It's moving in an almost geostationary orbit around this planet— like TV satellites orbit the Earth. But only *almost*, which is why it wanders so slowly across the sky."

"Only twenty-two-thousand miles above the surface of

the planet?" asked Ellen, who as a former astronaut understood something of what he was talking about.

"Yes, the mass of New California is similar to Earth's mass, so that's about right."

"Surely a moon that's so close to a planet would develop far greater forces."

"It's probably much smaller than the Earth's moon. Phobos also only moves around six-thousand miles above the surface of Mars, but it's only eighteen-thousand miles in diameter."

"I used to sail," said Lee Shanker. "If the moon is rising over the horizon now, the water ought to have reached its lowest level."

"In principle, yes—but the low tide is now over and the high tide has begun. We don't know the geography and the coastlines of this planet, but they're responsible for the tidal range as well as for the exact time that high tide begins."

"And what does that mean for us? How long will the high tide last? And when will it reach its highest point?" asked Marianna Waits.

"We don't know," replied the physicist. "It could last for years. On the other hand, it's possible that a huge wave *preceding* the actual high tide floods the lowland for a short time, and that the high tide itself is less dramatic. In that case, the water would disappear from the lowlands within a few weeks. Drew's geological findings suggest that the water flows back out relatively quickly. But the fact remains that the lowlands will be flooded. Everything else is pure speculation."

"And how long do we have until those beasts run us down?" asked Igor Isalovic.

"That's the bit we really don't know," answered Marlene. "We can only guess. A week, perhaps? Then the first big wave of wotans will flood to the observation post, and the barriers simply aren't strong enough to keep them out.

"And if we strengthen the barriers?" asked Ben.

Marlene shook her head. "Even the Great Wall of China wouldn't keep out those animals. There are millions of them and they have deep-rooted migration patterns. They want to get past precisely this point. The animals at the front would get crushed against the wall, and those at the back would simply climb over the dead bodies."

"Shit," said Ty.

"That means we have to escape?" asked Paulina Hall.

"That's exactly what we need to talk about," said Marlene.

Ernie Lawrence stood up, a spark of anger in his eyes. "We've bust our asses over the last twenty years for our colony and now we've finally got it to feel half-way like home, and don't have to worry every winter about having enough to eat. I'm not leaving here! At least not without a fight!" He sat back down.

"It probably won't work anyway," objected Jenny Baldwin. "We have nowhere to go. To the north are the mountains, to the west the highlands, and beyond that another range of mountains. In the space of a week we can't gather together all our belongings and drag them somewhere hundreds of miles away. We don't even know what lies beyond the mountains. Sure, we could take refuge in the high mountains for a while, but not for years. The fields haven't been harvested yet and without any corn we won't survive the winter."

"How much do we still have in reserve?" asked Marlene, turning to Ann Penwill.

"Not enough. Jenny's right. Fleeing into the mountains

isn't an option. Maybe we could escape through the transporter?" she added.

Linda Ladish in the row behind her snorted loudly. "Where to?"

Marlene agreed. "There's nowhere we can flee to. In the worst-case scenario, Russell's Planet would provide a refuge, but only for a while, until our supplies run out. And to transport enough supplies in the transporter for us all to survive in the medium term strikes me as impossible."

"We've worked our asses off for our colony! We should build a wall around Eridu and protect our city against these monsters," said Ernie Lawrence. He was in a militant mood. It was clear that he wasn't going to give up his life here without a fight.

Marlene shook her head. "Perhaps, if we had more time. But it would be impossible to construct the necessary fortifications in the space of a week. And anyway, we're back to the problem of the supplies. No, that won't work either."

Travis Richards groaned loudly. "And what do you suggest? Simply giving up?"

Marlene stood up. "No. Yesterday we put together a plan we'd like to put up for discussion."

A hush fell over the hall. She had the undivided attention of all of the colonists.

"Instead of strengthening the observation post, we could blow up the entire canyon at the narrowest point between here and the lowlands—right where the flood reaches its highest point. It would create a new, sheer cliff-face, a hundred and sixty feet high, which couldn't be crossed by the animals."

"Is that feasible?" asked Ty Grazier skeptically. Back on Earth he had been an explosives expert. "Do we even have enough C-4 left?"

Marlene shook her head. "That's precisely the problem. definitely do not have enough explosives left. Dr. Dressel proposes using one of the remaining atomic bombs."

Pandemonium broke loose. Russell had expected this. During the preliminary meeting, he himself had told the physicist that he was mad. It would be a drastic step to take.

"You must be nuts!" cried Stansilav from the back row.

"It's only three miles away from our settlement," shouted Rhonda Fielder.

"You'll contaminate us all!" said Dorothy Moore.

Marlene waited until the noise finally died down. "Let's at least discuss the idea, because we don't have any other options. Dr. Dressel will give you the details."

The scientist stood up and went over to the map. "It's true, the spot is only about three miles away. But we wouldn't be exposed to significant amounts of radiation." He stepped to the edge of the podium and waved his hands about nervously. "In order to cause the cliff to collapse, the nuclear explosive charge will be ignited inside a hole in the cliff face. A big part of the explosion's energy will be absorbed by the rock. The remaining fireball will have a radius of nine-hundred feet and glaze the rock surfaces—making it too slippery for animals to get over. We'll detonate the bomb in the early morning, when the wind should carry the radioactive fallout to sea."

"And the colony . . .?" asked Travis Richards.

"Eridu will only get a dose of gamma rays in the first seconds of the explosion—a dose too low to harm anyone. The shock wave will be deflected upward by the walls of the canyon and won't be felt here."

"I'm still against it," said Julia Stetson, who Russell

remembered had been an environmental activist in her youth and had demonstrated against nuclear power plants.

Marlene stood up again. "As I said, it is the only suggestion that appears to have any chance of success. According to Dr. Dressel, radioactivity is not an issue, but nonetheless, the plan still has other disadvantages."

She paused briefly because many people were still chatting. "The animals of the lowlands won't be able to get up here anymore. But we also won't be able to get down. At least not until the water has receded again. That means we'll have to manage without our oil spring and the refinery for a time. But they will be ruined by the flood in any case. Unfortunately, right now our supply of oil in the colony is as low as the tanks in the refinery are full. In order to continue operating our machines and vehicles, including the tractors, we'll have to make another expedition to the refinery before the pass is cut off. It's in our—"

"If the wind turns to the west during the explosion, we'll contaminate our fields with the radioactive fallout and starve!" interrupted Julia Stetson.

"If we flee, we'll definitely starve!" retorted Eliot Sargent bitterly.

Julia stood up. "Let's not build our future on atomic bombs! It would be a pact with the devil! It's bad enough that we still have this reactor here."

Lee Shanker grunted, stood up, and turned to Julia. Russell knew that they hated each other's guts. "The travelling wave reactor is completely safe. It regulates itself and doesn't pose a threat."

"I don't care! It's nuclear power, and we don't want that here!"

"Speak for yourself! Listen to what you're saying! You were happy enough that your laboratory had electricity before the refinery and the generator—"

"Enough!" said Marlene. "We're talking about our survival here. We don't have time for ideological debates. We'll vote on the plan."

"How long do we have to consider it?" asked Ann Penwill.

"None. Time is of the essence. We'll vote immediately. If a majority is in favor, we'll begin work on the detonation site tomorrow. Simultaneously, an expedition will set out to get as much petroleum, kerosene, and crude oil from the refinery as we can fit in the jeeps. Two days later, when the work is completed, we'll carry out the detonation!"

"In three days already?" asked Eliot Sargent.

"Yes. We don't know how much time we have left until before we can't defend the post anymore. I don't want to take any risks. Until shortly before the detonation, we'll have to triple the number of lookouts at the post. Until then, I'm going to withdraw all workers from the fields—and the jeeps. We need them here."

"But the harvest . . ."

"Yes, we will lose part of the harvest, but we can compensate with what we have in our reserves. This has absolute priority. If all goes well, the crisis will be over in three days. But we must not fail. I'll say it again, very clearly: our survival is at stake."

Chapter 20

"Not long now, and we'll be able to see the ocean from here," said Russell.

"Whatever the consequences, it will be a fantastic view." Ellen linked arms with Russell as they walked along the rim of the plateau. Eridu was still covered in gray mist, but on the distant horizon a red line indicated that the sun was about to rise. The lowlands, thousands of feet below them, were also covered in mist. Only a few treetops, like a sprinkling of dark-brown spots, peeked out of the blanket of gray. On the other side of the firmament, beyond the mountaintops, the moon of New California was getting ready to rise, even if up to now only a tiny corner of it had been visible.

Russell had gotten up early to prepare for the expedition to the oil spring. Ellen had woken up too, and they had decided to take a little walk before Russell had to set off.

"It all looks so peaceful," he said. "It's hard to believe that there are hordes of deadly animals down there just waiting to attack us."

"We'll stop them," said Ellen emphatically.

"Yes, we will. We'll definitely be able to defend the pass entrance until we detonate the bomb. We'll . . ." Russell was suddenly overcome by a coughing fit. He held his hand over his mouth. When the rattling subsided, his hand was full of blood.

"Shit," he muttered.

Ellen took a piece of cloth out of her jacket pocket and handed it to him. "It's getting worse."

Russell nodded. He knew that he looked awful. He couldn't sleep properly, because he had to cough constantly. And he had chest pains, which at least weren't unbearable. He had burst out laughing that morning when he had seen the dark rings around his eyes in the mirror. He looked in a worse state than a junkie. Although of course . . . now he was one.

"The effect of the medication is wearing off," he said flatly.

"Which shouldn't stop you from finishing off the dose of stimulants that Dr. Lindwall gave you," said Ellen.

"I've already asked for more."

"I think you should take it easy."

Russell rolled his eyes. They had talked about it at length the night before. "They need everyone they can get for this expedition."

"But not people who are terminally ill!"

"As long as I can stand up and hold a weapon in my hand, I will continue to help out," replied Russell. Of course he knew that Ellen was right. He ought to be in bed, not in battle. On the other hand, he couldn't be cured, so what was the point of resting? And in fact, secretly, he still hoped to die on a mission instead of slowly suffocating to death.

"You nearly died on your last adventure. And not just you, but our son as well!"

Russell put an arm around her shoulder. "You know that I hadn't intended to come back. That was the whole point. I'm sorry about what happened with Greg. I should have guessed. Planning the adventure wasn't the problem, but I should have been more careful. But today's mission is important. We need the petroleum."

"Maybe it was a mistake," said Ellen bitterly.

Russell turned to look at her. It was rare for Ellen to be so melancholy. "Maybe what was a mistake?"

"To destroy the transporter on Earth."

"You were in favor of it at the time. You encouraged me to set off the bomb, remember? As did the others."

"Yes, I know. And logically I still think it was the right decision. But I miss Earth. How safe and secure life was there."

Russell laughed. "Safe? Are you kidding me? At the end, you were a felon condemned to death. Like me."

It's not us I worry about so much, but the children. On Earth they could have grown up in safety."

Russell snorted. "Safe? On Earth?" He shook his head. "If I learnt anything from my time in the army it's this: nowhere on Earth is safe. Afghanistan and Syria were once also livable, pleasant countries, until they were wrecked by civil wars. Even if we lived in relative safety in the USA, it could have changed overnight. There were already signs of things falling apart before we left. There is no stability on Earth, only islands of calm in an ocean of war and destruction that rises up periodically and quickly recedes again."

"Aren't you exaggerating?"

Russell shook his head. "What would have awaited our children on Earth? With eight billion people, the world was so overpopulated it would have been impossible to feed everyone in the long term. The Earth can only handle the environmental footprint of a billion people. At most! Greenhouse gas emissions have pushed Earth's climate to the brink of stability. I'm absolutely convinced there's a point when global warming intensifies of its own accord—like a chain reaction. At some future date, conditions on Earth will be like on Venus. And you know what's so depressing about it all?"

He had worked himself up into a rage. "All the problems people have on Earth are self-inflicted. Here on New California we're fighting against nature. We're back where we were on Earth millions of years ago, when we had to defend ourselves against wild animals and adverse conditions. Once we solved those problems on Earth, we started to fight each other, and then humans became their own worst enemy."

"Here we have a chance to start from scratch, and to do it right," said Ellen. "If what you say is true, and people have ruined Earth, then our children and their children are perhaps the only chance for the continued existence of the human race. On an alien planet, beneath an alien sky. We don't even know which of those stars in the sky was once our home."

"The question is whether we have a chance of doing it right this time and of avoiding the same mistakes. It's possible that generations down the line, when our children and their children have colonized and conquered this planet, the same mechanisms of greed, materialism, and egotism will rear their ugly heads again."

"What does that say about us?" asked Ellen.

"It would mean we're programmed to destroy ourselves. In that case, humanity is doomed, regardless of whether they populate outer space or not."

Ellen shook her head. "I don't believe it, because I don't want to believe it. Our children are the future, and every generation can choose to change itself and learn from the mistakes of previous generations. Perhaps humankind hasn't yet grown up, but I firmly believe that it will one day. Here, and on Earth."

In the distance, Russell saw Eliot coming toward them from between the huts of their settlement, and waved.

"I think the expedition is starting. We better get back."

Russell turned around, but Ellen grabbed his hand and pulled him to her. "Promise me that you won't take any unnecessary risks!"

Russell looked her in the eyes. He hesitated before replying, because he still believed that dying in a fight was preferable to dying of his disease. He wouldn't provoke it, but if somebody needed to risk their life during the mission, then better him than somebody else. He didn't want to lie to his wife, so he decided not to answer her question. Instead he took her in his arms and kissed her softly on the top of her head.

"THIS IS THE SPOT!" called Drew Potter.

"Here?" Marlene stopped the jeep.

"Yes, right here! This is the narrowest point in the whole canyon."

Marlene, Drew, Ty Grazier, and Lee Shanker climbed out of the vehicle. Marlene recognized the place: it was where Russell had almost run over the geologist two weeks earlier. The gray cliff faces towered up at least three-hundred feet on either side. It was early in the morning. The sun was still low in the sky and the canyon shrouded in darkness. An icy wind whistled through the narrow valley and Marlene shivered. The cliff walls seemed to be closing in on her when she looked upward. She felt dizzy and she turned to look at Ty Grazier. "What do you think?"

The weapons expert chewed on a twig that he'd picked up from the ground, lost in thought. He continued to look around. The seconds dragged by. "It could work, it could work," he mumbled, barely comprehensible.

"Good. How shall we proceed?"

Ty pointed upward. "At a height of about thirty feet, we drill horizontally into the cliff face. Around a hundred-and-fifty-feet deep. When the bomb explodes, the pressure of the vaporized rock will cause the whole cliff to collapse. The rubble will fill the canyon and be glazed by the fire-ball. The barrier should end up being about a hundred-and-thirty-feet high and smooth as glass."

Marlene nodded. "That will do." She turned around to her chief engineer. "What needs to be done in preparation?"

Lee Shanker ran a hand through his prematurely gray hair, which tumbled in wild locks down to his shoulders. He sighed. "It'll be quite a job. We need to build a scaffold against the cliff face, and to operate the drill we'll need the compressor here. Our first job is to get that out of the workshop. How wide does the hole need to be?"

"Around twelve inches for the atomic bomb to fit inside," Ty answered.

Lee nodded. "No problem. The drill from the geology lab can do the job." He turned to Marlene. "It shouldn't be a problem."

Marlene smiled. "Good to hear. Will you manage in forty-eight hours?"

Lee whistled through his teeth. "Well, we should be able to get the scaffold up by this evening, then we'll need the night and all of tomorrow for the drilling. Hmm, that means we also need light. And we'll need the final night to get things finished. But yeah, it should be possible, if we work non-stop in two shifts."

Marlene nodded. "Start right away. I'll leave you two to divide up the work. This job has absolute priority. Whatever you need, you'll get it!"

"Good, I . . ." Lee stopped and listened. Marlene also noticed the sound of car engines and swiveled around.

The four of them sprang to the side as the first jeep raced around the corner. It was followed by three more. Ben was driving the first vehicle and raised his hand from the wheel to wave. Marlene nodded in response. The last vehicle had been converted into a semi and was pulling a trailer behind it, which looked like it had been improvised in a hurry. It was twice as long as the jeep.

"I'm glad I don't have to go out there," murmured Lee.

Marlene pursed her lips. Ideally, she would have liked to lead the expedition to the oil spring herself. But she couldn't do everything, and preparing the atomic bomb was more important. Despite his social shortcomings, Ben was a good strategist. Under his leadership, they would manage to get the oil supplies back to the colony. The six miles to the spring were familiar territory. Several years ago they had cleared about sixty feet of forest on either side of the track and put up a barbed wire fence. On the other hand, nobody knew how quickly the situation in the lowlands would come to a head. If the wotans were no longer able to defend themselves against the hordes of other animals moving in on their territory, all hell would break loose. In that case, the barbed wire around the oil spring wouldn't be much use. Anyone who went past the observation post at the bottom of the pass would be dead meat.

Chapter 21

"Jesus, it's unbelievable!" whispered Russell.

The road resembled a war zone. The fence had been torn down on both sides. Parts of it had fallen onto the road, and as they navigated their way through the carnage, they had to be careful not to puncture a wheel on the barbed wire. Some of the bodies were ensnared in the tangled remains of the fence and looked as if a huge mouth had bitten chunks out of them.

They drove through the killing field slowly.

"Was it those greyhounds?" asked Eliot, who was sitting behind Russell on the back seat. He was gripping tightly onto his weapon.

"I have no idea," said Russell.

"Quiet! Concentrate on what's going on around us!" barked Ben Hawke. "We've still got half the journey ahead of us."

"A whole herd must have stormed over the road here," said Eliot in a shocked tone of voice. He hadn't heard Ben's order—or didn't want to hear it. Ben shook his head, but said nothing.

"The barbed wire didn't stop them. They simply trampled over it and flattened everything," continued Eliot. "If a horde like that attacks our observation post, the lookouts won't stand a chance."

Russell nodded. "I don't like this one bit. It looks as if the wotans fled from something in a blind panic. That means they're losing their fight. We don't have much time left. I'm surprised they haven't attacked the observation post yet. I wonder what state we'll find the oil spring in? The area isn't much better secured than here."

"We'll soon find out," said Ben. "It's only a few more miles. At least everything seems to be quiet. Whatever came through here, they seems to have moved on."

"We definitely shouldn't stay any longer then we need to. We'll secure the wells, fill our tanks with petroleum and get out of there as quickly as possible," said Russell.

Ben turned around and glared at him. "I'm leading this expedition and I am the one who gives orders. Is that clear, Mr. Harris?"

He still hates my guts. Twenty years have changed nothing. Perhaps I should have stayed behind in Eridu, after all.

"It was just a suggestion, Ben."

"Save the suggestions. I know what I'm doing. And I don't want to hear another word until we're at the oil spring!"

Russell threw a glance at Eliot. He just shrugged and turned to look at the destroyed fences.

The silence was unnerving. Russell kept peering into the jungle. The vegetation was too thick here—it was impossible to see more than six feet into the thicket. Who knew what was lurking inside? If a group of snipers was hiding in the undergrowth, it could jump out and finish off the whole lot of them in the blink of an eye. They wouldn't stand the slightest chance.

But the rest of the drive was uneventful, and finally they rounded the bend to the oil spring. Russell jumped out of the jeep, opened the nine-foot-high gates that were covered in barbed wire and let the vehicles pass.

The cleared area measured roughly a hundred-and-fifty square feet, about the same size as a baseball stadium, and was filled with gravel. A wooden, fifteen-foot-high drilling rig stood in the center. They didn't need a pump, since the oil spring had enough natural pressure to bring the black liquid to the surface. An automatic valve regulated the stream. A pipeline led to a six-foot-high distillation column, which Lee Shanker had constructed together with Dr. Cashmore to separate the crude oil. Gasoline, kerosene, and fuel oil were conducted into man-high containers, the residues were pumped into a deeper-lying layer of rock via a second borehole.

The gasoline pumped out of here would have ruined a modern sports car engine in seconds, but luckily the jeeps had been designed to handle low-grade fuel from the worst banana republics, and could cope with the gunk they mined here. Their engineer and chemist had spent almost a month building the facility. The colonists had cleared the forest around the spring, erected the fences and set up the facility, while staving off attacks from the occasional wotan. Miraculously, nobody had been killed, and what they got in return was worth the effort and the risk: the oil spring and the refinery provided them with warmth, light, electricity, and mobility. Nobody wanted to live without it.

But all this would be flooded by the incoming ocean two weeks from now. When the floods finally retreated, they would have to completely rebuild everything. Then at least they would be able to work without the permanent threat of being attacked by wild animals, since they'd all have been drowned. And he himself would be long gone.

"Let's go!" Ben bellowed. "Everything as discussed! In two hours I want to be heading back home!"

Russell swung his weapon over his shoulder and climbed up the drill tower, at the top of which was a little viewing platform.

By the time he reached the top he was dizzy and sluggish; his head felt like it was wrapped in cotton wool. *That damn medication!* His heart was racing and the palms of his hands were covered in sweat. He balanced his weapon on the railing and looked through the scope. His hands were trembling.

Shit! If I'm trembling like this, I won't be able to hit an elephant from a distance of thirty feet!

Below him he heard Grant Dillon, who was swearing at the main valve of the oil spring. "The damn thing is jammed! I can't close it. Pump wrench. Someone bring me a pump wrench!"

Stanislav Radinkovic ran over to him with a metal case. "Why don't you have your tools with you?"

"Oh, screw you!"

Several feet away, Dr. Cashmore and young Peter Richards were busy with the distillation column. Although he was only fourteen, Peter was already nearly a foot taller than Dr. Cashmore. Marlene had agreed through gritted teeth that a few of the boys could join the expedition, because they needed all the help they could get. Both generations, Earthlings and New Californians, were fighting together for the future of their colony. The chemist and his helpers mounted a hose with which they could channel the precious liquid to the tanks on the trailer.

"We're pumping!" Cashmore called over to Ben, who was standing on the driver's seat coordinating the men and women.

"How much longer will it take?"

"About another hour."

"Good! Let's hope that we don't get any unwelcome visitors in that time."

Ernie Lawrence had positioned himself at the gate of the compound and had his eyes trained on the nearby forest, his weapon at the ready. His wife stood a few feet away from him and kept a lookout to the east. Sammy Yang and Allison Hadcroft were working on the refinery. They were both trying to secure it as firmly as possible, so that they could put it back into operation as soon as possible after the flood.

"Something's going on here," shouted Ernie Lawrence.

Russell looked over to him. The noise of all the work going on drowned out any sounds from the jungle. Every damn animal in the wider vicinity must have realized by now that they were here. But there was nothing to be seen.

Ben ran over to Ernie and the bullish soldier pointed in the direction of the nearby jungle. Russell could not understand what the two of them were saying.

Ben gave a short whistle and called over several men with automatic rifles. Eric Grant kneeled down and took aim. Cookie Shanker kneeled down next to him and also cocked his rifle.

Damn it, what's out there?

Russell aimed his gun at the spot beyond the outer fence and looked through the scope. He adjusted the focus, but could only see tree-trunks and leaves swaying gently in the breeze. Then he scanned the compound again.

Ernie whispered something to Ben and the officer craned his neck to look at the edge of the forest. They weren't moving, and clearly were waiting for something to happen. Whatever they had heard, it seemed to be close. After several long minutes, Ben relaxed and took a deep breath. Then he shook his head and turned around. Ernie took his hand off the trigger and shrugged.

False alarm! Russell breathed a sigh of relief.

But at that moment it happened. Three wotans shot out of the undergrowth and ran straight toward the perimeter fence of the compound. Ben screamed.

Holy shit!

Russell aimed quickly and pulled the trigger. The shot missed the creature at the back by a good three feet. A cloud of dust indicated the spot where the bullet had hit the dry ground.

Ernie also raised his weapon and fired. He hit the front wotan, which died mid-bound. Blood sprayed from the wound onto the animals storming up from behind. Due to its speed, the hulking creature collided full force with the perimeter fence. The steel post bent like a matchstick and the barbed-wire fence sagged to the ground. The carcass collapsed on top of the crushed wire. The other two wotans used the torn-down fence as a ramp to get across the inner barbed wire and leaped into the compound.

Eric Grant hit one of them from behind. The heavy-caliber shot tore off a complete leg. The acidic blood of the animal dissolved the metal of the fence. The third wotan ran full throttle at Eric.

Russell held his breath, aimed and fired.

Strike!

The dead body skidded across the gravel toward young Grant. It would squash him! Ernie Lawrence jumped and pulled the boy to the side, but his own leg got caught under the wotan. Lawrence screamed and tipped backward, his lower leg bent forward at a horrible angle.

Andrea raced over to her husband.

The whole spectacle had lasted no more than fifteen

seconds. Now they had one wounded man, a boy who had almost died and a big hole in the perimeter fence.

Holy crap! And that was just three of the beasts!

Why were the wotans so aggressive? Of course the monsters were dangerous, but the way they rushed in so wildly without regard for their own lives was something new. The beasts must be starving. What would happen if a whole herd streamed into the compound? Even with all their weapons, they wouldn't last five minutes. And the worst thing was: it was inevitable if they stayed here any longer than absolutely necessary.

Ernie Lawrence was writhing on the ground and grinding his teeth. The jagged end of a tibia bone was poking through his uniform, projecting from his leg like a bizarre clothes hanger. Ben held the brawny soldier down while Andrea Phillips tended to her husband's injury as best she could.

"How long do you need still?" Ben shouted over to Cashmore.

"Twenty minutes."

"Make it less!"

Ben turned to Eliot Sargent, who had appeared behind him. "Fix the gap in the fence. Put it back up and shore it up with logs."

Sargent nodded and went off. A few seconds later he reappeared with two men. Stanislav was holding a heavy pickaxe. He climbed on the fence and swung it into the body of the dead wotan. Together with Eliot he dragged the heavy carcass backward into the compound. The fence sprung up again slightly once it no longer had to bear the weight of the monster.

Maxwell Lindwall, the strapping son of the doctor, dragged over two logs and together with Eliot Sargent re-erected the fence.

Russell scanned the nearby forest edge through the scope of his rifle. There was nothing to be seen, but that didn't have to mean anything, considering how fast the three wotans had just burst out of the forest.

"We've secured the distillation column, the oil well is closed," Russell heard Dr. Cashmore call out. "The tanks on the hangar are nearly full. Two or three more minutes."

"We're almost ready," called Linda Ladish. "We're just loading the last barrel of kerosene."

"Good," said Ben. "It's time for us to get out of here."

"Damn! There's something in the forest again!" screamed Patrick Holbrook, who was guarding the back of the compound.

Ben and Eliot ran over to the boy. Russell couldn't see anything, but repositioned his weapon so that he could react quickly if necessary. *Damn!* The rectification column blocked his view of the back fence. *This isn't going to work.*

With a groan, Russell swung his weapon over his shoulder and climbed down, only to be suddenly overcome by a wave of nausea. He fell to his knees and feared he would have to vomit, but he spat only a bloody ball of slime onto the gravel. With a pounding headache, he stood up and swayed over to Ben, Eliot and Patrick, who were staring at the edge of the forest beyond the fence.

Now Russell could hear it, too. A constant cracking, rustling and hissing, as if a whole army were marching through the nearby forest.

There must be dozens of them!

"There are too many," he whispered to Ben, who gave him a brief sideways glance and then nodded.

"Retreat slowly," he said calmly, his weapon at the ready.

They had moved back barely fifteen feet when the forest exploded. Nine wotans rushed at the fence simultaneously. Russell had prepared himself mentally, and immediately shot down three animals, which fell on top of one another on the grass in front of the fence. Ben had also hit one, Eliot had missed his target and the five remaining wotans were now pounding against the fence. The force ripped two observation posts out of the ground. Entangled in barbed wire, the beasts flew into the compound.

Russell, Ben and Eliot didn't stop firing at the jumble of wire, bodies, and legs. Red and yellow liquid sprayed in all directions. Wherever it was hit by blood, the barbed wire dissolved with a hiss. The stench was almost unbearable, sweet and heavy like in a slaughterhouse where the slabs of meat were left untended for weeks. Russell retched. At least the beasts were dead. But a fifteen-foot section of the fence had been ripped down. And there were more cracking sounds coming from the forest.

"Jesus Christ!" said Ben. "Everyone over here!"

Andrea, Maxwell, and Stanislav ran over and directed their weapons at the gap. Ben shouted at Dr. Cashmore, who was still busy with the distillation column. "Stop pumping immediately! We have to get out of here."

Russell heard Cashmore cursing.

"Stop right now!" screamed Ben. "Leave everything and get out! Start the vehicles. Lee, open the gate and into the jeep!"

Ten wotans appeared simultaneously as if from nowhere. Russell shot, as did the other colonists beside him. Some of the animals dropped down dead, but others had reached the compound in a few quick bounds. At the same time, more beasts stormed out of the undergrowth. A seemingly endless stream came pouring out of the jungle. The onslaught had begun.

Russell killed another wotan that was coming right at him. The hulking creature slid forward a few more feet before coming to a standstill. Two others jumped over the dead body and were blown into pieces by a detonating hand grenade. Patrick screamed as his arm was hit by a spurt of acidic blood. He dropped his weapon and ran to one of the jeeps.

"Don't break formation! Keep shooting!" roared Russell.

The entire area between him and the edge of the forest was covered in blood, carcasses, and the body parts of torn-apart wotans. So far, they had managed to shoot them dead before they reached the barrier, but more wotans were appearing all the time.

"We have to leave! Come on, we'll give you cover," Russell heard Ben shout from behind.

"Fuck! They're also coming from the right," shouted Stanislav. Russell looked round. Dozens of the beasts had ripped down the fence on the right and were running toward the vehicles.

The engines roared. The convoy had started and had almost reached the gate.

"Run!" screamed Russell. He ran as fast as his painful lungs would allow him. There was no time for an orderly retreat. Now it was only about saving their own skins. He ran to the nearest jeep and grabbed a hand that was held out to him. Dr. Cashmore pulled him into the vehicle. Russell fell hard onto the back seat, but immediately turned around and shot at two wotans that were approaching from the side. He got the first one, then there was just a click.

Fuck! Empty again!

He grasped into his pocket to fish out a spare magazine.

Behind him the stragglers had made it to the last jeep. Patrick and Andrea jumped in. Two wotans had almost reached them. Ben put his food down hard on the accelerator. Stanislav, who had wanted to jump into the passenger seat, lost his balance. He stumbled und somersaulted onto the gravel.

"Stop, we've lost Stanislav!" shouted Andrea. Russell saw Ben looking round briefly before disengaging the clutch completely. The first monsters had already reached Stanislav. Russell turned around in order not to watch his friend being dissolved by the acid of these beasts of prey. But he couldn't block out the inhuman screams of pain. He looked stubbornly ahead, as the screams gave way to a weak gurgling. Then it was over and Russell breathed a sigh of relief.

His suffering is over! Thank God!

Then he was overcome by rage.

I'm the one with a ticket to the hereafter! I should have been in his place!

"They're pursuing us," screeched the chemist, sitting next to him, and shot wildly behind him with his pistol.

"Careful that you don't hit one of the jeeps behind us," Russell bellowed into his ear.

A whole herd of wotans had left the compound of the oil spring through the main gate. They were chasing them at over thirty miles an hour. The animals were faster than the fleeing jeeps, which kept having to swerve around pieces of fence and potholes. Patrick and Andrea fired in a frenzy. Scores of animals fell down dead on the stony track, but more and more came up from behind.

Ben shouted something to the young Holbrook, but Russell couldn't hear what. Patrick climbed over the seat onto the truck bed and busied himself with a barrel of kerosene.

Russell guessed what he was up to and hoped that the plan worked. The jeep swayed to the side and Patrick was almost thrown out, but he held onto the ropes with which the barrels were secured to the truck bed.

Patrick undid the ropes securing the barrel at the back and it fell to the ground with a loud thud before rolling across the tack. Andrea aimed and fired.

The barrel went up in a huge ball of fire. It was so bright that Russell had to shut his eyes. When he opened them again, the whole road up to the edge of the forest was engulfed in white flames. Even the jungle was shrouded in smoke. The stench of burning kerosene was so pungent, that Russell coughed and held his breath. The heat was almost unbearable. Patrick used a cloth to stamp out a little fire on the truck bed.

Finally, Russell took a deep breath. No wotan would make it alive through that hellfire. They'd done it. Despite the heat, he got goose bumps. Imagine what would happen if tens of thousands of these beasts attacked the colony?

Russell leaned out of the window of the jeep and vomited violently.

Chapter 22

Marlene looked at the two oblong holes in the ground and at the two coffins beside them. Paulina Hall was quite a talented carpenter—she had taught herself the craft after arriving in New California. She had had years to work on these two coffins and the other three that stood in the workshop.

Marlene tried to remember when the last funeral had taken place. The death of Jim Rogers was almost twenty years ago. She had always known that the time would come, and considering the dangerous wildlife of this planet, it was a miracle that it had taken this long. But she had hoped that during her time as president, she wouldn't have to conduct a funeral. Neither Igor nor Stanislav had been religious, so it fell to her to speak a few words. She waited until all the men, women, and children had gathered around the graves.

Standing next to Igor's grave were his wife Dorothy Moore and their three children. Igor and Dorothy hadn't fallen in love right away. Marlene still remembered how Dorothy had made fun of his first awkward advances. But the following fall, at the Thanksgiving party following the harvest, something had sparked between them. Or they had both decided they were sick of being alone; nobody knew for sure. In any case, Dorothy was now in floods of tears, even her children were unable to console her. Alexander, the eldest, kept speaking softly to his mother, and even the two younger children, Arkady and Natasha, seemed far more collected than Dorothy.

The other coffin was empty. They had had to leave Stanislav's body back at the oil spring. Marlene doubted that the wotans would have left any part of him in any case. They dissolved their prey with acid and absorbed the resulting liquid through their skin. Marlene shuddered. How Stanislav must have suffered in his final moment . . . a heavy animal on your back, immobile, as your own body slowly dissolved . . . Marlene would rather shoot herself than go through that.

Sophia O'Hara stood beside Stanislav's coffin with a blank expression. Her two daughters stood beside her and looked down at the grave with red eyes.

Only half of the colony was present. Ten men and women were guarding the observation post, and Ty Grazier and John Dressel were heading up the final preparations for detonating the atomic bomb. In two hours, it should be ready. Marlene would have preferred if the funerals could have taken place afterwards, but once the danger had been warded off, they would have to get straight back to working in the fields, in order to save as much of the harvest as possible.

Marlene looked up at the sky and saw a few thin wisps of cloud floating across the otherwise clear sky. A stiff breeze was blowing down from the mountains into the valley. The giant redwoods swirled the air around and gusts of wind kept blowing her hair into her face. The moon—

which could now be seen clearly—had risen in the west. Every day, a little bit more of its surface became visible. By now, a good half of the big white orb was looming over the nearby hill.

The murmuring died down, and Marlene seized the moment to make her little speech.

"When we came here, we all knew that we were up against a hostile, alien environment. That didn't stop us from conquering this planet. We defended ourselves against the wild animals that threatened us during the first winter, and banished them completely from our immediate environment. Although the odds were against us, we build a settlement in which we could live safely. We even survived the first years of food shortages. We sowed fields and brought in the harvests. In recent years, we started to feel increasingly safe, and to see this planet not just as a temporary refuge, but as a new home. Many of us, even if we were given the chance, would not want to return to Earth. We can be proud of what we have achieved here."

Marlene looked into the faces of as many of the people standing before her as she could. She knew that her speech was straying away from a standard funeral oration, but it seemed to her that the circumstances demanded something more. The very existence of the colony was under threat, at least until they'd cut off the pass. She was of the opinion that this crisis marked a turning point in their history on this planet, and she wanted everyone to grasp this. She hoped that it would forge a closer bond between the inhabitants of New California, because many of them still saw themselves as citizens of Earth.

"As colonists, we belong to a group of people that ceased to exist on Earth a hundred years ago. *Colonists* . . . you have to think about the meaning of this word and how it has shaped the history of humanity. Colonists are people who leave their homes to subjugate and settle in new lands. We are the first colony of humans on a distant planet. We have achieved something here that we can be proud of. Igor and Stanislav helped to fulfill this dream, and now they have died for it: in our fight against the environment and the dangers of this planet, and for our children, who, even more than us, regard this world as their home. Our grandchildren and great-grandchildren will look up into the sky and hardly be able to believe that we once came here from another planet. They will ask questions about us, the first generation. And they will discover the names of the fallen. The first ones to give their lives to secure their safety in this world were Igor Isalovic and Stanislav Radinkovic. They died as heroes and will be remembered in the history of this world as heroes."

Marlene paused briefly. Dorothy was still sobbing. Rhonda Fiedler had come up behind her and laid a hand on her shoulder. Russell was standing with his family at the edge of the gathering. He had another coughing attack, which caused him to sway. Ellen wanted to support him, but he pushed her hand aside. He looked terrible, and he had lost a lot of weight. For days now, Ellen had been worrying that he wasn't eating enough.

In a few weeks I'll be giving a eulogy for Russell. It's so unjust!

She turned back to the coffins. "Igor and Stanislav died because our new world laid bare a new danger and they helped to recognize and eliminate that danger. With the gasoline and kerosene supplies we'll be able to survive the coming months until the flood retreats and we find a new way into the valley. The preparations for igniting the bomb are almost complete, and once we've cut off the pass, no beasts of prey will be able to threaten our colony ever again. These two heroes will be the only ones to have lost their lives in the current crisis. When the sun sets tonight, the danger will be averted and we will be able to concentrate once again on building up our colony and conquering this world. The memory of how we overcame this crisis will remind us that we are the masters of this planet."

Marlene stepped back as a small group of men, led by Sammy Yang, slowly lowered the coffins into the graves. She had a bad conscience. In her talk she had said very little about Igor and Stanislav, as would have been appropriate at a funeral, but she didn't believe in retrospective adulation. Everyone had their own memories of the two men, and that would have to suffice. But she knew for sure that later in the day, Ben would accuse her of using the occasion for her own political ends, and perhaps he was right.

She hopped nervously from one foot to the other. She would have preferred to be in the canyon overseeing the preparations for the detonation. She hoped that everything there was going smoothly. She trusted Ty and Dr. Dressel, but the bomb was so important. She would only be able to relax again once the pass had been blocked.

Chapter 23

"How's it going, guys?" asked Marlene.

Travis Richards didn't remove his binoculars from his eyes. "Good. We killed three wotans an hour ago, and two snipers before that. We don't even wait for them to get close to the post, we just shoot 'em down as soon as they come out of the forest."

After the funeral, Marlene had driven straight to "Ground Zero," as Ty Grazier had started to call the spot which they were about to blow up. The explosives expert and the physicist had completed their work and Marlene had sent them straight up to the canyon entrance in the highlands. Here they had established a small command observation post in a cave, from where the detonation would be carried out remotely. Marlene had driven on to the observation post at the bottom to pull out the lookout team. In an hour's time they would no longer need this observation post.

"Good! Ty's ready to carry out the detonation. It's time for us to get back."

Travis laid aside his binoculars. "It's a good moment.

The animals are all in the forest at the moment. I'm telling you: we've heard some sounds that would make your skin crawl."

Marlene nodded. "That doesn't surprise me. The wotans are defending their territory against the invaders from the east. I was worried we wouldn't get the job done before the animals start to panic and disperse."

"When will the flood reach the observation post?"

"Dr. Dressel thinks in two weeks. But the animals will start migrating to the highlands long before that. Nobody knows when exactly, which is why it's high time to block their path."

"I always enjoyed my shifts here. Until recently there wasn't much danger, either. It always reminded me of my childhood. I often went hunting with my father. There are lots of woods in Maine. We'd spend the night in the hunting stand, and next day we'd often bring home a deer. Once we even shot a bobcat."

Marlene looked at him in surprise. She had never heard the usually uncommunicative Travis talk about his feelings. But she did not respond.

Travis climbed down from the lookout, followed by Marlene. At the bottom, Travis looked almost wistfully toward the jungle. "I'll really miss it!"

"Have you packed everything up?"

"Yes, all the weapons and equipment are loaded in the jeeps. We can leave right away."

"Then let's go. Ty is already itching to detonate the bomb. I don't want to test his patience for too long!"

"As long as the damn thing doesn't go off before we reach the top. . . ."

Travis called his men together. He made a short, unnecessary speech about duty and responsibility, which caused Sammy Yang to roll his eyes. Then they climbed in their vehicles and sped off. Marlene followed right behind.

Ten minutes later, they had reached Ground Zero. Marlene stopped, went to the little box on the wooden scaffold, and pressed a button. The remote detonation was ready to be activated.

Marlene looked around briefly. In a few minutes, once the bomb had caused the cliffs to cave in, there would be a wall of rubble here, over a hundred feet high. With a shudder she thought about what would happen to her if somebody now accidentally triggered the detonation. She would be dead in a split second.

She climbed back into her vehicle and drove to the upper canyon entrance. The last section was very steep and the engine howled as the jeep juddered up the final incline in first gear. The escarpment ended here and the grassland of the highlands began. Marlene took a sharp left and drove down into a flat hollow on the other side of the ridge. Two other jeeps were parked there already. Ty had blasted a cave into the rock, around fifteen feet deep. Grant Dillon was standing in front of the entrance, his head wrapped in a bandage. The master of disaster had been standing too close to the site of the explosion and a sharp stone had hit his forehead.

Marlene gave Grant a nod and entered the cave, which was to serve them as a bunker during the detonation of the atomic bomb. A generator in front of the entrance provided electricity for light and the detonation device. Ty Grazier, John Dressel, Russell Harris and Ben Hawke were standing in front of a table. They were debating something, but stopped when Marlene walked in.

"What's the status?" she asked.

Ty pointed at a green light that was glowing on a console. "Everything's ready for the detonation. The flow of electricity is constant, the detonator and the bomb are ready."

"Good. How's the weather?"

"Could hardly be better. The wind is blowing steadily at twenty knots from the west. It will carry the radioactive fallout far out to sea. Because we're detonating the bomb underground, only a little radioactive material will remain on the surface, and it will be washed away by the next rainfall. Theoretically, we could build a new road right over the site of the explosion without endangering anyone."

"We'll see in a few weeks when we've made the necessary measurements." Marlene turned to Ben. "Are all the colonists in safety?"

Hawke nodded slowly. "Yes, I just got the report that the lookout team arrived in the colony. Everyone's staying indoors until the explosion is over. Although . . ."

"Although what?"

"Although Donald Bell and a few others have set out for the mountains to get a better view. I couldn't stop them."

Marlene rolled her eyes. Couldn't people follow simple instructions for once? "Where did they go exactly?"

"They were heading for Devil's Cliff. Behind the spot where the whales sleep."

She signed. "That's far enough away. Let's proceed. Ty, I give you the green light to detonate. But can someone please get Grant and tell him to come inside?"

Ben went out and returned with Grant. Meanwhile, Ty got to work at the detonation device. His face scrunched up in concentration and, muttering under his breath, he flipped various switches. "Trigger circuit one on. Test OK. Alternative circuit on. Test OK. Synchronized ignition on. I have a green light from the electrical detonator." He took a key out of his pocket and stuck it in the console. "I'm activating the detonation mechanism." He turned the key and a white light went on. A warning signal rang out twice through the bunker. "Ready!" He laid his right forefinger on an illuminated red button. "Detonation. In five, four, three . . ."

Instinctively, Marlene shut her eyes. She prepared herself for a mighty tremor, when a few miles away, tens of thousands of cubic feet of rock would be displaced by the force of the nuclear explosion.

"Two, one—DETONATE!"

Nothing happened.

"What the . . ."

Marlene opened her eyes.

". . . hell . . .?"

She looked at Ty. "What happened?"

"Nothing, obviously!" whispered Ben.

"Shit!" Ty frantically checked the switches on the detonation device.

"Did the detonation fail?" asked Dr. Dressel calmly.

"No, dammit. The yellow light here says the detonation was successful."

"But nothing's happened," said Grant.

"I can tell that myself, smartass!" Ty rolled his eyes.

Grant turned on his heel and went outside.

"Obviously the bomb failed to detonate," said Marlene. "Secure the detonation device, then drive straight to the bomb and find out what happened." She grabbed the radio that stood on the table in the corner. "Eridu, report."

After a few seconds, Travis Richards answered. "Hello Marlene. What's going on? Haven't you detonated yet?"

"We just tried to. Unsuccessfully. Clearly the bomb isn't working for some reason."

"Oh Jesus!" static sounded over the loudspeaker.

"I need a troop at the observation post right away. Do

you hear? We need to secure the observation post again. Grab the last lookout team and drive down."

It took several seconds before Travis replied. "What if we drive through the canyon and the bomb goes off with a delay?"

"Ty is securing the detonating mechanism and driving down to Ground Zero himself. You don't need to worry. Make sure that you set off immediately. If the beasts invade the observation post, and we're not there to defend it, the colony is lost! Do you understand? Leave immediately!"

"Copy that, we're on our way!"

Marlene laid the radio aside and turned to Russell. He looked as tired as she felt. *This is all getting too much for me!* "What now?"

Russell coughed and turned to Ty. "What could have happened?"

"I have no idea. Something is wrong with the bomb. We'll have to get it out of the cliff and take it apart."

"We've got a second bomb in the warehouse, let's quickly bring it down to Ground Zero," Ben butted in.

"They were stored together and they're identical. We need to check out the first bomb before we try and do the same thing with the second."

"How long will it take? Will you be able to repair the bomb?" asked Marlene.

"We should take it to the workshop in Eridu. Then it depends how quickly we locate the problem. We should be able to find out something today."

"I hope so. Without blocking the pass, we're screwed."

Chapter 24

"Russell, you have to take care of yourself," said Dr. Lindwill sternly. He pointed to the latest X-ray, which he had taken the day before. "Half of the left lung is useless and the right one is full of metastasis. You can't carry on doing everything the way you are."

Russell looked at the picture lying in front of him on the table. He cleared his throat, but said nothing. The excitement of the last few days had done him good, despite all his ailments. He had the feeling that he was needed, and for hours at a time, he was able to forget about his illness—at least until he was overcome by another coughing fit or dizzy spell. Now, after the detonation had failed and the colony was in danger, there was so much to do. Russell desperately wanted to be there when Ty and his team examined the nuclear bomb. He was annoyed that the doctor had dragged him to the infirmary. He had wanted to resist, but Ellen had also insisted on it.

"Your blood levels also look—there's no other way I can put it—like shit. And I don't know if that's because of the cancer or the amount of stimulants and pain killers you've been taking the whole time."

"I refuse to lie in bed, while all around me the colony is in danger," retorted Russell.

"I'm not asking you to do that. But you have to accept that you're not as fit as the others. You need to rest and leave the difficult missions to them. If I'd known that you were planning to drive out to the oil spring, I would have told Marlene to withdraw you from the mission."

"That's precisely why I didn't say anything," replied Russell. "We lost a good man on that trip. Yes, the mission was dangerous, and that's exactly why I went on it. I'm as good as dead anyway, so it's better to put my life at risk than someone else's."

"But it's no use to anyone if you collapse in the middle of a combat mission. *That* would put the others in danger. I almost have the impression you're looking for an opportunity to die."

"And if I was?" The doctor had been clear about the fact that he couldn't save him. If Russell decided to die an agonizing death in battle rather than peacefully in bed, then that was damn well up to him.

Lindwall raised his arms. "I can't stop you. But I also can't endorse it. You should at least rest. Go home and go to bed. At least for today, okay?"

Russell shook his head. "No, I can't. We're about to examine the atomic bomb. Then I'm driving down to the observation post in the valley. Every man is needed there. Nobody knows when the beasts will start storming the barricades."

Dr. Lindwall shook his head slowly, the corners of his mouth pulled downward. "It's up to you." He went to the front door. As far as he was concerned, the session was over.

But Russell remained standing. "I need more Dexedrine."

The doctor swiveled around. "You won't listen to my advice and you want me to give you the strong stuff so you can kill yourself even faster?"

Russell stared at Lindwall. What was that about? He was as good as dead anyway. Nobody knew that better than the Doc; why did he have to make such a fuss about Russell wanting to spend the time he had left as productively as possible? After all, the colony was in grave danger!

Finally, the doctor sighed deeply and took out two little bottles from a cupboard. He looked down at them briefly before handing them over to Russell, who slipped them into the pocket of his parka.

"Thanks, Doc."

The doctor only spoke when Russell had opened the door. "What I wouldn't do for a cigarette . . . Just a single cigarette. . . ."

Russell went past the biology lab to the physics lab. After all these years, the containers looked considerably worse for wear. The once white-painted metal walls were full of black streaks, and the corners were covered in rust. Russell knocked and opened the door.

Pens, piles of paper, clips, cables, screws, electrical components, and other odds and ends covered the workbenches and dilapidated shelves that were gradually being eaten away by rust. LED ceiling lights cast a harsh, bright light. A big metal table stood in the center of the long room, and on an anti-static plastic mat lay the undetonated atomic bomb. Around the table stood Dr. Dressel, Ty Grazier, and Marlene Wolfe. Donald Bell was sitting in a corner taking notes. Ty looked up briefly and then went back to sorting his tools. Marlene and John Dressel were engrossed in a discussion.

"I have a bad feeling about this," said Marlene.

"Nothing can happen. Don't worry."

"What if it suddenly detonates? Maybe a part that was blocked will suddenly unblock when we take it apart."

"No, no. The detonation occurs electrically. If it isn't triggered, there's no way it will detonate without being repaired. And we don't have enough time to set up a lab outside of town anyway. That would take days."

"We could have examined it at Ground Zero."

"What? In the open air?"

"We could have put up a tent."

Ty Grazier put down his screwdriver on the table. He snorted. "We need a decent laboratory to work on it."

"Do you actually have any idea what you're doing?" asked Russell.

"Weapon design was one of my subjects at military academy," responded Ty.

"But you've never worked on an atomic warhead in practice," said Marlene flatly.

Ty threw the screwdriver back into the toolbox. "No, dammit, I haven't! But nor has anyone else here. Are we going to examine this thing now or not?"

Marlene raised her hands in the air. "Alright, alright. I just don't have a good feeling about this. I know we're screwed if we don't have a functioning bomb. But I want to know exactly what you're doing with this thing. You need to explain every step to me until I've understood it."

Ty grumbled something under his breath, took a set of precision engineering tools out of a black case, and pulled out a thin Phillips screwdriver.

Russell felt queasy as the weapons engineer removed the first screw from the bomb. This thing, hardly bigger than a basketball, could wipe out the whole colony!

The outer shell shimmered silver. There was an electric

control panel flange-mounted to the top. It consisted of a digital display, a switch and a dial for the time fuse. On the side, there were a series of plugs, presumably for remote detonation. After pulling out the fourth screw, none of which was more than two millimeters in diameter, Ty pulled the control panel out of the recess. A ribbon cable connected the detonation device to the explosive charge. Ty detached the cable and placed the control panel in a bowl on a little metal trolley.

"That was just the detonation device. Now I'm going to start actually dismantling the bomb."

Ty removed more screws, then gently jimmied the outer casing. The half sphere, which was barely three millimeters thick, loosened, and Ty carefully removed it. Meanwhile, he explained to the others what he was doing.

"The weapon lying in front of us is a W97 warhead. I downloaded the operating and maintenance instructions from our database. It's an advanced version of the W48 nuclear weapon that was already tested by the American Atomic Energy Commission in Nevada in 1957. This is one of the smallest explosives in our arsenal, but it still has an explosive force of one kiloton of TNT. This version of the warhead was used for tactical command missions."

"How much uranium is in there?" asked Marlene.

"No uranium. Plutonium 239. After Little Boy exploded over Hiroshima, almost no more uranium bombs were built. They're simple to produce, but considerably less effective."

"I didn't know that," said Russell. "I only know that when nuclear fuel undergoes fission, it somehow starts a chain reaction."

Dr. Dressel smiled. "It's easy really, once you've understood the basic physics." He pointed at the bomb. "Inside is a mass of plutonium 239. The number 239 refers to the number of protons and neutrons in the plutonium isotope."

"And how does the chain reaction take place?" asked Marlene.

"The plutonium atoms in the bomb split when they capture a neutron. Then they release energy, as well as two or three new neutrons, which in turn are captured by other plutonium nuclei. Then those split, make new neutrons, and so on. It's a self-perpetuating process. The final number of split atoms is unimaginably high, and thereby so is the energy that is released."

"You mean there's just plutonium in there and you shoot in a neutron?" asked Russell.

Ty laughed. "It's not quite that simple. Plutonium has the property of emitting neutrons itself. It would explode on its own if you tipped enough of the stuff on one heap. You need about twenty pounds of plutonium for an explosion. Once you have that much, it'll explode of its own accord. There are various ways of detonating a nuclear bomb. But ultimately they're all based on the same principle. Two subcritical masses are brought together fast enough to create a critical mass."

"Aha! So I simply bash together two chunks of plutonium and it goes bang?" asked Marlene.

"No, you would burn yourself and get a high dose of radiation. It's not that simple. The secret is to bring the two plutonium halves together into a critical mass *quickly enough*. You only have a few microseconds to assemble the critical mass correctly. The simplest nuclear weapon design is a simple gun barrel, with which you fire one piece of uranium-235 down the barrel of the gun to join another. That's quick enough. The Hiroshima bomb was based on such a design."

"But this doesn't look like the barrel of a gun."

Ty smiled. "That's true. The tactical explosive here is based on the two-point method. This core is egg-shaped, just about subcritical and surrounded by a cylinder of high explosive, which is detonated from both ends. The shock waves created by the explosive mass presses the egg roughly into a spherical shape. The surface area of the plutonium core is reduced, less neutrons can escape and . . . boom!"

"Well, the nuclear weapons program seems to have had many creative minds," said Marlene, barely able to suppress the sarcasm in her voice. How somebody could devote their life and their creative energy to building an atomic bomb was utterly incomprehensible to Russell, too.

"Some of the best," said Ty. "Some men, like Ted Taylor from Los Alamos, were living legends."

"Never heard of him," said Russell.

"Ted designed the biggest as well as the smallest atomic bomb tested by the USA. He and his colleagues at the nuclear weapons laboratory in Livermore competed to construct the smallest atomic bomb. In the process, he found out that you can build functioning bombs out of the tiniest amounts of plutonium, small enough to easily fit in a suitcase. This worried him so much, he spent the rest of his life warning against the dangers of nuclear terrorism."

"I've heard enough," said Marlene. "Could we please continue with the work?"

"Okay," said Ty, and removed another plastic husk from the bomb. A green mass became visible. "That's the explosive mass that presses the plutonium into the right shape in an explosion. Here on the side are the detonators." He loosened two plate-like inserts, one on each side of the bomb, and pulled out the thin, two-veined cables. "The detonators actually look fine." He passed the inserts to Donald. "Can you measure them? Thanks!"

Then Ty busied himself with the explosive mass. With a thin screwdriver, he pulled the two halves apart. He ended up with an oval, hand-sized mass in his hand. He laid the explosive in a plastic bowl.

"What is that stuff?" asked Russell.

Ty checked in the instruction manual, which was open beside him. "For the first atomic bombs they still used Baratol and RDX. In modern weapons they use new explosives like TATB. Makes it possible to reduce the diameter of the bomb from over three feet to this basketball size."

In a hollow in the bottom half of the explosive, a finger-long, shimmering silver egg could now be seen. Russell got goose pimples. There was something mysterious and powerful emanating from the small object. "Is that …?"

Grazier nodded. "Yes, that's the core of the bomb."

"That's the plutonium?" asked Marlene. Cautiously she took a step forward.

"Yes, although the surface is plated with a thin layer of nickel so that it's shielded from the air. Plutonium is highly reactive, it would immediately go up in flames if it came into contact with oxygen."

"It seems to emit warmth," said Russell.

"You're right. Touch it. Don't be afraid."

Russell cautiously touched the silver egg with his fingertips. He felt uncomfortable doing so. It was as if he were stroking the egg of a dragon that had brought a mystical power into this world. Then he very slowly laid his hand on the surface of the nuclear explosive. It was warm. Very warm, in fact, as if the stuff had been lying in the sun for hours. Russell couldn't shake off the feeling that the plutonium was alive, that it was in a feverish sleep and just waiting to wake up and unleash the fire of hell on them.

He could feel the hairs on the back of his hand standing on end. "It tickles!" Hastily he pulled his hand away.

Ty grinned. "The warmth comes from the decay of the plutonium. It's slightly radioactive and transforms with a half-life of around twenty-thousand years into uranium. Heat is released in the process. The core of the bomb also emits gamma rays.

Marlene immediately stepped back. "Isn't that unhealthy?" She felt very uncomfortable being in the vicinity of this dangerous substance.

Dr. Dressel shook his head. "No. The radiation is very weak. One X-ray puts a greater strain on the body than standing next to a plutonium core for a whole afternoon."

Ty Grazier took out his screwdriver again and stuck it in a barely visible gap on the equator of the bomb core. He levered half of the mass upward. With his gloved right hand he carefully, and with some difficulty, pulled out the top half of the bomb core. He set aside the screwdriver, took the plutonium core in both hands and carried it over to another workbench, on which various measuring devices were standing. "There shouldn't really be a problem with the core, but still, I'm going to measure the gamma rays it's emitting."

He fiddled around for a few seconds with an implement that sprung to life with a beeping sound, then returned to the table where the bottom half of the bomb core was still lying, embedded in explosive.

When he looked more closely, Russell could see that inside there was another little sphere, no bigger than a pea. He pointed at it. "There's something inside the plutonium core!"

Ty smiled. "Yes. That's the most complicated part of the whole bomb. The initiator!"

Marlene and Russell's eyes met. Russell shook his head.

Ty was clearly enjoying playing the atomic bomb expert. Dr. Dressel obviously knew enough about the principles of nuclear fission to look unimpressed.

When neither Russell nor Marlene responded, Ty continued. "The little sphere consists of a mixture of polonium and beryllium. Beryllium emits alpha particles which polonium turns into neutrons. The two substances are arranged in a complicated way, so that at exactly the right moment during the detonation, a large surge of neutrons is sent into the plutonium."

"And without this pea?"

"Without an initiator, you only have a rather elaborate, radioactive firecracker."

Marlene pointed at the parts of the bomb. "That's all well and good. That was an interesting lesson on how to build atomic bombs. But how does it help us? Why didn't the thing detonate?"

Ty scratched his head. "That's a good question!" he said histrionically.

Russell rolled his eyes. It was starting to get on his nerves that Ty was making such a show out of examining the bomb.

Donald Bell piped up from behind them. "The electrical detonator is working fine. And I've measured the ignition plate. All in order."

For the first time Ty looked baffled. "Strange. I expected there to be some problem there."

"Could it have to do with the initiator?" Russell asked.

"No, definitely not. It only starts working when the plutonium is pressed into the critical form by the explosive."

"Perhaps there's something wrong with the explosive?" suggested Marlene.

Ty looked at the greenish mass. "Hmm, it looks normal to me . . ."

"I thought you're the explosives expert," said Marlene. "It seems to me you know more about plutonium than normal explosives."

"Well, I've never had to deal with TATB," grumbled Ty.

Marlene sighed. She turned to Donald, who had placed the electrical detonator back on the table. "Please get Dr. Cashmore."

"What are we going to do if we can't fix the bomb?" asked Russell. His head was spinning again. He gripped the edge of the table to regain his balance, and hoped the others hadn't noticed anything.

"We could always try the second atomic bomb," suggested Dr. Dressel.

"We won't have any other option. But if it also fails …"

"Then we've got a real problem on our hands," said Russell. "We need to think of a Plan B."

"There is no Plan B. Using the atomic bomb is the only way of closing off the pass."

"Maybe we'll be able to defend the observation post if we strengthen it enough," said Ty.

"We've been through that already. We don't stand a chance against hundreds of thousands of wotans and snipers. And anyway, the post will be flooded. In two weeks it probably won't even be there anymore."

"And if we built a new observation post half way down the canyon? At the narrowest point? Wouldn't we have a better chance of defending it?"

Russell shook his head emphatically. "The animals will steamroll through everything. If we had more time, a few weeks perhaps, we could maybe build a proper wall. But in the space of a few days—impossible. We don't even have the building materials."

"Shit. There must be a way."

"The only other alternative is to flee," said Marlene, a note of resignation in her voice. "Into the mountains. Take as many provisions with us as possible and hope we survive until the flood subsides. But we don't know when the beasts will return to the lowlands. And our provisions won't last us that long."

The door opened and Donald came in with Dr. Cashmore. Marlene pointed at the dismantled bomb and explained what they had found out so far. "Could it have to do with the explosive?"

The chemist bent over the hemisphere. He frowned, and took a handkerchief out of his jacket pocket. With one corner, he brushed carefully over the greenish mass, held the handkerchief up to his nose, and sniffed at it.

"Aha," he said decisively and nodded.

"What?" asked Russell.

The chemist held the handkerchief up to Russell's nose. Right away he felt a burning sensation in his nostrils.

Cashmore threw the handkerchief in a bin and turned to Marlene. "The explosive material has decomposed. It's sweating hydrazine. Just like old dynamite discards nitroglycerine. You can see it at a glance. Usually TATB is yellow, not green."

"How can that be?" asked Marlene.

"Well, the bombs have been lying around here for twenty years. And not exactly in ideal storage conditions. I'm sure the high humidity here has played a role."

"And that means?" asked Dr. Dressel.

Cashmore turned around and shrugged. "It means that our two atomic bombs are just radioactive waste."

Chapter 25

"For Christ's sake, Ernie! What are you doing here? You should be in Eridu taking care of yourself," said Marlene, after she had climbed up to the viewing platform at the observation post. Ernie sat grinning on a chair, polishing his binoculars. His broken bone had been fixed after his return from the oil spring, and his leg was in a cast.

"Hell, what's the point of staying at home? If the wotans start attacking the observation post, I'll be needed here. It's our last line of defense."

"But only until the observation post also gets flooded."

Ernie shrugged.

"How are things?" asked Marlene.

"Strangely quiet. I've been sitting here for two hours and haven't seen a single one of the beasts."

"That'll change soon," said Marlene. She only hoped that by then they had found a solution to their problem.

Ernie looked over the wooden railing at the sweeping grassland. It was still early morning, and the grass glistened in the dazzling morning sun rising over the forest treetops. Swirls of mist rose from patches of lush green grass. There was not a cloud to be seen in the deep azure sky; it was going to be a hot day.

"In a few hours, Lee will be here with some men," said Marlene. "They're bringing materials with them to build a second barrier. Around sixty feet from the first one. That should help to withstand a stampede."

"It won't help much if thousands of the beasts attack at the same time," grumbled Ernie.

"Of course not. It's just to give us a bit more time. Nothing more."

"It sure sucks that the explosion didn't work."

"You can say that again!"

"What's the plan now?"

Marlene sighed. "We don't have one. But probably our only remaining option will be to flee."

Ernie snorted. "Flee? Flee where?"

"That's the big question. Originally I intended to pack together as many provisions as possible and to head for the mountains."

"I thought we don't have enough supplies."

Marlene nodded. "We don't."

"Great plan!"

"Russell had another idea. If it works, it could be a viable alternative."

"Russell? What's his plan?" asked Ernie.

"To use the transporter."

Ernie's jaw dropped. "The transporter? We haven't used that creepy thing since we got here. We can't get back to Earth. Where does he want to go?"

"He wants to talk with the sphere's artificial intelligence to find out if there are other planets with friendly environments that can sustain us."

Ernie laughed. "And that's gonna work? How will the

225

transporter know if there's something for us to eat on another planet?"

Marlene was unsure herself. She doubted that they would be able to find a suitable planet in the short amount of time they had left. Quite apart from the evacuation. But Ernie didn't need to know what she was thinking.

"It's worth a try. Unfortunately our options are narrowing."

Ernie grunted. "But flee to another planet? Leave behind everything here? It's taken us twenty years to make a home for ourselves here. We might be better off trying to take on the beasts."

"We don't stand a chance, Ernie. There are too many of them. It would be suicide."

Ernie pulled a hip flask out of his jacket. He unscrewed the top and took a big swig. Immediately his face turned red.

Marlene rolled her eyes. She wanted to make a pointed remark, but decided against it. Many years ago, Dr. Cashmore had found some plants that could be fermented into alcohol. She had wanted to forbid it, but obviously people would still make it in secret. Marlene looked over the parapet at the broad stretch of grassland and the nearby forest. How many animals were fleeing from the flood and heading in this direction?

"We're screwed," said Ernie and took another swig.

Chapter 26

Russell took a deep breath and laid his hands on the outer wall of the transporter. He winced when an opening appeared.

He hesitated. It had been a long time since he'd last set foot in the alien contraption. The transporter even looked sinister from the outside. The material of the outer shell was so black, it was impossible to make out any texture. From inside, a surreal gray light shimmered and awakened memories of his first missions with the transporter over twenty years ago. On a trip to a black hole, Russell had almost died. It was only thanks to a lot of luck that he had been able to return to Earth. Some of the others, like Sean O'Brien, had been less lucky. Sean had been transported to a planet with an atmosphere of sulfuric acid. Somehow he had managed to activate the return transport, but Russell and the other guinea pigs had had to watch as his body dissolved and he died an agonizing death.

Russell stepped into the contraption, a heavy backpack with sample containers and lab equipment slung over his shoulder. The inner walls were gray. Nobody had found out what emitted this diffuse light. It seemed to come from all directions, and Russell didn't cast a shadow. The interior was spherical in shape and had a diameter of about thirty-five feet—it reminded Russell a little of the inside of a gas tank. Even more sinister was the inner sphere, which hovered like a fifteen-by-fifteen-foot pearl in the middle of the room. This sphere was the actual teleportation device. When you stepped inside, you could be transported to countless other transporters around the galaxy.

Christian Holbrook followed him into the sphere a few steps behind. "I still get goose bumps when I climb into this thing. Even after all these years."

"Well, we haven't used the transporter for almost fifteen years."

"Yup, when we destroyed the sphere on Mars. And I keep asking myself if that was really such a good idea."

"We can't change it now," said Russell crossly.

Russell could feel the familiar pressure in his head, not unlike a headache. At the time, the scientists had thought it was a simple side effect of the magnetic fields that passed through the transporter. Then Russell had found out that in fact it was the device's artificial intelligence, trying to make contact by a kind of telepathy. After Russell had put himself into a meditative trance, he had succeeded in making initial contact, and gradually they had discovered the story behind the alien artifact. He hoped that the artificial intelligence would still talk to him.

"I'll start now," he said to Christian.

"Yes, okay." The astronaut hopped uneasily from one leg to the other. "We should have brought along two folding chairs."

Russell shrugged and sat down on the curved floor. Then he closed his eyes and began to meditate. He suppressed all thoughts until his mind was empty and all he could feel was the pressure in his head. Then he tried to make contact. He whispered so that Holbrook could hear the conversation.

"Can you hear me? Are you there?"

The answer came right away.

Yes, I can hear you.

It wasn't so much as if someone else had answered his question but rather as if he had had the thought himself. It felt almost schizophrenic. Like a mental disorder which caused him to wrestle with his own thoughts.

He quietly conveyed the answer to Holbrook.

"How are you, buddy?"

The sphere did not answer his question.

"I'm looking for another habitable planet."

Define habitable!

I'm looking for a planet with a similar environment to Earth's."

I don't know a planet called Earth.

Russell took a deep breath. How could he explain to the sphere what he was looking for?

"I'm looking for a planet with similar environmental conditions to this planet."

A galaxy appeared in his mind's eye. Billions of points of light blurred into a spiral-shaped cloud, until Russell could make out the Milky Way. Gradually the points faded, but ten thousand still remained. How was he supposed to select from all these?

"I need a planet with plants that humans can eat."

The data for this selection are insufficient. There is no information about the compatibility of plants for specific species.

"Damn! Show me the habitable planet closest to this one."

An image appeared in Russell's mind. It was of a desert of golden sand, with barren, craggy mountains rising high into the sky. The sky was blue, but that was the only friendly part of the picture.

"Show me another planet. I need one with plants and animals that eat only plants. Without beasts of prey that are a danger to humans. And no extreme seasons or weather conditions."

A new image appeared. Russell saw a black sphere lying in lush, green grass with a few trees and bushes. In the background he could see high mountains that rose up into a blue sky.

This planet is a hundred and twenty light years away. Average temperature seventy-seven degrees, sixty-eight degrees at night. Duration of days twenty-two hours and eight minutes. Gravity zero-comma-nine-five G. Atmosphere eighty percent nitrogen, nineteen percent oxygen, one percent argon.

Russell opened his eyes and passed on the data to Christian.

"Doesn't sound too bad," said the astronaut.

"Shall we try it?"

"Why not?"

Russell took the retractable ladder that they had brought with them from Eridu, and climbed up the steps to the inner sphere. The straps of the black backpack dug into his shoulders. He wheezed heavily and coughed.

"That doesn't sound good at all," murmured Holbrook, who despite carrying his own kitbag, climbed the steps with ease.

Russell was silent until he reached the little platform from where they could enter the sphere.

"Perhaps somebody else should make the trip with me?" offered Christian.

Russell grunted. "I'm fine." He was well aware how unrealistic that sounded.

"Didn't you speak to Lindwall yesterday? What did he say?"

"What's he supposed to say?" asked Russell. "I'm finding it harder to breathe from one day to the next, and there are moments when I can only stay upright using stimulants. The damn cancer is spreading like a wildfire. In two weeks it'll be hard for me to stand up at all, in four weeks I'll need oxygen if I don't want to suffocate. There's a bottle under my bed, and last night I almost used it. In two months, you'll all be standing around a pretty little grave and listening to Marlene making a speech in which she'll tell everyone what a nice guy I was, while at least half of the colony will be thinking the opposite."

"I'm sorry," replied Christian. He put his hand on Russell's shoulder.

"It's okay. Sometimes I manage to forget that I'm sick until someone asks me about it again."

"I won't ask anymore."

"Good." Russell entered the inner sphere. He laid the ladder flat on the floor and took off his backpack. Holbrook closed the opening and went over to the transporter's control column. He pointed at a black field on which a code was already visible. "Is that our destination?"

Russell nodded. "Yes, I told the intelligence to pre-select the destination for us."

Holbrook shuddered. "Even knowing that the destination has a friendly environment, it's still a horrible feeling to be transported. To be beamed across light years in the blink of an eye surpasses my powers of imagination. Particularly since we don't know how this thing works."

"I used to be afraid of flying," said Russell. "I especially hated taking off. And once we were up in the air, I would look out of the window and wonder how long it would take to fall back down to Earth. Eventually, I found a solution to my fear—it works here, too."

"And that is?"

"I simply don't think about it." Without flinching, Russell pressed on the illuminated field below the code.

There was a slight, hardly discernable jolt as the gravity changed. As if an elevator had started.

"You see. There already." Russell smiled. "And much faster than in an airplane."

His friend shrugged and opened the entrance to the inner sphere. "Can you pass me the ladder?"

They climbed down and opened the outer wall of the sphere.

The air was warm, dry and pleasant. He stepped outside and looked around, his right hand hovering over his holster. You could never be sure. . . .

An orange sun stood high above them. The deep-blue sky was dotted with little white clouds that drifted slowly toward the horizon. A light wind ruffled Russell's hair. The sphere was surrounded by grassy knolls and the occasional tree—just as the intelligence of the transporter had shown him. Fruit was hanging from some of the trees. To his left, a river meandered through a valley before disappearing into a forest.

"Looks nice," said Russell.

"Yes," agreed Christian Holbrook. "Reminds me of the orchards in New Hampshire or even more so in Europe. England, or northern France maybe. If it weren't for the orange sun, you might think you were on Earth."

"The trees don't look at all strange. That one over there with the red fruit looks like an apple tree. There are conifers in the forest over there. No mile-high giant redwoods or other exotic varieties."

"We should have taken Jenny with us."

"Yes, she would have had something to say about this. Even on New California she was surprised how the physiology of the plants and trees was so similar to on Earth."

"Apart from the fact that on Earth there aren't any wotans or other acid-spitting beasts," said Christian.

"Wrong," said Russell. "Ever heard of ants? What do they squirt?"

"Ant acid." The astronaut nodded. "One point for you. But they're a tad smaller than wotans or greyhounds."

"That's true. But it seems as if all Earth-like planets went through a similar development."

"Jenny said the same. At least, that similar environments inevitably lead to carbon-based life forms with a cytochemistry similar to on Earth. The differences are in the details. Shame that she can't return to Earth. With the results of her research she would win the Nobel Prize in Exobiology!"

Russell grinned. "We can offer an alternative prize. I think there are a few people in the colony who deserve one."

Christian nodded and chuckled. "Ernie would get the Golden Combat Boot for being the toughest soldier."

Russell chuckled. "And Doc Lindwall the Glass Ashtray for twenty years as an involuntary non-smoker."

"Dr. Cashmore told me that a while ago the doc asked him for some chemical—I can't remember the name of it anymore. Some awful stuff that's used for chemical weapons. When he asked him what he wanted it for, the doc beat abound the bush for a while and then admitted that he wanted to try and synthesize nicotine out of it."

"And?"

"Cashmore chased him out of the lab and since then has been regularly double-locking his chemical supplies."

Russell laughed. "Luckily, the doc has his own

drugstore. It wouldn't surprise me if he created something stimulating out of it from time to time. That's probably also why he's so stingy about handing out medication."

"Or he's just trying to make our supplies last as long as possible. We won't be able to produce a lot of it once it's used up. And we don't even have some stuff that we urgently need."

"Chemotherapeutics for example," said Russell bitterly. *Then I might at least stand a chance and wouldn't have to die a miserable death!* Now he had come back round to the subject after all.

Christian was silent.

Russell tried to shake off his negative thoughts. "Let's get our samples." He opened his backpack, took out a specimen container and scooped in some earth. Together they checked out the area, took samples of plants, fruit, and water from the river, and measured the natural background radiation.

They approached the conifer woodland, when Christian suddenly pricked up his ears. He turned around, and his eyes widened. Russell turned around, too.

An animal was standing no more than ten feet behind them and staring in their direction. Russell reached for his pistol and released the safety catch.

"It looks harmless," whispered Holbrook. The creature resembled a horse. It was a little bigger than a pony, with brown fur, a slightly shorter head and smooth tail. It lowered its head and snorted.

Obviously it was neither shy nor in any way aggressive. Its legs seemed powerful, but at the same time graceful. Its big ears were turned in their direction.

"It's standing between us and the transporter," said Russell quietly.

"I don't think we need to worry," said Holbrook, and walked slowly toward the animal.

"Don't!" whispered Russell. "Who knows what it'll do."

The creature made no sign of running away or attacking as Holbrook approached it. Russell felt uneasy. He pointed his pistol at the creature, ready to react quickly if necessary.

The astronaut slowly reached out a hand.

"Christian! For God's sake!" Russell hissed.

The animal closed its eyes as Christian gently stroked its head. Only now did Russell notice that his friend was talking softly to the horse. It opened its eyes again and sniffed at Holbrook's chest. Holbrook turned round to look at Russell triumphantly. After a while, Russell put the gun back in its holster and went over to the horse, but kept at a distance of over an arms length.

"What a lovely boy!" said Christian.

"Until it bites off your arm and has it for supper," said Russell drily.

"It's completely tame. Like the horses on my uncle's ranch. When I was young I used to spend my holidays there. In the afternoons, we often went out for a ride." He turned away from the horse and gave Russell a serious glance. "It should be possible to domesticate them without any problem. Imagine—if we had horses, we could use them for transportation or working the fields. We wouldn't be reliant on a couple of jeeps for everything."

"Seems to be paradise," grumbled Russell. In his opinion, his friend was getting excited about this world too soon. After all, they'd only seen a tiny part of it. They couldn't tell yet whether the soil was suitable for growing plant species from Earth, or whether the fruit on the trees was edible and the water drinkable.

"I'm sure we'll find more animals here. Maybe there

are also animals similar to cows or pigs. Something we can eat. I would so love to eat a steak again."

Russell grinned. He had nothing against that idea, either. "Maybe this guy here would taste good barbecued."

Holbrook looked at him sharply, grinned, and carried on stroking the horse creature. "Good boy! We won't be barbecuing you. You're much too sweet for that."

As if the animal had understood that they were talking about him in relation to food, he turned round suddenly and trotted off. Or perhaps he had just grown bored of the encounter.

"In any case, the animal wasn't afraid of us. And that suggests that there isn't much here that it has to be afraid of," said Holbrook.

"The artificial intelligence of the transporter seemed to suggest that there weren't any beasts of prey here. At least none that could endanger humans."

"Only here in the immediate surroundings or on the entire planet? How could it even know that?"

"No idea."

"I must say, I like it here. If the test results are positive, I'd say we've found a refuge."

Russell nodded. "At least until the flood is over. You don't want to pack up everything and move here?"

Holbrook looked at him and shrugged. "It would mean starting from scratch on a new planet and setting up a new colony." He hesitated. "On the other hand . . ."

"On the other hand what?"

"Well, in a way this planet is only three miles away from Eridu. All we have to do is go to the transporter. An hour's journey and you're here. We could live on both planets at the same time."

Russell nodded. His friend was right. "Perhaps we made a big mistake."

"What do you mean?"

"After we moved to New California, we only used the transporter to destroy the other spheres in the galaxy. For fifteen years we forgot about it almost entirely."

"Suppressed it, I would say. I reckon we just didn't want to see the thing anymore, after so many people died using it."

Russell nodded. "You're right. We were constantly complaining that we didn't have any livestock, that we didn't have more choice of food. And all that time, all the other habitable planets in the galaxy were just a stone's throw away. We didn't even go to the transporter and communicate with it. But I think we just didn't want to have any more to do with it."

"I guess so."

"Only now that the colony is in serious danger are we turning back to the alien technology. You can't describe our behavior as particularly logical."

"What does it have to do with logic?" asked Holbrook.

"We destroyed the spheres in the solar system so that the people of Earth don't destroy themselves."

"Yeah, and? I don't get it."

"But we left the transporter lying around for our own kids. At some point, they or their descendants will also start to play around with the thing, even if it takes a few generations. If we'd followed our idea through to the end, we would have destroyed the transporter on New California, too."

Holbrook remained silent as they traipsed back to the transporter with their backpacks full of specimens.

"Well, for now, we can be glad. Escaping through the transporter might be our last chance."

Chapter 27

"You wanted to speak with me?" asked Marlene, after she had pulled closed the door to the lab.

The dismantled atomic bomb was still lying in the middle of the room. Ty had now taken it apart completely, and the two halves of the plutonium core lay in plastic bowls. The initiator lay in a little black container. Dr. Dressel stood beside them, red-faced.

"Yes," said Ty. "We have another suggestion for how we could close the pass."

Marlene listened attentively. Perhaps the men really had come up with a feasible idea. Then they wouldn't have to evacuate. "Have you found a way of repairing the bomb?"

Dr. Dressel shook his head. "No. They're both dead. The explosive has decomposed. In principle——"

Ty interrupted him: "But would it be possible to take the cores of both bombs and construct a new one out of them?" He grinned, as if awaiting applause.

Marlene looked back and forth between the physicist and the weapons expert and raised her eyebrows. "Gentlemen, what am I to make of this? First you say the bombs don't work anymore because important components no longer work, and now you're saying you want to build a new bomb? I think you need to give me a little more information before I can respond."

Ty's grin faded and after a moment he nodded. "Of course we can't build a bomb that works in the usual way, in other words, one that's detonated with an explosive, because we don't have a suitable explosive. And even if we did, we wouldn't be able to position it around the core with the necessary precision to produce a symmetrical shock-wave for the detonation. So I thought that we could initiate the chain reaction the same way it's done with uranium bombs, by fusing two subcritical masses into a critical one." With a gloved hand, he took out one half of the bomb core and laid it on the other, so that they formed a silver egg. "The plutonium of the bomb is sub-critical in this form, until it's turned into the right form by the detonation of the explosive mass."

Marlene nodded. "We knew that already. Continue!"

"Together with the other atomic bomb over in the warehouse, we have two sub-critical cores. We'll build a device that lets the two bomb cores slam into each other fast enough to create a supercritical mass."

"Without an explosive?" asked Marlene. She had difficulty imagining this.

"Exactly!" said Ty. "We'll take a tube, around thirty feet long, put the plutonium from the first bomb at the bottom and drop the other plutonium from the top. When the mass from the top hits the one at the bottom, we'll have our atomic explosion!"

He grinned again, as if he'd just discovered the cure for cancer.

Marlene shook her head. "That simple? We let one

mass drop onto the other and that'll result in a nuclear explosion? Didn't you say the other day that it wasn't that simple?"

Dr. Dressel shook his head. "That's just the basic principle. It's far more complicated in practice. The two subcritical plutonium masses not only have to fuse quickly, they also have to stay together long enough for fission to occur. The height of the fall has to be calculated precisely and I doubt whether thirty feet will be sufficient. We could add some of our remaining C-4 and make a canon, like with a uranium bomb. That way we could make a rudimentary bomb that would be considerably less efficient, but ought to do the job."

"You keep talking about a uranium bomb. But these are plutonium cores. Doesn't it make a difference?"

Dr. Dressel shook his head again. "Normally yes, but in this case we're lucky." He nodded to Ty. "Show her!"

Ty reached for a yellow box and took out a thick rod connected to a device with a black cable. He pointed the measuring instrument at the bomb core lying in front of him and looked at Marlene. "This is a neutron counter. Do you notice anything?" he asked with a grin.

Marlene felt anger welling up inside her. Ty had no idea how much he got on other people's nerves with his excessive posturing. "Talk!"

"It's not ticking," he said triumphantly. "No neutrons."

"So?"

Ty looked at her like she hadn't understood the punch line of a joke.

Dr. Dressel shook his head and Marlene wondered whether he was doing it because of Ty's behavior or because he thought she was being dense. "Normally plutonium emits far more neutrons than uranium. That's why plutonium bombs work according to the implosion method and not the gun-type method. The chain reaction would occur too early, because weapon-grade plutonium 239 is usually contaminated with plutonium 240, which is a strong neutron emitter." He pointed at the bomb core. "This bomb core doesn't appear to be contaminated with Pu-240. They must have found a new production method."

Marlene had difficulty following the conversation. She had to trust that the men knew what they were talking about. "And that means . . .?"

"That means we can detonate this plutonium bomb in the same way you would detonate a simple uranium bomb."

Marlene didn't know what to make of this information. "What do you mean with 'simple'?" What will it involve? How long will it take? And above all: what are the chances that your improvised atomic bomb will work?"

Ty hesitated. "Unfortunately, there's a lot to do. We have to drill a deep hole in the canyon in order to install the device inside it. Because it isn't a bomb in the conventional sense, but more of an apparatus with the dimensions of a building. The shape of the plutonium core has to be changed. We have to melt it and combine both bomb cores into a hemispherical shape. That's not so easy, because we can't do it in an oxygen atmosphere, as it would catch fire. But we have the necessary equipment. Then we have to carry out a few tests to work out the necessary speed of the falling plutonium half. Then we'll know if we need to also create a booster out of C-4, which would make it all more complicated."

How much time did the men think they had left? In a few days, the colony might be overrun by those damn monsters. "Anything else?" she asked sharply.

Ty nodded. "The initiator needs to be adapted. With this method it won't be compressed enough to mix the beryllium with the polonium. But I have an idea of how it could work."

Marlene sighed. "All I'm hearing is 'could', 'would, 'might'. How long will it take?"

Ty swayed his head from side to side. "Good question. We might encounter some problems that we haven't thought of. Five days, maybe?" He looked at Dressel.

Dr. Dressel shook his head again. "I would say a week, if all goes well."

Marlene laughed. "We don't even know if we have two days left before the beasts overrun the post. What are the chances that your plan will work?"

Ty looked at his feet. "Fifty percent, maybe?"

"At most!" added Dr. Dressel.

Marlene whistled through her teeth. And that was supposed to be a serious suggestion? She looked at the men in turn. "Gentlemen, we find ourselves in a life-threatening situation. In a few days, perhaps in a few hours, hundreds of thousands, perhaps millions of starving beasts will storm our settlement, and we won't stand even a chance of defending ourselves. If we don't find a failsafe solution we will all die. And you two want to start your private Manhattan project, which might take weeks and which doesn't have a great chance of success." She looked at the two men angrily. Then she turned on her heel and marched out.

"What should we do now?" asked Ty.

"Nothing!" called Marlene and slammed the door shut behind her.

Chapter 28

"It's not looking good," said Jenny. "It's not looking good at all!"

Marlene and Jenny were sitting at a long table in the mess room together with Russell, Dr. Cashmore, and Ben. The biologist had asked to have a meeting and Marlene had rounded up the team. Jenny projected an image onto the wall using her computer—one of the few that still worked—and the last projector they still had. In the early days they had used the projector for movie evenings, but after the penultimate bulb had broken ten years ago, they had stopped using it for recreational purposes.

Russell tried to interpret the image. The background was black. A white outline presumably indicated the boundary of the lowlands. A blue point far in the south marked the observation post and the beginning of the pass. Green, yellow, and red structures were dotted around the lowlands. They looked like bubbles in a bubble bath. In the north-east they merged into a thick, scarlet stripe. Almost like a work of art, thought Russell.

Jenny stood up, took a stick and pointed at the scarlet area. Above it everything was black.

"These pictures were taken with our drone and infrared optics. The red area is the main wave of animals running away from the flood. Black indicates the extent of the flooding, which is gradually moving inland. It's black because there's nothing living there anymore."

Marlene nodded. "Of course. And the bubbles below it?"

"That's the most interesting part. At the edges of these bubbles large number of animals are gathered. I presume they indicate the boundaries between different hunting grounds. That's where fighting is taking place."

Marlene gave Russell a sideways glance. The area was no more than twenty miles from the observation post, he thought. Marlene turned back to the biologist. "We reckoned with that. What's new about it?"

Jenny pointed the stick at the red line. "Two things are new. One is that we can now roughly work out when the main wave of animals will reach the observation post. That will happen in six to seven days. Meaning shortly before the flood. Originally, I thought that it would happen earlier—particularly after the expedition to the oil springs where we saw how aggressive and panicked the animals were. But there's less pressure on the wotan territory than we thought, and that gives us the chance of holding out for longer. Still, we need to reckon with massive attacks on the post every time a territory collapses."

Russell wasn't sure what to make of Jenny's presentation. On the one hand, the biologist was telling them that they had more time than they had expected; on the other hand, she was suggesting that the observation post was already in danger. It was hard to know what to make of this information. It just looked prettier with the colored areas on the map.

"Good. Thanks, Jenny," said Marlene. "What's next on the agenda. Oh yes, Russell. Did you find a planet that we could possibly escape to?"

Russell nodded. "Yes, it looks good. The environment is pleasant and there are even animals there that don't immediately attack, like here on New California. But I can't say if the soil is fertile or if the fruit we found is edible." He looked at the chemist.

Cashmore cleared his throat. "I've analyzed the specimens that Russell and Christian brought back. The atmosphere is clean and the soil contains all the nutrients necessary for growing plants, although of course I can't guarantee whether the climatic conditions are ideal. The fruits are edible. Interestingly, they even contain pro vitamins, which our bodies can utilize. The trace elements that we require are also all contained in the fruit. However, they lack any kind of protein. If we think about evacuating to this planet, we will need to take foods like soya and potatoes with us."

"The soya is almost all gone, but we still have a lot of potatoes," said Marlene.

"It could also be that the animals on the planet are good sources of protein." The chemist looked at Russell reproachfully. "It's a shame that you didn't bring me a specimen of the horse-like animal with you."

"What were we supposed to do?"

"Well, shoot it and bring it with you. At least a piece of it. With all due respect to Holbrook's love of animals, but this is extremely important! If we have to evacuate in such a short space of time, it is vital to know what resources we have there."

"So we could live on this planet?"

Cashmore tilted his head to one side. "Well, I didn't find anything in the specimens that speak against it. But to make a decision like that based on one single visit would be very risky."

"Ultimately we don't have a choice. We can't stay here," said Marlene. She turned to Ben. "How long do we need for the evacuation?"

Ben pulled some papers out of a folder. "I worked out a schedule. I based it on the assumption that I would have half of the colony available as a workforce, while the other half would be defending the post." He looked at Marlene. It hadn't escaped Russell's notice that Ben hated having to have his plans approved by Marlene. For somebody who always demanded obedience, he had an alarming problem with authority.

"Yes, good. Continue!"

"I sorted the work according to priority. The most important thing is a basic supply of food, weapons, tents, medical supplies and equipment. That could be done in a day, if I can get three jeeps for the job. On the second day we'll start dismantling the lab containers and other infrastructure. And we'll take apart one jeep that we'll take with us to the other planet. At the same time, we'll transport other supplies such as benzine and kerosene as well as weapons, so that on the fourth day our whole camp is there. Finally, the other jeeps and the weapons that we still have here for defending the observation post. The evacuation will take a week."

"A week!" groaned Marlene. "That's very tight."

"And we need more information about the target planet. We need to find out more about the plants and animals and check out the wider area around the transporter," said Jenny.

"Alright," answered Marlene. "You and Cashmore will

go tomorrow with the first evacuation team. Russell will accompany you. I can't spare any more people. Ben, you take over command of the observation post. One of the civilians can lead the evacuation mission." She thought for a moment. "I'll ask Sammy: he's already mastered quite a few logistical challenges."

Ben nodded. He was visibly relieved to be freed from this task.

"Shouldn't we wait for the research results before we begin the evacuation?" asked the chemist.

"We don't have any time for that, unfortunately," said Marlene. "The countdown has begun. We have one week left—if we're lucky."

Chapter 29

"What are you doing?"

Drew had just started to pack her backpack when Ben appeared behind her. She winced at the sound of his voice. She had thought he was already on his way down to the observation post in the valley. Perhaps he had forgotten something.

She stood up and turned to face her husband. "Russell has asked me to accompany him on the reconnaissance mission to the other planet," she mumbled with a lowered head. "He reckons it wouldn't be a bad thing to find out something about the geology there."

"Russell . . ." Ben nodded slowly. "Is that so?"

"Yes, I'm sure I could find out where the ground-water level—"

Ben made a lightning-fast movement and his hand was on her throat. Drew gagged. She couldn't get any air. "Ben, please . . ." she croaked.

"Are you fucking with me? You were waiting for me to disappear, and now you're plotting against me with that motherfucker behind my back?"

"Ben, please . . ."

He squeezed a little harder until she saw stars in front of her eyes. Her feet dragged across the floor until she felt the wall against her back. She tried to get out of Ben's grip but didn't stand a chance. She was close to losing consciousness when he finally let go. She dropped to her knees and retched.

"I'll teach you respect! By God, if you ever try to go behind my back again, you'll see my true colors!" he said in an icy tone of voice.

What did I do? I just wanted to help!

Drew sobbed. "I'm sorry. You've got so much going on. I didn't want to upset you."

"Well you've managed to do just that!" He left her lying on the ground and turned around. He rummaged around in the cupboard and took out a night vision device. As Drew began to pick herself up, he turned to face her again. "I want you to stay here and not move from the spot until I come back."

"But I already said I'd go," cried Drew in despair.

Benn stepped closer. His eyes glinted and he raised his right hand. "What did you say?"

Go to hell, Ben! Who gave you the right to treat me like a slave?

This brief flash of defiance disappeared as quickly as it had come. She didn't stand a chance, anyway. He would grab her and strangle her again until she said what he wanted to hear.

Drew looked at the floor. "Nothing."

"What will you do?"

She sobbed. "I'll stay here."

Ben nodded. "That was the right answer. I'll talk to Russell myself. And I want to—"

"What's going on?"

Catherine had appeared in the doorway unnoticed.

"Leave us, it's none of your business!" hissed Ben.

"Why can't you leave Mom alone?"

"Ask your mom! If nobody around here has any respect anymore, I'll just have to demand it."

"You won't get any respect by shouting. All you're doing is making Mom afraid of you."

"Good. That will stop her from doing any more stupid things." Ben looked at the backpack that his daughter was carrying. "And where do you think you're going?"

"I'm going to Jim's. We're helping Sammy to load the supplies into the sphere."

"Didn't I tell you that you should stay away from Jim Harris?"

She put her hands on her hips. "I'm eighteen! I can decide for myself who I spend my time with!"

Ben pointed an accusatory finger at her. "As long as you live under my roof you'll do what I say, young lady!"

Cathy snorted. "Then it's about time I left your house. It isn't a home anymore, anyway. Take a look at yourself. Do you think your regime of terror makes it fun for anyone to live with you?"

"Watch what you say, or you'll be sorry."

"If you ever dare to hit me, you'll never see me in this house again!"

Ben turned around to Drew. "It's all your fault. See how you brought up your daughter? It's all your fault."

He picked up the night vision device and stormed out of the house.

Cathy ran over to her mother and took her in her arms.

"I'm sorry. It *is* my fault," sobbed Drew.

"No it's not," said Catherine and stroked her hair. "It's not your fault. It's his fault. He shouldn't treat you like that."

"I just can't seem to do right by him."

"That's not your job," whispered Cathy. "If he can't stand himself, that's his problem. I don't understand how you can stick it out with him."

Drew was silent.

"If I were you, I'd think about leaving him."

Drew wiped the tears out of her face with her sleeve. She'd thought about it herself from time to time. But she also knew that she didn't have the strength to do it.

Chapter 30

"What's with the rice?" Sammy Yang, small and slightly overweight, stared at Russell through the thick lenses of his glasses.

Russell kneeled on the driver's seat and fished around for the checklist that was on the truck bed. "Twenty sacks. That's all that we had left in storage."

Yang nodded. The lab assistant looked younger than his forty years, and was one of the youngest of the first generation of settlers. He had come to New California at age twenty, had spent half his life here and settled in surprisingly quickly. Right from the start, he had helped Marlene to plan and expand the colony and had proven to have a real talent for logistics. Yang was also very popular in the colony, and many people believed he would be voted President at the next election if Marlene didn't run again.

"Good," said Sammy. "Then the first load is complete. The other vehicles are ready too. Let's get going." There was a loud crash behind them, and Sammy turned around sharply. "Robert! You have to secure the pallets better. If the planks break, we'll have problems building up the new camp."

"Sorry!" called the young Cashmore. He jumped down from the truck bed of his vehicle and heaved the parts that had fallen down back into the vehicle. Carrie Phillips helped him.

Sammy shook his head. "Nineteen years old and a head full of shit."

Russell grinned. "Were you any different?"

"I guess not. Okay, let's get going to the sphere. Has the planet we're visiting got a name already?"

"Not an official one. Christian referred to it several times yesterday as Asylum."

Sammy shrugged. "Kinda fitting. In any case, we'll set up the depot and the first tents. That'll take about five hours and require several transports, because we won't be able to fit everything in the sphere. I suggest you go first so that you have some time for your reconnaissance."

Russell nodded. "Good plan. Jenny and Cashmore are already on the way to the transporter by foot. I'm actually still waiting for Drew. She wanted to come with me to get an idea of the geology of Asylum." He looked around. "I don't know what's keeping her. She should have been here ages ago!"

Sammy looked up briefly from his checklist. "Perhaps he can tell you where she is."

Russell looked around, confused. "Who?"

"Harris!"

Russell turned around and saw Ben trudging toward them. He was wearing a threadbare, beige army uniform, and a heavy olive-green backpack. He had shouldered his automatic rifle. His stony face didn't bode well.

"Hi, Ben. Everything okay?" Russell jumped out of the driver's seat and walked over to him.

Ben stopped an arm's length from Russel. "Two things, Harris! Now listen up!"

Russell gave him a puzzled look. *What's this about?*

"First: If you want something from my wife, you come to me first. Got that?"

Russell blinked. "I only asked her if she wanted to accompany us on our expedition. We could do with a bit of data about the geology of Asylum and it isn't dangerous at all."

"I don't give a damn! Next time you come to me, got it?"

Russell could see that Ben was simmering with rage. His face was red and his nostrils were quivering. Russell raised his hands conciliatorily. "Calm down, Ben. It's okay!"

"Second: Tell your wayward son to keep his hands off my daughter!"

This is getting better all the time! It hadn't escaped Russell's notice that something was going on between Jim and Cathy Hawke. He wasn't bothered by it and surely Ben must also be able to see that they were both adults and could decide for themselves who they started seeing.

"Now listen, Ben, I . . ."

"I don't give a shit what you have to say on the matter. I want your son to stay away from my daughter!"

Sammy acted as if he were busy with the checklist, but his shocked face revealed what he actually thinking.

"I will not dictate to my son who he can and cannot see," said Russell. "And if I get to hear that you've been pressuring him, don't expect me to take it lying down!"

"Are you threatening me, Harris?" Ben's voice trembled, he clenched his fists.

"I'm not going to let you treat me like this, Ben! If you can't stand me, that's fine. I can live with that. But don't start making other people suffer because of it. Your wife and your daughter are both adults and perfectly capable of making their own decisions. Leave them alone!"

Ben pursed his lips, his face was twisted with anger. For several long seconds the men confronted one another. Ben's facial muscles twitched. Russell's glance fell on Ben's weapon.

He wouldn't hesitate to shoot me if he had the chance!

Suddenly the former lieutenant grinned. "You know what I'm looking forward to, Harris?"

Russell was silent.

"In a few weeks' time, you'll be lying in bed gasping for air, while your cancer eats up your lungs bit by bit. In the end you'll suffocate to death after you've wasted away to a skeleton," Ben hissed. "While your family stands beside your deathbed crying their eyes out, I'll be standing next to them laughing. And you know why, Harris? Because you'll finally be getting what you deserve!"

Ben turned on his heels and marched off.

Russell stared after him, stunned. He'd had to take a lot from Ben over all their years on New California. But for him to outright wish him a horrible death came as a shock. Ben would never forgive him for preventing a return to Earth. Not until one of them was dead.

Sammy lowered his checklist. He was open-mouthed. "My God. I knew that Ben didn't like you, but I didn't realize that he actually *hated* you!"

After a few long seconds, Russell shook his head vigorously as if he wanted to free himself of the words that had been flung at him. Then he climbed into the driver's seat of the jeep. "Let's go," he said quietly.

During the drive, Sammy made several attempts at starting a conversation, but Russell just sat brooding behind the wheel. After twenty minutes on the bumpy track, they reached the transporter.

Dr. Cashmore and Jenny were sitting on the grass in front of the sphere. With them were several second-generation colonists, including Eric Grant, Anthony Neaman, and Edward Grazier.

Sammy jumped out of the vehicle and began divvying up the work. "Robert! Unload the pieces of the containers and lay them out in front of the transporter. Neatly please! Maxwell, you can help me get the supplies from the jeep!"

"Where do you need them?" asked the tall blond boy. The son of Dr. Lindwall was too thin for his height and his gangly limbs made Russell think of a puppet.

"Put them in front of the transporter. Cover the stuff with a plastic sheet so that the sacks stay dry, in case it rains." He turned round to Jack Neaman. "After everything's been unloaded, drive back and get the next load. And don't mess around! All clear?"

"All clear," said Jack.

"Great. I'll go first with Russell, Jenny, and Cashmore to get an idea of the planet and decide where we'll set up the camp. Carrie, you come with us!"

The seventeen-year-old with the cropped hair nodded.

Sammy turned round to Russell. "Shall we?"

Russell took his rucksack out of the jeep and hurried over to the transporter. He laid a hand on the black shell and stepped inside. Something was bugging him, but he couldn't work out what it was, and then he was distracted by Sammy, who came in behind him.

"Can you write down the code for the target planet for me somewhere?"

Russell nodded and took a piece of paper out of the chest pocket of his combat uniform. "I almost forgot. I've got the code here." He gave Yang the piece of paper with the alien signs, and Yang put it in his pocket. Then they went up the steps they had installed the day before. With the next load, they would take along some more steps to replace the retractable ladder in the target sphere.

Russell opened the inner sphere.

"We could take along a first load of supplies," suggested Jenny Baldwin.

Sammy shook his head. "No, I want to check out the place first and then I can think about the order in which we'll take the stuff over."

Dr. Cashmore closed the wall of the sphere behind him.

"I'm scared," said Carrie.

Russell turned to her. As he looked into her anxious face, he realized that nobody from the second generation had ever been transported. Since the trip to Mars fifteen years ago, the transporter had been taboo. The children knew about the trips in the transporter only from their parents. Of course the youngsters knew about the sphere, which was located not far away from the colony in the woods, but nobody had expressed a desire to be transported. Most of them were scared of it, and some of them had even been afraid of entering it on the annual school trip to visit it. One exception had been young Cookie Shanker, who one day had declared to his friends that he intended to take a trip in the transporter the following night. Luckily the adults had got wind of his plan. In a hurry they had gathered together all the children and shown them horrible photos of the victims of the first transport attempts. The photo of O'Brien disintegrated by the sulfuric atmosphere had had a shattering effect. Obviously the images were still fresh in Carrie's mind.

"You don't need to be afraid. We know the target planet and there are no dangers there."

"Will the transport hurt?" asked Carrie.

Russell laughed quietly. "No. You won't even notice that anything is happening. Perhaps a slight jolt. Like in an elevator."

"What's an elevator?"

"Oh, of course. Well, let's just say, you won't notice anything!"

Carrie nodded slowly. Russell smiled at her again and stepped over to the console. He stuck out a finger to set the code of the target planet.

What the hell . . .?

He blinked in irritation.

"What is it?" asked Dr. Cashmore and came up beside him.

Russell pointed at the black surface. "It's not showing the code. Usually you can see the code of this sphere. Now there's nothing!" Carefully, Russell tapped on the field, but nothing happened. "It's not reacting at all!" He tried with more force—but again without success. "I'll try to make mental contact with the intelligence of the sphere."

As he spoke the words, he suddenly realized what had irritated him when he entered the sphere. He hadn't felt any pressure in his head, like he usually did. He closed his eyes and focused, but he could feel immediately that it wouldn't work. He had always concentrated on the dull pressure in his head, which eventually established the tele-pathic communication. What should he do now?

Can you hear me?

No answer. There was nothing from which he could form an answer.

Can you hear me?

It was pointless.

Russell opened his eyes. "Nothing!" He shook his head numbly. "The sphere is dead!"

Jenny looked at him with big eyes. "I thought these things have existed for millions of years. They can't just give up the ghost overnight."

Russell raised his arms. "Yesterday it all worked perfectly—the transporter and the communication with the sphere. I just don't get it."

"Maybe the thing just needs to be charged," said Carrie.

"No, that would contradict all the experience we've ever had with the transporter!"

"What can we do?" asked Dr. Cashmore in a hoarse voice.

Russell stared at him. He felt numb.

"Nothing!" He blinked. "Absolutely nothing!"

"The thing is dead," said Sammy bitterly. "And I have a feeling it's going to stay dead."

Russell bit his lips. "The transporter is our only chance of escape."

"We could still flee into the mountains," said Jenny, despairingly.

"We don't have enough to eat for everyone. We'll die in the mountains," said Dr. Cashmore.

"Well then I guess that's that," whispered Russell. "We're dead!"

Chapter 31

Drew was sitting in Marlene's office when Ty Grazier came strolling in. He blinked in surprise. "Where's Marlene?" he asked.

"She's gone home to get some rest. You'll have to come back later," she said flatly. The fight with Ben had rattled her. She had spent the whole morning lying in bed crying, before finally pulling herself together and coming here. Her laptop had broken some time ago and Marlene had offered her use of her computer to do some calculations. Drew was still feeling wretched and was finding it hard to concentrate.

"Doesn't matter. Wasn't that important, anyway," said Ty with a dismissive wave of his hand. He hesitated. "Is everything okay? You look pretty under the weather."

She avoided looking him in the eyes. "It's nothing, I'm okay." But as she spoke, tears welled up in her eyes.

Ty walked up to her tentatively and pulled up a stool. "It doesn't look that way." He took her hand.

Drew was about to pull it away, but the gentle touch felt good.

"Ben?" whispered Ty.

She wanted to shake her head, but didn't have any strength left to lie. She nodded slowly.

"Honestly—why do you put up with it?"

"You don't even know why we argued," she said with a flash of defiance. What did it have to do with him?

"No, I don't know, and that's neither here nor there. Whatever it was, it's no reason for him to treat you badly all the time." He hesitated. "Or to hit you."

She looked up and had no idea how to respond. Did he suspect? Or did he know?

He looked at her intently. "The whole colony knows," he said quietly.

She started to sob. She could feel all the resistance inside her collapsing like a house of cards. "I'm always trying to do right by him, but it's never good enough. No matter what I do, he always finds a reason to quarrel."

Ty didn't speak. Drew had never spoken about her problems with a man before. She didn't know why she was doing it now, but it felt good and she had always liked Ty. It was true that he could be a bit full of himself, but he was always in a good mood. In the early days of the colony they had been good friends and he had always made her laugh. Then he had got together with Ann, which had caused her a stab of jealousy, despite the fact that she was together with Ben. Their friendship had petered out, but if there was anyone in the colony with whom she could speak openly, it was Ty. The dam had broken and it all came gushing out like a waterfall.

"Ben was always short-tempered when something didn't go his way. I knew that when we got together, but he also always gave me a feeling of security, especially after we were stuck on this planet. When the children were born, he was a really good dad, and for a long time I thought I'd made a good catch. But for the last few years, I simply haven't been able to do anything right. Cathy became rebellious when she hit puberty, and he blamed me for encouraging her, which simply wasn't true. She has a strong character, that's all, and I can't do anything to change it."

Ty moved closer to her pulled her head to his shoulder. His warmth felt good.

"It's not your fault," whispered Ty. "Stop blaming yourself. He simply has no right to abuse you and it isn't your duty to put up with it!" He was silent for a moment. "I knew a woman once. An incredibly pretty woman who I fell in love with at first sight. She was full of joy and saw only the good in other people. She loved her work and above all she knew what she wanted from life."

He looked deep into her eyes. Drew was a little surprised by his frankness, but she had guessed at the time that he had wanted more than a platonic relationship. But it had never turned into more, not least because at the time she hadn't wanted to jeopardize her relationship with Ben.

"I haven't seen that woman for a long time," whispered Ty. "I would love to see her laugh again."

For a long while she said nothing and just looked into his big, blue eyes. "Why didn't you say anything back then?" she said at last in a husky voice.

He shrugged and smiled uncertainly. "I never had the guts—and you were already taken."

His face was nearly touching hers. Drew pulled back. Ben would kill her! On the other hand . . . It had been such a long time since anybody had made her feel desirable. She briefly felt an impulse to ask Ty how his wife was doing, but then all resistance melted away and their lips met.

Chapter 32

"Thirteen wotans! They're starting to approach the observation post," whispered Ernie Lawrence, without looking up from his night vision device."

Eliot, who was sitting beside him on the floor of the lookout polishing his weapon, stood up and leaned over the railing. "I can see them. The light from that crazy moon is bright enough. Thousand-five-hundred feet away. Shall I raise the alarm?"

"No. Let's wait and see what they're up to."

"Jesus Christ, it almost looks as if they were running in formation."

Ernie nodded. "Yes, a V formation. The leader's at the front. The others are following at a distance of six feet behind and the same distance to the side." He switched the device into infrared mode and zoomed in. Red flickering shapes against a black background. It made the animals look positively demonic. As if Satan himself had sent out his hounds of hell to attack them. Ernie adjusted the focus. "There are more of them on the edge of the forest. But they're not moving. It looks as if they're watching the vanguard advance."

"Maybe those beasts are more intelligent than we thought."

"We don't really know anything about them, except that they could be the death of us. But we know even less about the other monsters. In any case, I prefer wotans to snipers. Another six-hundred feet to the first barrier!"

"What should we do?" Eliot balanced his weapon on the railing and got it in position.

"We'll wait."

"It doesn't look like an attack. Jesus, what are they planning?

Ernie was silent.

"Should I ring the alarm bell?"

"We'll wait," said Ernie sharply.

"Damn, I hope you know what you're doing!"

"Three hundred feet." Ernie put the night vision device to one side and picked up his own weapon from the floor. "You take the leader at the front."

"I'm already aiming at him."

"Good, I'll take care of the ones behind. But only shoot when I say."

Ernie watched as the first wotan stopped in front of the barbed wire, which blocked the pass about three hundred feet from where they stood. They had secured the terrain in between with landmines. The other wotans also stopped without changing their formation. The leader of the pack paced back and forth. It looked as if it were sniffing the metal—but since wotans didn't have a head, and nobody knew for sure where their olfactory organ was, they couldn't be sure. Jenny's theory was that lots of sensory receptors were spread out over their brown, leathery skin.

The monster took another step toward the wire, until it made contact with its skin. The metal dissolved with a hissing sound.

"They want to get through the wire," said Ernie quietly. "Okay, let's get him!"

Eliot fired. The wotan fell to the ground and stopped moving. At the same time, the others turned around and ran back toward the forest at lightning speed.

"Let's kill'em!" cried Ernie.

"Why? They're running away anyway."

"Do it!" Ernie fired, followed by Eliot. Within moments, several wotans lay dead in the grass. But they didn't get them all. At least five of them made it to the forest and disappeared.

"Fuck!" Ernie cursed.

"What is it? What's the problem?"

Ernie laid his weapon on the floor and reached out again for the night vision device. "I reckon they were checking out the observation post. I wish they hadn't made it back to the forest."

"Do you mean they're going to get reinforcement?"

Ernie shrugged. "I don't know. But I bet you they have some kind of plan."

Linda came clambering up the ladder. "Everything okay?" She sounded drowsy.

"We got a visit from a few wotans," said Eliot. "But we chased them away."

"They'll be back," said Ernie sharply. "And then there'll be more of them. Many more. How late is it?"

"About another hour till sunrise," said Linda.

"We'll wait till then. But then I want to talk to Marlene. Something's going on here. I didn't like the look of that foray one bit."

"But we've been attacked often enough!" said Eliot.

"That wasn't an attack. I don't know what it was, but something is definitely brewing."

Chapter 33

"Where is he?" asked Russell. He felt totally beat, and didn't want to wait any longer. "Do I have to come too?"

"I would prefer it if you did," replied Marlene. She was about to say something else when there was a knock at the door and Ty finally entered the meeting room.

"Sit down!" said Marlene. The sun had not gone up yet, and only a pale blue stripe on the horizon gave an indication that dawn was approaching.

After they had given up hope of escaping with the transporter, they had spent the whole night talking. Russell looked in the mirror on the wall. There were dark rings around his eyes, caused partly by tiredness and partly by his illness. Ben didn't look much better: he had spent the whole of the previous day at the observation post and had only got back to Eridu around midnight, when he had immediately joined the urgent meeting in Marlene's office. Russell noticed with amazement that he acted as if nothing had happened between them. In fact, he was almost friendly toward him. The three of them had discussed every remaining option. There weren't many, and none of them guaranteed the colony's survival.

Ty sat down next to John Dressel, who had reached the barrack a few minutes earlier. The physicist was unshaven and his hair stuck out in all directions. Russell leaned against the wooden wall. He was afraid of falling straight to sleep if he sat down on a chair. What he wouldn't have done for a cup of coffee! But their supplies had been used up over ten years ago.

Marlene sat down at the table opposite Ben and stared at Ty from beneath her drooping eyelids.

"You made a suggestion to me two days ago."

Ty nodded.

Marlene leaned forward. "Do you still think it's possible?"

Ty and Dressel glanced at each other. "Yes, I still think that we could build a new bomb," confirmed Ty.

Marlene nodded. "Good. Start straight away. You have four days, no more. You'll get everything you need. Take as many men and women as you need."

Ty blinked. "Why the sudden change of heart?"

Russell stepped forward. "The plans for the evacuation have gone to dust. The transporter is dead."

Dr. Dressel opened his eyes wide. "The transporter's dead? How . . ."

"We don't know," said Marlene. "The control panel isn't reacting, and neither is the sphere's artificial intelligence. Something has paralyzed it."

"A defect?" asked the physicist.

"We don't know."

"Shall I take a look at the transporter?"

"Would you be able to fix it?" Marlene snapped.

The physicist was silent. Russell remembered his own dismay when he had realized that that the transporter was dead. Ever since, he had desperately been trying to think of an alternative plan, but he had come up with nothing. If the plan they had hatched last night failed, they were screwed.

"You and Ty get to work on the bomb—that's all I want you to do. The situation is critical. Activity has been reported down at the post. We don't know how much time we have left until those monsters beat a path to our door. You won't sleep or rest until the job is done. If necessary, get Doc Lindwall to prescribe you some stimulants. Our survival is at stake here. Your construction is our last hope. If you fail, we all die. Have you got that?"

Ty and John exchanged brief glances and nodded in unison.

"Good! We'll check on a daily basis if the transporter is working again, but I presume that once the thing is dead, it's dead." Marlene turned to Ben and Russell. "You get a few hours' sleep so that you can think clearly again. Ben, you have supreme command of the observation post. Think about what we could do to improve our defenses. We have to survive the first wave, at least."

Hawke nodded.

"Russell, you're going to rest for a while!"

Rest? Of course, he was dead beat, but there was so much work to be done. The survival of the whole colony was at stake, and she wanted him to rest?

"But . . ."

"No buts! You look like shit. If you collapse, you won't be of any use to us at all. You'll oversee Ty and John's work and give me regular updates. I'll coordinate all the other work from here."

Russell nodded. Once again he was impressed by Marlene. She was a born leader, whether as a soldier or as the head of a civilian government. For as long as he had known her, she always put her own needs and opinions to one side. She never complained and she could work until she dropped. Plus she understood how people ticked and what they were capable of. She knew exactly what each and every person under her command could achieve. She drove people to their limits, but never beyond.

Russell had known many people with leadership qualities, but most of them had made irrational decisions under pressure. Not Marlene. Even in this seemingly hopeless situation, she quickly but carefully weighed every possible option and selected the most viable one. In his whole life, he had only met one other person who was just as effective: General Morrow. Russell suddenly wondered what had become of his former superior. He would have certainly taken the blame for the loss of the transporter on Earth. Having already fallen out of favor over another incident, the disaster with the sphere would have guaranteed the end of his career. Morrow had been almost sixty. He had probably died years ago. Now Russell would never find out.

"Perhaps you should also hit the sack," he said to Marlene.

She smiled at him weakly. "Later. First I have to talk to some people who can help with the new project. If you want to do me one more favor, please wake up Lee Shanker and Dr. Cashmore and send them over here. I'd like to talk to both of them as soon as possible."

Chapter 34

"Four, three, two, one, detonate!" shouted Lee, and turned the lever on the remote control.

The blast was so loud that Russell thought his eardrums had burst. The ground shook, and stones, rubble, and dirt flew out of the tunnel entrance. They were immediately enveloped in a cloud of brown dust and Russell had to sneeze.

"That was stronger than planned," said Sammy. "It would have worked with a little less explosive."

Lee just grunted. Once the cloud of dust had settled he stepped forward. The road below the tunnel entrance was covered with rubble. Lee called Max Dressel and some of the other second-generation helpers. They began to clear away the debris.

Lee, Sammy, and Russell walked to the foot of the scaffold and climbed up the steps until they were standing in front of the tunnel entrance, which still had grey dust pouring out of it.

Sammy coughed. "Let's wait a few more minutes until the smoke has dispersed."

Lee nodded and rifled through some papers.

"And what was the point of that explosion?" asked Russell.

It was already late afternoon and the canyon walls cast dark shadows across the floor. Russell had slept the whole morning, and felt better after he woke up. Despite all of Ellen's protests, he had taken two of Dr. Lindwall's tablets and driven to the construction site with Sammy. He wanted to get an idea of the situation and see if he could help out in any way. But the men and women at the site were making good progress.

"We have to create a big cave in the tunnel to set up the drilling equipment," said Lee. He waved aside a cloud of smoke, turned on his flashlight, and stepped into the tunnel. Sammy and Russell followed him. The floor of the cave was covered in a fine layer of dust that immediately covered their boots. Russell coughed.

After about sixty feet, the tunnel opened out into a big cave about the size of their mess room. The ground was covered in pieces of rock and debris. They would have to carry the stuff out by hand.

"Looks okay," Lee grinned.

"Luckily. Our supply of C-4 is running out. We've only got four pounds left, and Ty and John need that to detonate the bomb," said Sammy.

"I say we drill the hole right in the middle. Here!" said Lee and pointed at the spot. Sammy marked it with a wooden stick.

"And what's the hole for?" asked Russell.

Lee seemed to have a clear idea of how it all worked. "We'll drill a hole here with a diameter of about six inches, and line it with a steel tube that Albert is finishing off in the workshop. Then we'll lower down half of the pluto-nium. For the detonation, we'll drop the other half of the plutonium from the top, and on top of that a metal mass and a charge of C-4, which will be detonated shortly before the moment of impact. The speed of the fall and the force of the exploding charge will combine the two plutonium halves into a super-critical mass," he explained. He paused for a moment. "At least that's how I understood it."

Ann Penwill entered the cave. "Travis has just arrived with a jeep, he's got the drilling equipment on the back. Shall we bring it in?"

Lee shook his head. "No, we have to get rid of the rubble first. Please get Manuel Sargent and the other boys. They should start on it right away."

The former lab assistant disappeared back down the tunnel.

"How long will it take to drill the hole?" asked Russell. He still doubted if the plan was viable. Ty and his home-made atomic bomb? It would never work! But what other option did they have?

"We'll work through the night, and as long as no problems crop up we should be done by sunrise. In the morning, the workshop will deliver the steel pipe."

"Sounds like it's all going according to plan."

Lee laughed gruffly. "This is just standard stuff. Ty and John definitely have the bigger challenge. I wouldn't want to be playing around with plutonium." He laughed again. "And Ty even seems to find the whole thing fun."

Sammy nodded. "Yeah, he was talking about what the two remaining nuclear warheads could be used for years ago. I was there when he suggested to Marlene that we detonate one of them north of the crop fields in order to create an artificial lake for bathing. You should have seen her face!"

"A lake?" asked Russell in disbelief.

"In his defense, he was drunk as a skunk at the time."

"I reckon Ty is a pyromaniac in disguise," said Lee. "And what could be more appealing to a pyromaniac than a nuclear fire!"

"If he's successful, I don't care if he's out of his mind or not," said Russell. "Because if he doesn't succeed with his bomb, we're dead meat."

"I still think we should have escaped into the mountains," said Lee.

"We don't have enough supplies," said Sammy.

Lee shrugged and turned his attention back to his notebook.

Manuel Sargent and three other youths entered the cave.

"So shall we get rid of this stuff?" the wiry seventeen-year-old asked eagerly.

Russell said goodbye and headed back to the colony with Ann Penwill.

"Do you think we'll manage?"

Russell turned to face the petite woman who was steering the jeep dexterously through the twists and turns of the canyon. He wondered if she was interested in his honest opinion, or just wanted him to put her mind at rest. He decided on the former. "I wish I knew."

"Ty is sure he will," she said quietly. She and Ty had two children. Edward was Grace's age and Russell had often seen the two of them playing together.

"And what do you think?" he asked.

"I know Ty well. He throws himself into new projects full of optimism. The more complicated the better. But more than once he's come home subdued, and admitted that he was in over his head. The fact that he's now playing around with atomic bombs frightens me."

"Well, he's the only person who has any idea about this stuff."

Ann guffawed. "He doesn't actually have a clue. He may have read a few books on the subject, but that's about it."

Russell looked at her, dumbfounded. He couldn't believe what he was hearing. "Read some books? I thought he he'd studied nuclear weapons technology."

"Ha! That's what he wants you to believe! He's never had anything to do with atomic bombs. And I'm scared he'll get his fingers badly burnt in this experiment."

Russell swallowed. He knew that Ty wasn't a nuclear weapons expert, but that everything he knew was self-taught was hard to get his head around. At least he had Dressel helping him. But he also only had a basic under-standing of nuclear technology. He felt his pessimism turning into sheer despair.

"I guess he knows what he's doing," said Russell, trying to sound as convincing as possible. Without much success.

Ann didn't say anything for a long while. "I doubt it," she said quietly. "He always talks about what he wants to do and everything he'll take care of, and then nothing happens. That's one of the reasons we want to split up."

Russell was surprised. He had no idea about this—in a colony where rumors spread like wildfire.

"Are things that bad between you?"

Ann shrugged. "I don't know. I can't say it's going badly. It's just not going. Everything he says, everything he does—I just don't care anymore, and I think he feels the same about me."

"Maybe you've just grown apart."

"Could be. It's been like this for years. We've talked about it endlessly but nothing's changed. There's just nothing left to hold us together. The children are at an age where they'll understand, so we'll go our separate ways. If we survive this crisis that is."

They were nearing the settlement and Russell asked Ann to drop him off at the entrance to the physics lab. As he took his backpack from the back seat, she said: "But please still keep an eye on him."

Russell smiled and waved goodbye, and the jeep roared off toward the camp.

Russell took a deep breath and opened the door to the lab container without knocking. Ty and Dr. Dressel were standing in front of the lab's cupboard-shaped furnace, immersed in an animated discussion.

"I don't know enough to be able to judge," the physicist was saying crossly. "I think Cashmore should take a look at it first."

"That's really not necessary. I don't see why . . ."

"What's going on? What are you two arguing about?" asked Russell.

"Ty wants to melt down the plutonium of the first bomb to get it into the hemispherical shape that we need," said Dr. Dressel. "I've been saying that we need our chemist to look over it first."

Russell nodded and unclasped the radio attached to his belt. "Marlene, can you hear me?"

"What are you doing?" asked Ty. Russell cut him off with a wave of his hand.

"Marlene here, what's up?"

"Please send Dr. Cashmore to the physics lab."

"Will do."

Russell reattached the device to his belt and turned to Ty. "You're not dealing with gelatin here. If one of you is unsure of how something needs to be done, then choose the safest option, is that clear? And if one of you wants to involve someone else, then that's what will be done!"

Ty folded his arms in front of his chest. "I've taken all necessary precautions. I filled the oven with helium to prevent a fire breaking out. I've already scratched off the nickel using the glove box, and nothing happened. I also used tungsten for the mold, as it has a much higher melting point than plutonium."

"I believe that you've been careful—but surely it wouldn't harm to let someone with a better knowledge of chemistry to take a look," said John.

"It'll take ages, if . . ."

There was a knock at the door and Dr. Cashmore entered the container. "What's going on?"

"We want to be on the safe side and have you look over what we've done so far before we continue," explained Dressel.

Dr. Cashmore paused and looked at Ty and then John. Then he cleared his throat. "You weren't seriously planning to melt down the plutonium?"

"Of course we were," replied Ty. "We need to get it into a hemispherical shape. Why shouldn't we melt it?"

Dr. Cashmore walked up to the glass door of the oven. "You took all the plutonium out of a bomb and want to melt it down to one piece?" His voice sounded as if Ty had suggested repairing a computer chip with a crowbar.

"Won't it work?" asked Russell.

Cashmore sighed and shook his head. "No, it won't work. I thought you knew how to build a nuclear weapon."

Ty seemed to deflate. "I . . ." he stuttered. "What's the problem?"

"The different allotropes of the plutonium are the problem. Damn it! I should have been involved in the plans from the start!"

"Allotrope? What's that?" asked Russell. He'd never heard the term before. Yet again, he was coming across as the dunce.

"Plutonium comes in different forms, depending on the temperature. A bit like diamonds and graphite are two different forms of carbon. At room temperature, the gamma phase dominates, with a medium density. If you heat up the material, it mutates into a different phase. At higher temperatures, shortly before it melts, you reach the epsilon phase, which has a high density. That means that at five-hundred degrees Celsius, the stuff contracts abruptly." He looked at Ty sharply. "And what happens when a sub-critical mass of plutonium suddenly contracts?"

The weapons expert sunk his head. His face turned as red as a beetroot.

"You get a super-critical mass!" whispered Dr. Dressel.

"Exactly!"

"You mean, the plutonium would have exploded here?" asked Russell.

"No. But it would have turned into a pure nuclear reactor. In the end, the stuff would have evaporated and killed us all with the radiation!" said Dr. Dressel, visibly shaken.

"But we need to get it into a hemispherical shape," said Ty feebly.

Dr. Cashmore looked at him without blinking. "In the delta phase, plutonium is malleable. You heat it up very slowly to four-hundred degrees, then you can form it into the shape you need using the press. Four-hundred degrees and no higher! If you gradually increase the pressure in the press, the phase won't change."

Russell groaned. Ann's words about Ty echoed in his mind. He turned to Dr. Cashmore. "I want you to help them every step of the way! Nobody does anything if the other two aren't present. Is that clear?" He grasped Ty by the shoulder. "Is that clear?"

"Yes," said Ty, and looked at the ground.

Chapter 35

"I thought he knew what he was doing," said Marlene angrily.

Russell didn't reply and leaned back into the armchair. "I get the feeling he's trying to prove something to himself."

Marlene stood up and paced back and forth behind her desk. "I don't give a damn what his reason is. He's a bullshitter. I always thought he'd at least completed some kind of official training. Now I discover that nuclear weapons are just a hobby of his. An obsession, nothing more. If the beasts don't kill us, Ty will—by playing around with radioactive material in the middle of the colony!"

Russell could understand why Marlene was so angry. He had felt the same after talking to Ann. Ty had acted as if he were a specialist when it came to atomic weapons. Now it turned out it was all a lie. "When he took the bomb apart, I really had the feeling he knew what he was doing. He explained every step in minute detail."

Marlene stopped pacing and placed her hands on the back of the chair. "Superficial knowledge can be more dangerous than lack of knowledge. Particularly when someone is a good actor."

"I don't even think he's acting. I think he really believes he knows what he's doing."

"Even worse," said Marlene gloomily.

"What do you want to do? Call a halt to the project?"

Marlene groaned. "That's what I would like to do. By God I would like to stop it. But this suicide mission is our last chance. If I stop it, I really don't know what else to do."

"There's still the option of fleeing to the mountains," said Russell.

Marlene shook her head. "The supplies!"

"How many people could survive with the food we have"

"Based on the assumption that we have to hold out for half a year? Twenty. At the most!"

"And if we send twenty people into the mountains? Then at least some of the colony would survive," said Russell. It was a stupid suggestion, and he immediately regretted voicing it.

She shook her head again. "I've been through it with Ben already. The colony couldn't survive with twenty people. And what happens to the rest of us? Fight to the death? We don't even know when the animals will return to the lowlands. It isn't a solution."

"So . . .?"

"So we continue with Ty's plan, as lousy as the chances of success are."

"At least he has Dressel and Cashmore helping him."

She looked at Russell testily. "How many people were involved in the Manhattan Project in Los Alamos?"

Russell shrugged. "No idea. A few thousand?"

"At least. The best scientists in the USA worked

together to build the world's first atomic bomb. And it took them years. If it's a physicist and a chemist doing it under the direction of an amateur Oppenheimer—in four days—it makes me feel sick to the stomach that our lives depend on it."

Russell was silent. Marlene sat down and rapped her fist on the table. From the dark rings under her eyes, it was clear to see that she hadn't rested after being awake all night. Her face was drawn and gray. The commander suddenly seemed much older than her fifty-five years. She opened the bottom drawer of her desk, a relict from Earth, and pulled out a half-full bottle of whiskey. She put two glasses on the table and filled them halfway. She pushed one of the glasses across the table to Russell.

"Looks expensive," said Russell and took the glass.

"It was already expensive on Earth. Here it's priceless."

"But it lasted a long time!"

"Perhaps we only have a few days left to finish it."

Russell lifted the glass to his lips and let the liquid fire trickle down his throat. It immediately made him cough.

"I miss Earth," whispered Marlene.

Russell had heard this sentence so often in the last twenty years, spoken by many different people, and he always felt responsible. He had destroyed the transporter. It was his fault that that all the people around him could never return to their families and friends, to their home. And he still regarded it as a miracle that so many of the colonists had forgiven him. But he had never heard the words spoken by Marlene.

"I'm sorry."

She looked up from her glass. "I didn't mean it like that. . . ."

Russell swilled the whiskey around in his glass. "Would you have destroyed the sphere on Earth?"

"No. I was a soldier and would have listened to orders —not my conscience. I wouldn't have had the guts." She took another sip. "But it's good the way it turned out. At least that's my logical take on it." She hesitated. "Emotionally, it's a little different."

Russell studied her face. They had spent a lot of time together over the years. But Marlene had always put up an armor, which made it difficult to know what she was really thinking. She always seemed so logical and confident, but she was careful to hide her true feelings from the outside world.

"I wanted to marry. Back on Earth, I mean."

Russell looked down at the floor, embarrassed. He felt awful. "I didn't know that."

"How should you? Once there was no way back, I had to forget about it."

"Which makes me all the more sorry."

"I told you, I don't blame you. I pursued a career as a soldier in the full knowledge that I could die on a mission or be so badly injured that I could no longer live a normal life. After the sphere on Earth was destroyed, I concentrated on the here and now. I've tried to see the good side of our situation, and to be a leader of the first colony of human beings in another solar system. Who knows— perhaps I would have chosen such a mission voluntarily. And I've always been happy here, even though it destroyed my hopes of having a family. My marriage back on Earth might have failed too, so I see no reason to lose sleep over what might have been." She paused. "But sometimes, especially when things aren't going too well, I start thinking about the life I might have had if things had turned out differently. And right now, things couldn't be worse."

Once again, Russell was overwhelmed by a feeling of

respect for Marlene. "That's a very rational way of looking at things."

"Maybe. I guess it's just the way I am." She picked up her glass and finished her whiskey. "What about you? How are things?"

Russell knew that she wasn't talking about the work on the bomb. "Quite frankly? Terrible. I've started to notice with every breath I take that my lungs are no longer functioning properly. Without the pills, I probably wouldn't be able to stand anymore."

Marlene nodded. "Others would feel sorry for themselves and wait to die in bed. I think it's amazing that you can still throw yourself into work."

"Well, to be honest, it's my way of running away from my problems. I guess it's just the way *I* am!"

Marlene grinned and poured them each another whiskey. "Let's drink to that."

"I'm not really supposed to drink when I take these pills," said Russell with a smile. "But I guess I don't really need to worry about damaging my kidneys anymore."

They clinked glasses and Russell was about to take a big gulp, when the door burst open, banging against the shelf. A few books flew to the ground.

Jenny was standing at the door, out of breath. "It's started. The first wave has started to attack the post."

Marlene put her glass back on the table. "The first wave? What—"

"We just took new infrared pictures with the drone. One of the territorial borders beyond the wotan territory has fallen. The pressure is driving hordes of them toward the post."

"How many?" Marlene stood up and supported herself on the table.

"I can't say exactly. A few hundred, perhaps?"

"Oh God," whispered Russell.

"How long do we still have?" asked Wolfe.

"An hour. At most."

"Okay. Grab every available colonist. Including any older children who know how to use a weapon, and bring them all to the workshop. We'll leave in a quarter of an hour!"

The children? Are you sure?" asked Russell, in despair. It couldn't be. It shouldn't be. The children were the ones that they most wanted to protect.

"We need them. If the barrier falls now, we're all dead."

"I had hoped we'd have a few more days."

"It could be worse," said Jenny. "It's only the first wave, and it's only a few hundred animals."

". . . only animals," Russell heard Marlene whisper.

Chapter 36

"If they're going to come, then please now. The sun will have set in half an hour. I'd rather fight the beasts in daylight," said Lawrence, his weapon at the ready.

"I agree," said Russell, who was standing next to him on the lookout and adjusting the scope on his gun. They had been able to mobilize fifty men, women, boys, and girls. A little over half of the colony. Some of them were manning the lookouts, the rest were behind the barbed wire fence and earth wall, which they had quickly erected to provide cover. Marlene had taken over supreme command, which Ben had grudgingly accepted. Beside Russell and Ernie, Eliot Sargent and Ryan Dressel were also standing on the six-foot-wide platform.

"Was it really necessary to deploy the kids?" asked Ernie.

"It was Marlene's decision," said Russell. It distressed him to know that even his fifteen-year-old daughter was lying behind the wall with a gun. "I'm as unhappy about it as you are, but if the animals break through the barrier, we're done for anyway. We're all fighting for our survival here."

Ernie grunted and looked through his binoculars. "Nothing to be seen. Are you sure this isn't a false alarm?"

"I think Jenny's able to estimate the movements of the herds pretty accurately. I bet we're going to have our work cut out for us during the next hour or so. We just fooled ourselves into thinking we were safe up there in our settlement."

Ernie nodded.

"Drew was always saying we needed to do more research," said Russell despondently.

"Instead we sent her up into the mountains to look for crude natural resources and gave her shifts in the fields like everyone else. If only she'd found out earlier about the regular floods . . ."

". . . then we would have shut off the pass years ago with a sixty-foot-high wall," Russell finished off the sentence of his comrade. "Now it's too late, and we're atoning for our mistake."

"What a pile of shit!"

Russell looked to the right. The sun was disappearing behind the craggy peaks of the nearby mountains. In an hour it would be pitch dark. "Do you see anything?"

"Nothing. All quiet."

Russell turned to Ryan. "Better get more ammo from the hut. I'm sure we're going to need it."

The boy nodded and climbed down the ladder. A few minutes later he returned with a bag and tipped the spare magazines into the green ammo crate.

"Careful!" cried Russell. The boy gave a start.

"They aren't toys, for God's sake!" Russell shook his head. Although they had taught the children to use weapons, their shooting practices in the forest could hardly be described as military training. Russell's hopes lay with the adults who had been soldiers back on Earth. Even the scientists had had to do some basic training before joining the military mission. But all that was twenty years ago now.

Russell looked at Ernie, who continued to scour the area with his binoculars. He obviously noticed Russell's look, because he slowly shook his head.

"This goddamn waiting," murmured Eliot, who was fiddling around with his jacket.

"Yeah," replied Russell. "Going into battle is bad enough, but waiting for one that could take us by surprise at any moment is even worse."

From the corner of his eye he saw Ernie flinch. "What?"

Ernie adjusted the focus of his binoculars. "I can see them," he hissed. "Wotans! A whole army of them. They're running out of the whole width of the forest. Dozens, if not hundreds of them."

Someone else had obviously seen them too. Russell gave a start when the warning bell went off. Ernie put his binoculars down and grabbed his weapon.

"Here we go. Get ready!" shouted Marlene from the neighboring lookout. "Only fire when they're closer than six-hundred feet. I'll give the command!"

Now Russell could also see the approaching herd. A brown mass was flooding out of the forest and storming across the grassland. From this distance, it looked like a giant herd of buffalo, ready to flatten everything in their path.

"I'm scared." Ryan Dressel tugged at Russell's uniform.

Russell gave him an encouraging smile. "Don't worry, they're only animals." *But a hell of a lot of them.*

"One thousand-five-hundred feet," whispered Ernie and cocked his semi-automatic rifle.

The ground was vibrating under the weight of the oncoming herd.

"One thousand three hundred."

"What we could use now is some good artillery," murmured Eliot.

There are quite a few things we could use now. But we don't have any of them.

"One thousand."

"Look out!" cried Marlene.

The wotans were moving in such a tight formation, it was hard to distinguish one animal from the next. And there was no end to the deluge. Russell estimated that there were at least a thousand of them.

"Fire!"

Russell squeezed the trigger.

The sound of fifty automatic rifles being fired simultaneously filled the air. The noise was so deafening, Russell feared he would go deaf. A number of wotans in the first row fell to the ground. Those behind tripped and tumbled over as they were hit by more volleys of gunfire. Others ran straight over the bodies without slowing down.

Russell shot blindly into the mass of animals. He couldn't say how many he had killed, but the herd continued to stampede toward the barrier. *Like trying to drive back the ocean with a shovel.*

"My weapon is jammed," shouted Ryan.

"Rotate the cylinder!" commanded Russell.

"They're nearing the barbed wire," cried Ernie.

The first wotans mowed down the outer fence. Three got caught in the safety wire, and tore horrible wounds into their bodies. There was a loud bang, as a beast stepped on a mine. Dirt, blood and acid sprayed high into the air and covered the animals coming up from behind. A second explosion tore apart three more wotans.

Another remained twitching on the ground, with its abdomen lying three feet away from it. The wave of animals changed direction and surged into the gap that had been created.

"Concentrate on the gap in the fence," shouted Russell. His weapon clicked. The magazine was empty. He grabbed some more ammunition and racked the slide before firing again.

More mines exploded. A whole mountain of dead wotans was piling up in the gap in the fence. The animals that followed simply used it as a ramp.

"There are too many," shouted Ernie. "We don't have enough mines."

"Keep firing! Don't stop!" cried Marlene.

"Fuck, they've made another gap in the fence," Eliot sounded frantic.

"That's good. It means they'll spread out across the minefield." Russell had already emptied another round. He pulled a hand grenade from his belt, pulled the safety ring and threw the egg-shaped grenade into the minefield, right in the center of a group of wotans. A shower of dirt came down on the colonists.

Now mines closer to the barrier were exploding. It was only another hundred-and-fifty feet until the wotans would reach the main fence and the people behind it. But the piles of cadavers were slowing down their advancement. The beasts had to go round the mountains of bodies, which drove them into other mines. The noise of the exploding mines every few seconds was deafening.

The first wotan reached the main fence. Travis Richards stood up behind the earth wall and shot it dead. A second one threw itself full force against the fence. It died immediately in a hail of bullets, but its weight flattened the barbed wire.

"Careful down there!" cried Marlene. "We've got a hole in the main fence. Focus on the gap!"

Two wotans used the bodies of the dead animals as a springboard, and jumped the fence. Travis ducked to the side at the last second. The two wotans, and four others that came storming up right behind, died in another hail of gunfire.

"Jesus fucking Christ. They're storming the fences as if they were made of paper," Ernie cursed, before reloading.

Russell allowed himself a quick look at the grassland. There were no more animals coming out of the forest. Most of the herd was between the two fences or just outside. But there must be at least another hundred animals storming forward.

My God! We'll never manage!

"They're getting through the gap," warned Ernie.

"Get away from the gap in the fence!" shouted Marlene.

Camille Ott, Julia Stettson, and Edward Grazier threw themselves to the side. Wotans were still rushing forward.

"We're running out of ammunition," gasped Ryan.

"There are just too many," shouted Eliot.

He's right. And they're coming through the gaps. We have to defend the gaps!

"I'm going down," said Russell. He put two spare magazines in his pockets and slid down the ladder. The colonists were pressed up against the cliff walls. A good dozen wotans had already stormed to the other side of the earth wall and were attacking the frantic colonists. One by one, the animals were shot dead, but they were immediately replaced by stragglers. The sound of exploding mines still echoed through the valley. The ground vibrated with every detonation and Russell struggled to keep his balance. Beside him, someone screamed. Maxwell Lindwall tipped backward. Steam was rising from his chest. He must have been hit by some of the acid spraying out of the dying wotans. Russell kneeled down beside the eighteen-year-old and ripped open his shirt. It smelled terrible, but it was only a surface wound. The young man was trembling all over.

"Take care of him, he's in shock," said Russell to Cookie Shanker, who was running toward his friend.

"What should I do?" asked the boy in a quivering voice.

"Dab away this shit from his chest. Then make sure that he doesn't fall unconscious. Talk to him!"

Russell didn't wait for an answer, but kept running toward the gap in the fence. He fired at a group of wotans. One of them took five bullets before dying. Russell stopped in between Andrea Phillips and Chris Neaman, who were firing non-stop, to reload.

"Die, you motherfuckers!" Chris roared.

Russell had the feeling that they had been fighting for their lives for hours, but the sun had hardly moved. No more than a few minutes could have passed since the first shot had been fired. Hundreds of dead animals lay on both sides of the ragged remains of the fence.

"Watch out, Russell!" he heard the hysterical voice of Sophia O'Hara behind him. From the corner of his eye he noticed a movement, a shadow that was approaching fast. Instinctively, Russell jumped back, pulling Andrea back with him. He stumbled and she fell on top of him. They tumbled over each other, and Russell threw a protective arm around the gasping woman. A scream! From where he had just been standing. It was an inhuman scream and stopped as quickly as it had started.

Russell wanted to stand up, but stumbled over Andrea. He fell down again, and rolled on the ground. When he stood up, his left knee was crippled with pain and his leg gave way again.

In front of him, a new gap had appeared in the fence. Underneath a dead wotan, lay Chris Neaman in a pool of blood.

"Fuck," Russell swore, but he felt nothing. That would come later. If there was a later.

He hobbled over, dragging his left leg behind him and, with Andrea's help, heaved the dead monster off Chris. What he saw made him want to retch: acid had sprayed onto Chris' head and eaten away half of his face. His left eye was wide open with a look of total surprise. To the right of it was nothing but a hole, out of which dripped a hissing white liquid.

"Russell, watch out!" Andrea pulled him back. He almost stumbled again. A good dozen wotans were stampeding through the gap. Russell grabbed his weapon and fired. It only clicked. "Oh fuck!" He would never be able to jump out of the way in time!

But at that moment, the wotans exploded in the gap in the fence. Someone had thrown a grenade, and dirt, entrails, and white liquid flew in their direction. Thinking fast, Russell threw himself to the ground and protected his head with his hands. He was immediately covered in dirt, some of which he breathed in. It burned like hell. Coughing, he tried to get the stuff out. At least he hadn't been hit by any acid. He tried to stand up, but a new stab of pain in his knee caused him to fall screaming back to the ground. He saw another shadow flying toward him, scrambled for his weapon in the dust and fired. Click.

The magazine is still empty, you idiot.

A loud bang right beside him. Someone had saved his ass! The monster flew over him and fell to the ground several feet away from him. Russell rummaged around in his pocket for the last magazine and groaned as he racked the slide.

"Help! Help me!"

He recognized the voice. It was Patrick Holbrook. Russell couldn't see what was wrong with him.

I have to get away from here!

He dragged himself forward, bit by bit, foot by foot, away from the gap in the fence, while all around him, wotans fell dead to the ground. Bullets whistled so close to his ears that he could feel the gusts of air.

It was difficult for Russell to concentrate on anything except the pain in his knee. He crawled on, as if in a trance.

I have to keep going! I have to get away from here!

Somewhere behind him a grenade exploded. The blast almost took his breath away. After a few long seconds he turned around.

I'm far enough away from the gap. Get up! Now!

He screamed as the pain seared through his knee, but by propping himself up on his weapon, he finally managed to get to his feet. He looked around. It was a scene from hell. The cadavers of wotans were piled up in great heaps in front of, on top of, between and behind the fence. Many of them had terrible injuries and missing limbs after being crushed underfoot by the animals streaming from behind. Some of them were just a slimy mass, torn apart by explosions. In between, people—streaming with blood, unconscious, screaming in pain or dead. A few feet away he saw Patrick Holbrook. The boy was lying in a sea of blood, his spine twisted at a bizarre angle.

And it wasn't over yet. More wotans were surging through the fence toward the observation post.

Russell lifted his weapon and emptied the magazine into the herd. He screamed, but over the sound of the

shots and explosions he couldn't even hear his own screaming. He took one out. And another. From the corner of his
eye he could see the muzzle flare of his comrades. Row by
row, the wotans went down. But one was still racing in his
direction. Russell took aim and fired, but his last magazine
was empty.

He threw himself to the ground, but as he was falling,
something heavy collided with his head. He felt a flood of
pain, which obliterating everything else.

Fuck!

He was enveloped by darkness.

Chapter 37

"He's coming to."

He heard the voice before he opened his eyes.

I'm alive!

It was the first thought that shot through his head.

I'm alive!

The next thing he felt was pain. Pain in his leg, pain in his chest, and his head felt as if it were being squeezed in a vice. Slowly he opened his eyes. In front of him, the face of his wife swam into view. She was smiling.

"Ellen," he croaked.

Then Dr. Lindwall was looming over him, and a flashlight being shone into his eyes.

"Can you hear me, Russell?" the voice droned through his head.

He nodded weakly. "What happened?"

"You were concussed, which is why you probably have a terrible headache. And your knee is badly bruised. You'll probably be hobbling around for a few more days, but otherwise you're fine." He hesitated. "Apart from your cancer."

"The observation post?" groaned Russell. *The dead! The injured!*

"We drove them back," said Ellen. "It was close, but in the end we killed all the wotans. Unfortunately we lost some people."

In his mind's eye, Russell could see Patrick, dead in a pool of his own blood. "Who?"

"Holbrook's son is dead. And Chris Neaman and Ryan Dressel."

"Ryan? He was next to me on the platform. How . . .?"

"A wotan caused the lookout to collapse. Ernie and Eliot suffered slight injuries, But Ryan fell right in front of a monster."

"Three dead?"

"And twice as many injured. But Marlene is glad that we were able to survive this wave."

Russell nodded. As sad as the losses were, he was surprised there weren't more. Especially as he had doubted they would be able to defend the observation post at all. He had led military missions with more casualties. But children had died here, and consequently he couldn't feel happy about their victory. "Ty?"

"I don't know. They've been working through the night. Even when John found out about his son's death he only went to see his wife briefly before disappearing back in the laboratory. Marlene is at the observation post. They're re-erecting the torn-down barrier and laying new mines."

Russell gripped the edge of the bed and tried to sit up. The pain in his head was hellish. He let his feet drop to the floor. His legs were trembling.

"Russell, what are you doing?" asked Lindwall. "You can't get up yet."

Ellen forced him back into bed. "I won't allow it," she

said softly but firmly. "You need to rest. At least for a few hours."

Russell did not put up any resistance. He sank back into bed and drifted into a restless sleep.

WHEN RUSSELL WOKE up a few hours later, he felt strong enough to sit up and eat the bowl of stew that Ellen had placed on the table beside his bed. His headache had subsided to a dull throbbing. Pushing aside the empty plate, he stood up and hobbled over to the washbasin. When he looked at himself in the mirror he got a fright. His face looked gray and sunken. His left cheek was caked with bits of dry blood, and a thick bandage was wound around the top of his head. There were dark shadows under his eyes.

Ellen had put out clean clothes for him on the chair. His threadbare combat uniform reeked from the open hamper in the corner. He hobbled over and searched the pockets until he found the little box with the medication. He opened it, swallowed two of the stimulants, and staggered over to the door of the infirmary.

The infirmary was located at the edge of the housing settlement. There was nobody in sight. Most of the colonists were probably at the observation post helping with the clean-up operations. But he heard a woman sobbing from Christian Holbrook's hut. It was Paulina, crying over Chris, her fallen son. Should he go and see her? He decided against it. The fight wasn't over yet. If Ty and his atom bomb failed, then all of the colonists would be dead after the next onslaught.

He turned right and dragged himself over to the physics laboratory, the door to which stood open.

John Dressel stared at him from bloodshot eyes. In front of him lay sheets of paper with complicated-looking calculations. Ty stood a few feet to the side at a table and was stacking up gray blocks with gloved hands.

Russell shuffled over to the physicist and grasped his shoulder with both hands. "I'm so sorry," he said huskily.

"It's okay," said Dressel. "I know that you were with him at the start of the battle. It's not your fault that the damn tower fell down later."

"Don't you want to take a break?"

Dressel's face was rigid as a statue's. "I couldn't save Ryan, but I have two more children. Once we've finally blocked the pass and are safe from these damn beasts, there'll still be time to mourn."

Russell nodded and turned to Ty. "How's it going?"

The weapons expert pointed at a table beneath a window. Two metallic corpuses lay on the table, similar to the egg-shaped halves of the bombs, but now perfectly hemispherical, and bigger. There was a small indentation in the flat end of each one. "Cashmore was right. With the hot press, we were able to reshape the plutonium cores quite easily. Those are the two halves, which we will later combine into a supercritical mass in the cave. This part of the job is complete."

"What else do you need to do?"

"Detonating the bomb using this method is extremely inefficient, because we can't compress the plutonium. Only a small percentage of the atoms will be split during the chain reaction. That's why we're trying to reflect back as many of the neutrons that first escape from the core by surrounding the steel pipe with graphite at the point of the explosion."

"Graphite?"

"Yes, Cashmore still had a couple of pounds, which he took out of a spectrometer in his lab." Russell looked at the gray slabs on the table. Ty continued. "Graphite is an excellent neutron reflector and during the early stage of the explosion it'll reflect back a large part of the neutrons into the bomb, like a mirror. We hope that'll compensate for the loss of efficiency."

"So you'll just set up these slabs around the steel pipe in the cave?"

Ty shook his head.

"Unfortunately it's not that easy. Each of the two bomb halves is already almost at critical mass. If I simply put the graphite next to them, there's a risk that the reflected neutrons would start a chain reaction on their own. Not like in a bomb, but like in a nuclear reactor. It's essential that the chain reaction only starts *after* the detonation, so we need to work out exactly how much graphite we can use."

Russell noticed the pile of paper in front of the physicist. "And that's what you're calculating now?"

Dressel nodded. "No problem in theory. But in practice it is, because the graphite is unfortunately impure."

Ty grinned. "Tomorrow morning, when we're finished with converting the initiator, we'll carry out an experiment and tickle the dragon's tail."

Russell stared at him blankly. "You want to do what?"

"We'll gradually surround the bottom half of the plutonium with graphite, until we reach a K-factor of one. In other words, until a chain reaction starts!"

Russell shuddered. "You want to start a chain reaction here? Are you serious?"

Ty's grin broadened. "Don't worry. Once you have just enough mass for a chain reaction, you get delayed neutrons first. They ensure that the fission rate only increases at a snail's pace. It isn't dangerous and we'll stop the experiment as soon as we've reached that point. Then we'll know what we need to know."

Russell felt uneasy: a chain reaction here in the middle of the laboratory? It sounded dangerous. He turned round to the physicist. "What do you think about this?"

"If we proceed cautiously, I don't think we'll have any problems. We just have to be careful that we don't emit any prompt neutrons."

Russell looked puzzled, so he continued. "During a chain reaction, both delayed neutrons and prompt neutrons are emitted, which immediately split into new nuclei. As long as you only work with the delayed neutrons, you can control the process, but if you amass too much reflector material at once, there's a danger that the chain reaction will be driven by the prompt neutrons alone. If that happened, I wouldn't want to be present."

Russell frowned. Compared to Ty's explanation, this did sound dangerous. "And what then? Would there be an explosion?"

"No, but the process is equivalent to an out-of-control nuclear reactor. Like in Chernobyl, a huge amount of radiation would be emitted and the core of the atomic bomb would melt."

"And you seriously want to carry out this experiment here?"

John Dressel waved his arms around helplessly. "What other choice do we have? We need precisely the right amount of graphite so that we don't just end up with an expensive firework."

Russell shook his head and left the laboratory. Ty and Dressel reminded him of two children who had discovered their mother's lighter and were now playing around with it in the garden shed. Only that the two children here in this laboratory were playing around with an atomic bomb. In the middle of their settlement!

Chapter 38

"Was it really necessary to take the children down there?" asked Russell.

After visiting the laboratory, he had hobbled home but couldn't find any peace of mind. After lying in bed for a few hours, he had gone to Marlene's office.

She was pale, and her eyes were bloodshot. Her hands were trembling, and Russell wondered when she would collapse. She was sitting in her armchair and had put her feet up on the table. A cup of something steaming was balanced on top of a pile of paper.

"I would have preferred not to," she said quietly. "But we needed them. We could only defeat those monsters by mobilizing all our forces. The youngsters made up half our line of defense. Without them, the beasts would have run us down."

"But the children should be the future of our little society! Now we're sending them to slaughter!"

"What choice did we have?" asked Marlene irritably. "Should we have tried it with just the adults? Then I can guarantee you the beasts would have made it into the canyon."

"Perhaps we could have found another solution!"

"Yes, perhaps. And if you hadn't blown up the transporter on Earth, then *perhaps* we wouldn't be in this shitty situation," Marlene's voice was trembling.

Russell was silent. Her last words hit him hard. *When the shit hits the fan, people say what they really think.*

But it didn't change the fact that she was right. What right had he had to decide over the lives of forty people? The question was in fact easy to answer: he simply hadn't thought it through.

"I'm sorry," he whispered.

"Yeah, me too," said Marlene. "There's no point throwing accusations around like this. We're still in a critical situation."

Russell rubbed his throbbing knee. "Perhaps we should see it from this perspective: at least we can hope again."

"Can we?"

"We managed to defeat the first wave. That's more than we dared to hope for yesterday."

Marlene groaned. "The situation hasn't changed at all. The wave of wotans yesterday was smaller than we predicted. We cleared away around a thousand dead wotans. The next wave will be bigger. Much bigger. I spoke to Jenny this afternoon; she's taking new infrared pictures. She thinks something is brewing again. The former wotan territory has been infiltrated by other animals who are themselves on the run. Jenny reckons that the next wave will drive at least twenty thousand beasts into the canyon."

"Twenty thousand," repeated Russell numbly. It was hard to even imagine such a number.

"Correct. The next wave will overrun us if we don't

manage to seal the pass first." She picked up her cup. "What's the latest?"

Russell sighed. "The work at the building site has been completed. The new bomb core is finished and the initiator should be done tonight. But both of our bomb constructors want to carry out an experiment tomorrow morning and turn the plutonium into a critical mass, in order to determine the amount of graphite necessary."

Marlene looked confused. "To turn it into a critical mass?"

Russell shrugged. "They said they have to carry out this test. Ty's explanation frightened me."

"I don't have time to deal with this. Please be at the test and make sure they don't do anything stupid."

Russell gave a despairing laugh. "I have absolutely no idea what they're up to." He hesitated. "I'm surprised that Dr. Cashmore wasn't in the lab with them. Perhaps it would be better if he monitored the test."

Marlene shook her head. "I took him off the bomb project."

"Really?" asked Russell.

"Yes. Ben had an idea of how to create more firepower for the observation post, in case we really have to defend ourselves against another wave. I need Cashmore to implement Ben's idea."

"What does it involve?"

"That's none of your concern. We don't even know whether the idea is feasible or not. You just concentrate on your bomb. It's enough for me to know that you'll put the brakes on Ty if Dr. Dressel has any doubts."

"Okay."

"When will the bomb be ready?"

"If the test tomorrow morning works, we can start on

the final stages in the canyon. Perhaps the day after tomorrow very early, with a bit of luck tomorrow evening."

Marlene leaned over her desk and looked Russell straight in the eyes. "We can't afford any delays. None. If it's in any way possible it should happen tomorrow. We don't know when the next wave will swarm toward the observation post, but if the bomb isn't ready to detonate, we're all dead."

Chapter 39

"It already stinks like hell," said Ernie Lawrence. He looked at the huge heap of dead wotans three-hundred feet away on the other side of the fence. The sun had just gone up. It looked like it was going to be a nice sunny day, but Ernie still had the shivers. They had spent the whole night piling up the bodies of the dead wotans into a huge heap, so that they would have a clear line of fire if it came to another battle. Lee had welded a shovel to one of the jeeps so that they didn't come in contact with the acid.

"Can you imagine how bad they'll stink when they start to really decompose?" asked Dillon Grant, who was standing next to him on the lookout. "Maybe we should have burnt them."

"We can't be wasting any fuel. And anyway, the fire would probably have attracted more of the beasts," said Ernie.

"At the moment they're still doing their own thing. But eventually they'll come back," said Dillon. He had a deep crudely bandaged gash on his forehead from the last battle.

Thankfully, no more animals had come near the post since the attack.

"Hey, there's our egghead. What's he doing here?" asked Ernie.

Dr. Cashmore pulled up under the lookout. On the truck bed were three shimmering, silver objects that looked like little canons with long levers at one end, and the same number of metal containers. Ben hurried over and Cashmore shook his hand.

Ernie and Dillon leaned over the railing. "What's he up to? He's never shown up at the post before."

"I have no idea. If you gave him a gun, he'd probably shoot himself in the foot by mistake," added Dillon.

Ernie grinned. Cashmore might be a genius in his laboratory and he was not bad as an engineer—after all, he had built the refinery together with Lee. But as a soldier? Ernie remembered a drill with hand grenades, where the nervous chemist had only thrown away the safety pin. Fortunately it had been a practice grenade that couldn't explode.

"Don't stand around gaping! Help me and take this thing off my hands!" yelled Ben, who was climbing up the ladder with one of the objects from Dr. Cashmore's jeep.

Ernie knelt down and grabbed it. The thing was heavier than it looked. Grunting, Ernie and Ben placed it on the front of the platform, while Dillon helped the chemist up onto the lookout. When he reached the top, Cashmore held onto the railing, gasping for air.

Ernie eyed the construction. What he had just taken to be a cannon resembled, on closer inspection, the spraying device of a fire truck. "What's it supposed to be, Ken?"

"A little surprise for the next lot of beasts that get it into their heads to attack the observation post," said Ben.

"That's a spray nozzle," explained the chemist. "A hose

will be attached to the other side, and down there we'll install a pump, which will pump the contents of the vats into the nozzle. Albert will bring the pump down in the next hour or so, once it's cleaned. Then you can spray the stuff over the beasts."

"The stuff? What's in the vats?" asked Dillon.

"Napalm," replied Ben with a grin.

"Napalm?" repeated Ernie and Dillon in unison. This wasn't the Vietnam War. Back then the stuff had caused enormous damage—particularly to the civilian population. Ernie shook his head. "How did you get hold of it?"

"Fresh from the lab. Napalm isn't difficult to produce," answered Dr. Cashmore. "It's basically kerosene gelatinized with additives. It's easy to extract the necessary aluminum soaps from aluminum hydroxide, cyclopenthan and cyclo—"

"Spare us the lecture, Ken," interrupted Ben. "The other two also need to be installed."

Cashmore shrugged and started going back down the ladder.

"A flamethrower?" asked Ernie.

Ben nodded. "Like in Vietnam! With the pump that Albert's bringing over soon, we can spray the stuff up to three-hundred feet on the other side of the barrier. The gel sticks to the beasts and the burning kerosene will finish them off in seconds. Unfortunately we don't have much of it. It'll probably take a minute to empty one vat, but at least the fire will keep burning for some time."

"If only we'd had this two days ago," said Ernie despondently. Maybe then Chris and the others would still be alive.

Ben nodded. "The annoying thing is that it won't help us much against the next wave. There'll be too many of them. The napalm will hold them back for a bit. But no more."

"Better than nothing. Is there any news about how long we've still got?"

Ben grimaced. "No exact information. Jenny thinks it'll be sometime between this afternoon and tomorrow morning."

"And when is our amateur Oppenheimer blowing up the canyon?" asked Dillon.

"It's planned for this evening."

"Great," said Ernie, his voice dripping with sarcasm. "Let's hope there's still someone left by then to ignite the bomb."

Chapter 40

"We can start right away. But first I want to show you something." Ty walked around the table and took a silver, marble-sized ball out of a container. He held it under Russell's nose.

Russell took a step back. "Is that the initiator?"

Ty nodded. He was in his element. "The initiator has elements of beryllium and polonium. When it's compressed by the implosion of the bomb core, the elements fuse and the initiator emits the neutrons into the plutonium."

"You told me that already," said Russell irritably.

Ty's posturing was getting on his nerves again.

"Oh . . . Well, in any case, we don't have an implosion, so it wouldn't work. Instead, I've opened up the initiator and slotted the individual elements directly into one another. And I've brushed a thin layer of nitrocellulose in between."

"Aha."

"Nitrocellulose is more commonly known as guncotton, and it's impact-sensitive. At the moment it isn't emitting any neutrons, since the alpha particles emitted by the beryllium are being absorbed by the thin layer between the elements. But when the second plutonium half hits the bottom half at the moment of detonation, the nitrocellulose evaporates and moves through little ducts to the outside. The beryllium comes into contact with the polonium, and neutrons instantly stream outside."

Ty clearly expected some sign of comprehension, but Russell did not do him the favor. He turned round to John Dressel, who was standing apathetically in a corner of the room. The physicist's eyes were red and puffy and he was staring numbly at the ceiling, lost in thought. Russell asked himself how he would feel if he had just lost a son. But it was no use. Somebody with the right knowledge had to supervise Ty's work.

"What do you think? Will it work?"

The physicist didn't react.

"John!" said Russell and took a step toward him.

The physicist gave a start, looked at him in momentary confusion and then nodded. "We did a test with a little piece of the initiator. It'll work."

Russell turned back to Ty. "Good. Now what? Shall we start the experiment? Time is of the essence."

Ty nodded and waved Russell over to the test setup on a table. It was shielded on three sides by twelve-inch-high blocks of lead. In the middle lay the bottom half of the new bomb core. A row of graphite slabs surrounded the plutonium. Ty carefully placed the initiator in a depression in the center.

"After re-forming it into the hemispherical shape, we poured nickel tetracarbonyl over the plutonium. As a result, a thin layer of nickel formed on the bomb core, which prevents contact with the surrounding air, so that we can work with it safely. We set up a neutron source below the table, and are measuring the level of neutron multiplication in the core." He pointed at an oscilloscope-like instrument with several digital indicators. "At the moment the k factor is at 0.9. That means that through nuclear fission, per neutron an average of 0.9 new ones are being generated." He flipped a switch on the measuring device. An irregular ticking could be heard from the loudspeakers. "Every click represents a captured neutron, like with a Geiger counter."

Russell could feel himself breaking out in a sweat. The whole thing was uncanny. "That means the core is now emitting radiation?" He found himself taking a step backward.

Ty laughed. "Don't worry. We're working with very few neutrons. We're not in any danger. In any case, we will keep putting graphite around the core for as long as it takes to reach a k factor of precisely one. That is the precise value of the critical mass. And we will then position exactly that amount of graphite around the core in the bomb cave." He turned to John. "Are you writing down the values?"

The physicist nodded weakly and picked up a clipboard with a table for filling in.

"Good, let's get started. The test setup has exactly ten kilograms of graphite. The k factor is 0.905. Now I'll lay more blocks around the core." He picked up a plastic container, which was filled with grey cuboids.

Russell wondered how many scientists in the early days of the US atomic bomb program had been exposed to radiation during such experiments. He wished Dr. Cashmore could have been here to monitor the experiment.

"Twenty-six point five pounds of graphite. 0.951," said Ty.

John Dressel added the values to the table. It seemed to

Russell as if the clicking from the loudspeaker had become faster, but he could be imagining it.

"Twenty-eight point five pounds. 0.986. Now it's getting interesting." Ty picked up more graphite blocks.

"Twenty-eight point five," murmured Dr. Dressel.

Ty carefully laid another block next to the plutonium and looked at the measuring device. "0.998. Twenty-nine point five." He looked at Russell. "Now I'll take a smaller block, then we should reach a stable chain reaction."

Ty's hands were shaking. Russell automatically took another step back.

"1.001 at exactly Twenty-nine point nine six pounds." Ty looked at his test setup almost lovingly. "That gives us a stable chain reaction." He grinned. "What do you say now? We've made our own atomic reactor."

The ticking from the loudspeaker became faster without Ty adding any more blocks. Russell was sure he wasn't imagining it. "And now a chain reaction is taking place in the material?"

Ty beamed and nodded, and waved his arms around. "Yup. We exceeded critical mass very slightly. The nuclear fissions will continue to accelerate on their own, even if I switched off the neutron source. But it would take a long time until it was strong enough to expose us to radiation, because we're still in the area of delayed neutrons."

He was making a real show of this actually dangerous experiment. Suddenly Russell heard Dr. Dressel make a choking noise. The physicist was chalk white.

"What is it, John?"

"I don't feel well. I'm dizzy."

"No wonder," said Ty. "You haven't eaten anything since last night."

"I wasn't hungry," said the physicist in a husky voice.

He can't cope with his son's death.

"Wait. I'll take you outside into the fresh air." Russell took John by the arm and led him toward the door. As they went, he turned to Ty. "Are we finished with the experiment?"

Ty nodded. "Yes, we know what we need to know. You can go outside, I'll dismantle everything."

Russell opened the door while propping up the physicist. He was about to sit him down on a wooden bench next to the door in the sun, when Ty let out a piercing scream. Russell spun around. A blinding, bluish light radiated out of the lab and cast a shadow of the door on the dusty ground. The ticking that up to a moment ago had still been regular was turning into an ear-splitting buzz. It only lasted a moment, then the light was gone again. The buzzing from the loudspeakers subsided and eventually fizzled out completely.

Russell stormed into the building. "What was that?" He was irritated. The experiment had been over.

Ty's eyes were ripped open wide and his face was even paler than Dr. Dressel's. His lips were quivering.

"What is it?" shouted Russell. Something had obviously gone very wrong.

"I wanted to gather up the graphite blocks," whispered Ty. "I held the container at a slant, and a big block slipped out and fell straight onto the bomb core. It bounced off, but . . ." He stared straight through Russell. "Oh my God!"

Dr. Dressel pushed past Russell, doubled over. "What does your dosimeter say?" he asked quietly.

Ty put down the container with the blocks and with trembling hands took the film badge dosimeter out of his chest pocket. He looked at the reading and his eyes widened even more.

"It's at the top of the scale. Over twenty sievert!"

Russell looked back and forth between Ty and the physicist.

Ty's face, which a moment ago had been chalk white, was turning red. "Twenty sievert," he repeated quietly. He started to cry.

"What happened?" Russell asked.

Dr. Dressel turned to look at him. "Get Dr. Lindwall. Right now!"

Perplexed, Russell left the barrack and made his way to the doctor.

Chapter 41

"Here comes Marlene," said Dressel.

Russell spun round. *Finally!*

He, John Dressel, and Lee Shanker were standing in front of the entrance to the infirmary, when Marlene appeared. Lee had a bandage on his right hand. He had hurt himself with a saw at the building site in the canyon and Dr. Lindwall had just been treating him when Russell alerted the doctor.

"What happened?" asked Marlene, catching her breath.

"Ty was radiated in the experiment with the plutonium," said Russel.

"Is it bad?"

"He got twenty sievert," said Dr. Dressel.

"Is that a lot?"

Russell looked at the ground. He felt guilty. Marlene had asked him to supervise the experiment. And now this!

Dr. Dressel nodded. "The dosage is lethal."

Marlene's jaw dropped. "How could it happen?" She turned to Russell.

He was just about to answer when Dr. Dressel stepped in. "It's my fault! I felt sick and Russell had to take me outside after the experiment was actually completed. Ty was in the process of dismantling the experiment, when a graphite block fell on the plutonium core. The graphite bounced straight off, but it was enough to turn the plutonium into a powerful nuclear reactor for a fraction of a second. Ty was standing right next to it and . . ."

"Jesus Christ," said Marlene. "I knew that this playing around with nuclear shit was going to end in a disaster. If only I hadn't gone along with it."

The door to the infirmary opened and Dr. Lindwall stepped outside. He dabbed the sweat from his forehead with a handkerchief.

"How's it going, Doc? How's the patient?" asked Russell.

The doctor shook his head. "Bad. He keeps passing out. I've given him a strong painkiller."

"A painkiller? Nothing else?" asked Marlene. "There must be something we can do for him."

Dr. Lindwall shook his head. "There's nothing we can do for him. He got such a strong dose of neutrons, that everything metallic he was wearing has become radioactive. The cells of his body are already dying. He'll die within the next twenty-four hours from multiple organ failure."

"Oh my God!" said Marlene. "We need to tell Ann."

"I already have," said Lee.

"She's with him now," added Dr. Lindwall.

Marlene nodded. "What about the bomb?"

"What do you mean?" asked Russell.

"I want to know if the bomb is ready for action!" she said. Her eyes had narrowed to slits.

"You really want to continue with this crazy plan?" said Lindwall in amazement.

"Unfortunately we don't have a choice. So, if the bomb core wasn't damaged in the experiment, I would like you to get straight back to work!" Her eyes flicked from Russell to John Dressel.

Russell was silent. The shock of what had happened to Ty had hit him hard. He could feel an almost physical resistance inside him to carrying on with this madness — not least since the driving force behind this hellish project was now lying on his deathbed.

"I don't want anything more to do with this bullshit," said Dr. Dressel with a blank expression.

Marlene stepped forward and grabbed him by the collar. "Now listen to me! Fifty men, women, and children are lying in the mud down at the observation post waiting for the next wave of monsters. And there is no way we will be able to defeat them this time. Max is down there too. I know how upset you are by Ryan's death—and what just happened to Ty—but I can't take your feelings into account here. Apart from Ty, you're the only one who has any clue how this damn thing works. I want you to complete the job, transport the explosive to the canyon, and save our lives!"

"We don't know if our bomb is strong enough or if it will even work at all," said the physicist. He started to cry. First the death of his son, and then Ty. It was too much for him! "Nothing makes sense anymore. We bit off more than we can chew. Look at Ty! I'll never forget the look in his eyes when he realized that he was going to die."

Russell laid a hand on his shoulder.

Marlene cuffed the physicist round the ears. "You will pull yourself together and continue with the work. Immediately! We don't know when the next wave will attack the observation post. Every second counts. And if the whole thing fails on account of you losing your nerve, I will personally throw you to the beasts. Do you understand?"

Dressel was shocked. He stared at Marlene with his mouth agape, and didn't move.

"Do you understand?"

Finally the physicist nodded.

Marlene turned to Lee. "How far along are you with preparing the cave?"

Lee moved back a step.

Russell had never experienced Marlene like this. It was as if she'd lost control of herself, but he knew she hadn't. The way she had handled Dressel was cleverly calculated. She knew how she had to treat him to get him to finish the job.

"The bomb construction site is completed. We're just waiting for the bomb core and the graphite."

"Then go!" she said. She turned to Russell. "Now take the physicist to the lab, for God's sake!"

DREW HEARD SHOUTS OUTSIDE. Something was going on in the infirmary, and when she stepped inside to look, Russell shuffled past, dragging along Dr. Dressel behind him. Both their faces were like stone, and she knew that something terrible had happened.

"What is it?"

Russell turned round and looked her in the eyes. "There was an accident with the plutonium in the physics laboratory. Ty . . ."

Drew began to tremble and she could feel her legs giving way. Their encounter in Marlene's office . . . She'd had a terribly guilty conscience, but had been aching to see Ty again. She'd been trying desperately to think up a way of meeting him again in secret. That one kiss had given her back a tiny bit of courage and optimism, and for the first time in years, the future didn't seem so bleak. She knew that Ty was on the brink of separating from his wife, and she'd been thinking about her own relationship with Ben, and the scales had suddenly fallen from her eyes. She didn't want to delude herself any longer, or put up with the way Ben treated her. There were other possibilities; there could be a different future. Perhaps even one with Ty.

"What's up with Ty? Is he okay?"

Russell looked at the ground.

"No, he's not okay!" answered Dr. Dressel angrily. "He was exposed to a high dose of radiation. He's dying."

It took a moment for the words she was hearing to sink in.

Ty is dying!

Instinctively, she wanted to race over to the infirmary to see him. But she knew that his wife would be there, or at least on her way there, together with their children. It wouldn't be right. If it was true that he was dying, she would never see him again.

At that moment something broke inside her. As if part of her had also died. Any hopes she had had for the future seemed to melt away in the early morning sun like ice in a volcano.

Chapter 42

The workshop was empty. Russell presumed that Albert and his helpers were either working at the bomb-construction cave, or had been sent down to defend the observation post. It was strangely quiet in the settlement, the rumbling of the jeep's engine echoed from the walls of the huts.

On the way back to the lab, Russell made a quick stop at his hut to get more medication. His legs trembled as he got out of the jeep and staggered the few steps to the door. As he entered the hut he bumped straight into Ellen, who was just about to leave. She had put on her old army combat uniform which still fit her perfectly. Over all the years, she had managed to stay in great shape.

She hugged him. "I heard about Ty. How is he?"

"Bad. He probably won't survive the day."

She groaned. "That bad?" she whispered.

"He got a full dose of radiation in the accident."

"What about you? How do you feel?"

"I was with John in front of the door. Luckily we didn't get any of the radiation." He touched her backpack. "Are you going down to the observation post?"

322

"I'm no use here. If we have to fight for our lives, then I'm not going to stand back and watch."

"Where are the kids?"

"Greg is with Julia Stetson and the other young kids. Jim and Grace have been at the observation post since morning. I couldn't stop them, so I'm going too."

Russell nodded. He wasn't happy that his family was on the front line against these beasts, but what could he do? He knew that everyone who could fight was needed. And he also knew that Jim and Grace wouldn't try and hide somewhere in a situation like this.

"I'd rather be with you down at the observation post than monitoring this crazy nuclear project I don't even understand."

Ellen took his hand. "I know you'd rather fight. But the bomb is our only chance. It will make me feel a lot better knowing that you are supervising the work. And as you found out today, it's just as dangerous to be working on the bomb as being down at the observation post."

Russell shrugged. "We're about to take the plutonium and the other nuclear material down to the canyon. I'm not sure how long it will take to set it all up. A few hours, maybe."

"I hope we can defend the pass for that long."

"And I hope that this damn plutonium doesn't just turn out to be a dud."

Ellen kissed him tenderly. "I'm convinced everything will work out okay." She smiled.

He returned her smile, but he had lost his optimism. Ty lay dying in the infirmary and John Dressel was a physical wreck. And there was still so much that could go wrong.

Ellen let go of his hand reluctantly. "I have to go. We'll see each other when it's all over."

"Take care of the children!" he said quietly. That should have been his job. It made him feel sick!

His face dark and brooding, he watched Ellen disappear around the corner of the hut. Would he ever see his family again?

"Damn it!" he swore aloud. He hobbled over to the shelf, found some pills and put them in his pocket.

Dr. Dressel was already waiting at the entrance to the lab container. Wordlessly, Russell helped the physicist load the jeep. They put the plutonium cores of the bomb in two lead boxes on the back seat, together with the measuring devices. The container with the graphite blocks lay on the truck bed and a little box containing the initiator was on the physicist's lap as Russell started the jeep.

Only once they had left the settlement behind them did Russell speak. "Will it work?"

Dressel's face was expressionless. "I have no idea."

Damn it! This had *also been his idea!*

"Come on, John. You're a physicist. For the last few days you've done nothing except prepare for the detonation."

"I'm not a nuclear engineer. Nor is Ty. We did everything that we could. But I have no idea whether or not we overlooked something. I've tried to estimate the explosive force of our construction, but I don't have enough knowledge of the substance. In Los Alamos, they used computer codes for something as complicated as that. I can only make rough estimates. Just one or two neutron generations too few and it won't be enough! It's nothing more than an experiment!"

Russell veered around a pothole only to land in the next one. The boxes on the truck bed bounced. "Unfortunately it's an experiment on which all our lives depend."

Chapter 43

"Ben, I need to know where . . ."

But Ben wasn't listening. Among the vehicles that had just arrived, he had spotted his wife. "I'll be right back."

He hurried over the dusty track, along the rows of barbed wire, which they had raised to a height of six feet. Albert's workshop had hardly been able to keep up with the production.

"Ben, shall we use the time to raise up the earth wall a bit higher?" called Sammy.

"Ask Marlene!" he replied gruffly and carried on without even looking at Sammy.

After a few seconds he had reached his wife, who was just pulling her backpack out of the jeep. Beside her stood Ellen, Manuel, and Andrea, who had come down with her.

He grabbed his wife roughly by the arm and pulled her to the side.

"What are you doing here, dammit!"

She didn't seem surprised. Ben was irritated. There was a spark in her eyes that he hadn't seen for many years: defiance!

"I will fight here for our children and our future. Along with everyone else!"

Ben's voice became louder. "I told you to go to Julia and to look after the other children with her! You will drive back to the settlement with the next jeep."

With a quick movement she shook off his arm. "It's over, Ben! I won't let you order me around anymore."

"Excuse me?" His lips trembled. Somebody must have incited her. Probably it had been his daughter. He would give her a talking to when all this was over.

"I'm trying to defend the colony here, and you stab me in the back like that? Have you gone mad?" he hissed. "I wanted you to stay in the settlement for your own safety. But once again, you were too stupid to realize that."

"From now on, I make my own decisions. If you don't like it, that's your problem. And if you ever dare to hit me again, I will leave you!" She turned around and stalked off, without waiting for an answer.

Ben shook his head. What had he got himself into with this woman? Not long after the start of their relationship she had become rebellious. She simply wasn't able to grasp the fact that in a family, only one person could make the decisions. When the children came along, she had seemed to come to her senses and become more compliant. But now that Catherine was growing up, his wife was also becoming increasingly stubborn. Once or twice he had thought about simply throwing her out of the house, but he didn't want people gossiping and thinking he couldn't handle his wife. But when this thing was over, she had a nasty surprise coming. He had dealt with worse.

On the other hand: if this ridiculous plan with the atomic bomb failed, which he was sure it would, then he wouldn't need to think about this or any other problem anymore, so for the time being he was concentrating on his work.

Earlier in the day he had been rejoicing. He was the commander-in-chief; he was leading the sixty men and women into battle. Finally he had gotten what he had always wanted to achieve on Earth: his own command.

But then Marlene had turned up and taken over. Yet again he had been demoted to deputy. He hoped that soon she would hightail it back to the bomb-construction site— or to the settlement, where she belonged. On the other hand . . . perhaps she would be the first to fall at the start of the battle. He wouldn't be sorry.

He grimaced when he heard her querulous voice somewhere behind him. "Ben!"

He turned around and forced himself to give a friendly wave. Marlene was standing next to Jenny Baldwin in front of the entrance to the barrack, calling him over like a lowly henchman.

He strolled over to her with a deliberate air of nonchalance. "What's up?"

"Jenny has new data from the last scouting reconnaissance flight of the drone. I wanted you to hear this, too."

The biologist pointed at an infrared photo that she transferred onto her tablet. There was a broad red line to be seen on it. "The ocean has moved another six miles inland. The creatures are fleeing in panic. We have about one more hour."

Marlene looked at the long red line. "How many? How many are coming?"

Jenny looked up grimly.

"All of them!"

Chapter 44

"Here they come with the bomb parts from hell," said Albert caustically, as Russell and Dr. Dressel, each holding one box, entered the cave.

"Save yourself the comments and help me," grunted Russell. "This stuff is heavy."

Although he was ten years older than Russell, Albert Bridgeman took the containers from his arms and carried them over to a wooden table with ease. The plutonium and the lead containers weighed around forty-five pounds combined, but the weight didn't seem to bother the former military pilot. He had always been physically fit and had done everything necessary to stay that way as he got older.

Russell leaned against the cave wall and coughed.

"You should take care of yourself, Russell," said Lee, who was standing next to the borehole.

With difficulty, Russell pushed himself away from the wall and limped over to the engineer. With his threadbare jeans and his pointed brown boots, he reminded Russell of a young Clint Eastwood.

"So this is it," said Russell. He was looking down into a

deep hole with a diameter of about eight inches. The end of a steel pipe stuck out of the top. Wooden struts held it exactly in the middle of the hole in the ground.

Lee nodded. "It's all ready, we were just waiting for you."

Dr. Dressel opened the container and waved to Max Lindwall, who was standing at the entrance of the cave. "At the back of the jeep there's another box containing graphite and a few measuring instruments, and on the passenger seat there's another case. Can you get them, please?"

Max nodded, grabbed Peter Richards by the arm and pulled him outside with him. Russell watched Lee, who was adjusting something on a bracket above the hole. Wires led from the contraption up to a winch on the ceiling. "What is that, Lee?"

Lee answered without looking up. "We need to somehow lower the bottom half of the bomb into the hole. I'm attaching a thin hemisphere out of steel to the winch, which will be suspended from the wires. The plutonium half will go inside it. At the bottom of the borehole is a strut which will center it precisely."

"And here comes the first half of the plutonium," said Dr. Dressel impassively. He carried the bomb material to the borehole. He was wearing thick gloves.

"Good, just put it in the bracket," said Lee, who was holding on tight to the steel cable under the winch, so that it didn't sway back and forth.

"We need to be careful that we don't damage the nickel layer on the plutonium," said the physicist and let the bomb material glide into the hemisphere like a raw egg. "There, that's done."

"What now?" asked Russell, as he watched the men at work.

"Now we wait for the boys and the initiator," said Dr. Dressel.

"Coming," called Max from the tunnel. He ran into the cave and almost stumbled.

"Careful!" shouted the physicist and hurried over to the boys. "The initiator is impact-sensitive." He ripped the little case out of Maxwell's hand.

"Cool it, man," said the young Lindwall. "It's okay."

"I should have brought in the initiator myself," said the scientist crossly.

Russell shook his head in despair. This was all ridiculously unprofessional. It wouldn't work. It *couldn't* work!

Dr. Dressel took the little sphere out of the case with trembling hands and placed it in the cavity on the plutonium half. Then he took a syringe out of his bag, with which he squirted a little liquid into the narrow gap between the plutonium and the initiator. "I'm putting a bit of fluoride-containing nitric acid into the gap. That will adhere the initiator to the plutonium."

"Won't that dissolve the layer of nickel on the plutonium?" asked Lee.

"Yes, but it doesn't matter. But it *does* mean we can't separate the components anymore. There—done."

"So I can lower the stuff into the hole now?" asked the engineer.

Dr. Dressel nodded and Lee slowly turned a switch on the winch control system. The steel cable with the half of the bomb was slowly lowered into the hole. After a few seconds it had disappeared into the steel pipe. "Precision work," said Albert, standing proudly in the background.

"I never dreamed that one day I would help to build an atomic bomb," said Lee drily.

"It's certainly strange," remarked Russell. "On Earth we built nuclear weapons in the hope that we would never have to use them. And here we're building an atomic bomb on which our lives depend."

"I wish we'd been able to find another solution," said the physicist. "Then Ty would still be alive."

"But he still is!" said Lee, indignantly.

"No," said Dr. Dressel with conviction. "He died the moment he was exposed to the radiation."

Lee shook his head but didn't say any more. Suddenly the winch stopped. Lee looked at the digital display and nodded in satisfaction. "The bottom half of the bomb is now in position. I'm going to release the wire and pull up the steel cable. Then we can lower the graphite."

"Alarm!" screamed Maxwell Lindwall, as he came stumbling back into the tunnel. He looked frightened. Russell knew immediately what was happening.

The observation post!

"I just had Marlene on the radio. The next wave is approaching the post."

I knew it! "I'd hoped we would have more time."

"Me too! We're nowhere near done here. We need more time."

But time, thought Russell, *is precisely what we don't have!*

Chapter 45

"Everyone in position!" Marlene shouted into the megaphone. "They're coming!"

Travis Richards and Sammy Yang immediately finished their conversation in front of the door to the narrow barrack, hurried to the earth wall that separated the entrance to the canyon from the open grassland, and took up their positions. Thirty men and women lay behind the cover of the barbed wire and the earth wall waiting to take aim at the first wave of beasts.

Marlene looked over to the other two lookouts. Dr. Cashmore was on the next one, fumbling with the flamethrower. The chemist hadn't wanted to miss the opportunity of putting one of his constructions to use. He seemed nervous—perhaps not surprisingly since he had never been involved in a battle. Marlene turned around to Eliot Sargent, who was leaning casually behind the flamethrower of their lookout. His rifle was slung over his shoulder. "Is that thing good to go?"

Eliot nodded. "The pump is running. I'll ignite it as soon as the first creatures come running out the forest."

"We don't have much fuel. The vat with the napalm will be empty in a matter of seconds," said Ernie Lawrence, whose weapon was propped on the railing.

"That's why we'll only use the flamethrowers one by one and only on my command," replied Marlene.

"Then I hope that Cashmore doesn't lose his nerve. I'm guessing he isn't particularly reliable in battle."

"For that reason I'll let him shoot first. Also to test the effect it has on the oncoming herd. *Our* flamethrower has to cover our retreat. So don't even think of using it before you hear my command," said Marlene, looking at Eliot. "In fact, leave it standing there for now and grab a weapon. We need to defend the observation post until the bomb is ready. At all costs."

"I only hope they manage in time," Ben commented grimly from behind.

"I just spoke to Max. He's with Russell and Lee. He reckons they still need a while."

"Oh great," said Eliot. He picked up the binoculars that lay beside him on the ammo crate and peered over the railing. Marlene squinted into the sun, her eyes focused on the edge of the forest. There wasn't a cloud in the sky. It was warm, but a light, cool breeze blew down from the mountains into the valley. It was hard to believe that the fate of their entire colony would be decided on a day like this. And yet a blanket of fear, heavy as lead, enveloped the men and women. There were only two possible outcomes: either the plan worked, and they could defend the observation post until the bomb was ready, or they would all die here in the next few hours.

Marlene looked down at the colonists with a grim expression.

Not all of them will survive this day!

"I don't see or hear a thing," said Ernie quietly. "Are

you sure Jenny didn't make a mistake? Where is she, anyway?"

"Somewhere down there. She didn't make a mistake. I saw the drone's infrared photos. Anything and everything with legs is heading this way. She couldn't say exactly how far away they are, but it's only a few miles."

"Be quiet!" said Ben. "Can you feel it?"

Marlene stopped talking and concentrated on the silence. Ben was right. The whole lookout was shaking slightly. And it was getting stronger.

She looked at him and nodded. "This is it. They're coming." She leaned over the railing and tried to see something through the trees on the edge of the forest, but it was impossible. But now she could hear the trampling. Like a gigantic herd of buffalo, getting ever closer.

"They still seem pretty far away," remarked Eliot, white as a sheet. "But it sounds terrifying."

"Like every goddamn animal on this planet is headed this way," whispered Ernie. Ernie rarely lost his cool, but now he looked terrified.

The trampling noise turned into a droning that drowned out everything else, accompanied by the sound of thousands of branches being trampled to the ground.

"There!" screamed Eliot. "They're coming!"

Marlene grabbed the binoculars. At that moment, thousands of creatures came running out of the forest into the open grassland. They could see wotans, snipers, hyenas, and some other kind of beasts that they had never seen before. These ones, in particular, filled her with fear. They were as big as cows, had razor-like rows of teeth and sharp claws that looked as if they could tear apart a whole human with a single blow. And they were definitely powerful enough to tear down the barbed wire fence.

From down below she could hear screams of horror

from the ranks. Young Nicole Grant threw her weapon to the ground and ran into the canyon. Rhonda Fiedler screamed at her to come back.

Marlene grabbed the megaphone. "Everyone stay in position. Start firing only on my command. Flamethrower one at the ready."

She looked over to Dr. Cashmore. He was white as a sheet, but nodded. With trembling hands he brought the flamethrower into position.

Marlene looked over the railing again. The oncoming herd had already crossed a third of the open grassland. In less than a minute they would be at the barrier. And more and more animals were streaming out of the forest.

Marlene shook her head.

There must be thousands of them!

The animals had turned the plain into a sea of brownish-green. The creatures would simply steamroll through the barbed wire. With so many animals, even the mines would be useless.

Now they had almost reached the barrier.

"Flamethrower! Now!"

A fountain of liquid fire shot out of Cashmore's flamethrower and burst over the rampaging animals. The fire was so hot and bright, that Marlene had to force herself not to look away. Within seconds, dozens of animals were on fire and fell to the ground, where they rolled around in the dirt helplessly. Thick, black smoke rose up into the air. The chemist screamed as he swung the flamethrower to the right and the burning napalm spread across the whole width of the canyon entrance.

"My God," whispered Marlene.

It was an inhuman, ghastly sound. Marlene knew that she would never forget the appalling howls of the dying animals for as long as she lived. The whole entrance to the valley was up in flames. It was so hot that Marlene had to cover her face, and the stench of charred meat was unbearable. She breathed in the remains of unburned napalm, making her retch.

But the flames stopped the monsters from advancing, while the animals coming up behind were driven into the burning cadavers and immediately caught fire themselves. The black plumes of smoke rose high into the sky and partially blocked out the sunlight. The observation post was now illuminated only by yellow and white flames. Marlene shuddered. It was like a scene from the apocalypse.

With a final fizzle, Cashmore's flamethrower went out. The vat was empty. It had lasted no more than fifteen seconds. But the gel continued burning on the three-feet-high pile of dead animals.

It will provide us with a few minutes' breathing space, thought Marlene. *But no more!*

Chapter 46

"Ready! It can go down!" said John Dressel, who had carefully angled the graphite into the bracket.

Lee nodded, and let the ring of graphite glide slowly down the borehole. It encircled the steel pipe almost exactly.

Russell watched the work and shuffled his feet nervously. It was taking too long. He wondered if the observation post was already under attack. What was happening to Ellen, Jim and Grace? He would have much preferred to be at the observation post and help fend off the attack. There wasn't much he could do here. He briefly considered disobeying Marlene's order and heading down on foot. He bit his lip. Marlene trusted him. She needed him here. "Shit," he said under his breath.

"What is it?" asked Lee, without looking up.

"S'alright. It's just taking too long."

"If we don't do it carefully, we might as well leave it altogether," said Dr. Dressel. His pessimism had given way to fierce professionalism. The work was obviously doing him good.

"It's down," said Lee. "I'll release the steel cable and pull it back up." A few seconds later, the loose end of the cable was dangling on the winch above their heads. Lee rolled a huge plastic container up to the hole and opened a spout. Sand poured into the borehole around the steel pipe.

"That's to fill up the empty space. It should help to keep the graphite in position during the early stage of the explosion," explained Dr. Dressel, who had noticed Russell's confused expression.

When the hole was filled up to the top, Lee closed the container and rolled it to the side.

"Now comes the tricky bit," said Lee. "Help me!"

Russell and the others followed him to an approximately six-foot-long steel cylinder that Albert had welded together in the cave. He had carefully filed down the weld seams, so that there were no protruding parts. They rolled the cylinder to the borehole.

Coughing, Russell watched as Lee connected a hook to the steel rope of the winch.

At the same moment, Maxwell stormed into the cave. He was holding the radio in his hand and was very pale. "The animals have reached the observation post; they're at the barrier. They're fighting. I could hear the sound of the fighting in the background. It was horrendous!"

Russell's eyes met Dr. Dressel's. "We have to hurry. Every second counts!"

Cursing, Lee turned the switch of the winch control and the steel cylinder was pulled upward until it hung exactly over the borehole. The engineer stopped the swaying movement with his hands and waved over Dr. Dressel, who had taken the second plutonium half out of the lead container.

Russell felt nauseous, and he pulled the box of pills out

of his pant pocket. He flipped open the lid with his thumb and gulped down one of the pills. It must be the fifth one he'd had that day.

Groggily, he watched as Lee hooked the second bomb half to the bottom end of the steel cylinder and screwed it in place with two wing nuts.

"What's with the long steel cylinder?" asked Maxwell from the entrance to the cave.

"If we let the upper bomb half drop straight onto the lower half, it will start the chain reaction right away," explained John Dressel, as he worked out the correct alignment of the plutonium hemisphere with a measuring device. "The pressure of the released energy will try to drive the upper bomb half explosively upward through the pipe. The inertia of the steel mass plunging down will counteract this pressure and ensure that the two bomb halves stay together in the first nanoseconds of the explosion and create the necessary number of neutron generations for our explosion."

"And what happens with the C-4?" asked Russell, pointing at the explosive, which was ready and waiting.

"We'll get that to explode twenty inches over the ground. As a result, the steel mass with the top half of the bomb will be fired into the lower half with even greater force. Right, I'm done, it's perfectly positioned."

"Okay, then I'll start," said Lee, and lowered the long steel cylinder into the pipe in the borehole. First the plutonium hemisphere disappeared. After a few seconds only a small part of the steel cylinder was still sticking out of the hole. Lee immediately got to work on it. "I'm going to attach the explosive bolts. Then we'll ignite them from a safe distance and the steel mass and plutonium will plunge down into the hole.

"What happens if the thing falls down now by accident?" asked Russell. He had to think of Ty and how he had sealed his own fate in the space of a second.

"Then all that will remain of us is atoms," replied Dressel drily.

"Quiet!" said Lee. "I'm attaching the detonating wires, and don't want to make a mistake."

Dr. Dressel stepped back and stood next to Russell. He wiped the sweat from his brow with a handkerchief.

"Okay, that's done. The explosive bolts are doubly secured. They'll only ignite if there is tension on both cables. The cables lead to the bunker at the upper end of the canyon."

"So we're finally ready?" asked Russell.

"No, not quite. I'm going to screw the lid on the contraption and then we have to evacuate the borehole."

"Evacuate? You mean, pump out the air?" asked Russell. "Why?"

"Because otherwise the air down in the pipe will create resistance and counter the pressure of the falling plutonium," said John.

Lee rolled a petrol-driven pump up to the hole and connected the hose that was hanging out of it to a nozzle on the steel pipe. He flipped a switch, and the pump sputtered to life. The exhaust fumes were conducted out of the cave by another hose.

"How long will it take?" asked Russell nervously.

"About quarter of an hour. Then we're done."

Chapter 47

The wall of flames had protected them for ten minutes. But gradually the flames began to die down. The harrowing sound of animals being burnt alive could be heard across the battlefield.

Soon the first beasts will start storming through the remaining flames.

She grabbed the megaphone. "Get ready to fire!"

She put the megaphone aside and reached for her automatic rifle. Less than ten seconds later she heard the first firing of guns. Cookie Shanker shot at a hyena that came rushing through the fire. It was unnecessary, because the animal burned and stumbled before it had even reached the minefield.

The animals now came one by one through the wall of flames that was starting to fizzle out. A sniper stepped on a mine and was torn to shreds. Its innards shot several feet up into the air. Next to Marlene, Ernie fired at a wotan that had made it through a gap in the fire unharmed and was rushing toward the barbed wire barrier. Struck and killed, the animal rolled over and came to a stop just before the fence.

"Motherfucking beasts!" cursed Ernie.

Further detonations caused the ground to shake. In dozens of places, wotans, hyenas, and snipers broke through the smoking heap of dead animals.

Marlene heard Camille Ott scream loudly. Directly in front of her, one of the cow-like beasts had broken through the fence. It had simply ripped it down. The animal was bleeding from dozens of wounds, but still continued its rampage. Dorothy Moore shot it, while Camille jumped to the side to escape the dead body flying in her direction.

A few seconds later, the barrier had been broken through in two more spots. Beside one of the gaps, Jack Neaman was lying on the ground in a strangely distorted position. He didn't move. When Marlene looked more closely, she noticed with a shudder that the boy no longer had a head.

We don't stand a chance! There are too many of them!

Marlene grabbed the megaphone. "Flamethrower three: fire when ready!"

She looked over at Andrea Phillips on the furthermost lookout. Beside her stood Grant Dillon and his son Eric. Both of them were firing at animals that were approaching the fence. Andrea waved to Marlene, then opened the valve of her flamethrower.

There was a dull bang, and the three-feet-high jet of flame engulfed the entire watchtower. It rose into the air like a little mushroom cloud.

"Andrea!" screamed Ernie. He threw his weapon to the ground and swung down the ladder, wailing in despair.

All that remained of the lookout was a burning wooden frame. Colonists who had been standing beneath it ran off in all directions, screaming.

"My God!" gasped Eliot. "What happened?"

"The flamethrower obviously malfunctioned," murmured Marlene.

We're dead.

Chapter 48

Damn, damn!

Russell paced back and forth beside the vacuum pump. Lee kept checking the pressure gauge, followed by a shake of the head.

"Still not enough."

"We're losing valuable time," moaned Russell. "Can't we just let the pump run and in the meantime make our way to the bunker?"

"No," said Lee sharply. "Afterwards I need the generator of the pump as a power source for the explosive bolts.

Damn, damn!

Russell wondered how things were going at the observation post. Was the barrier still standing? Had colonists already died? What was happening to his wife and children? He bit his lip. Marlene hadn't reported back since letting them know that the attack had started.

"For God's sake! Please tell me the fucking bomb is going to work!" Russell spurted out angrily.

Dr. Dressel didn't even look at him. "We've done everything in our power!"

That's not what I wanted to hear.

"Shall I drive down to the observation post with the boy?" asked Albert, who had remained in the background the whole time. "Maybe we can help."

"No," said Lee, who was looking at the pressure gauge again. He looked up and smiled tentatively. "It's ready. There's no more air in the pipe. I just need one more minute."

The engineer disconnected the pump, but left the generator running. He checked the safety relay again, which would prevent the bomb from detonating by accident. "Finished. Let's get out of here. To the bunker!"

Finally!

The men ran out of the cave, through the short tunnel and climbed down the scaffold to the jeep. Russell grabbed the radio as Lee started the motor.

"Marlene, Russell. Report!"

No answer. The queasy feeling in Russell's stomach intensified.

"Marlene, please report!"

"Marlene here," came the rustling reply through the little loudspeaker. In the background, Russell could hear the sound of the battle. Shots. Detonations. Then a blood-curdling scream that made the hairs on Russell's neck stand on end.

"We're finished. I repeat: the bomb is ready to detonate. You can retreat."

"Understood."

"How is it down there?"

"We've suffered heavy losses. No time!"

Then there was silence again.

Damn, if only those beasts had given us one more hour!

"Sounds pretty bad down there," said Max.

Nobody answered. The jeep roared along the bumpy

track. Russell hoped that they could clear the observation post in a halfway orderly fashion. Dr. Dressel sat silently beside him. He stared into space. Russell knew exactly what the physicist was thinking, because the same thing was going through his mind.

Hopefully the bomb will detonate!

Chapter 49

Marlene put down the radio and picked up the mega-phone. "Everybody prepare to retreat." She turned to Eliot. "Prepare the flamethrower!"

He looked at her in horror. "Are you crazy? Did you just see what happened with the other one?"

"Damn it, we need the wall of fire to cover our retreat, otherwise we don't stand a chance. The monsters will run us down while we retreat!"

Eliot glanced uncertainly at the nozzle of the flamethrower, as if he were looking at a wotan that could attack him at any moment. "I . . . I . . ." he stuttered.

Marlene shoved him aside. "Everyone down. I'll do it myself. Go!"

A few seconds later, Marlene was standing alone on the platform. She also didn't trust the construction of the flamethrower, but she had no choice. She threw a quick glance over the railing. Men, women, and teenagers were fighting for their lives. The fence had been broken through in many spots. Dead animals lay next to dead and injured colonists. Under her lookout, sixteen-year-old Edward

Grazier was doubled over and screaming with pain. There was a gash up the length of his thigh, and red muscle mass hung in ugly shreds out of the wound. Several feet from him, Linda Ladish lay under a dead sniper. Blood was trickling out of her mouth, her eyes were blank.

Let's finish this!

Marlene pointed the nozzle of the flamethrower at a point directly beyond the fence. She closed her eyes and pressed the trigger. There was a loud hissing noise as gelatinous kerosene spouted out of the tube and immediately ignited. Liquid fire rained down on the hordes. Marlene swung the flamethrower back and forth until a thick barrier of yellow and white flames blocked the pass completely. Her face felt as if she were standing in the middle of the fire herself. With a short burst, the last drops of napalm from the empty vat spurted out of the flamethrower.

Marlene grabbed her weapon and scrambled down the ladder from the platform.

"Retreat! Retreat! Everyone in the vehicles. Take the wounded with you!"

She almost tripped over Dr. Cashmore. The chemist was bleeding from a deep wound on his chest. He groaned, as Marlene propped him up and dragged him to the nearest jeep. With the help of Sophia O'Hara, she heaved the wounded man onto the trailer, on which several groaning and screaming colonists were already lying.

She hurried back to the barbed wire fence and helped Christian Holbrook carry the body of Lucia Sargent. The fourteen-year-old's face was covered in blood. She was spitting and wheezing, so at least she was still alive.

The first vehicles started to move. They laid Lucia down on the truck bed of the next jeep, then jumped into the back seat next to Holbrook. Marlene looked back and saw William Lennox, another one of the injured, lying on the truck bed of the last vehicle. Further behind, Ben was staggering toward the jeep, a lifeless body in his arms.

"Come on! The fire won't last forever," she bellowed.

William waved to her to start, then jumped into the driver's seat of his jeep.

Marlene turned around and sank back in the seat. "Go!" she said to Ernie Lawrence, who was screaming the name of his dead wife. She was beyond tired and her mind was numb.

The cries of the burly soldier were swallowed up by the sound of the motor as he turned the key.

"That was close!" groaned Holbrook. He had a wound on his shoulder, but it didn't seem to be very deep.

"So many dead! But at least we did it!"

Marlene looked him coolly in the eyes. "We've only done it when this damn bomb has detonated!

Chapter 50

"They're on their way," said Russell.

"Casualties?" asked Lee.

"Marlene reckons there are at least ten dead and as many injured."

"Ten," repeated Lee. "Did she say who?" His wife and his eldest son had fought at the observation post.

"No, I have no idea," said Russell tonelessly. He couldn't stop thinking about Ellen and the children, how they had lain in the dirt at the observation post and fought against the wotans. He could barely contain his worry.

Lee raced with squeaking tires around the last curve. Dirt and stones were thrown into the air. The jeep reached the grassland of the plateau and turned left, toward the bunker.

The vehicle had barely come to a stop when Lee and Dr. Dressel jumped out and hurried to the cave. Maxwell and his buddies ran toward the pass to greet the returning fighters from the observation post. Russell resisted the temptation to follow them. He remained with his radio in his hand next to the vehicle. Making contact with the vehicle in the canyon was difficult enough. In the bunker they would definitely have no reception. Albert came and stood next to him, in silence. He fished a little package out of his pocket and held it up to Russell.

Russell raised his eyebrows. "Where did you get that?"

"Saved it for a special occasion. Help yourself."

Russell hesitated. "I don't know. With the state of my health . . ."

"You've already got lung cancer, so what the hell?"

Russell shrugged and pulled a cigarette out of the packet. He couldn't help grinning.

"How on earth were you able keep these hidden from Lindwall?"

"To be honest, I stole them from his infirmary," admitted Albert. "Years and years ago."

Albert took one and put the packet back in his jacket. Then he lit it with the cigarette lighter next to the driver's seat in the jeep.

"This is horrendous," whispered Russell. "I can't bear it anymore!"

"You mean, wondering if the bomb will explode, or who will return from the observation post alive?"

"Both! But mostly, wondering if one of my family has died. . . . At times like this, there's an advantage to being single. You can be glad that you don't have to go through this torture of not knowing."

Albert smiled weakly. "You're wrong."

Russell was silent.

"There was someone I was particularly worried about," said his friend.

Russell smiled. "You sure know how to keep a secret! Who . . . Hang on. You said *was*!" His eyes widened. Up to now they only knew for sure that one person had survived the attack. "Marlene?" he asked in amazement.

Albert smiled.

"How long has this been going on?"

"Almost twenty years."

"Why did you both keep it secret?"

"Because . . ." he stopped. Lee came out of the bunker, white as a sheet.

"What . . .?" asked Russell.

"We have a problem," croaked the engineer. "Come inside."

Russell dropped his cigarette.

In the cave, Dr. Dressel was wrestling with the electrical detonator and cursing.

"Leave it, it's no use," said Lee. He pointed at the red light and turned to Russell. "The safety relay isn't working. We can't detonate."

"What?" Russell felt the blood draining from his face.

"I told you from the start that it was a bad idea to use that old relay," said Albert angrily.

"I wanted to prevent a bolt of lightning or some other voltage spike from detonating the bomb while we were still in the cave or on our way back. After all, there are several miles of cable," shouted Dr. Dressel. He was angry— whether with himself or the broken mechanism was hard to tell.

"We shouldn't have used that damn relay!" Albert couldn't hide his anger.

"Enough!" said Russell in a loud voice. "What can we do?"

"Somebody has to drive back to the bomb and discon- nect the relay," said Lee.

"Damn it, the barrier is unprotected," countered the physicist. "Thousands of these creatures are storming into the canyon as we speak. Whoever drives down to the bomb now will run straight into the beasts."

Russell planted himself in front of the engineer. As if he didn't know! "Tell me exactly, what I have to do!"

"It's quite simple," Lee explained. "You take out the two red cables from the relay and connect them directly to one another. Then we can detonate from here."

"That's it?"

"That's it."

Russell turned around without a word, ran out of the bunker, jumped into the jeep and started the engine. Maxwell and his friends stared after him, dumbfounded, as he raced past them.

He had hardly gone more than three-hundred feet along the dusty track when the first jeep from the observation post came racing toward him. His heart jumped for joy when he saw Ellen, Jim, and Grace on the back seat. As he drove past he waved at them encouragingly, as they stared after him in horror.

We have to detonate this fucking bomb!

BEN HAD BEEN STAGGERING NUMBLY through the smoking debris when he'd stumbled over the body of his wife. There was no visible wound, but her eyes were devoid of life. Ben stood for a long time, unable to feel anything. Finally he kneeled down robotically, picked up Drew's body, and carried it to the next jeep. Slowly, almost tenderly, he laid it on the truck bed.

"Come on, man! We have to get out of here, before the fire goes out!" shouted William Lennox from the driver's seat. Without replying, Ben swung himself into the passenger seat. Bill stepped on the gas and cursed as the gear stick jammed briefly.

Behind him, Paulina Hill was moaning on the back seat. "Was that your Drew?" asked Bill. "Is she . . .?"

"Dead," said Ben. From the corner of his eye he had seen his daughter jump into another jeep. She was alive. She didn't know yet that her mother was dead. If only Drew had stayed in Eridu, as he had ordered her to do! He should have felt rage, but there was none. Neither rage nor sorrow . . . nothing.

They rounded a curve and the bomb construction site came into view. Ben gasped as he saw Russell racing toward them in a jeep, which came to a halt in front of the scaffold of the cave.

Bill slammed on the breaks and stopped with the engine still running. "What's going on?"

Russell had difficulty breathing. He looked as if he were about to collapse. "The detonating mechanism is malfunctioning. I have to bypass the safety relay." Coughing, he climbed up the ladder.

Ben stared after him, in two minds.

"Jesus Christ, did you see how he looks?" asked Bill. "Russell is going to collapse at any second. And this bomb is our last chance. We should help him."

Ben hesitated for a moment as he thought about his daughters, but then he jumped out of the jeep. "I'll do it. You drive with Paulina back to Eridu. She needs medical attention."

He followed Harris onto the scaffold.

HARRIS STUMBLED along the tunnel to the cave. The generator was still making a noise.

Where is the damn relay?

"What's the problem?" asked Ben, coming up behind him.

"The safety relay is broken. It's blocking the remote detonation of the bomb. We need to disconnect and bypass it."

Russell had found the relay, and dropped to his knees in front of it. He began to disconnect the cable, but was overcome by a coughing fit. Ben pushed him aside. "I'll do it!" Hastily, he disconnected the last cable from the relay in the little plastic box.

"You have to connect the two red cables," said Russell, his voice rattling.

Ben jiggered the thin wires apart until he had found the red wires. Then he groaned. "It doesn't work! They have different plugs!"

"What?" said Russell, aghast.

Damn Dr. Dressel! He hadn't said a word about that!

"I said, they have different plugs. I need some pliers, so I can disconnect the plugs and twist the wires together."

"Lee took all the tools with him, but I saw a toolbox in the car."

"Then get me the pliers. Quick!"

Breathing with difficulty, Russell climbed down the ladder and stumbled over to the vehicle. He heaved the heavy toolbox out from beneath the driver's seat and searched for the pliers. He paused as he noticed a tremor and looked down the canyon. The ground was vibrating.

What the hell is that?

Then he heard the stampeding.

My God. They must be close.

Russell grabbed the pliers and was about to climb back up the ladder, when a lone wotan came around the bend. Instinctively, Russell dropped the pliers and grabbed his pistol from the holster. He still had time for two shots, then the beast would be on top of him. Russell fell to the ground and protected his head with his hands. He screamed as something hit him on the left shoulder. The animal flew over him and Russell rolled over to fire

355

again. The body hit the support of the scaffold. Massive planks of wood snapped in two like matches, and with a huge crashing noise, the whole scaffold collapsed. Only a few struts of the ladder remained. The creature was dead.

Ben appeared at the entrance to the cave and looked down. He must have heard the noise. Thirty feet of smooth cliff-face separated him from the ground of the canyon. He had no way of getting back down. Then his eyes fell on the cable leading out of the cave. It was severed just below the entrance to the cave. The collapsing scaffold had torn it into pieces. There was now no way the bomb could be ignited remotely.

"Ben!" screamed Russell.

Ben's face distorted into a grimace. "The pliers!"

Russell looked up at Ben, aghast.

What's he planning to do?

"Throw up the goddamn pliers!"

Russell swung himself up and threw the pliers to the entrance of the cave. Ben caught them.

"The beasts are nearly there. I'm going to ignite the bomb from here. Go! I'll give you five minutes."

"Ben!" screamed Russell. There must be a way of getting him down. But the sound of the animals thundering through the canyon was getting louder by the second.

Ben held up his right arm with the pliers. "I've always hated you, Harris!" he bellowed. "I'll see you in hell!" Then he disappeared back into the cave.

For several seconds, Russell stood as if petrified in front of the scaffold, which lay around him in ruins. Then he hobbled back to the jeep. He wanted to turn, but heard a loud bang from the engine compartment.

Oh God! The transmission must be broken!

The engine made a yowling noise. Russell wanted to try another gear, but the gearstick was jammed.

Five minutes!

Russell jumped out of the jeep.

I'm standing on Ground Zero of an atomic bomb, I've got no vehicle and only five minutes!

Russell briefly played with the idea of simply sitting on the ground and waiting for the end. It's what he'd wanted. His wish of not dying slowly from cancer would be fulfilled. But then he saw the faces of Ellen and his children when they had passed him in the canyon. They had survived the battle.

No! I want to hold them in my arms. At least one last time!

He mustered all his strength and started to run. He ran as fast as he could. He gritted his teeth and tried to ignore the pain in his knees.

How far will I get in five minutes?

The ground was vibrating. Small pieces of rock loosened from the sides of the cliff and rolled onto the track. Russell kept on running until his lungs were on fire.

BEN WALKED along the narrow tunnel. He felt completely numb.

This is the day I'll die.

He stood in front of the borehole and the thick metal pipe. He thought of the lifeless body of Drew on the back of Bill's jeep and didn't know what he should feel.

He had loved Drew once, but it was a long time ago. The more she had caused him problems, the more he had fallen out of love. His children were also nearly grown up, and no longer as easy as they had been as children. Cathy's stubbornness made life particularly hard, and recently it had dawned on him that she might actually hate him.

Perhaps he just wasn't suited to family life. Just as he wasn't suited to the life of a settler on this godforsaken planet. So it was really for the best if he took the highway to hell with these beasts. He couldn't remember when he had last been really happy. And who was responsible for that? Harris! Why had he even given that bastard five minutes? It would have been more than fair if Harris had died with him. It would have been one last triumph.

With a grim expression, Ben went down on his knees, snipped off the plug of the red cable and pulled off the plastic cladding until only bare copper stuck out.

If I connect it directly to the pole on the generator, the circuit will be complete.

He pulled the cable over to the generator, which had a plug similar to a car battery. He was silent for a moment.

Here we go!

There was a small spark as he connected the wire to the pole. A bang and a grinding sound were the last thing he heard.

RUSSELL DIDN'T KNOW for how long he had been running. He kept on going up the slight incline of the canyon. He had just turned another curve when he stumbled. He flailed his arms around to try and regain his balance, but without success, and fell headlong to the ground. This saved his life.

He was surrounded by a bright light, brighter than a thousand suns. He screamed, as searing heat singed his hair. There was a terrible rumbling sound, but he only heard it for a second before his eardrums burst. Pieces of rock started to break off the canyon wall and poured over his battered body.

Chapter 51

When Russell came to, his surprise was boundless. He opened his eyes, but the brightness blinded him so much that he immediately closed them again.

I should be dead! The atomic bomb! The exploding rocks! Or am I in fact dead?

He felt pain in his knees and back.

The dead don't feel pain!

Tentatively, he opened his eyes again and forced himself to keep them open.

Gradually he got used to the light. He recognized the infirmary. The light came from the sun that was shining through the window straight onto his face. He turned around and saw Ellen's face. She was smiling. She said nothing, but stroked his cheek with her hand.

"I love you!" whispered Russell. He could not remember when he had last spoken those words. The face of the doctor appeared beside his wife's.

"How many lives do you have, actually?" Lindwall smiled.

"I'm guessing I've used them all up now," croaked Russell.

"And he hasn't lost his sense of humor, either."

Russell propped himself up with difficulty, tensed his muscles and one by one, moved each of his limbs. It seemed he hadn't even broken anything.

"How . . ." he began.

"How did you survive?" his wife finished his question. "It's thanks to your radio. The talk button was pressed down the whole time. That way we were able to find you under a foot of debris. It's lucky you weren't any nearer the explosion. The whole canyon is buried.

"The explosion . . . It worked!"

Dr. Lindwall nodded. "It did. At Ground Zero there's a sheer, hundred-and-thirty-foot high barrier. No animal in this world will be able to get over it. Unless it has wings."

"It was awful," said Ellen. Her voice was trembling. "We went down shortly after the explosion and looked over the edge. The beasts had torn each other to bits. A few hours later the flood came, and drowned any that were still alive."

"How long was I out for?" asked Russell.

"Two days. You had a bad concussion. The doc put you into a deep sleep with a bit of medication, so that you could recover."

Russell coughed. He had difficulty breathing, and he remembered that his survival would only be short-lived. He wanted to run his hand through his hair, but his hand touched nothing but naked skin. It must have been the radiation from the bomb! "Will I end my life like Ty's?" he asked blankly.

Dr. Lindwall shook his head. "You didn't get any radiation, although you were less than a mile away from Ground Zero. The bomb exploded below ground. Only a small amount of gamma radiation was emitted. The heat singed your hair, but you don't have any critical burns. This evening you can go back home."

"The children?"

"They're fine. Greg and Grace were here until a few minutes ago. Jim is with Cathy and her sister. Another two children who have to carry on without their parents."

Ben!

Slowly, Russell remembered the last few minutes before the explosion. "How many dead? How many victims?"

"Ten dead and fifteen injured," said Ellen. "It could have been worse. We survived." She leaned over and kissed him gently. "And we have you to thank for that."

Russell shook his head. "No, we have Ben to thank for it, and above all Ty. In the end his plan worked. And the men and women who sacrificed their lives for the colony down at the post."

"We all fought for it," said Ellen. "But we won! We saved our colony!"

Russell could feel all the strain of the last week in his bones. He sank back down on his pillow.

"Rest now. Try to sleep a little. This evening at sunset there will be a memorial service for the dead." She smiled. "Well, and to an extent of course it is also a victory cele-bration. I'll come and collect you with the children and we can go together.

Russell smiled weakly and fell back to sleep.

Chapter 52

"I had hoped we wouldn't have to hold another memorial service," said Marlene. "But unfortunately it has come to pass."

Twelve graves had been dug in the hurriedly extended cemetery. Because they did not have enough coffins, they had lowered all the dead directly into the ground, filled the holes and scattered them with fresh flowers. A single candle flickered on each grave. Wooden crosses were adorned with the names of the fallen. In the coming weeks, they would be replaced by individual gravestones.

All of the surviving colonists had turned out, apart from Sarah Denning, who was still lying in the infirmary. Marlene's head was bandaged; the heat of the flamethrower had burnt her scalp.

"Ten people gave their lives to defend our colony at the observation post. Ty died constructing the bomb. We owe our lives to his idea and to his zeal, and to Ben, who detonated the bomb, in full knowledge that he would die in the process. All of these brave people gave their lives for us, the survivors. Together, we mourn the loss of the men and women from our midst and, even if the pain subsides, we will never forget that they died to secure the survival of our colony."

Marlene paused for a moment.

Survive. We will carry on living!

Two days ago she had no longer believed it. When she had seen the hordes of beasts approaching the observation post, she had been sure her life was over. She would never forget that sight and that feeling. It would haunt her for as long as she lived. Her hands hadn't stopped trembling since the battle, and she couldn't do anything to stop it. At some point it would subside. Along with the pain and the memories. But the scars would remain. They had fought, they had won. That was what counted!

"I know that some people in our community have always struggled to see this planet as their home. But that is precisely what we fought for over the last few days, and what the fallen died for: our home! Let's continue to work together to improve life in our colony and to give our children a solid foundation for their futures. It may take hundreds more generations, but I am convinced that our descendants will spread across the whole planet. I am also convinced that the names of those killed in action from the first and second generations will always be remembered by our descendants. And it goes without saying that we ourselves will never forget their sacrifice."

Marlene paused. She could hear sobbing from the crowd. Many had lost mothers, fathers, husbands, wives, and children. It would take a long time until the sorrow and the horror of the last few days faded.

Marlene gazed toward the horizon. The air was incredibly clear. The radioactive wave had been blown out to sea. The setting sun had turned red and would disappear over the horizon in a few minutes. A few bright stars already glimmered in the sky. The moon was just coming into view over the cusp of the horizon. Despite the many victims, Marlene wanted to face the future with optimism.

She turned back to the waiting colonists. At the edge of the crowd she could see Russell, who was leaning against Ellen and coughing. She was glad that he had survived the explosion, but it made it all the more distressing to know that soon she would be conducting another funeral service.

"Today is a time for mourning, but it is also a time to celebrate. Our colony has survived, and once again we can look to the future full of hope. We will wait until the flood has subsided, and make our way back down to the lowlands. Since all the monsters are dead, we can go down there for the first time without fear. We will put the oil wells back into operation and step up our efforts to explore and understand our planet. The events of the last days have taught us that we cannot afford to isolate ourselves in a single settlement and focus only on ourselves. We need to build a future not only for the second generation, but also for the third generation, which will hopefully soon see the light of day. And we can do so with less obstacles than before, which is what we want to celebrate today."

She paused. "I can understand that many of you are not in the mood to celebrate, but I would ask you to still come to the mess hall, because we want to spend this day together."

She nodded and stepped aside. One by one, the colonists walked past the graves and laid down flowers. After a while, the crowd dispersed and trotted in little groups back to the settlement.

RUSSELL AND ELLEN walked slowly over to the mess hall. She had to support him. He felt weaker than he had ever felt in his life. And yet he was in good spirits. All the exertions of the last days and weeks had been worth it. Despite the advanced stage of his cancer, he had contributed to the survival of the colony. His family was alive, and considering the many victims, that was not to be taken for granted.

When they arrived at the mess hall, somebody pressed a glass into his hand and he took a big gulp. The moonshine had been diluted with some juice and tasted awful, but the warmth in his throat felt good.

Marlene came up to him and smiled. "We haven't seen each other since you woke up. I wanted to come by the infirmary, but there was just too much to do." She squeezed his hand and he smiled back weakly.

"It's okay, I can imagine you must be up to your ears at the moment. Thanks for organizing this little party."

She helped herself to a full glass from the tray and toasted with Russell. "It seemed wrong to go straight back to the normal routine. I hope this will mark a symbolic end to the crisis. Despite the mourning, we will continue with our daily lives tomorrow. We need to get back to the fields urgently, and save whatever we can of the harvest. Some of the vehicles are damaged and need to be repaired. God, there's enough to be getting on with."

Russell nodded. "I'll help as much as I'm able."

Beside him, Ellen rolled her eyes and groaned.

Marlene laughed. "You've already done more than anybody ever expected of you. You will stay at home with your family and let yourself be taken care of."

"But—"

Marlene interrupted him brusquely. "No buts. If I catch sight of you anywhere near the workshop or the fields, I will have you dragged away and chained to your bed." She grasped his hand. "I know exactly what keeps you going. You've still got a bad conscience because it's because of you that we're all stranded on this planet. But you've made your contribution. Over all these years, no task was ever too much for you, and even in the last few days, despite your illness, you risked your life to save the colony. And you nearly died in the process."

"Everyone risked their lives," said Russell flatly.

"Yes, the crisis of the last few days was a turning point. It marks the start of a new beginning for our colony. Now we definitively leave the past behind us and live only for the future. Whatever debt you felt you owed our community, it's been paid, once and for all. That's the way I see it, and so will everyone else."

Russell stared into his half-full glass. The brownish liquid swilled back and forth.

Marlene clapped him on the shoulder. "Stop moping about, and enjoy the time with your family." She smiled at him and Ellen again and then disappeared into the crowd.

"She's right," said Ellen. "Be happy that you're alive and that *we're* alive. Let's celebrate a little longer."

He hugged her and smiled. "Okay!"

Chapter 53

They had stayed till long after sundown, shaken many hands, exchanged hugs, and drunk several more glasses of the terrible swill. They had celebrated with some and mourned with others. Then Russell had been overcome by exhaustion and they had returned to their hut at the edge of the settlement.

Despite his tiredness, Russell was unable to fall asleep for a long time. Beside him, Ellen was also restless.

"It was so close!" said Russell.

"Yes. I was scared. I was sure we would die. I was even more afraid than in the transporter all those years ago."

"The transporter. I simply don't understand why the sphere suddenly stopped working. I mean, those things were built to last hundreds of millions of years. I just don't get it."

Ellen didn't seem too bothered by it. "Everything breaks at some point."

Russell shook his head. "But not those spheres. You know yourself that those things work without a hitch in even the most adverse environments. I would love to know why the transporter gave up the ghost precisely when it did."

Ellen cuddled up to him. "Stop thinking about it. We'll never know."

Russell sighed. "You're probably right."

"What will you do now?"

He looked at her in confusion. "What do you mean?"

"Will you leave us again?"

Russell frowned. That evening he had managed pretty well to forget about his cancer. But he also knew that Ellen was waiting for an answer.

"No," he said quietly, and held her tight. He had wanted to spare his family the sight of a dying husband and father. But he had been wrong. If he just went, and left Ellen and the children in a state of not knowing, it would probably be much worse for them. Here they would be able to bury him and mourn him.

"I'm staying!"

They lay in each other's arms for a long time until they fell asleep.

WHAT WAS THAT?

Russell awoke from a horrible dream. He had been startled out of his sleep by a noise. There! Again he heard something clattering outside, somewhere close to the hut. Had somebody at the party had one too many? He turned around and tried to get back to sleep. Then there was a scream. Russell sat up in bed.

Jesus, what's going on?

He heard footsteps on the other side of the wall.

Hastily, he shook Ellen, who woke up groaning. "What is it?"

"Shhhh! Something's going on outside!"

He swung himself out of bed and pulled on his pants, which were lying on a chair. Again he heard the sound of heavy boots on the gravel. Crouching, he moved over to the window and peered out. It was pitch black, but from somewhere came the beam of a flashlight. He could make out silhouettes—of humans, not animals.

Who the hell is that?

Russell opened the bedroom door and ran to the cupboard, where he kept his gun. Ellen followed him. She blinked drowsily. "What is it?"

"There are figures creeping around the houses."

"Figures? Who—?"

"I don't know," he hissed. "But I'll be damned if it's someone from the colony. Go to the children!"

Russell was about to insert a magazine, when the front door burst open. Ellen screamed. Six people stormed into the house. Two of them grabbed Ellen and held her mouth closed. Russell wanted to raise his weapon, but four powerful arms grabbed him and pressed him against the wall. He tried to defend himself, but his opponents were clearly well trained. One of them took him in a headlock, the other ripped the gun out of his hand. Two others stood against the wall, weapons at the ready.

"For fuck's sake! Who the hell are you?" Russell exclaimed. He didn't get a reply. Instead, a flashlight was shone straight into his face.

"It's him, Sir. We've got him," called one of the men.

Russell tried to wriggle out of the man's grasp, but didn't stand a chance. He stood silent as someone came through the door. The person stopped a few feet away from Russell, but because of the light in his face, Russell couldn't see him properly.

"How nice that we finally meet again, Harris!"

Russell felt the hairs on the back of his neck stand on

end. The voice was seething with hate, but that wasn't it. He knew the voice. He couldn't place it, but he'd heard it thousands of times before in his life. He hadn't imagined he would ever hear it again.

"Who are you?"

Another flashlight went on. The man lit up his own face.

That face! It was furrowed and haggard. Much older than he remembered. Short, snow-white hair peeped out from under a cap. But the eyes were still bright and sparkling.

"General Morrow!" croaked Russell. "How the hell—?"

The General nodded to a man at his side and the last thing Russell felt was an explosion of pain, as a rifle butt hit him on the head.

———

END

More books by Phillip P. Peterson coming 2017:
  Transport 3: The Zone
  Paradox - On the Brink of Eternity

DON'T MISS PHILLIPS HOMEPAGE. For updates and notifications about new releases feel free to subscribe to the newsletter: http://petersonauthor.com/

THANK you very much for reading this book. Although the translation from german language has been made by a professional translator in cooperation with an editor and additional proof-readers it's hard to get a text 100% error free. Thus any editorial recommendations are highly welcomed and I will incorporate them into the book rapidly. Thanks again.

IF YOU ENJOYED this book please consider writing a short review at amazon or at the blog of your choice.

CONTACT:
  contact@petersonauthor.com

FOR UPDATES, questions and new releases you can also find the author at Facebook:
  https://www.facebook.com/PetersonAuthor

TWITTER:

Made in the USA
Middletown, DE
15 December 2017